"DON'T YOU WANT TO KNOW WHAT I PLANNED TO DO ONCE I'D SEDUCED YOU?"

Elizabeth stared up at Lucien, waiting for him to tell her.

"I was going to ask if you wanted to become my mistress," he explained.

She blinked, wondering what to say. Well, she knew what she'd like to say, or rather, what to call him, but the unladylike words would not cross her lips.

"You must surely be the most base, depraved male of my acquaintance."

"Do you think?" he asked.

"I do. But I would not be proud of the fact, your grace. I would look in the mirror. See what it is you have become. I fear you will not like what you find."

"No?" he asked, his eyes appearing to be genuinely curious. "Do you not wonder what would happen if you did the same? Are you not tired of being such a perfect lady?"

"This one is headed for your keeper shelf."
—Amanda Quick,
New York Times bestselling

Please turn to the back of this book for a preview of Pamela Britton's upcoming novel, *Tempted*.

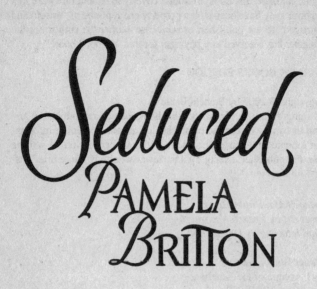

Seduced
PAMELA BRITTON

WARNER BOOKS

An AOL Time Warner Company

WARNER BOOKS EDITION

Cover design Diane Luger
Cover art by Franco Accornero
Hand lettering by David Gatti

Warner Books, Inc.
1271 Avenue of the Americas
New York, NY 10020

Visit our Web site at www.twbookmark.com

ⓦ An AOL Time Warner Company

Printed in the United States of America

First Printing: April 2003

10 9 8 7 6 5 4 3 2 1

This one's for the man upstairs. I gotta admit, there were times when I thought You had it in for me. But You know I was never truly angry with You. (All right, maybe a little.)

And then You gave me Michael.

And then Codi.

And before that the best parents in the world. Not to mention three supportive, ever proud siblings. I lost sight of that for a while, and I sometimes wonder how I could ever have thought You didn't care.

Thank you, Lord, for the blessings in my life. And especially for giving me this wonderful, though sometimes painful, ability to write. May Your touch always guide my hand.

Seduced

PROLOGUE

I t was a well-known fact amongst society that to love Lucien St. Aubyn meant your death.

Oh, it wasn't as if everybody who'd ever cared for the man had died, just almost everybody.

Take, for example, his governesses. Four of those good ladies had died before Lucien ever reached his prime, one, it would appear, from nothing more than a headache. That the young earl's groom had passed away, too, seemed most coincidental. But 'twas after the death of his best friend that people began to cross themselves. After all, a man could only be surrounded by so much death before it seemed, well, *odd.*

Losing one's best friend would not be such a terribly strange occurrence. After all, people died. Rather, it was the way Lucien's best friend died that truly frightened the more superstitious lot.

Marcus had died from a rock. That the rock had been thrown up from the wheels of Lucien's carriage seemed most ironic. That Lucien had been on his way to see Marcus, and Marcus on his way to see Lucien, seemed ironic, too. But that the rock had struck Marcus in a spot so rare, so hard to hit, the doctors proclaimed it hardly believable that it could happen at all, well, that was the final irony. And then when Lucien was twenty, his father had died, at which time people recalled that Lucien's mother had died in childbirth, and, well, it didn't bode well for Lucien's social life that dowagers all but clutched their daughters to their bosoms whenever he was near.

A part of Lucien was troubled by his past, too. After all, it seemed most bizarre that so many people of his acquaintance resided underground. Could there be some truth to the rumors that he was cursed?

His concerns, as silly as it may seem, plagued him to the point that one day he found himself broaching the subject with his brother. Henry, whom Lucien thought about the most sensible person on God's green earth, actually laughed.

"Lucien, old man," Henry had said, "you must be daft to believe in all that rot."

Lucien had been greatly comforted by the words. Still, a part of him wouldn't let the issue rest.

"And 'tis not as if they all died suddenly," Henry had further pointed out. "You've gone years between deaths."

"Yes, but 'tis a lot of deaths."

"And they all died of natural causes," Henry had continued, "including Father."

"A chicken bone is natural?" Lucien had asked.

Henry'd shrugged. "'Tis not as if the chicken flew down his throat."

To which Lucien had laughed. Henry was a master at stating things in a mundane, yet humorous way. To tell the truth, Henry hardly seemed concerned about anything. And why should he be? Henry had been born first;

thus guaranteeing his brother sixty thousand pounds a year, a dukedom, acres of land, and his pick of the season's beauties. Lucien had been born second, thus guaranteeing him a pittance of Henry's fortune, an earldom, and a castle whose walls crumbled into the ocean.

But even though Henry's inability to be ruffled irked Lucien to no end, he still loved his brother. Yes, he was a bit jealous of the bounder, and he ofttimes made his jealousy known, but that was to be expected: all second sons were jealous of the firstborn.

"So you do not think it odd that so many people who have known me are dead?"

His brother gave him a gamin grin. "Not at all odd, brother. After all, you haven't killed me yet."

Two months later Henry was dead.

It was then society began to call Lucien the Duke of Death, a sobriquet Lucien had tried to ignore, yet deep down inside his worry had tripled. Nine people had died knowing him, the last, his brother, the most horrible death of all.

Henry had been shot. But what made it all the more worse, what made it scarcely believable, was that Henry had taken a ball from a pistol Lucien himself had shot.

Henry dead.

Wonderful, sanguine Henry, the only family Lucien had had left.

For the first time Lucien knew the true meaning of grief. Nothing, not even his father's death, had hit so hard. It didn't help that society whispered behind ornate fans that perhaps the new duke had purposely killed his brother.

And as the rumors grew in volume, it became clear

many people thought him guilty of the deed. Oh, society still accepted him, but it was under duress. Whereas before Henry's death Lucien had been invited to the most prestigious of parties, a year after the death he was hard-pressed to receive above twenty invitations a season.

So it was that Lucien found himself rather at odds with society. They didn't like him. He didn't like them. But still he forced himself amongst them almost as if to damn them all for daring to show their animosity to his face. And as the years passed, as the memories of the deaths faded, he became more and more accepted.

But Lucien never forgot. Perhaps as a way of hiding his pain over being responsible for his brother's death, perhaps as a way of thumbing his nose at those who thought him guilty of such a deed—whatever the reason— he grew quite reckless, doing things no young buck in his right mind would do: seducing innocent women (well-bred innocent women), racing through London's winding streets at breakneck speed. Holding wild parties at his estate. He became something of a rake. Well, more than that. He was the king of all rakes.

The Rake of Ravenwood.

Oddly enough, his new sobriquet only increased his appeal. Women would sigh whenever he entered the room, the younger ones fantasizing about being the one to bring such a devilish duke to his knees. Older women, women of an age to remember the scandal associated with his brother's death, found his dangerous past alluring, not to mention his sin-with-me green eyes, wide, strong shoulders, and masculine, square jaw. Even those matrons hired to keep such men away from their charges—the chaperones—fanned themselves whenever

he drew near. Never mind that the duke had been rumored to ruin more than one of their charges.

Lucien grew bored. Who wouldn't when you could
have your pick of women, behave any way you wanted,
and get away with it? He was the result of an
overindulged mind. He didn't believe in love, thought the
emotion a scam, a fairy tale invented by poets and novel-
ists to entice young ladies into reading their words (and
paying for the privilege).

No, love did not exist, and if it did—a statement he
was known to utter aloud on more than one occasion—it
would certainly never find him.

Or so he thought.

Elizabeth Montclair didn't belong. She knew it. The
ton knew it. And, lord help her, the London papers knew
it.

It wasn't that she wasn't titled. She was, after all, the
daughter of an earl. The problem stemmed more from
where the title had come from rather than the title itself.
After all, earning an earldom simply because one was—
as George III had put it—"A damn fine cobbler," wasn't
exactly, well, *romantic*. One needed to slay dragons, or
depose princes in order to gain the respect of the populace.

So it was that while growing up Elizabeth became
quite used to the scandalized looks she received. It didn't
help matters that the carriage she rode in had a half boot
inside the crest. Her grandfather, almost as crackers as
the king, had thought the idea hilarious at the time.

Society was *not* amused.

Elizabeth ofttimes thought that it was from her grandfather that she had inherited her somewhat unconventional and unusual mind, a mind, it seemed, often plagued by odd thoughts. But she accepted the fact that whilst in the midst of a curtsy she might have a sudden urge to spring into an Irish jig. Or perhaps slide down the banister rail and into the ballroom. They were odd thoughts, to be sure, thoughts she always contained, but there nonetheless. Then, too, her departure from normaldom might have had something to do with her aunt's marriage to Lord Harry Ludlows.

Now, a marriage would not normally have had such a radical effect on a young girl, but this had been no ordinary marriage. The Montclair family had been rather shocked by the aunt's announced nuptials. The woman had been on the shelf for nigh on twenty years (owing, no doubt, to her father's smelly profession). But upon meeting the groom, her aunt's father had understood only too well. Lord Ludlows was the infamous Ludlows heir, a miscreant of such reputation even the newly styled earl had heard of him. Ludlows had been sent to the Continent as punishment for one of his more sensational escapades, and it was upon the Continent that Aunt Lilibeth (as she was called, having been named Elizabeth, too . . . as was every firstborn daughter of Sheffield, all two of them) had met her beau. There she'd fallen in love with her "reformed" rake. And there she'd married him, much to her family's dismay.

Elizabeth had been befuddled by her grandfather's anger over the marriage. Her aunt had always told Elizabeth to marry for love, and now her aunt had done so. Was there a more perfect end to a more perfect fairy tale?

As mentioned before, Elizabeth was young, too young to realize that things were not as they seemed.

Lord Ludlows took his return to England with a certain degree of jubilation. Ripe new pickings for his roving eyes. Never mind that he was newly wed. He made it abundantly clear to his new wife shortly after their marriage that he'd only married her because she was an heiress. Nothing else could have persuaded him to marry—good God—a commoner. He'd needed money, and Aunt Lilibeth had seemed the best way to gain it.

And so when Elizabeth found her aunt crying in the family solarium one day, at first Elizabeth had thought her injured.

"Why, Aunt, what ever is amiss?"

In response, her aunt began to sob in earnest, Elizabeth thinking she must surely be in pain to carry on so. And instead of doing what most children her age would have done—run off to tell an adult, or begin crying herself—Elizabeth had gone to her aunt, doing a very odd thing for a child her age by cupping her aunt's face with her hand. "Are you wounded?" she had asked, genuinely concerned.

Her aunt had sniffed a few times before managing to say, "Aye, child. I am hurt."

"Where?" Elizabeth asked.

"Here," her aunt had said, drawing back from Elizabeth and pointing to her heart.

Elizabeth had looked perplexed when she spied neither blood nor even a cut in her aunt's lemon-colored gown. She looked into eyes near the same sapphire blue as her own and frowned. "I do not see a wound, Auntie."

Her aunt used her free hand to wipe at her tears. "That is because the hurt is deep inside."

"It is?"

Her aunt nodded, looking away for a second, her eyes filling with tears again.

"If I kiss it, will it make it better?" Elizabeth had asked.

"No, dearest, this kind of hurt will never go away."

A frown had settled upon Elizabeth's face, for she didn't understand.

Her aunt must have seen her confusion, for it was her turn to frame Elizabeth's face with her hands. Skin—so smooth it looked like poured milk to Elizabeth's young eyes—filled with color. Her aunt's eyes glistened with tears as she stared down at her. "Poor dear. You have no idea of how miserably the *ton* will treat you, do you?"

Elizabeth, who thought a *ton* was something that weighed a lot, merely shook her head.

"They will eat you up and spit you out," her aunt predicted. "Especially if you marry as miserably as I have done." And then her aunt did a startling thing. She bent her head so they were nose-to-nose. Her expression turned somewhat fierce. "You must promise me something, Elizabeth. Something very important."

Elizabeth, who would have done anything for her aunt, nodded.

"Promise me you will never marry one of *them*."

Elizabeth felt her brows lift. "One of *who*?"

"Them," her aunt all but growled. "Men. Scoundrels. Fiends, all of them: Never to be trusted."

The words shocked Elizabeth, as well they should, for her aunt had always preached that every girl should marry, but more than that, marry for love. "But . . . I don't understand."

Aunt Lilibeth had drawn back, her face turning sad all at once. "You will in time."

Elizabeth doubted it, but she was not truly a normal child, and so she resolved to give her aunt's warning some serious thought, enough so that she never forgot her words.

As it happened it wasn't until two years later that she finally understood. She'd been sent to her aunt, something that Elizabeth never minded, thus when she arrived she didn't wait for the butler to announce her. She'd burst into the drawing room. And caught her uncle atop one of the upstairs maids.

Elizabeth had been horrified, puzzled, then, with a surge of maturity far beyond her years, she'd finally understood. Her uncle didn't love her aunt. He loved the maid.

But it wasn't until two years after that she completely understood, for it was then when she made her bow to society.

A comeout ball. Who wouldn't be excited? And Elizabeth was, as every girl her age, very excited indeed. The weather that night had been splendid. Clear. Warm. Magical. Her mother, a Hartnell of the Cheshire Hartnells, had prepared her well for the day. Elizabeth had lain down to rest early on (so that she wouldn't have bags under her eyes, but she was so excited she could barely lie still). When the time had come she'd donned the prettiest gown (a white satin dress with silver thread shot through it so that it looked like stars glittered upon her skirts). Her black hair had been washed and combed to such a shine one would have a hard time picking out the coronet her grandfather had purchased from an impoverished viscount. And as she stood, poised at the top of the stairs, Elizabeth had felt like a princess.

Too bad a prince hadn't shown up.

Nor a duke.

Nor even an earl.

Just the youngest son of an impoverished baron along with fifteen other guests.

It was a humiliation of the first order, and her mother had never recovered. And as Elizabeth danced with the one eligible young man who'd deigned to show up, she'd finally understood her aunt's dire words. The rest of the guests had looked on, most of them family members from her great-uncle's side, all of whom had shown up to gawk at their wealthier relative's household goods. (Elizabeth had caught one distant cousin stuffing a napkin holder into his pocket. She could only guess he'd thought it a bracelet.) No matter that she'd been educated at a proper boarding school. Nor that she had the manners and grace of a duke's daughter. As her aunt had warned, society looked upon her with disapproving eyes.

It was a heartbreaking realization, and some young ladies might not have borne it.

Elizabeth did. She realized nothing she could say or do would change matters. She accepted that she would never be good enough for the *ton* in the way that most people accepted the color of their hair. And if sometimes certain barbs hit home, she ignored them. She behaved perfectly. Attended parties. Danced sedately.

But deep down inside, buried far in her heart, Elizabeth wondered if it was all a farce. Perhaps one day she would rebel. Perhaps one day people would see her as she truly was, a commoner masquerading as an earl's daughter. Perhaps one day she would do something truly shameful. After all, no matter how perfectly she behaved, she would always be the granddaughter of a cobbler.

And the offspring of a shoemaker did not, as a rule, marry into the nobility.

Or so people thought . . .

Everyone ought to bear patiently the results of his own conduct.

—PHAEDRUS

CHAPTER ONE

There was a certain amount of freedom that came along with being a rake. A glorious liberation that made the black coat and tails Lucien St. Aubyn wore almost worth the effort it took to button himself into it. Almost.

Clutching a crystal-tipped walking stick, the duke of Ravenwood stepped down from his carriage. The air was chilly, the heavy clouds that had hung low over London's hazy sky having dropped to the ground. He took a big whiff of moist air, letting it invigorate him, before patting his chest to ensure his quizzing glass was where it should be and stepping toward the huge mansion that belonged to one of society's premier families: Lord and Lady Derby.

Rolling off into the night, his massive black carriage pulled away as he climbed the steps of the brick mansion, ignoring the curious and excited stares he received as he followed the crowd toward a rather grandiose and ostentatious ballroom that near deafened him from the number of voices coming from within. Some half-wit, his hostess no doubt, had come up with the brilliant idea of having rose petals tossed down from the balcony that encircled the ballroom. As a result the petals dotted the guests' clothes, hair, and foot bottoms. Frankly, he was surprised Lady Derby hadn't dressed young children in loincloths and fake fairy wings and suspended them from the ceiling. Then again, he should probably be thankful she hadn't thought of the idea. Like as not she'd have nailed the wings to the childrens' backs, causing an unholy racket.

He shook his head, pausing for a second in the doorway. Through a snowstorm of white and red petals he watched as couples danced in the center of the room, the season's offerings lined up before one wall like carp at a fish mart, minus the smell, of course. Well, in some instances.

Gold-gilt mirrors projected their backsides, more the pity. There were no balcony doors, just long, paned windows that sat between the ornately etched mirrors. Most of those windows were open, though nary a breeze ruffled the feathers stuffed into the elaborate hairstyles of the debutantes, nor dispersed the smell of bodies long overdue for baths.

Lucien surveyed it all and sighed. Another night. Another party. Odd's teeth, it bored him to tears.

He lined up to greet his hostess. The woman, who was a veritable old hag by society's standards, thirty-seven (seven years older than he), tried to pretend she hadn't noticed the passage of time by clothing herself in a dark blue gown better suited to a woman half her age, or half her breast size. She was quite in danger of falling out, Lucien noted.

"Lady Derby," he drawled as he stopped before her, his weight leaning on his walking stick. He leered at her breasts rather shamelessly as he gave her a smart bow. "I must say, you look *outstanding* this eve. Your *modiste* must be commended for managing to, er, keep you contained so well."

Her cheeks filled with sudden, instant marvelously unflattering color, given her spotty complexion. "My lord Ravenwood, what a surprise to see you here," she said with a polite smile pasted upon her pale face. She had the sad misfortune of having frizzy red hair, the result being that she resembled an orange poodle right down to the pointy nose and snip-at-your-heels eyes. "Especially since I do not recall inviting you," she added.

He allowed a patently false, yet thoroughly smug smile to grace his face. "Ah, but you didn't."

She drew herself up.

"I assumed, however, that your lack of an invitation was an oversight. Therefore, I took it upon myself to rectify the situation since I knew you could not possibly be upset with me still for refusing your advances."

Frankly, she did look upset. Her hands clenched. Her canine brown eyes glittered. "If your father were here, he'd box your ears," she said after first eyeing those nearby to ensure they wouldn't overhear.

Lucien felt no such restriction. He leaned toward her, mere inches away. "If my father were here, you'd still be sleeping with him, which is why, of course, I would never have slept with you, assuming, of course, that I was interested, which, I assure you, I was not."

Her glare all but boxed his ears.

Lucien smiled. "If you will excuse me," he said with false politeness, "I do have business to attend to." He looked past her. "Although it appears your husband has already finished his business." He *tsked, tsked* in disapproval. "You might want to tell him to tuck in his shirt. Terribly gauche to walk around like that."

He didn't give his hostess time to respond; rather, he turned on his heel and headed for the edge of the dance floor, the tip of his cane *click-clicking* as he did so, a smug smile upon his face.

But the boredom returned almost as quickly as it had disappeared. Sighing, he headed for the dance floor in search of more people to amuse himself with, only to be brought up short rather suddenly. A young man stood blocking his path, the youth so completely engrossed in showing his (apparently) new gold cuff links to his chums that he hadn't spied Lucien coming up behind him. Lucien reached into his pocket and pulled out his monocle, adhering it to his right eye as he looked the lad up and down.

Young men these days. Not only did they dress funny, but they had no respect for their elders. Witness this youth. His shirt collar was so high he was in danger of gouging his eyes out. He wore an ornately embroidered waistcoat, the color of the thread gold, the color of the jacket a blue Lucien had only seen on bottle flies and scarabs. To top it off, he wore his hair combed over to one side like blades of grass crushed by a bovine.

He waited for the young man to notice him, and when he didn't, switched his cane to his right hand, raised his left, and tapped him on the shoulder. "Excuse me, young man," he drawled.

The youth turned, spied Lucien looking at him, gave him a do-you-mind-I-am-talking look, then promptly turned his back to him.

Lucien's monocle popped off. He drew himself up, quite horribly shocked. Did the young man not recognize him? Did he not know he was the Duke of Death?

He looked around, trying to determine if the youth's shocking lack of respect had been noted.

And that was when he saw her.

Lady Elizabeth Montclair.

She twirled around the dance floor in the arms of a man so old, his shoulders were as hunched as a statue of Atlas. But Lady Elizabeth didn't seem to mind, for she apparently hadn't noticed the view it gave his lordship of her breasts. The lavender gown she wore was a tad low. The beads sewn upon it sparkled as they caught the glow of the candles above. Her hair lay piled atop her head in some loop-type design that gave the appearance of naturalness but that Lucien knew had taken hours to sculpt around her coronet. She had a figure that, while elegant, lacked a certain robustness some men preferred and light blue eyes that most men found beautiful and startling, for they stood out even from a distance. Her face was all that was classic, from the tilt of her snub nose to the heart shape of her face. Too bad she was of common blood. But that blood didn't preclude her from being, in a word, striking.

And she hated him. It was wonderful. They had met two times, and both of those occasions she'd done her best to convey that loathing in the most creative and rudest of ways. The first time she'd called him a murdering whoremonger, a sobriquet that while not entirely accurate, did have flair. The second time they'd met was aboard a ship when both of them had had the sad misfortune of being in the wrong place at the wrong time, that is, aboard the same ship. She'd made it clear whilst they'd been together, however briefly, that she didn't like him, would never like him, and wouldn't bother to *pretend* to like him. The attitude, coming as it did from the granddaughter of a cobbler, had at first shocked him, then amused him. Damned if he didn't admire her cheek.

He'd watched her from a distance from that time on, though he doubted she knew it. He thought of her rather like he would a bug, one that bore examination, for he found it rather remarkable that given her lineage she would be so high in the instep. One would need a pry bar to get beneath her skirts.

He straightened.

And for the first time that evening, nay, the first time in months, Lucien felt his ennui fade. Why hadn't he thought of it before? he wondered. What he needed was a diversion. A challenge. Someone who wouldn't come crawling to him with a mere look.

What he needed, he realized, was to seduce Lady Elizabeth Montclair.

She wanted to run from the ballroom.

Lady Elizabeth Montclair probably would have, too, if she hadn't been in the middle of a dance floor with hundreds of people gazing upon her as she danced with a man so old she was surprised he hadn't dropped to the floor dead from apoplexy, or at the very least, fallen to the ground after one of his creaking legs snapped from old age.

Rather a macabre thought, she admitted, but there you had it. Dancing with old Lord Luthgow would give anybody macabre thoughts. Perhaps it was the face paint. His lordship had used so much of it tonight he looked like a child's painting experiment gone bad. Perhaps it was the way his hands had a tendency to drift over parts of her body, in some instance actually squeezing. Or perhaps it was that his lordship was as deaf as lead pipes. Whatever the cause, Elizabeth would do something drastic if he didn't look up from her breasts and meet her eyes.

It didn't help matters that she could feel society's censorious stares as she twirled around the floor with him. Such was always the case when she danced with one of society's elite. His lordship was a baron, from a very old and very distinguished family. The *ton* considered it a travesty that one of their most illustrious peers would deign to dance with a woman whose family had become rather destitute in recent years.

"So you like to ride a spirited horse, eh, my lady?"

Startled out of her thoughts, Elizabeth forced herself to pay attention. She hadn't said anything of the sort. They'd been talking about Brighton. Elizabeth had said that she'd been in awe of a tide's force. But his lordship had thought she'd said horse. Now he was utterly convinced she was an equestrienne who wanted nothing more than to talk about horses. And while she did, indeed, love horses, it was rather maddening to have to shout to be heard.

"Indeed I do," she found herself saying, some little imp she should probably have ignored making her add, "Next to orangutans, they're my favorite animals to ride."

To her surprise, his lordship nodded. "Aye, like the Arabians myself. They've improved the Thoroughbred blood monumentally, do you not agree?"

She stared up at him, unbelieving that he could so

completely mishear her. She tried again. "Certainly, sir. The influx of monkey blood has been of tremendous benefit. Why, just the other day I heard a horse grunt like a chimp, a definite improvement over a neigh."

He nodded. Actually nodded. *Unbelievable.*

And so it might have gone on all night but for the fact that the music came to an end.

Thank you, Lord, Elizabeth silently prayed.

"A pleasure dancing with you, my lady," his lordship said with a bow, peering down her dress as he did so. The old buzzard.

"I wish I could say the same, your lordship, but dancing with you fair made me want to cry." She gave him a small curtsy.

He smiled at her magnanimously. "Now, now, now, my dear. Do not flatter me so. My ability to dance should not move you to tears."

Elizabeth gawked, bit her lip, then nodded, giving in to a little chuckle that turned into a cough before murmuring, "Just so," then turning and all but racing to her mother's side. Of all the ridiculous conversation . . .

"How was his lordship?" her mother asked.

"Quite, ah, talkative," Elizabeth supplied. She supposed she ought not to have done such a deplorable thing, but truly, she couldn't help herself. Perhaps she should apologize to his lordship. Then again, chances were he would likely mishear her again, thinking she was sorry over the demise of the English Thoroughbred or some such nonsense. Bother.

She turned to her mother, as grandiose a figure as ever there was one in her red-and-gold gown—the season's "in" colors. Her gray hair, naturally curly, sprang around her face for all that it was pulled back in a chignon. She had not aged well, the skin around her eyes sagging as if giving up all hope of ever being young again. Yet she still held herself as if she were a great beauty, something she had been as a young woman. It was that beauty her father had offered for. She'd been, to put it bluntly, sold to the highest bidder, and nearly bankrupted her father's family in the process.

"What did you talk about?"

Elizabeth blushed anew. "Horses."

Her mother nodded, light blue eyes glittering. "Good, good, for while his lordship is old, he is very, very wealthy, and *very* good *ton*. You would do well to encourage him."

Married to that lecherous old fool? Not likely, Elizabeth swore to herself. But she could never voice such thoughts aloud. This was to be her last season, the family funds having finally run out. But no one knew that yet, and no one would if her mother had her way.

"My lady?" a masculine voice greeted.

Elizabeth turned, eyeing a servant standing nearby.

"My lady, this is for you." He bowed slightly, the outdated wig their hostess forced him to wear nearly matching the dark gray of his jacket.

"A note," her mother trilled. "Oh, my dear. Likely another sonnet from one of your admirers." The words were said loudly so as to be heard by all the other matchmaking mamas nearby, and, in the process, make them obscenely jealous that their own daughters hadn't received such a missive.

Elizabeth, who had never received such a sonnet in all

her life, took the envelope curiously and opened it. A piece of paper nearly fell out.

Beth, I must see you right away. Something terrible has happened. Meet me in Lady Derby's drawing room. Alone.

Lucy

If someone had been watching Lady Elizabeth closely right then, that person would have noticed a dramatic transformation come over her. Her face paled. Her hands clenched.

"Why, Elizabeth, whatever is the matter?"

"Ah. Nothing, Mama."

"What does it say?"

Elizabeth debated with herself what to tell her mother, but she knew to confess the truth would not be wise. Not after what happened the last time she'd gone to her friend in a time of need. Indeed, she'd nearly sailed to Spain with the Duke of Death thanks to her rather clumsy friend.

"Elizabeth?" her mother asked.

"It says," Elizabeth stalled, her mind furiously trying to come up with an appropriate sonnet. "Roses are red. Violets are blue. You hair is very pretty, and I love you."

She smiled miserably at her mother, knowing that good lady would see right through her lie. But her mother was too busy acting delighted by the words.

"Why, my dear," she trilled loud enough for residents of France to hear. "You have a secret admirer."

"Indeed, Mama, I believe I do."

Her mother actually looked pleased about something, for once.

Elizabeth could barely stomach it. "Er, if you will excuse me, Mama. I believe I shall go refresh myself in case I am asked to dance by my new, ah, friend."

"Oh, indeed, indeed," her mother encouraged, shooing her away.

Elizabeth felt sick, knowing it was wrong to lie. Another part of her knowing that her mother had never liked Lucy, never *would* like Lucy, and always frowned upon seeing Lucy, especially since that same Lucy had become a marchioness. It irked her mother to no end to be outranked by Elizabeth's best friend.

She caught the eyes of the servant who'd brought the note, and who'd obviously been told to wait for a reply. "Where is she?" she asked, when they were out of earshot.

"Follow me."

"Elizabeth," her mother called.

Elizabeth stiffened, turned back.

"Do be sure to pinch your cheeks. You look as pale as a corpse tonight."

Elizabeth blushed scarlet. "Oh. Ah, yes, Mama. Of course." She turned. Of all the things to say. But her embarrassed pique faded as she followed the servant, her worry about her friend doubling. Lucy was with child, and it suddenly dawned on Elizabeth that there might be trouble with the pregnancy. But then wouldn't her husband Garrick come to fetch her?

Barely paying heed to the petals that rained down upon her, or to the faces she passed—all of whom smirked at her as she glided by—she followed the servant past their hostess, out of the ballroom, and into the main hall. The sudden drop in noise was a welcome relief. So was the smoky-cool air wafting through the hall. A vase filled with multicolored tulips sat before a mirror. Her reflection was sent back to her as she passed before the drooping blooms. Various closed doors lined the main hall. A stairway lay at the end, hugging the right wall, then turning left. There was a door at the foot of them, and it was there that the servant led her.

She opened the door. Elizabeth, spying Lucy immediately, was relieved she had reached her friend undetected. Lucy sat in a beige armchair, a purple cloak covering her. She stood the moment she heard Elizabeth enter.

Two things hit Elizabeth at once. One, Lucy had grown a great deal since she'd last seen her. Two, marriage had not flattered her friend at all, for either she'd grown very masculine looking, or the person staring back at her was . . .

"You!" she hissed, stopping abruptly.

His grace, the duke of Ravenwood, bowed slightly, "My dear Elizabeth, we meet again."

Lucien watched as a comical mix of disbelief, outrage, and accusation filled her ladyship's face.

"Why, that is mine," she accused, pointing to the cloak he wore.

"Indeed it is," he said, stopping. "Do you think it flatters me?" He pulled the bottom half over his face in a feminine gesture, mimicking a female voice in a way that would have done a Shakespearean actor proud. "I confess, I told the servant who fetched it for me that I thought the color might make me look a bit sallow."

She just stared.

He waited for her to react.

But she didn't react.

He shoved the hood off his head.

She still didn't react.

It was, truth be told, rather disconcerting. He'd been hoping for a scream—a raised voice perhaps—at which point he would move in, kiss her senseless, perhaps even have his wicked way with her—if she were lucky—after which they could both retire to the study and smoke cheroots. Or at least, *he* would smoke a cheroot. He was utterly confident *she* would feel like having one, too, if he hadn't lost his touch.

Only she wasn't cooperating with his plan.

He removed the cloak with a dramatic flair, allowing her to see him in all his masculine garb. Perhaps that had been the problem. After all, he reasoned, it was hard to bring a woman to her knees when one looked like Mary the maid. He straightened, letting her eyes take their fill of him, watching as she looked him up and down, a part of him wanting to stand extra tall as she did so. Through the oak-paneled walls one could hear a violinist strike up a spunky tune. Lucien waited.

Then she did something that truly baffled him. She placed her hands on her hips, slowly, deliberately. Then lifted a black, perfectly plucked brow in a rather chastising way. She held that position for exactly ten seconds before clucking her tongue, and saying, "It occurs to me, Your Grace, that you must have some nefarious and scandalous reason for summoning me here tonight. Truth be told, I'd far rather you simply spit it out than keep me waiting."

Lucien gawked.

"If I am incorrect, of course, then tell me otherwise. If, perhaps, Lucy sent me word of her plight through you, then I would rather hear what is wrong."

What? No screech? No pointed fingers? No, "You horrible rake," yelled at him? Granted, he hadn't had a private tête-à-tête with her in almost a year, but the last time they'd parted company he'd been sure she despised him. Not surprising. He despised himself.

She waited, left brow lifted.

He said, "You think your friend would actually ask for my help?"

She shrugged, those small breasts of hers plumping as she did so. "Why not? She seems to like you, though I've no idea why. She trusts you. So, yes, she would do something that unbelievably silly."

Lucien didn't know what to say. He didn't know what to do. And it wasn't her condescending attitude that threw him. It was her belief that someone in London might actually *like* him that stymied him.

"So, what is it, Your Grace? Why have you brought me here? I know it can't be my charming company you seek."

"You think not?"

Her eyes narrowed. "You know how little I like you."

Indeed, he did. Unlike most of society, she didn't hide it. He supposed it had something to do with his brother's death, but he wasn't sure. Who knew the workings of the female mind?

"Well?" she prompted.

Good God. She actually tapped her left foot, giving him a look of impatience.

"I brought you here to give you my kiss of death," which, of course, wasn't what he was here to do at all, but he felt the sudden urge to see how she would react to those words.

She didn't. She just pursed her lips in an impatient way, saying, "I would recommend you save those for your courtesan, whomever that unlucky woman might be."

Unlucky? And by now Lucien had grown a bit miffed. He straightened, putting on his best I-am-the-Rake-of-Ravenwood-and-I-am-here-to-steal-your-virtue look.

She didn't flinch.

Damnation. Very well. Let us see how she reacted to spoken words. "I brought you here to seduce you." Once again he waited for her reaction.

He had it a moment later.

She snorted.

CHAPTER TWO

E lizabeth couldn't help herself. Certainly it was an unladylike sound, but what he said sounded so ludicrous.
"You want to seduce me?" she repeated sarcastically.

"I do," he said.

"And why," she asked, "have you decided to seduce
me?"

He shrugged, appeared to consider his words, then
said frankly, "Because you despise me."

The words settled over her slowly. But it was the look
on his face that finally convinced her he might be telling
the truth. "You, duke, are a demented fool."

"I beg your pardon?" he asked.

"You heard me correctly. What is more, my words are
true. Witness your behavior of late. Oh, yes," she said
when she noticed his upraised brows. "It may have been
over a year since that debacle of a scandal wherein rumors of your ruining me on that awful ship surfaced, rumors, I might add, that you never bothered to deny. But
during that time, I have kept my eye on you, mostly in the
hopes of steering clear of you. As a result I know of the
horse race down Durry Lane. The fisticuffs at the opera.

Even the cockfights you attend. What is more, I know the cause of it all."

"Indeed?" he asked. "Pray, enlighten me."

"You are bored, Your Grace. Utterly and completely bored. You like to bully society with your arrogant looks and outlandish behavior, and now you have apparently decided to bully me. Well, I will have none of it, for I am leaving. Forgive me for spoiling your plans for my seduction."

She turned, lifted her nose, and made to exit the room.

He was at her side in an instant, and for the life of her Beth didn't know how he managed to move so fast. But a hand shot out to stay her, lightly clasping her forearm. She gasped at such forward behavior, then stared at that hand pointedly, telling him without words to unhand her that instant, yet oddly lost for a moment as she stared at his tan fingers against her pale flesh. She looked up at him sharply, disconcerted to realize how close he was.

"You truly *do* despise me, don't you?" he asked softly, those tarragon-colored eyes of his looking at her in a way that startled her. He almost seemed to care about her opinion of him. Ridiculous.

"I do," she admitted, though, truth be told, she didn't really hate him. Elizabeth didn't hate anybody.

He still hadn't let her go, and so she was conscious of that hand on her flesh, oh how she was conscious. It irritated her to the point that she jerked out of his grasp.

"How utterly surprising," he murmured.

"What is surprising, Your Grace, is that someone has not put a ball through your heart."

"Are you volunteering for the job?" he asked, looking almost hopeful.

"The only thing I would volunteer for is to beat you with a club. Now. Let me go."

He did. She felt buoyed by her triumph. But it was a triumph that was short-lived, for he stared down at her intently, his gaze sweeping her up and down yet again. "I must say, your hair looks quite pretty like that."

"Indeed, sir. I am most flattered. Coming from a man whose wardrobe most likely consists of red capes and pitchforks, I will take the compliment to heart."

"I wonder how you manage to keep it in place. Sewing pins, perhaps?"

He was jesting, of course, but she could jest right back. "Certainly, duke, the same pins you must use to keep your horns in place."

He smiled, a smile that looked genuine, his eyes appearing surprised. And intrigued. "Touché, my dear."

"I bid you *adieu*, Your Grace," she said, turning to the door when it appeared obvious that he wasn't about to leave. "Do have a pleasant journey back to Hell."

"Don't you want to know what I planned to do once I'd seduced you?"

She told herself to keep walking. Told herself not to stop. But she did stop. Looking back on it, she realized it was that one action that changed her life irrevocably.

She stared up at him, waiting for him to tell her.

"I was going to ask if you wanted to become my mistress," he explained.

She blinked, wondering what to say. Well, she knew what she'd like to say, or rather, what to call him, but the unladylike words would not cross her lips. "You must surely be the most base, depraved male of my acquaintance."

"Do you think?" he asked.

"I do. But I would not be proud of the fact, Your Grace. I would look in the mirror. See what it is you have become. I fear you will not like what you find."

"No?" he asked, his eyes appearing to be genuinely curious, then considering. "Do you not wonder what would happen if you did the same? Are you not tired of being such a perfect lady?"

"I've no idea what you're talking about. What's more, I do not care to know."

"Ah, but I think you know well indeed what it is I am talking about."

She drew back as his hand lifted.

"What is the matter, my dear? Would you rather I ply you with soft words? Perhaps tell you your lips look as soft as rose petals?"

She stared at his lifted hand, the skin oddly callused for a man who did no labor. "Do not flatter me, sir. It will get you nowhere."

"But I'm not flattering. It's true. You *do* have lips like rose petals."

"And *you* are a poor liar."

"And *you* have a piece of petal stuck to you lower lip."

She drew up.

"Here," he said, touching her, bending toward her, his lips mere inches away. "It fell from your hair when you turned."

Elizabeth felt her whole body tense, then tingle, then, gracious, she didn't know what. She looked up at him, so near, his breath drifting lazily across her face. She almost she closed her eyes, though she told herself to draw back. To pull away. To slap his lordship soundly across the face. Experience warned her that the duke was not a man to be trifled with. But wouldn't you know it? She just stood there, motionless, as his finger dragged across her lower lip, leaving a trail of heat in its wake.

"Oh, I *do* beg your pardon."

Elizabeth jumped. So did the duke. They pulled apart, both turning toward the door.

"Your Grace," their hostess trilled, her haughty face filling with sudden, unmistakable malice. "I had no idea the business you needed to attend to was her ladyship."

And Elizabeth knew. She knew what would happen once Lady Derby left the room. A whisper here, a hint of what she'd seen there. Elizabeth's reputation would dissolve. For while the *ton* danced a mere few rooms away, she'd been alone with a man, unchaperoned, and that man had been touching her. Intimately touching her. And not just any man: Ravenwood. A man whose name had been linked to hers in the past.

She was compromised.

By the Rake of Ravenwood.

CHAPTER THREE

A pall hung over the Montclair household the next day, a pall that could be felt in the very framing of the home. A stillness settled over everything. No boards creaked. No windows slammed. No voices dared to be heard.

Elizabeth pushed aside a heavy, blue velvet curtain as she stared out her bedroom window and down at the cobbled street below. The sun shone off stones that seemed to be glinting happily at the unexpectedly beautiful day. It glared into her eyes, prisming off the gossamer stands of a web a spider had spun on the other side of the glass. She felt rather like the mummified fly she saw in that web. Trapped. Helpless.

She inhaled deeply, the better to keep herself from crying. She wouldn't cry, she told herself. She would not. It seemed ridiculous to cry when there was nothing she could do about what had happened.

Ravenwood.

That devil. No. Not devil. The Antichrist.

Bitterness made it hard to swallow. She turned away, unable to stand the sunlight a moment longer. Her reputation had been destroyed last night. Utterly and completely destroyed. And if Ravenwood behaved up to par, it would sink even lower, for she doubted he would marry her. The man would slither away unscathed, but she, *she* would be left to pick up the pieces of her damaged reputation, if such a thing were possible given her already low position.

And so now what? She had no dowry. No reputation, nothing to recommend her to a man. Not that she particularly wanted to marry, not after watching what Lord Ludlows had done to her aunt. But she knew her choices were few and far between. Her family was out of money. Nothing bore the evidence of that more than her room. Where once before the blue curtains had been new, now threads hung from the seams, the fabric unraveling near the bottom. The floral carpet looked worn, the coverlet on her bed that matched her velvet curtains having aged as poorly as the rest of the room. There would be no season for her next year, Elizabeth having assumed—and accepting—that she'd become a governess once her mother accepted defeat.

But not now. Not ever. Not with her reputation.

A sudden racket from down the street caught her attention. She turned back to the window and looked down the lane. Other faces peeked out of other windows as people in the brownstone neighborhood rushed to see what passed by.

A carriage came at them. Six dappled gray geldings, two outriders, and one red-and-purple-garbed coachman accompanied it. 'Twas the shiniest, biggest, most grandiose carriage Elizabeth had ever seen, and it jingled and creaked like a Mayfair parade. Gracious, but her father would give his left arm for such an equipage. A bird dived toward it, only to turn around at the last moment as if frightened away. The lead horse on the left tossed its white mane and swished its white tail as if to chastise that bird for such impertinence, the horse's silver-and-black tack gleaming in the sun.

Elizabeth, who thought she'd seen everything, felt her jaw drop. Gracious, it must be the Prince of Wales.

And then she saw the crest on the door.

Two black birds, each facing the other on a shield of red. Ravenwood.

Not a prince. A duke.

Her teeth clenched. She turned away from the window again, a myriad of emotions cascading within her. Relief. Anger. And oddly enough, hope.

So, he had decided to come? She'd wondered if he would. All night long she'd fretted, conjecturing on what would be worse: his grace proposing or his grace not proposing? She'd wanted to ask him last night as her mother had hastily shooed her out the door, but not one word had been exchanged, not one look from him that promised he would make things right. As such she didn't know what to expect. She still didn't know even though his carriage was outside. Why, he might be driving by, his face pressed to the window, thumbs stuffed into his ears, taunting her with his tongue as he drove by.

But the carriage had stopped. She could hear that it had. She looked toward the fireplace in the corner of her room and the clock that ticked on the mantel. Fifteen minutes went by before she heard a knock on her door.

"My lady?" a maid called.

Elizabeth turned back to the window, staring blindly

out of it. She knew, she just knew Lucien St. Aubyn, the Duke of Death, the Rake of Ravenwood, had asked her father for her hand.

God help her.

She was to become his duchess.

"You will accept him," her mother said when she was shown into the family's private parlor fifteen minutes later. It had taken Elizabeth that long to compose herself. And yet still her hands shook. Still her mind spun with the disbelief of it all. "You will accept him and be grateful for it, for I do not need to remind you that we cannot afford to give you another season. This is the one reasonable proposal we've received, and you will accept it."

It hadn't been a proposal. She'd been ruined. But Elizabeth didn't remind her mother of that fact.

"You should be pleased," her father added from his corner. His horseshoe-shaped hair looked mussed, his blue eyes as hard as spearpoints. And even though he was shorter than she, he suddenly felt twice the size this morn. "For you shall become a duchess." He stood near a suit of armor that had been purchased at auction and was meant to fool guests into thinking their lineage more noble than it was. "'Tis a title your mother and I could only dream of securing for you."

The Duchess of Death. How lovely.

Still, she nodded, not looking either of them in the eye, especially her mother. She hadn't been able to look her in the eye since Lady Derby had regaled her with all that she'd seen.

Ravenwood had been touching her lips, Lady Derby had hissed loud enough for half her guests to overhear.

Elizabeth would never forget the look on her mother's face. Never forget the look of dismay followed by relief followed by triumph. It had obviously never crossed her mother's mind that Ravenwood might not come up to scratch.

"Elizabeth, are you listening?" her father asked, his blue eyes, so like her own, narrowing.

She started. "Of course, Papa."

Her father nodded, exchanging a look of approval with her mother before the countess went to the door connecting the two rooms. She motioned her in, Elizabeth doing as bid. Her mother didn't leave the door open, as was proper. Elizabeth found that wildly amusing, although she was hard-pressed to understand why.

"My dearest Lady Elizabeth."

She turned to her right as the door closed. The drawing room overlooked the street, and so she had a perfect view of his grace as he knelt on one knee before the massive bow window. He had a shiny, black top hat clutched to his chest, a bouquet of hothouse roses in his right. A great black cape was thrown over his shoulders, his boot polished to such a shine she could see white bars of light from the reflection of the window.

"I have come to ask for your hand in marriage."

Elizabeth blinked at the sight. Blinked, then gasped, then horrors upon horrors, felt tears build. She tried to stifle them, inhaling then exhaling then inhaling again, hands clenching. Oh, how she tried to stop them. But she couldn't. She watched as he knelt there. A tear escaped. She wiped it away angrily. He must have seen it, for he slowly got to his feet. She watched as he stared at her for a second, then tossed the flowers and hat aside.

"Well, now," he said. "I never expected my proposal to move you to tears."

And the dam burst.

"You beast," she said. "Have you any idea of how much I despise you?"

Lucien started. What was this? *Tears?* "Despise me?" he asked.

"Yes," she sniffed.

She had the most damnable way of crying, he noted. They weren't sobs. She didn't whine. She made these little snuffle noises that sounded like a clogged waterspout.

"By why?" he found himself asking.

The snurfle noises increased. "Lady Elizabeth, please. I see no reason to carry on like this."

"See no reason?" she all but shrieked.

He jumped, actually jumped like a frightened man. And who wouldn't be frightened of the harridan coming at him? She suddenly looked like a character from *The Taming of the Shrew.* Her hand was outstretched as she came at him, little wisps of her upswept hair trailing behind her like smoke from her ears. Call him mentally challenged, but he actually had no idea what she intended until she came to a halt before him and slapped him full in the face.

His cheek stung from the force of it.

Her hand must have hurt, too, for she cried, "Ouch," just before she shook her fist at him. "You have a face as hard as your fiendish head."

He had faced women in pain. He had faced women in pleasure. He had never, ever, faced a woman as angry at him as Elizabeth Montclair.

And she had a right to be.

He knew it. He admitted it. 'Twas why he stood before her even though he knew marriage to her would be a consignment to Hell. He'd told her he'd wanted to seduce her, only he'd ended up ruining her, and now some long-forgotten sense of chivalry had him rethinking his morals . . . or lack of them. She hated him. No, she despised him, she had said. And she would be his wife. Just as soon as he calmed her down.

"Lady Elizabeth, please." He held his hands up. "Can we not discuss this like civilized human beings?"

"Civilized," she screeched, and suddenly Lucien was held captive by the sight of her. Her hair was drawn back loosely, the style flattering, the angry color in her cheeks even more flattering. Her eyes sparkled, her chest heaved. She was, to his eyes, quite splendid.

"Civilized," she repeated, chest still heaving. "Is that what you call your behavior?" She changed the expression on her face to one of polite disdain. "Why, I'm here to seduce you," she mocked his words. "Why, I ask," she parroted her own words. "Because," she mimicked again, "you *deserve* to be seduced."

"I never said you deserved it," he interrupted.

Interrupting an irate woman in the middle of a tirade was not, perhaps, the best thing to do. Gone were her tears; in their place was the feistiest, most attractive woman Lucien had ever seen and damned if he could figure out where she'd come from.

"You didn't have to say it," she hurled at him. And then, as suddenly as it'd come, her temper fled. "You didn't have to say it," she repeated, tears entering her marvelous, beautiful blue eyes again. "Because I know why you chose me. I am the cobbler's granddaughter, a man who by some miserable streak of misfortune was made into an earl. Yet no one respects that title. Not you. Not society. Not even the populace. As such if you'd succeeded in seducing me, society would have looked the other way. If you'd failed, somehow *I* would have been made to look like the fool, not you."

"You make it sound as if I ruined you on purpose."

"Didn't you?"

"Good heavens, no. I only wanted to *bed* you."

Oddly enough, the words made her stand up straighter, made a combination of pain and wounded pride enter her eyes. "I see," she said, though it was clear she didn't.

And suddenly, he realized she was right. He *had* chosen her for the very reason she claimed. She was an outcast. He was a duke. Society would ultimately turn the other way if he refused to marry her. He had known that. He simply hadn't cared.

And that made him feel as low as the slugs that wiggled on the bottom of upturned rocks.

Why, he didn't know. Frankly, he'd thought he'd outgrown any semblance of a conscience. Apparently not.

He stared at her, wondering what to do. Females enjoyed hugs. At least, the females of his acquaintance did. So he went to her and pulled her into his arms, holding her for the first time in his life. Wondering why he hadn't held her before.

"I'm sorry, Elizabeth."

But she was like a fence post. She immediately jerked out of his embrace. "Sorry, Your Grace?" she said with a voice gone hoarse. "Well, I am sorry too. Sorry that I ever met you. Sorry that I am forced to say yes to your offer." She swallowed, wiping at her eyes and leaving flat roads of tears on her face. "Sorry that I will follow in my aunt's footsteps and be wed to London's most notorious, black-hearted rake."

More tears escaped, but she swiped them away, too. "But I promise you this," she gritted out. "We may become husband and wife, you and I, but you will never, ever have more of me than the finger you place your ring upon."

She glared up at him. Lucien was torn between saying something sarcastic and admitting he deserved her words. Instead, he found himself bowing. "As you wish," he replied, surprised at the sharp stab of regret he felt.

CHAPTER FOUR

And so it was that the duke of Ravenwood was finally brought up to scratch. One can only imagine the stir such news brought to the *ton*, many of whom had heard the infamous tale of Lady Elizabeth's compromise and could scarce believe that he actually offered for the chit. Then, too, there were those matrons who cursed their own luck that it was the countess of Sheffield's daughter, and not their own, who'd managed to pull off such a trick.

And trick it was, although no one actually believed the infamous duke would walk down the aisle. In fact, White's had nigh on fifty bets connected to it, bets that ranged from when the duke would flee London, to how long Lady Elizabeth would stand at the altar before admitting that his grace wasn't going to show. The *Gazette* carried the story, the general populace then reading about it. Everyone who was anyone wanted to witness the spectacle.

All of this Elizabeth knew, and all of it served to make her quite ready to throw herself out her bedroom window on the eve of her nuptials. Well, not really, but it was an appealing momentary thought.

Instead she sat before her sitting room fireplace, a swarm of embers dancing amongst the chimney's updraft before shooting away. No one kept her company, her mother purportedly having, "Worked her fingers fair to a nub," which Elizabeth took to mean that the servants had been run ragged in the three weeks the duke had given them to make the arrangements. Three weeks. And not a word from him since.

And though she told herself not to, Elizabeth studied the gown that hung in the corner of her sitting room, her throat tightening in what could only be described as fear as she did so. There was no doubt it was beautiful. The white lamé was beaded with pearls. The long, tight sleeves embellished with silver-and-blond lace. The train—which reminded Elizabeth of a foresail it was so long—was made of the same lamé. She would look stunning in it tomorrow. That is if the duke made an appearance.

And if he didn't, what then?

She didn't want to focus on that too much, for she knew only too well what would happen. Her reputation would be lost, for engagement or no, what she needed was a wedding to remedy her compromise. And yet odds were six to one at White's that her fiancé would jilt her, odds she privately agreed with since she'd seen neither hide nor hair of him. For all she knew he could be on his way to the Indies, celebrating with a slew of drunken sailors his narrow escape from the parson's noose.

Shaking her head, she realized if he were on a ship, there was naught she could do about it. She would know on the morrow what her future held. For now she needed to wait. Wait and sleep, if such a thing were possible.

She rose from her chair, turning away from the fireplace and drawing her cotton wrap around her as she left her sitting room. It would be a long night.

"Good evening, Elizabeth."

Elizabeth came off the floor—all ten toes exiting the well-worn carpet as if they'd stepped on glass. A man reclined in a manner of sublime contentment against one of the posts of her bed, a man she only too easily recognized, the scurvy knave.

"You!" she hissed, disbelief making her blink.

"You," the duke of Ravenwood mimicked, straightening away from the bed, the black jacket he wore falling open.

He looked like he'd been on a drinking binge, for he had stubble upon his chin, his normally tidy black locks in disarray. They hung past his shoulder, Elizabeth realizing that when they weren't swept back, they were rather long. His white shirt appeared wrinkled, the cravat he'd worn loose around his neck, the ends of it almost dragging on the floor.

"My dear Elizabeth," he drawled with a smirk, "you must start greeting me with something other than *you* every time you see me."

Perhaps not drunk, but certainly having been drunk, for she could smell the faint aroma of brandy that hung on his breath. She tried not to gawk, tried, but couldn't help herself. "You're in my bedroom," she accused.

He looked around. "I am? Funny, I thought this was the drawing room." He turned to the blue floral-covered mattress, stroking his chin in thought. "Though I suppose that explains the presence of the bed."

"You're in my bedroom," she repeated, with an edge of anger.

His brows lifted. "Yes, I do believe I gleaned the meaning of your words the first time."

"My bedroom," she repeated again.

"Your bedroom," the duke repeated. "Quite."

"What are you doing here?"

He lifted a brow again. "Why, I should like to talk to you, of course."

She felt her brows lift. "Talk to me? Now?"

"Do you always repeat the words spoken to you, or have you suffered a sudden, debilitating loss of hearing I should know about?"

"You needed to talk to me tonight," she stressed, ignoring his words. "Not three weeks ago when you gave me the ultimatum of preparing for our wedding? Not two weeks ago. Not even this morning? Now?"

"You sound rather peeved."

"Get out," she ordered, pointing to the door, suddenly recalling that she wore nothing more than a wrap with lace flounces, the edges of it scratching at her neck. She drew it around her tightly, catching a piece of hair, which she'd yet to braid for the evening. "Get out. Whatever it is you have to say can certainly wait until the morrow."

"No."

"No?" she huffed.

"No," he repeated. "You may not know this, but I went to quite a lot of trouble to get up here. Why, it took me nigh on fifteen minutes, then another ten to find your room. I'm quite exhausted."

"You're mad."

"Am I? How reassuring to know. That explains quite a

lot. But my mental state aside, I shan't leave. And if you're worried I might compromise you, I shouldn't fear," he said with a wicked smile. "It would be rather hard to ruin you a second time, I believe."

She blushed. "Go away, you insufferable man."

"No," he answered firmly. "What I have to say will only take a moment," he added. "Surely you can give me that?"

She clutched the wrap around her even more tightly. "You may speak with me on the morrow."

He lifted his brows, pacing a look of horror upon his face. "On our wedding day? But that is bad luck."

"I wouldn't worry, Your Grace. You are long overdue for a bolt of lightning."

He pursed his lips, nodded. "Yes, I know. So I rather thought I might give the good Lord above another reason for striking me down by coming to your room to discuss our impending marriage."

He was going to call it off, she realized, trying not to panic. For a second she forgot her anger, forgot that she wore a wrap with a gauzy chemise beneath . . . forgot everything but a sudden, unexpected panic.

He couldn't call it off. Her family couldn't weather the shame. As it was, their position in society was precarious. If he were to jilt her on the morrow he would ruin them all, and bankrupt them in the process, for her family needed her to marry well in order to restore their fortunes. Ravenwood had been made to pay for ruining her, and pay dearly. Her father had been overjoyed.

"I have a question for you."

"A question?" she squeaked, her mind whirling. Perhaps she could conk him over the head. Render him unconscious, then arrange to have his body propped up near the altar in the church somehow?

"You know, Elizabeth, I really am worried about your hearing. Do reassure me that you haven't suffered a disease in the three weeks since I last saw you."

"My hearing is quite fine," she said. "And I wish that if you are going to call off the wedding, that you would do so now."

"*Me* call it off?" he asked, his black brows lifting. "I want *you* to call it off."

"Me?" she breathed in shock.

He lifted a hand to her chin, touched her as he had on the day of Lady Derby's ball, that disastrous day that had led to this very moment. Next he leaned close to her, saying very clearly and succinctly, "Yes, you." Then he straightened, though he didn't release her. "I thought that since you obviously do not want me as your husband." He dragged his finger down the side of her jaw. She tried not to shiver. "And I obviously don't want you as a wife, that you might want to jilt me tomorrow."

She didn't move, couldn't move. "But I cannot jilt you," she said, her breath drifting back to her.

"Why not?"

Think, Elizabeth. She blinked, stared at his lips. *No, no, no. Not there.* She looked away, focused on his left ear. *There. That was better.* He had tiny down hairs growing from the lobe of his ear. How . . . unexpected.

"My family would not weather the scandal." She dared to meet his gaze again. *Mon dieu*, but he was close. And his thumb. For the second time she found herself thinking how coarse it was for a man of leisure. "If I jilt you, I will be deemed an outcast."

"Women jilt men all the time," he argued.

"Not a duke. Especially when that woman has been ruined by that duke."

"A trifling matter," he said.

"I hardly think so," she huffed.

"But I will pay you to do so," he said softly, almost devilishly.

She blinked, hardly trusting her ears.

"I shall pay *you,* not your father," he said, a wide, temptation-filled smile upon his face. "Pay you enough money to live on your own, in comfort, somewhere far away, where you could behave and do whatever you like. Having a sullied reputation shall not matter a whit."

She drew back, though it took a monumental effort on her part to do so. Drew away from his disturbing touch. Drew away from him. His hand fell to his side.

"Surely you jest?"

He straightened. "Indeed I do not, my lady." His gaze darted down. Only then did she realize that she'd let her hands fall loose. The glint in his eyes returned.

It was that look combined with the contents of his words that made her step away, made her place her hands upon her hips. "Why, you wretch," she gritted out. "You are trying to pay me off."

He blinked, met her gaze, then changed his smile to one of happiness. "Yes, I believe that is what I just said."

She stared at him, wondering how it was possible that she felt the thoroughly unladylike urge to slap him. Again.

He lifted his brows again. "Are you going to strike me again, for if you are, I'd just as soon move out of the way."

She blushed that he could so easily read her mind. "I cannot believe you would ask such a thing."

"Why not? It makes more sense than *me* calling it off. If I jilt you, you will be shunned, considered demoralized, seduced and then abandoned by the wicked duke," he added with a smirk. "You will not recover."

She stiffened, knowing he was right, angry because of it. "As if my reputation matters to you."

He clutched his chest as if wounded, his demeanor turning into that of an adorable scamp. "But it does."

She didn't believe him, not for a moment. Like as not he only cared that his jilting of her might result in society's disfavor of him. Why, he might actually be shunned by society. The man already trod a fine line, what with all the suspicion surrounding his brother's death.

"But putting that aside," he continued, "you must see what a brilliant idea it is."

"Brilliance for someone of your low intellect is not a remarkable thing."

"Ouch, my lady. You do wound me with your words."

"One can only hope. And I shall not do it. I have family to think of—"

"A family you will have enough money to visit upon occasion."

Not if her father was in debtor's prison. She pressed her lips together before continuing. "Not without causing them great shame," she said, assuming her father had not told him about their near financial ruin. "And I have friends, too, friends whose husbands would object to my shameful presence should I visit."

"You can make new friends."

She held on to her patience only by the thinnest of threads. What he asked was unconscionable.

And tempting.

"You ask too much," she hissed, angry with him for daring to corner her in her room, to propose such a preposterous thing. And angry at herself for even considering it.

"Why? Surely what I propose is no worse than what you propose. You wish us to bond in matrimony, to become man and wife. We shall be forced to endure each other's company for the rest of our lives. Frankly, I believe I'd rather tie stones to my ankles and fling myself from Westminster Bridge than endure that."

She lifted her chin. "I feel quite the same."

"See. If you were to jilt me on the morrow"—his tone all that was reasonable—"you would be able to seek your own future. Marry a man of your choice, marry nobody if that is what you wish, but you would be releasing us from a marriage neither of us wants."

He was like Hades, come before her to tempt her with a deal. Even the fireplace cooperated with the image, the flames suddenly flaring to life on a smoke-scented breeze. And she was tempted. Gracious she was startled at how much she had to fight back the urge to agree. But along with a longing to do as he asked came a fear of what would happen if she actually did. Her family would suffer the consequences of her selfishness. They would be penniless, shunned, while she lived her life in comfort. Oh, she could share her wealth with them, but she knew her father well enough to know he would never accept charity from her. And who was to say that her reputation might not follow her? If she agreed, she might have nothing, perhaps not even a husband, for what man would marry a woman with such a sullied reputation? Ruined. Then branded a fool for refusing to restore her reputation. Her father in debtor's prison.

"No," she all but groaned. "I cannot." She met his gaze, his green eyes looking almost black in the light. "What you propose is preposterous. You ask that I give up everything that is dear to me so that you may go on living your life as you please. That I shall not do."

She was proud of herself, proud of the way she held herself—no matter that he was so near. Proud that she didn't tremble though the blood rushed through her ears. Proud, most of all, that she'd had the courage to say no.

"Will you give me an heir, Elizabeth?"

The blood drained from her face like liquid from an upturned cup.

"Will you?" he asked.

He moved toward her again, only a scant inch, but it felt like he all but pressed himself against her. "Will you mind me doing this?"

He leaned toward her and, before she gleaned what he intended to do, covered her lips with his own. Shock made her drop the lapel of her wrap, made her place her hands against his hard chest. He angled his head. "Are you ready for this every night, Elizabeth? For that is exactly what I will ask," he murmured against her, his hot breath fanning a heat inside her, a heat she hadn't even known could exist.

She tried to move her head away, but quick as lightning, he moved to cup her face. Spots danced before her eyes as he forced her against a wall she hadn't even known she'd retreated to. Spots of anger, she told herself, but, no, what his kiss stirred in her was not anger. And for the first time she admitted that she'd always wanted to be kissed thus by a man, wanted to have him up against her, to have him take his taste of her. A part of her had wondered, however briefly, what it would be like to be kissed by *him*.

Wicked. Wicked. Wicked thought.

And it horrified her so much she used all her strength to push him away. Only he didn't move, just drew back, saying, "Perhaps you won't mind giving me an heir after all?" with a gleam in his eyes.

"Bastard," she hissed the unladylike word, then slipped away, her lips buzzing from the pressure of his mouth. She swiped at them, turned back to face him, shoulders square, hands clenched. "You shall beget no heir off of me." She looked into enigmatic green eyes. "But why do I have the feeling that you do not truly care about an heir?"

Something flickered in his gaze, something like surprise, followed by anger. Gone was the charming rascal. In his place stood a man who appeared as sinister as many claimed him to be.

"Do not expect me to be faithful," he growled.

"Do not expect *me* to be faithful," she hurled right back.

Silence descended.

"Very well," he said, stepping back from her. "As long as we understand each other."

"We do," she snapped. "You shall have your lovers, and I shall have mine."

"As you wish," he said.

"I do."

"Then I shall see you on the morrow?"

"Will *I* see *you*?" she asked.

For a second she thought he might deny it—her heart actually stilled as she waited for his reply—but he didn't deny it. He didn't say anything. Without another word he turned and left her room as soundlessly as he'd come. Elizabeth collapsed into a chair.

"Good heavens," she murmured. *How can I be so base as to enjoy his unwanted touch?*

And how can I marry him tomorrow?

And across town, far away from prying eyes and eavesdropping ears, two gentlemen discussed the coming marriage, too.

"Should we warn the family?" the Attorney General asked, his arms relaxed as he reclined in a plush red armchair in a secluded corner of White's. It always struck people as odd that the man should have the looks of a kind puppy, with his brown eyes and equally brown hair, when, in fact, he was something of a bull terrier when it came to convicting criminals.

"Warn them of what?" The Lord Chancellor shook his head, his gray hair meticulously styled, as was the rest of his toilette. He took a deep sip of brandy before saying, "That new evidence might be presented confirming that the duke might have killed his brother? 'Tis no more than what has been flying about society for years."

Brown eyes narrowed. "Yes, but this is the first time we might actually be able to prove the matter."

A frown, and then another shake of the chancellor's head. "Even so, I do not think it would change the earl's and countess's minds. They want too badly for their daughter to become a duchess. Do not forget, the earldom is new, and from what I hear, the family is near penniless, what with giving their daughter nearly three seasons. No. I'm sure the earl negotiated a bride-price in exchange for the scandal he caused them. They will not want to give that up."

The magistrate's brows lifted. "But it is preposterous that they would allow their daughter to wed such a man."

"Quite the contrary," his lordship contradicted with a wry smile. "With the scandal of his brother's death having faded, the duke is looked upon with near favor by many members of the *ton*."

"Not for long."

"Indeed," he said with a wave of his elegant hand. "But rest assured, I have already warned the earl as best I could. To say more might cause him to go to the duke, or do you not care that his grace might flee the country before you bring him to trial?"

The Attorney General released a breath, knowing his lordship had a point. "I pity the lady. It will not be easy for her to bear the scandal."

"She is used to scandal."

"Not this sort of scandal."

"She is the granddaughter of a shoemaker. Their kind can weather the storm. They always do."

The difference between war and marriage is that in marriage you sleep with the enemy.

—ANONYMOUS

CHAPTER FIVE

Like a fairy-tale wedding, the day of Elizabeth Montclair's marriage to the duke of Ravenwood dawned bright and clear. The air fair sparkled with sunshine, nary a cloud in the pretty blue sky. It was one of those rare, beautiful days when the dew sparkled off blades of grass, the air blew warm with the promise of a perfect, sunny afternoon, and flower petals glowed with a vibrancy that almost hurt the eyes. Fabulous viewing weather for the people who lined the streets leading to St. George's Church. But unlike a traditional wedding wherein people came to gawk at the bride and her maids, it was the groom people had come for.

A carnival atmosphere prevailed. Those who weren't lucky enough to wake up early to find a spot on the road found themselves ten people back instead. Street hawkers, quick to seize an opportunity, sold fruit to those who'd bypassed breakfast. Dandies dressed in their morning finery, mixed with servants dressed in their Sunday best, the ladies wanting to know if the fairy-tale prince—or duke as the case may be—would show up to sweep the fair maid off her feet. Or not.

One problem marred it all, not that the populace knew. The bride hated the groom.

Well, perhaps "hate" is too strong a word. But the morning after her tête-à-tête with the duke of Ravenwood, Elizabeth Montclair still felt as steamed as a teapot. As to the kiss, well, she'd shoved that thought to the furthest corner of her mind, an oak door covering it and the words Not to Be Examined painted upon its surface. Instead she focused on the duke of Ravenwood, the stress of having to marry a man within three weeks of being ruined by him combined with not being able to sleep the eve before, and, well, to say she was rankled would be a severe understatement.

She was ready to draw blood. Ducal blood.

The energy generated by her anger helped to cover her nervousness as she donned her wedding finery—something that took nigh on two hours. Helped her to focus as she was pampered and primped and made to look like a princess bride. One thought emerged. *He better bloody well show.*

And yet, what could she possibly do if he didn't?

"There, m'lady," her maid said, stepping back.

Elizabeth forced her troubled thoughts aside, looking at herself in the mirror. What she saw startled her, for as her mother was fond of telling her, she was no classic beauty. And yet, today she looked rather fine. At least she thought so.

"You've done well given what you had to work with," her mother said from her position standing in the corner of Elizabeth's room.

"Thank you, my lady," the maid bobbed.

Elizabeth studied her reflection again, admitting her

mother was right. The dress was shaped to accentuate her bust. It lifted, pushed her breasts up so high she wagered she could balance a plate upon them. Her hair, too, had been teased into an elegant mass reminiscent of the Georgian era, three black curls left to dangle down her right shoulder. And the white gown, rather than wash out her coloring, made her skin look even creamier, her blue eyes more startling. There was very little beading upon the gown—there hadn't been time—but the seamstress had managed something rather clever. What pearls she had sewn upon the fabric were shaped to resemble ivy, the vines seeming to sprout from her waist, creeping toward her toes and neckline in S-shaped patterns.

"Shall I call for the carriage?" the maid asked.

"Yes," her mother breathed softly. "She is ready to be viewed."

Ready to be viewed? Elizabeth thought, feeling an unruly reaction come to mind. Was she an exhibit? Was there a sign upon her rear requesting a shilling per view? Ready to be viewed, indeed.

"Now, my dear," her mother said, "when you enter the church I want you to pause in the doorway. Let society get a good look. Goodness knows St. George's doesn't seat a lot of people, so I want those we were able to invite to be able to recall perfectly how expensive yet tasteful your gown looked."

Oh, bother.

"Then, just when the music reaches a crescendo, I want you to stroll, not walk, down the aisle."

Wasn't a stroll a walk?

"Once you reach the duke, pause again—"

"Mother, please," Elizabeth dared to interrupt.

Her mother's words abruptly stopped, her eyes narrowed.

Elizabeth felt her heart begin to race at her daring, but, she reminded herself, this would be the last day she would have to listen to her mother's orders. "I understand what to do."

"I hope that you do," her mother snapped coldly. "This is an important day."

"Yes, I know." This was the day the family fortune was restored. "I know what you want me to do, but for now, I want to be alone."

"Alone. Do not be ridiculous. You are about to marry a duke—"

"Mother," Elizabeth dared to interrupt again, only more firmly. "Please."

The countess's mouth flopped open and shut a few times, but Elizabeth held firm. But then her mother's eyes swept her up and down. A self-satisfied gleam entered her gaze.

"Very well," she said at last. "I suppose it will not hurt to let you alone for a moment."

"Thank you. I promise not to slit my wrists."

"Elizabeth, do not even jest about such a thing," her mother gasped. "Why, I forbid you to do it."

Forbid it? Elizabeth felt like laughing. Even if she was desperate enough to do such a ghastly thing—which she wasn't—she doubted her mother could stop her. "I beg your pardon, Mother. That was in poor taste."

"Indeed it was. And just for that, I will expect you downstairs in two minutes."

Elizabeth merely nodded and, when she was alone, turned toward her window, only to realize she could barely move her train was so heavy. Anchored to the floor, she contented herself with viewing the sky, sending a short prayer heavenward for help.

Ah, but what kind of help? Elizabeth asked herself.

If the duke didn't appear, she might—just might—be better off than she was before. Jilted sounded better than ruined. If she were jilted, she might be able to marry someone else.

Yes, but your family will be destitute.

So? That didn't mean she couldn't wed.

Like who? An undertaker?

At least he wouldn't be Ravenwood.

An undertaker would be better than Ravenwood?

She thought about it for a moment.

Yes!

The carriage Elizabeth rode to the church in was magnificent. And rented. It had three large windows, one on each side and one in the back. Its black paint gleamed majestically, as did the four white horses pulling it—not a speck of dirt marring their coats—two servants riding postillion wearing green and gold livery. A giant bouquet of red roses sprang from the roof—an idea her mother stole from a marchioness—the blooms bobbing in the slight breeze. She was to ride in it alone, like a princess on her way to meet her prince.

Hah.

It was disgusting, Elizabeth thought. One might actually believe they were true peers of the realm, or that her mother expected the duke to show.

She climbed into the coach, her heart pounding in her chest, her palms sweaty.

Gracious heavens, she needed to get control of herself. But as the door closed behind her with a *snick*—the fresh air sucked out of the interior like a casket—she felt more alone and frightened than she ever had in her life. Longing for her friends overcame her. But Lucy was eight months with child—her first—her other good friend, Salena, in a similar state. Matrimony, it would seem, was not the least bit disagreeable to her bosom friends.

And so the panic increased.

Not a good thing.

Not a good thing at all.

She barely noticed the ride to St. George's Church, deathly afraid the evidence of her nervousness stained the pristine white fabric of her underarms. The carriage door opened. The sharp gust of wind that blew in did little to alleviate the cloying sense of suffocation that had overcome her. Someone handed her down—Elizabeth would never recall whom. Her legs nearly collapsed as she stood upon the hot pavement. Her breath grew labored. The distant cousin whom Elizabeth had never met before and who acted as bridesmaid handed her a bouquet of white lilies and red roses. Elizabeth clutched them. Her mother went inside but Elizabeth held back, the blooms shaking so badly they looked scared. Barely breathing, she watched as the church doors swallowed her mother. Would that they could swallow her, too. And spit her back out. Somewhere on the other side of London. Bother that, the world.

Was he inside? she wondered. *Had he arrived?*

No one told her. No one said a word.

It was too much for Elizabeth. She *had* to know. Slowly, she approached the door, one of the ushers waving her away. Yes, yes, yes. She knew it wasn't time for her to go down the aisle. She just wanted to peek. Just one tiny peek. She leaned forward, her train tugging at her waist. The light inside the church was muted, as if not even the sun would dare to shine brightly in such a holy place. Mahogany pews to the left and right of the main aisle were packed with people, their heads dipping and bobbing as if from a wind. One would think their attention would be taken with the painting of the Last Supper that hung at the altar. But no. They were all looking at *him* . . . at Ravenwood.

He'd shown.

Emotions pelted her. Relief. Disappointment, followed by an overwhelming urge to put a pistol between his grace's legs and pull the trigger (oh, yes, she knew how to wound a man). Certainly not a very ladylike thought, but there you had it. Elizabeth Montclair had reached the end of her rope. She'd hit the wall. Taken the final step off a short pier. The spectacle of her marriage combined with the lack of sleep after her midnight rendezvous with him all culminated to give her a sudden and thorough steaming head of temper.

Oh, gracious, was she ever mad.

He kept his back to her. It was as if he couldn't be bothered to turn. As if in showing up he'd done his part, now it was up to her to come to him.

Elizabeth grew even more furious.

Come to him, eh? She'd go to him alright.

Anger suddenly propelled her forward. The bridesmaid yelped, pulled forward and off her feet by Elizabeth's sudden dash.

The musicians hiding in the second-floor alcove must

have glanced down, seen her coming, then hurriedly started to play the wedding march. People quickly rose, bumping into each other in the process.

And Elizabeth stomped. Oh, how she stomped, not strolled, not floated, not any of the things her mother had ordered her to do. The string quartet played faster and faster, trying to match the music to her pace. She flew down the aisle, her train so heavy, she felt rather like a draft horse, all but grunting as she leaned into it. She came to a halt at the front of the church, next to Raven-wood.

The duke who still refused to turn.

The curate, who looked startled by her heaving walk down the aisle, stared between the two, his bespectacled eyes appearing huge behind his glasses.

"Ahem," he coughed, trying to alert her groom that his bride had arrived.

But his grace *still* didn't turn.

Hateful man.

"So glad you could make it today," she hissed.

Finally, slowly, he turned.

Elizabeth stiffened.

It was utterly maddening. The cad looked resplendent. Unlike last eve, he appeared ready to cut a fine swath this morn, his cravat tied in a subtle, yet sophisticated style. He wore a dark blue jacket with tails, his tan trousers nearly as pristine as her wedding dress. His hair slid back over his head like it existed only to make him look even more suave. But it was the look in his green eyes that stood out most. He laughed at her. Faced her as if this was all a fine joke and she the butt of it.

Ooo, the wretch.

"So glad you could make it, too," he responded, though not as softly as her. "You look rather well."

"Thank you." She smiled tightly. "You look rather ghoulish."

"Why thank you," he replied, equally polite.

If anyone thought it rather odd that the bride and groom were chitchatting at the altar, no one commented. Then again, they were probably too busy trying to hear what was being said.

"Shall we begin?" the duke asked after turning back to the befuddled curate.

The man blinked behind his glasses. "Begin what?" the curate asked.

"The ceremony."

The man jumped, saying, "Oh, ah, certainly. Certainly."

Elizabeth watched as he took a deep breath, seemed to clutch his Bible as if praying for divine intervention, then began, "Dearly beloved. We are gathered here in the sight of God . . ."

And that was when Elizabeth truly began to panic. The marriage ceremony had begun. He had shown up. She would be wed. To the duke of Ravenwood.

Dear God.

Suddenly the duke's idea of throwing oneself off the Westminster Bridge didn't sound like such a bad notion.

It was unfortunate timing on the curate's part that he came to, "therefore if either of you know any impediment, why ye may not be lawfully joined together in matrimony, ye do now confess it," right at that moment.

Elizabeth thought and thought and thought. Run? Stay? Swoon? Stand?

"I don't suppose if the groom is suspected of murder that would be considered an impediment?" she asked in desperation.

The poor curate went goggle-eyed.

"Elizabeth," her mother hissed. Someone gasped.

"I," the curate stuttered, "I don't believe so. He, ah, would have to have been *convicted* of such a crime, I believe."

"Oh," she responded dismally. She glanced at the duke, expecting him to be furious. Instead he looked down at her approvingly, nodding his head. "Too bad. It was a rather good idea. I never thought of paying someone to object." He turned back to the curate. "Is it too late to do so?"

"To do what?" the curate asked.

"Pay someone to object?"

The poor man began to sweat, giant beads of it dripping down his head. "I should say so, Your Grace."

"Hmm," the duke murmured. "Pity. Very well, proceed."

The clergyman's mouth gaped. It was a moment before he looked back at Elizabeth. "As you wish," he said, staring between them both like they were a ball bouncing between walls. "Then, ah," he began, blinking a few times before looking down at his prayer book, "if no impediment be alleged, then I ask you, wilt thou, Lucien Albert Zavier St. Aubyn, twelfth duke of Ravenwood, thirteenth earl of Chalmly, sixteenth baron of Blackwell have this woman to be thy wedded wife to live together after God's ordinance in the holy estate of matrimony? Wilt thou love her—"

Elizabeth snorted.

"Comfort her."

Not if I can help it.

"Honor her—"

She snorted again.

"And, ah, keep her in sickness and in health." The curate paused as if waiting for another noise from her, and when none was forthcoming, said in a rush, "forsaking all others, keeping thee only unto her, so long as ye both shall live?"

Elizabeth waited. The congregation waited. Likely God waited.

"I will," Ravenwood answered.

Someone sighed. Her mother, likely. The poor curate turned to her, his eyes wide, his lips quivering nervously. "Wilt thou, Elizabeth Montclair, have this man to be thy wedded husband, to live together after God's ordinance in the holy estate of matrimony?"

"Noooooo," she said, at least, that's what her mind screamed, but in reality she said, "I will."

"Wilt thou obey him—"

"Only if he's quite lucky," she said softly.

"And serve him—"

"I wouldn't wager upon it," she added.

The clergyman faltered. "Ah, er. Wilt thou," he seemed to wince. "Wilt thou love him—"

She snorted again.

"Honor him," the curate continued, "and, ah, keep him in sickness and in health?"

"No," she answered.

The curate almost dropped his prayer book. "You shan't?" She shook her head. "I cannot guarantee to keep a man healthy when everyone knows he regularly tries to drink himself to death."

The man's mouth dropped open. Elizabeth waited, breath held, for the duke to erupt. But he didn't. She darted a glance up at him again. The wretch was staring at his nails. *His nails.* Looking down at them as if a potential hangnail concerned him quite a lot indeed.

"Well, then, ahh. Do you, er, do you promise to *try,* my dear?" the curate asked.

Knowing if she disagreed the whole farce of a ceremony would come to a grinding halt, she looked back at the curate, knowing that the final chance to object was at hand.

But had she really ever had a choice?

"I will," she choked.

The curate rocked back on his heels, apparently weighed with himself if he should continue, looked at the duke, then apparently decided he should. "Very good. And do you promise to forsake all others, to keep thee only unto him, so long as ye both shall live?"

She didn't say anything.

The silence in the church was complete. She could hear someone scratch themselves, their nails raking fabric.

"Do you, my dear?"

"I am wondering if a bolt of lightning will strike me down should I say yes."

Laughter from the audience mixed in with the furious hiss of her mother, "Elizabeth, I will surely disown you if you do not say I will."

Elizabeth looked up at the duke once more. He turned to her, lifted a brow, just raised it as if to say to her he cared not a whit what she did.

All the fight drained out of her. Goodness knew why, but she just gave up then.

The curate looked at her as if her head had cracked upon and pigeons had begun to fly from it. People had started to murmur. Elizabeth debated—debated and decided—lifting her chin before saying, "Very well, I will."

"Bravo," someone called from the back. A person clapped. The duke turned to her and said with a twinkle in his arrogant eyes, "Good choice, my dear."

Elizabeth looked away, a sudden misery choking her with its intensity.

And that was when it hit her, though why so late, she didn't know. That was when she realized what it was she'd committed herself to. A farce. A parody of a marriage. She was married to his grace, and they would be nothing more than polite strangers. There would be no children. No little ones to keep her company, not even the daughter she'd always yearned for. It would be she and he and a lifetime of loneliness.

Just like her aunt.

"You are an embarrassment. A disgrace. How could you *do* this to me?" her mother cried from inside the church.

"If you were still under my care, you would be made to pay for your behavior," her father added, blue eyes glittering. "The Lord Chancellor was here today. You can be sure your disgraceful behavior will be related to every peer in London."

They were standing near the door, her mother having stomped up to her practically the moment the little church had emptied.

"Ravenwood," her mother said, turning to the duke, "I would not blame you in the least if you wanted to disown her."

Ravenwood smiled enigmatically. "On the contrary, my lady. As a new husband, I shall do nothing of the sort."

If her mother caught the duke's clipped tone, she didn't reveal it. Nor did her father. It caught Elizabeth's attention, however. She glanced up at the him. No. At her husband. She gulped. *Husband.*

"You are more forgiving than I, duke," her father said.

"How will I hold my head up?" her mother added. "How will I ever live this down? She has made a farce of my beautiful marriage. I tell you, a farce."

"I thought it was my marriage, Mother?" Elizabeth finally gained the courage to say.

Her mother drew herself up, the blue gown she wore all but popping its seams. "Do you hear this, George? Do you see what I have been dealing with since her come-out? She is willful and outspoken. I wonder that the duke doesn't ask for an annulment right now."

Elizabeth glanced at Ravenwood. There was the oddest expression on his face.

"If I might interrupt?" he asked politely.

Her mother and father looked at the duke.

"I have decided Elizabeth and I are going to Raven's Keep for our honeymoon." He smiled widely. "We leave now."

Elizabeth gasped.

Her mother gasped, too. "You *what?*"

"Here now, Ravenwood," her father said, "there's no need to hide your head in shame. I understand that my daughter's behavior was reprehensible today, but you do not need to run. If you put a brave face upon it, you should be able to weather the scandal nicely. Goodness knows, you've weathered worse."

Elizabeth tensed.

"I assure you, sir," Ravenwood answered, though his teeth seemed to stick a bit, " 'tis nothing to do with Elizabeth's somewhat unorthodox idea of wedding vows. Quite the contrary. Considering the circumstances, I thought she behaved rather well. Most brides would have swooned when under such stress. Besides, anything she could do couldn't possibly be worse than what I myself have done in the past, as you yourself just alluded to. No, I wish to leave because the journey will take two days. More if the roads are rough. Much as I enjoy society's company, I wish to enjoy my new wife's company more."

Elizabeth's mouth dropped open. It hung there like a giant fly trap as the duke's words ran through her head. *Leave? Today?*

"But the breakfast guests," her mother wailed. "What will I tell the guests?"

The duke smiled. "Why, exactly what I told you." And with that, he took Elizabeth's arm. "Shall we?" he asked.

Escape. He offered her escape.

Suddenly she didn't care that it was Ravenwood who did the offering. She turned toward the door. But it wasn't as easy as that.

"Elizabeth, you will *not* leave," her mother ordered.

Elizabeth straightened, looking her mother full in the eye. "On the contrary, Mother. I believe I shall."

Her mother's eyes all but goggled. Elizabeth felt a

fledgling sense of freedom. She bent, gathering her massive train while somehow holding on to her flowers, all the while expecting her mother to protest further. But she didn't. Her father remained strangely quiet, too. Nor did they follow her when she peered over the fabric of her train and followed the duke to the door, though she could hear them whispering furiously as they exited.

He paused at the entrance. She stopped next to him. Elizabeth blinked at the sudden sunlight.

A cheer went up.

"By George, she brought 'im up to scratch," a lady yelled. "Bully fer you, yer ladyship."

Hundreds of people stood outside the church, some of them the remnants of her wedding guests, their faces filled with curiosity, others perfect strangers.

"Yur Graces," a red-and-purple-liveried servant pushed through the crowd and bowed. "Managed to squeeze yur carriage through a wee crack. If you'd follow me."

Ravenwood nodded, his grip tightening as they pressed through bodies. She was glad for his helping hand, though she hated the way his touch made her feel. Almost relieved.

Some of the bystanders snatched at her: at her dress, her train, anything they could get their hands on. But the duke's tall form helped to keep any but the most bold at bay. Still, she was grateful when they reached the waiting coach, the familiar coat of arms—two ravens facing each other—gleaming from its doors. A tiger stood by the horses' heads, trying to keep them calm. But even the blinders the horses wore didn't help much. She could see their skins twitch nervously, their ears swivel back and forth. Two outriders on matching gray horses stood in front of the team, their backs ramrod straight as they stared straight ahead.

"'Ere ya go," the coachman said. "And may I be one o' the first to wish ye the best?" he added.

"Thank you, Cedric," Ravenwood answered as he helped her into the carriage. There was just one problem.

Her train wouldn't fit.

Ravenwood stuffed the material inside, having to stuff some more when it still spilled out. For some reason, the sight of him shoveling her dress made her want to laugh. Hysteria, she supposed. When he finished, the satin surrounded her like foam waves.

"You could ride upon the roof," she said to Ravenwood upon noticing there was no room for him to sit.

He met her gaze.

And smiled.

It wasn't a cynical smile. It wasn't that irritatingly scampish smile . . . the one she wanted to smack off his face. It was a genuine smile. The first she'd ever seen from him.

Good Lord, it changed the whole look of his face.

"Yes, I suppose I could," he said, "though I rather dread the thought of my face colliding with bugs. No, I'd much rather sit in here with you."

She swallowed. Nodded. How could a man look so masculine yet so perfectly handsome at the same time?

"Lovely flowers," he drawled, his smile creeping higher.

She looked down. The flowers she'd clutched so diligently were nothing but stems with a few broken leaves.

"Perhaps if we locate a pair of scissors, I can rid you

of some of this fabric," Ravenwood said dryly, eyes shifting to her dress again.

Elizabeth stiffened. She'd been half-tempted to take a pair of scissors to the gown from the moment of its creation. Instead, she tossed her stems outside the still-open carriage door. The crowd outside scrambled for them like they were guineas, then she grabbed an armful of fabric and made just enough room for the duke to sit down on the opposite seat. When she released the fabric, neither of them could see their legs.

She felt very, very hot of a sudden.

"This must have been what Moses felt like as he crossed the Red Sea," he said, a faint hint of his breath reaching her. Lemon. His breath smelled of lemons. How . . . odd. "I only wish I had a staff and a fake beard. I should like to see the looks on peoples' faces as we roll by, me with my arms stretched out over a wedding dress sea. Most biblical."

Elizabeth didn't comment. What was there to say? Was he trying to be amusing? And if so, why? Heaven knew nothing he could say would make her relax. She felt as charged as static on silk fabric during a thunderstorm.

The carriage shook a bit as the coachman climbed up the side of it, then took his seat. In the back, she could hear the tiger settle himself in the exterior rear seat. The brake lever released with a groan. She felt her nerves stretch taut as she waited for them to move forward, though why the prospect made her suddenly more nervous, she couldn't say. She supposed 'twas because they were leaving London. She was going to a place she'd never been before, with a man she hardly knew.

Her husband. Her *handsome* husband.

"Cold?" he asked.

Had she shivered? She shook her head, refraining from acting on the urge to rub her suddenly chilled arms.

And as if the horses couldn't wait to be off, the carriage lurched suddenly. She leaned back, her heart clattering nearly as loudly as the crowd that cheered as they began to roll down the road. A shadow enveloped them, then more and more as they passed between buildings. An occasional stab of light illuminated his face in a sudden burst, the interior of the carriage seeming to be lit from within. 'Twas the same coach she'd seen clatter down the road outside her home on that long-ago day when he'd proposed. The inside was everything the outside promised it to be. Luxury enveloped her, the plush, red velvet seats peeking out from behind his back. Mahogany panels gleamed with a fervent shine, silver fixtures—and she was sure they were real silver—flashed brightly. Even the carpet beneath her slippers felt lushly woven, and Elizabeth, who prided herself on never feeling intimidated, felt extremely out of place.

Her eyes caught on her ring. An oval-cut diamond surrounded by baguettes. Pinpoints of light spotted the carriage roof when the sun caught the stones, like a tiny constellation of rainbow stars. 'Twas easily the biggest ring she'd ever seen, and it illustrated the phenomenal wealth of the man she'd married.

"A ring befitting a duchess," he said, obviously following her gaze.

She nodded, and Lucien, who for some odd reason felt the need to converse with her, tried again. "Do you like it?"

She nodded again before looking away, her face in profile as she stared out the window. So much for conversation.

The carriage picked up speed. *Either the crowd is thinning or the coachman has decided to run people down, one of the two,* Lucien thought. Whichever, the quick jerks and starts of the vehicle smoothed.

And Lucien merely stared. If he'd thought Elizabeth stunning the night of the Derbys' ball, that was nothing compared to her now. With her hair drawn up and her skin glowing from the reflection of her gown, she looked like a sea goddess come to tempt him to a watery grave.

"You're staring at me," she said, her voice all but startling him.

"Am I?"

"You are."

She met his gaze directly, trying to assess him. That was what he liked about Elizabeth Montclair, no, St. Aubyn now, he corrected. "If I am, 'tis because I find myself rather flummoxed to think of you as my wife."

She didn't look pleased by the reminder.

"In fact, I find myself wondering what to call you. Shall it be wife? Mrs. Duke? Or simply the Leg Shackle? I confess myself rather partial to the last."

Her blue eyes didn't grow amused, as was his hope. Instead, she took his comments seriously. He hated when people did that.

"You may call me Elizabeth," she offered.

"Well, I should certainly hope so, my dear. After all, one of these days you shall bear me a child. 'Twould destroy the mood if I had to call you Lady Ravenwood during the marriage act." He placed an index finger upon his chin thoughtfully. "Speaking of which, when do you want to consummate our marriage? I quite look forward to seeing how you look out of that gown." He allowed his smile to grow in volume. "Then, too, there's something to be said for simply lifting your skirts and having a go at it right now."

The color drained from her face.

He threw back his head and laughed. He couldn't help it. She looked so genuinely terrified. And from nowhere came the thought that her fear of him was most ego deflating. Didn't she know that his skills as a lover were quite renowned amongst the *demimonde*?

Apparently not.

"Surely you are not serious?" she asked.

"Oh, but I am," some little devil prompted him to respond. "Or didn't you realize I was serious last night about begetting an heir?"

Her mouth opened, then closed. "You—" But then her eyes narrowed. She didn't say anything, merely stared hard into his eyes. "You are teasing me," she pronounced.

Yes, he was, and damned if he knew how she knew that. The only other person who had been able to read his jests so easily had been his brother.

Instantly, he sobered. His brother would have liked Elizabeth, he admitted. Henry would have approved.

"You have found me out," he admitted.

"Our marriage is not a game, duke," she chastised. "Indeed, whilst we are on the subject of our marriage, let us get a few things straight." She pulled herself up as if there was a little string attached to her head. "When you compromised me, you ruined your chances for begetting an heir."

Bloody good thing I don't really want an heir then, Lucien thought.

"What is more, I insist we go our separate ways once this farce of a honeymoon is over." She paused, as if waiting for him to object, and when he didn't, said, "I've been thinking about our discussion last eve. We both agreed we did not want to be wed to each other. Likewise, we both agree that we will be miserable in each other's company. As such, I insist we set up separate houses. I will not bother you, nor condemn you for any mistresses you might take; likewise, you shall not condemn me if I decide to take a lover."

As her words sank in, Lucien felt himself grow oddly perturbed. "How utterly civilized."

"Yes, it is. Further, while I will not mind you having a paramour, I insist you be discreet. I shall, of course, be the same. There is no reason for either of us to cast shame or embarrassment upon the other for all that we dislike each other."

"Are you done?" he asked, wondering how the hell he was to tolerate such a shrew of a wife.

"No," she said. "I wish to know how long we will be in northern Wales?"

"Three months," he said, the first thing that came to mind.

"Three months?" she gasped.

"Yes, three," he snapped. "And now I wish you to understand some things." He leaned toward her. "While I agree that we should both be allowed lovers, we shall each wait until after the honeymoon to find our prospective partners."

She ignored his words. "But that is a ridiculous amount of time for a honeymoon."

"We are not going to Raven's Keep for a honeymoon. I wish to conduct business there. "

"Can you not conduct your business in a shorter amount of time?"

"Actually, no. I need to supervise a project. 'Tis something I wish to handle personally."

She didn't look as if she believed him. No matter.

"One month," she tried to negotiate. "I will allow you one month, nothing more."

"Two," he countered, not really caring if she stayed a week, just as long as she stayed some small amount of time. Silly, he knew, but he wanted people to think them married in the truest sense, at least for the first month or so.

"One-and-a-half," she bargained.

"Done," he agreed, having expected her to stay for less.

She looked startled by his easy acquiescence. "I shall spend a month and a half at Raven's Keep, after which I will be free to go," she reiterated as if she didn't believe him.

"Exactly."

She settled back against her seat, sunlight flickering in and out of the carriage. Her eyes looked luminous as she stared across at him, luminous and uncertain.

"And one more thing," he said silkily. "You *will* sleep with me."

CHAPTER SIX

Elizabeth jolted away from her seat. "I beg your pardon?"

His left brow lifted. "Is your hearing going again, my dear?"

Elizabeth narrowed her eyes. " 'Sleep with me'?"

He smiled complacently. "So you did hear me. Good. Then hear this, too. I wish to give people the impression that we're trying to make a go of it," he said. "At least for a little while. After that you may sleep alone to your heart's content." He studied her for a second, his expression heating in a way that made her distinctly uncomfortable. "Though I rather doubt that will be the case for long."

"You lied to me," she accused.

"Lied to you? What do you mean, "I 'lied to you'?"

"You said it would be a marriage of convenience."

"Yes, and it is convenient that you sleep with me."

"That is not what you meant, and you know it."

"Do I? Then explain it to me, Elizabeth. What do you think I mean by a marriage of convenience?"

"You go your way, and I'll go mine," she instructed. "You sleep in one bed, I'll sleep in another."

"No," he said.

"No?" she snapped back, clutching the hand strap as they rounded a corner. "And what if I insist we sleep in separate beds? What will you do? Lock me in your room at night?"

"I might."

She wished the hand strap was his throat. "You jest."

"I only jest on Tuesdays and Thursdays," he quipped. "And as this is Saturday, I assure you, I am not jesting. I merely wish to present to society the appearance of a marriage, at least for the first month. After that, we will go our separate ways, as we already agreed upon. 'Tis done all the time. A few weeks of communal bliss that all of society knows is a sham, then we lead separate lives. Surely you understand how the game is played?"

She could think of not a single word to say, for she did indeed understand . . . all too well. The coach lurched over a bump. Elizabeth looked outside, her eyes unseeing as they passed through the London streets.

"My dear Elizabeth, don't look so terrified. You will quite enjoy sleeping with me."

"No," she breathed, her gaze snapping back to his.

"Although I believe I snore," he stated matter of factly. "At least, that's what my chums at Oxford told me, but I'm quite sure you shall get used to it. They did."

He couldn't be serious. And yet she could glean no trace of humor in his eyes. None whatsoever.

He *was* serious.

Ravenwood, the Duke of Death, the Rake of Ravenwood, was going to force her to bed with him.

"You will not touch me," she ordered.

"My dear, of course I shan't touch you. Nor will I force myself upon you, for if you will recall, there was a time not too long ago when I could have easily taken advantage of you, and yet I didn't. I behaved the perfect gentleman."

He was referring to their time aboard that ship, something she still wished to forget. And yet she couldn't. He had seemed different then. More cold.

But sleep with him? She didn't think she could do it.

What choice do I have?

"Why?" she breathed, only then realizing she'd whispered the question aloud.

"Because that is what I wish."

His green eyes were unwavering, his thick lashes framing eyes of utter seriousness.

"Why?" She insisted upon knowing the answer.

He considered her words. "Because," he finally answered, "I refuse to be the laughingstock of society. Because I refuse to have my chums know that I couldn't get my new wife to sleep with me. Because I am many things, Elizabeth, but I am ultimately a man. My pride is all I have."

She stared up at him, his words startling her.

"Do you understand?" he asked.

She didn't. And yet . . . she did. All too well. Sometimes when society or her mother belittled her she, too, depended upon her pride to see her through. She might be publicly humiliated at times, but she never let the public see that humiliation.

"Well?" he prompted.

"As you wish," she said, feeling her heart begin to

pound in an oddly sympathetic way. And then she had a thought. She stiffened. Gracious, what would she wear? The blood drained from her face.

What would *he* wear?

It was a question that plagued Elizabeth for the whole long ride that day. They were to stop just outside Oxford. From there they would leave the next morning to push on to Wales, a journey that would normally take them two days, but that they would try to do in one, or so Ravenwood told her. They were almost the only words he'd spoken to her since their earlier conversation, not that Elizabeth minded. She still tried to come to grips with the fact that he expected her to sleep with him.

The countryside they drove through was some of the most beautiful in England. Gently rolling hills with stone or wood fences that marked the property lines. Fat cows or fluffy white sheep grazed in fields shaded by giant elms with emerald green leaves that sometimes dropped onto their carriage as they passed beneath. The road was smooth, even though it had obviously rained recently. But it always rained in England. The weather today, however, was as scenic as it'd been in London. Fluffy white clouds. Soft, warm breezes, the sky nearly as blue as the tail of a peacock.

"We are almost there," Lucien said, interrupting her thoughts. His green eyes resembled the color of a fern as sunlight filtered through them. "I expect you shall want to change." He smiled. "Unless you like dragging that material behind you?"

She shook her head, looking away from him, her eyes catching on a beam of light that slid its way along the interior of the carriage, turning the red velvet almost orange wherever it touched.

"I'm relieved to know that," he said. "I'd begun to wonder if this massive amount of fabric wasn't a ploy to keep me at bay during our ride."

She looked up sharply. "If I thought such a ploy would work, I would wear it to bed tonight."

He lifted one side of his mouth in a naughty smile, green eyes glittered. "You're quite right. Such a scheme wouldn't have worked. As you may have heard, I am most adept at relieving women of their skirts."

"I thought it was at lifting them?"

He looked as surprised that she would say such a thing. Truth be told, Elizabeth was surprised at herself. But her nerves were stretched so tight, she felt capable of saying anything.

"Has someone been telling tales about me?"

She hated when he smiled at her thus. It made her feel as if she rode with Eros. His grin seemed to say, "I am a *very* wicked man. Be wicked with me?"

She swallowed, telling herself that she should be impervious to that smile. Alas, she was not. It made her feel very, very naughty in return . . . almost like she'd felt when he'd kissed her.

She'd lost her mind.

"All of society talks of your reputation," she said, having to wet suddenly dry lips. It didn't help that he followed the motion with his eyes. Her insides coiled. This was why she hadn't encouraged a conversation between them up until now. For every time they conversed, Elizabeth felt like she was prodding a cat with a stick.

"Hmm. Yes, I suppose they do. Although if I'd had as

many lovers as society claims, I'd have long since died of exhaustion."

And, of course, she hated the way he made her want to laugh sometimes. How could that be? Gracious, she didn't like the man. He was forcing her to sleep with him. He shouldn't want to make her laugh.

It didn't help matters that at that very moment, the carriage slowed. Elizabeth stiffened, darting a glance outside. She'd been so busy with the duke, she hadn't noticed that they'd entered a small town.

Quaint homes faded into two- and three-story stone or wood buildings. The streets were wide with well-dressed citizens strolling along them. A hay cart pulled by a chestnut draft horse rolled by, the driver trying to peek into their window.

They glided to a stop, glided because it truly felt as if they rode upon Aladdin's carpet. She looked out the window on her left. A sign bearing the name of the Duck and Swan swung on a gentle evening breeze. Above the wooden roof clouds had thickened, as if fog hung in the sky only a few miles away. And indeed it did, for as the carriage door opened, she could see it rolling toward them, a giant gray wall that seemed almost ominous in size. So much for sunshine. She shivered.

"It looks a bit muddy outside," the duke observed before stepping down. A liveried servant stood at attention while holding the door. Elizabeth, who could count the number of servants her father employed on one hand, found it a bit disconcerting to have not only a coachman, but a tiger and two outriders. Obscene.

The duke's gaze swung back to hers. "I'd offer to carry you, but I doubt I could get close enough to lift you."

"I'd like to change right away," she murmured.

"No," he said, shaking his head. "I've decided that you shall walk around naked. Much more enjoyable that way."

Her gaze darted to his, but his expression was absolutely blank. "You're teasing me."

"Indeed, but you must admit, 'twas an intriguing suggestion." He smiled, that lovely warm smile that made her feel . . . odd. "I had one of my servants fetch some clothes for you whilst we were getting married."

Married. Oh, how the word hit her sometimes. Married to one of London's most notorious rakes. A ne'er-do-well who enjoyed his drink and cigars more than managing his estates. Who spent most of his life making a jest of things and would no doubt trot off to London the moment their "honeymoon" was over.

Well, bully for him, she thought. She would be off to live her life, too. That was the bargain they'd struck after all.

"If you're ready to disembark, I will help you down. Frankly, you might be able to make a jump for it. I imagine your train is so large it will immediately fill with air, thereby allowing you to float to the ground."

She gave him a look. It quite irritated her, for there it was again: the urge to laugh.

And yet she couldn't deny it. He did amuse her.

She watched as he used his hands to shovel away her skirts, and, when he was done, he held out his hand. "My lady," he said, palm up, his fingers wiggling when she didn't immediately take his hand.

She reluctantly reached for him, using her other hand to clutch the frame of the carriage. Somehow she managed to leave her train in the carriage, her body hovering in the doorway.

One minute she was in the carriage, the next she was in his arms.

"Sir," she gasped.

He looked down at her, their faces close, his breath whispering over her. She could smell him, a combination of lemon and mint soap. She could feel him, too, the heat of his body startling against the cool lamé of her dress. His eyes looked dark, nearly as dark as his ink black hair, and yet she could see something flicker in them, something gentle, yet hard and that made her pulse leap.

"Look at that," he said softly. "I could get close to you after all. Perhaps we should take that pair of scissors to your train after all. That way, we could do this more often."

Elizabeth felt her whole body go still as she looked up at him. "If you destroy this dress, my mother will have your head."

He kept staring at her, his eyes seeming to twinkle as he gave her a look of consideration. "Have you ever thought just how morbid a thing it is to 'have' one's head?"

And once again, she felt the urge to smile. "No," she answered back softly, finding it odd that she could be so still on the outside, yet moving so violently on the inside. "I confess, I never gave it a thought."

"Well you should. Deuced damn thing to do to a person, taking his head."

She merely stared.

Ravenwood, as if giving up, looked away, nodding at

one of his servants to catch her train before it fell out of the carriage.

"Put your arms around my neck," he ordered.

Elizabeth hesitated, but when he started to move, she realized she would indeed need something to hold on to. *Him.* Bother. She encircled his neck with her arms.

"There," he said. "That wasn't so bad, was it?"

She didn't answer, trying her best to keep her body from touching his. He chuckled softly as if he knew what she was attempting.

Like an elephant, the servant followed behind her whilst holding the tail of her train. Beth felt snugly warm as Ravenwood held her against his chest, her hands resting against the nape of his soft—surprisingly soft—neck. But with that warmth came a sensation of not being able to breathe. She told herself it was because he held her so tightly, but she wasn't at all convinced that was, indeed, the reason. There was an unreal quality to being held by him thus. She supposed it was because the person who held her was the duke of Ravenwood. Gracious, she still couldn't believe it. She was his duchess. And the way he held her. So firm, his body so tall, she so petite. She felt utterly feminine and completely surrounded by him. She didn't like it *at all*.

"Right this way," the innkeeper said, leading them into the establishment.

"Put me down," she hissed, the moment they were inside. The smell of stewed beef made her stomach growl, the crowd inside quieting a bit when they spied them in the doorway of the warm room. "Put me down," she repeated, trying not to blush at the stares they received, mostly from men, not surprising since the bottom floor of the inn was a tavern.

"Not yet," he answered, stepping into the room.

"But there is no need to carry me thus."

"Do you want your train to become entangled with the tables and chairs?"

He had a point.

She hated when he had a point.

"I didn't think so," he said.

She frowned, resigning herself to her fate. Truth be told, she'd never stayed at an inn before. When one was a Montclair, one had enough relatives to cross England without ever needing to secure public lodging. The patrons who sat at this particular inn looked to be mostly locals, as did those that sat on tall stools before the bar, their tankards of ale sweating big droplets of water and leaving rings behind when they lifted them to their lips. The inn's walls were made of stone, thick, dark beams supporting the second floor. Of Norman vintage, she supposed. A stairway cut into the middle of the room. The section to the right appeared to have been walled off. Either that, or the innkeeper led them to a broom closet.

"I hope you do not mind, but the room is a bit chill. We were not expecting any visitors of your rank."

Of our rank. Elizabeth closed her eyes. It still seemed unreal. As if it had happened to someone else. Three weeks ago she'd been living her life. Attending a few parties. Trying to please her mother (usually, unsuccessfully). And now here she was, on her way to northern Wales, a place she'd never been before, with her new husband, a man suspected of killing his brother.

Marvelous.

"A fire has just been started," the innkeeper said, "and your meal will be brought to you shortly." He bowed as they passed. "Please ring if you need anything else."

Ravenwood paused just inside the doorway, ignoring the man. Elizabeth waited for him to let her go. And yet, he didn't immediately. She looked up, startled to note his eyes fixed upon her.

"Are you certain you don't wish to proceed directly to the bedroom?"

Her body tensed. She glanced behind her to the servant who was very obviously trying not to appear silly whilst he carried her train.

"We could make a night of it," the duke added, his tone dropping a octave. "Quite a night of it."

She peered back up at him. "No thank you, sir. Feel free to enjoy your own company. I shall certainly not miss *you*."

Her sarcastic words made him give a bark of laughter. "Jamie," he said to the servant, "do you see what it is I've married? A smart-mouthed shrew." He looked back at her, his laughter fading. "In time you will learn to miss me, my dear." His smile grew as big as a jack-o'-lantern's. "In time."

"That, I doubt," she muttered.

"Would you like to change before or after dinner?" he asked, ignoring her words.

"Before, please."

With a wordless nod, he slowly let her go, but not quickly. No, he set her down in such a way that their bodies rubbed together. Inch by inch. Belly to belly. Thigh to thigh.

Her mouth dropped open. She snapped it closed, not at all affected by the feel of his body against her. Not at all.

The servant gently laid down her train, then turned, apparently on his way to go fetch her trunk. Elizabeth watched him go, feeling very alone suddenly and very vulnerable, with her train all but bolting her to the floor. The room was paneled in golden oak, the flames in the hearth seeming to set the walls aglow. A faded red carpet covered the floor, an ornately carved table in the center of the room. Two single chairs added to her sense of loneliness, one at each end of the table. She wondered what the innkeeper did if there were more than two guests.

"Do you need me to carry you up to our room?"

"No," she said, forcing herself to meet his gaze. "A maid can help me upstairs."

"Are you sure?" he asked with a wicked smile.

Dratted man. "Positive," she added.

He smiled, that mischievously boyish smile that she loathed.

"Then perhaps," he said, "if you won't let me help you to our room, you will let me help you get undressed?"

"No, thank you," she gritted out.

He bowed his head, smiled, his green eyes all but twinkling. Elizabeth wanted to poke them out.

Something needs to be done, Elizabeth thought as she dressed. *Something drastic.* But she could think of nothing that would change her present circumstances. Nothing except to show his grace that she would not be intimidated by his sexual innuendos and crass comments. Quite the contrary. Two could play at that game.

To that end she donned a dark blue, high-waisted gown

that highlighted the blue-black of her upswept hair and made her eyes appear huge. For added effect, she didn't wear any petticoats. She also dampened her skirts. The finished result looked quite shocking. And daring. So much so that she felt almost liberated as she made her way downstairs, the damp dress clinging to her legs most revealingly.

She would show his grace that she was no milk-and-water miss.

But something was wrong because no one gave her a second glance as she entered the main room. Oh, men looked, but their gazes just as quickly shot away. She felt her brow wrinkle, then glanced down, assuring herself that nothing was out of place. She looked fine. Perhaps it was the way she moved. She'd heard tale that courtesans had a way of walking that drove men wild. They swung their hips, she remembered. She tried doing that, swishing her rear from side to side like a pony.

"So did you see the McGregors' cow?" a man asked as she walked by.

Elizabeth almost stumbled. Cow? She was strutting quite noticeably, and they were reminded of cows?

And then she spied her husband by the parlor door. He stared at her, and his eyes weren't narrowed heatedly as they swept her up and down, they were . . . they were.

Laughing.

She stiffened. He laughed at her.

Oh! She almost turned around and went back to her room, embarrassment making her feel as hot as the tavern ovens. Had he noticed what she tried to do? Lud, she hoped not.

But any hope that he hadn't was erased the minute he said, "My dear. If you're going to attempt to draw a man's attention, I would suggest you lower the angle of your nose. Having salacious thoughts about the queen of England is unlikely at best."

The queen? She hadn't looked like the queen, had she? But then she realized she shouldn't reply, for to do so would admit what she'd done.

"I don't know what you're talking about," she lied, lifting her head as she walked past him and into their private room.

She thought she heard him chuckle as she passed, thought, but she couldn't be sure.

Dratted man. She was still piqued as he helped her into her seat, although the minute she sat, her stomach turned. Soon they would go upstairs, and he would—she gulped—he would what?

She didn't know. Didn't want to even attempt to guess.

So it was that the meal passed in a blur. All too quickly Ravenwood was saying, "Are you ready, my beloved, to engage in our night of passion?"

Elizabeth could have been eating wood chips, for all the notice she'd taken. Those wood chips instantly petrified. Into cement. She put her fork down. Ravenwood did, too, a wicked smile upon his face, his green eyes flickering in the firelight.

"I know you are as anxious as I," he added. "So let us be off."

Elizabeth didn't move. Oh what she wouldn't give for a magic wand to whisk her away.

"Come, my love," the duke prompted as he stood and held out his hand.

"I am not your love," she said slowly and succinctly.

"No, but you will be loved by me," he wiggled his

eyebrows. "Thoroughly, loved," he added with a suggestive leer. "Come." He waved his hand.

Swallowing, Elizabeth clutched her skirts and stood. No sense in delaying matters. She was wed to him, and that was that.

But when he held out a hand, the ruby signet ring he wore flashing, she ignored it, lifting her skirts as she exited the room. Her heart beat so fast, she was afraid it would stop in exhaustion.

"Give it to 'er, mi lord," a drunken voice yelled.

There were echoes of, " 'ear, 'ear," around the room.

"Ride 'er 'ard," another yelled.

Lucien caught her hand, forcing her to stop so that they faced the crowd. She tried to pull her hand away, but he forced her around by crooking his arm through hers, swinging her as though they were in the midst of a country dance.

"I assure you, gentlemen," he called out, patting her hand lovingly, "I shall do my best to show the lady a *very* good time."

The men erupted into laughter. Elizabeth felt her cheeks sting. And yet, she didn't cower away. Instead she straightened, one of those odd thoughts coming into her mind. She wanted to say something shocking. Wanted to set his lordship on his ear. She wanted to say, "It's his lordship that needs to worry," in a calm, clear voice, yet disconcerted to realize that she had, indeed, spoken the words aloud. But she had everyone's attention now.

"And why is that, my love?" Lucien asked with a leer.

"Why because, my sweetling," she gritted out, " 'Tis *I* that shall wear *you* out."

She had the wonderful experience of seeing Lucien's

eyes widen with surprise. She gave him a smile as sub-limely false as his own.

"Give 'im 'ell, Duckie," a barmaid called.

"Wear 'is bleedin' cock off," another one added.

Holly berries could not possibly be as red as she felt, Elizabeth thought. And yet she also felt, well, *smug*.

"My, my," Lucien drawled down at her, green eyes glinting. "Perhaps you're not such a stick-in-the-mud after all."

"Do not, for one moment," she hissed through her false smile, "think I spoke the truth."

He didn't answer, merely sent her an enigmatic look, a look, Elizabeth felt sure, that was meant to worry her. Oddly enough, it didn't. She didn't know what had happened to her as she stood in that room, but she suddenly refused to take any more.

Without another word the two headed up the stairs, the crowd's ribald comments following them the whole, long way. And yet with each stair, a bit of Elizabeth's bravado faded. It was odd.

Their room was all the way at the end of the hall, and Elizabeth's heart beat faster and faster as they neared the door. The wood floor creaked as they made their way toward it, flickering wall sconces shedding muted light. By the time they reached their room, her palms were as sweaty as the insides of gloves.

He opened the door for her, and more of her resolve fled. The room was large, surprisingly large, for it didn't look like the inn was that big from the outside. Two of the walls were made of stone, an arched hearth embedded in one of them. A fire snapped, heating the room to a nearly unpleasant temperature.

They were supposed to spend the night out of their clothes.

Gracious, what a thought.

Her eyes caught on the giant bed, which sat opposite the hearth, the finely woven dark blue coverlet turned back to reveal pristine, white sheets.

She gulped.

"Feel free to disrobe at any time. I shan't peek, I promise," he said, his breath wafting over her. Lemons again.

"Why," she snapped, "do you always smell like lemons?"

He looked startled by her question, only he recovered quickly. She watched as he opened his mouth, and then, good heavens, showed her his tongue. The remains of a tiny yellow candy hung upon it. "Drops. I like them."

Why she should suddenly want to laugh, Elizabeth had no idea. Likely hysteria again.

He closed his mouth again. "Well," he asked, "are you going to undress?"

She glared up at him. And yet no teasing look glinted from his eyes, no playful smile tugged the edges of his mouth. His expression was blank, and yet . . . not.

She swallowed again. Her mouth grew dry as sun-baked dirt.

And then he blinked, and the teasing look slipped back on his face, his eyes glinting nearly as brightly as her wedding ring. He smiled, that roguish smile that always reminded her of a schoolboy up to mischief.

"Or are you afraid I might lose control of myself and cork you right where you stand?"

If he had tried to embarrass her, he'd succeeded brilliantly, but she refused to let him see that. Not for nothing had she been a social outcast. She knew how to control her facial expression—rather well—she might add.

"Not at all, duke. The only thing you will be corking tonight will be a bottle of brandy."

He smiled, nodded. "Very good, my dear. I see you've developed some spine again. Rather like downstairs. I like that." His smile grew. "And, since you appear not to be intimidated by my, ah, suggestive comments, why don't you turn around so that I may help you with your stays."

Everything inside of her screamed the word, "No," but she turned her back just the same.

"Try not to scratch me with your rough hands," she ordered.

"Oh, but I heard you liked it rough."

She turned her head, giving him her profile. "I believe you are confusing me with one of your mistresses."

Oddly enough, Lucien had to force himself to move forward. "Believe me, my dear, if I'd confused you for one of my mistresses, we would not be standing here talking."

"Mmm mmm," she said, turning her face away from him, her curls sweeping over one shoulder. "No doubt you are correct. You would be enjoying yourself immensely, I'm sure, whilst your mistress would no doubt be *pretending* to enjoy herself."

He almost laughed. The urge surprised him. He forced himself to lean toward her and not touch.

"Women don't have to pretend with me," he said into the soft pink curves of her ear.

She shrugged, almost as if the feel of his breath disturbed her. "With the money you pay them, I'm sure you're correct."

By God, but she *was* sparring with him. The shrew had disappeared. How intriguing. "Most of the time, they offer to pay *me*," he added.

"And yet they never have, " she murmured. "I wonder why?"

Her words suddenly challenged him, made him want to kiss her. To trace his tongue over the tip of her delectable ear. To kiss the side of her neck. To suck her sweet flesh and leave his mark upon her.

Down, Lucien. She is not for you.

"Not all the women I bed are paid to be there."

She gave him her profile and a half smile. "Ah, yes, I forget. You like to seduce innocents."

"They weren't innocent by the time I was through with them."

She didn't say anything, merely faced forward again. Did his dastardly reputation worry her? he wondered. He hoped it did. After all, what was the fun of being a rake if not to frighten little innocents like Elizabeth?

He straightened, chagrined to realize that he'd leaned so close to her he could smell the sweet scent of roses that lingered from her toilette this morning. Damnation, it surprised him how much he wanted to touch her. He had to clench his hands to stop from doing so. Had to steel himself to undo her first stay. He didn't deserve to touch her. Didn't deserve anyone.

He touched her.

She jumped.

He almost did, too. Almost splayed his hands against her back, almost leaned into her. But he didn't, just forced himself to stand behind her, her warmth resonating through his fingers. If only . . .

"Your hair is thick," he heard himself say, trying to turn his thoughts with mundane conversation.

"Aye, it is."

Forcing himself to lift his hand again, he dragged his fingers across the sensitive skin above the edge of her gown. Obviously he liked to torment himself.

"Why do you not cut it?" he asked, breathing upon her neck as he did so. She smelled sweet and innocent and all too alluring. "Short hair is all the rage."

"My mother refused to let me," she said, only her voice sounded uneven. He watched a pulse beat near the base of her neck. Rapid. On edge. "She said it was my best feature."

He undid the second catch, slowly, carefully, making sure he didn't touch her, and yet it couldn't be helped. The tip of his thumb skated over her flesh. She jerked. He forced himself to breathe.

"She was wrong," he said.

"Oh?" she croaked.

His manhood warmed.

Control yourself, Lucien.

"Your best feature is your eyes."

He waited for her response, waited to hear that breath-less quality to her voice again. But she didn't say anything.

"Elizabeth?" he queried, wondering what she thought of his compliment. Wondering why he cared.

"Do you mind finishing, sir?" she asked, her face in profile again. "I am quite exhausted and wish to go to bed."

The words stung, which he supposed they were meant to do, but he was surprised at how much her cavalier attitude bothered him. "In a hurry, are you?" he asked in an attempt to set her at odds like she did him.

"In a hurry to retire," she corrected.

"Are you not afraid to share a bed with me?" he asked as he undid the catch.

"You promised not to touch me," she said, her shoulders tensing as his fingers dropped lower. He could see the cords of her back through the thin chemise. And from nowhere came the image of him kissing that flesh. Oh, how he wished he could.

"And what if I accidentally do?" he asked, popping another stay free. "What if I am overcome by the urge to touch you?" He leaned closer to her, some urge he couldn't resist wanting to prick at her self-assured bubble. "To do this," he whispered, lightly brushing her neck with his lips. He told himself he touched her thus to prove he could do so without reacting.

Pity it didn't work.

She jumped, whirled, her hands clutching at her dress, the ring he'd spent hours and hours picking out glinting on her finger. "Do not do that, sir," she ordered, her blue eyes wide with shock and something else, something dark and warm. Could that be desire?

"Do what?" he asked, his manhood suddenly hardening like candy. "This?" He brushed his lips against hers.

She drew away, the dress sliding down farther. One dusky nipple teased him through the chemise. The urge to taste that nipple made him feel as randy as a seventeen-year-old.

"Stop it," she ordered. "Stop it right now."

He stared down at her, pulling on a bland face only by sheer force of will. Odd's blood, what had happened to his willpower? Taking a deep breath he attempted to do what he always did when faced with circumstances out of control—he assumed an aloof attitude. Straightening, he said, "Alas, I suppose you're right. I wouldn't want you to go to bed too aroused. 'Tis not good for one's sleep."

But it was *he* who would go to bed unsatisfied this night, he found himself admitting. And he did, Lucien tossing and turning as he slept on the floor, all the while admitting that she was right. Sleeping unsatiated was devilishly uncomfortable. And he wasn't at all sure he could take another night.

Every woman is at heart a rake

—IB, EPISTLE

CHAPTER SEVEN

Elizabeth felt quite sure she looked like a troll the next morning. A baggy-eyed troll. It didn't help that Lucien appeared to have slept well, for no lack of sleep showed on his handsome, fiendish face. He wore a dark green jacket that caught the color of his eyes perfectly, turning them a lighter shade of green. His cravat was loosely tied. His jacket hung open, the buff-colored trousers he wore ending above dark brown half boots. He looked a veritable *pink of the ton*, in a Beau Brummel sort of way. She, however, hadn't slept a wink, his snoring was so loud that she was surprised the people in the room next door hadn't banged upon the walls.

"Did you sleep well, my dear?" he asked as he came up next to her.

They were outside the inn awaiting their carriage, people scurrying about, even at this early hour, lampposts with baskets of flowers hanging beneath them casting pools of light at their feet.

"Indeed I did," Elizabeth answered, turning away. A vegetable vendor across the street lost an onion on the ground, the little man stopping to pick it up and toss it back in his cart, but the smell of it lingered in the air before being replaced once again by flowers. " 'Twas you that no doubt slept ill," she added, despite the evidence to the contrary. "I imagine the floor was most hard."

" 'Twas not the hardness of the floor that kept me awake." She darted him a look, the feather in the regal blue hat she wore tickling her face. Crude, rude, and vile man, for she knew exactly what he meant. He purposely tried to make her blush. Well, it wouldn't work. Not this morn. For the first time in her life she refused to squelch the unladylike urges that overcame her from time to time.

"Indeed," she drawled, her expression filled with mock sympathy. "I hear that can be quite uncomfortable. You have my pity. Though I do hear there are ways for a man to relieve himself of so uncomfortable a problem. Feel free to engage in such an act, though I feel sorry for the sheep." And with that she turned away—triumph filling her at the shocked—and dared she say stunned?— expression on his face.

Take that you nasty man, she thought. *I can be just as crass as you.*

'Tis not something to be particularly proud of, said the prim and proper side of Elizabeth.

Who bloody cares? said the Elizabeth who suddenly realized there was no point in being ladylike when one was married to the duke of Ravenwood.

She had the pleasure of watching him have to snap his mouth closed before he said, "Where in the devil have you heard about men relieving themselves in such a way?"

She colored. "Lucy."

The duke considered her response, a myriad of emotions flitting across his face. "I see," he said.

"There is much Lucy taught me."

"Indeed?" he asked. "And what other things would that be?"

Elizabeth knew she was in way above her head, and yet she refused to back down. She shrugged, deciding to brazen it out. "Different positions one can be in. Different methods of gaining a man's pleasure. Things of that nature." She tried like the dickens not to blush.

His grace appeared to consider her words. Elizabeth decided it was quite worthwhile to say such brazen and crass things if it meant the duke would be quiet.

Alas, he wasn't for long. "And where did Lucy learn about such things?" He held up his hands. "Never you mind. I do not need to know the answer."

"She had a book," Elizabeth answered anyway. "*A Hundred Ways to Seduce a Man.* I was quite scandalized when she began to read me passages, but when one is aboard a ship, there is little else to do but read."

"Ah. The ship," he said.

"Yes, the ship," she echoed.

He stared at her for long, long seconds.

"You would have been interested in it, too, I wager, for it dealt in gaining a man's release. Rather an interesting subject."

He blinked. She smiled bravely. His eyes glowed in an odd way as he said, "Perhaps you could show me some of what you learned later tonight."

"I wouldn't wager upon it, Ravenwood," she said, watching as a groom led the coach and four toward them, his red-and-purple livery nearly as colorful as the flowers that hung above them. Then she added, "Has anyone told you that your servants' livery looks like a bruise?" As a way of changing a subject she had no desire to explore.

"Alas, no. I don't believe so."

"Well, it does."

"What a charming observation."

"I was merely thinking of what I'd like to do to your face when the idea came to mind."

He chuckled. Just a single bark. Like a seal. "Indeed, how very bloodthirsty you sound. It quite makes me wonder if I should share the breakfast I had packed for us."

"Only if I'm allowed to poison your portion of it."

He laughed again. "My, my. Such barbs this morning. Did we sleep on the wrong side of the bed, my dear?"

"I would wager I slept better than you. Or perhaps you're used to sleeping on the floors with the other dogs."

He lifted his hands. "Enough. You quite outdo me with your bloodletting words. I surrender."

As ill-natured as it might have been, she felt moderately better. Sometimes, one needed to vent on any hapless male who came by. That this hapless male happened to deserve it made her feel even more vindicated.

She stared at the carriage that stopped before them, at the splendid dappled gray horses that pulled it, and even though she despised Ravenwood, she couldn't help but notice he had magnificent cattle. It was a weakness of hers, this penchant for horses. Unfortunately, her family only ever rented vehicles, for Elizabeth would have loved to own even a swaybacked nag.

Something of what she felt must have shown on her

face because he said, "You like horses," in such a way as to make it a statement.

"I do," she admitted.

"We'll have yours brought up from London."

"I don't have one."

He looked at her like she'd said she didn't have a leg. "Why ever not?"

She straightened, refusing to let him see her humiliation. It wasn't her fault that her family didn't own horses. Lots of families didn't own horses. Just not noble families.

"Your father couldn't afford them."

She turned to him, prepared to lie and say she was allergic to them, or some such nonsense. But then he said, "I'll purchase one for you when we get to Raven's Keep."

"You'll *purchase* one?"

"Yes."

"No."

"A duchess should have her own horse." He lifted a brow. "You do know how to ride, don't you?"

She didn't answer. What could she say? It was hard to become an expert equestrienne when all you had was a stick horse.

"That well, eh?"

"I rode at my friends' homes. During the summer. Whenever I was allowed to visit." Which hadn't been often since her friends were, in her mother's words, "beneath you."

"I see," he said. "Well, we'll just add that to the list of things you need to learn how to do, right underneath your strumpet walk."

Her gaze darted to his. "Strumpet walk?"

He smiled at her, his green eyes sparkling like he hadn't a care in the world. And likely he didn't. "Do not try to bamboozle me, my dear. I saw what you attempted to do last eve. You were trying to walk like a member of the *demimonde*."

"I was not," she cried. Horrors, had she been that obvious?

"Indeed you were, only you were too engrossed in your acting to realize that your attempt fell rather flat."

"It did not fall flat," she denied, then blushed upon realizing she was supposed to deny it.

"Yes, it did, my dear," Ravenwood contradicted, ignoring her blunder. "You looked like a whore with gout."

"A whore with *gout*!"

The coachman came around the back of the carriage, Elizabeth catching the lifted brow the servant shot at the tiger who'd already taken his place. When the man opened the door for them, Elizabeth tried not to blush. Horrible Ravenwood. Perhaps she could slam the door in his face and make him ride with his servants.

Alas, it was not to be.

Ravenwood climbed in right behind her. "You did," he said, taking the seat opposite. The morning light was a muted gray, but it still allowed her a perfect view of his twinkling, obnoxious eyes. "And your nose was so high in the air, I'm surprised you were able to see where you were walking."

Ooo. Insufferable man. She lifted the aforementioned nose, hoping she gave him a good look up her nostrils. "I have no idea what you're speaking of."

He chuckled. Elizabeth's gaze narrowed. He laughed again. *Laughed.*

"Yes, you do. And if you're honest, you will admit you know you were a failure."

She was about to admit no such thing, but something, something she couldn't identify made her sink back against the seat, made her lower her nose, made her stop glaring. The fight just seemed to drain out of her. Mayhap it was his offer to buy her a horse. The chance at a life-long dream must have weakened her mind. "Was I horribly bad?"

He leaned back, too, a look of surprise coming to his face. The carriage whip cracked. The coach sprang forward. The duke nodded. "You were."

And from nowhere came the urge to smile. She let the grin slide upon her face, let her eyes give him a look of chagrin.

"It was, wasn't it?" she asked.

"It was, my dear."

And then she laughed. It came from nowhere, but Elizabeth delighted in that laughter. Her heart was still sore over saying good-bye to her home. She was still rattled over her marriage, but her laughter helped to soothe the edges of her frayed nerves.

Ravenwood's mouth dropped open.

And that made her feel good all over again, for there was a look in his eyes that made her feel suddenly beautiful. "Did you see the one gentleman duck his head so far he fair dipped his nose into his stew?"

He seemed to gather his thoughts before he said, "No, I did not, but I would have paid money to do so."

Her smile grew. "I thought the poor man was going to beg my pardon for daring to look at me."

"*I* was about to beg your pardon for daring to look at you."

She tilted her head. "You were?"

"I was."

"But what did I do wrong?"

If either of them found it odd that they were conversing like normal people for the first time in their lives, neither mentioned it either by look or deed. Instead, the duke appeared to consider Elizabeth's words. "You were too priggish."

"What do you mean?"

"Well, for instance, your walk. It seemed as if you'd severed a limb at some point in your past, then had it sewn back on." He smiled. "Backward."

"I didn't?" she huffed on a laugh.

"You did."

Elizabeth nibbled her lip, wishing she knew what she'd done wrong. How was she ever to attract a man's notice if she couldn't even get one to look at her? And she was determined to get them to do so. She refused to be like her aunt, hiding behind her sham of a marriage. She would live life to the fullest. "I had no idea."

She felt Ravenwood's stare, for the first time didn't feel self-conscious about it. "You need my assistance."

The carriage lurched in and then out of a rut. Elizabeth clutched at the hand strap. "I beg your pardon?"

He smiled at her, that gamin, boyish grin that made Elizabeth not quite despise him anymore. "I shall help you."

"Help me with what?"

"Learn how to seduce a man."

"*What?*"

He nodded.

"Why ever would you offer to do such an outlandish thing?"

But there was no trace of collusion on his face, no glint of deviousness in his eyes. "Because it would amuse me," he said, and when she didn't say anything further, he added, "Surely you realize we'll need something to do while we're at my home?"

"I thought you were working on a project."

"I cannot work on my project at night."

She wondered if he really did have a project. "And so you propose to teach me how to, how to—"

"Bring a man to your bed," he finished for her. "Since you so obviously lack the necessary skills."

"I see," she said, trying not to color. "And you would do this while we are in Wales?"

He nodded.

Elizabeth just stared at him, thinking surely that he was mad. What type of husband taught a wife to lure men into bed?

The duke's type, that's who, a voice silently answered. For coming from him, the idea did not sound odd at all. Certainly unconventional, but 'twas exactly the type of thing he had a reputation of doing. At least, from what she'd heard about him.

She looked away from him, trying to gather her thoughts.

It was madness. Utter madness. She would no doubt be putting herself in his grasp for she was no fool. Ravenwood would use his "lessons" as a way to seduce her himself; after all, he was exactly the type of man her aunt had warned her about.

And yet . . .

Who better to teach her what she needed to know than the master of seduction?

"Let me think on it," she said, meeting his gaze again.

For a second, no more than a heartbeat, really, she saw something flash in his eyes, and then it disappeared. But just that brief glimpse was enough to worry her. What had she seen?

"Well, do not think upon my offer too long. I am apt to withdraw it if I think too long upon the problems it will cause me."

"What sort of problems would that be?" she queried.

He leaned forward, the carriage walls seeming to instantly shrink up.

"Such as the fact that in teaching you the fine art of seducing a man, I may well want to seduce you myself."

She felt herself shiver. He had voiced her fears aloud.

"You would have a devil of a time trying."

"Is that a challenge, my dear?"

Be bold, Elizabeth. *Do not let him see that your hands shake. Or that your heart pounds.*

"No, it is not." But she could tell by the look in his eyes that he did think it a challenge. And that he thought she wouldn't take him up on the offer because of it.

"Very well," she heard herself say, knowing that she said the words out of pique more than anything else. "I will accept your offer, Ravenwood."

"Lucien," he corrected. "If I am to teach you how to stuff your tongue down other men's throats, please call me Lucien."

Miserable wretch. He had baited her, but it was too late to back down now. "As you wish, Lucien," she agreed with a nod. "You may teach me how to stuff my tongue down other men's throats." If she were to embark upon such madness, she'd best learn not to mince words with him.

"And other things," he added, his gaze unblinking.

Elizabeth tried not to squirm for his words made her feel . . . *Wicked*.

They made her feel naughty and if she were honest with herself, the sensation was just a little bit nice.

The Lord Chancellor was taking his tea when he receive the following missive from London's Attorney General:

> *My Lord,*
> *I feel it my duty to report that the witnesses confirm what was rumored to be true. As such, I fully intend to charge Lucien St. Aubyn, duke of Ravenwood, with the murder of his brother. You may wish to take the appropriate action to alert the peers of the coming trial. I trust, however, that you will wait to do this until after he has been apprehended and charged.*
>
> *Yours, etc—*
> *Robert Peters, Attorney General*

CHAPTER EIGHT

They arrived at the coast of Wales just as the sun began to sink below the horizon, the sky an amazing blend of colors. Dark gray, then abrupt streaks of vibrant orange followed by lighter streaks that faded through a spectrum of colors: yellow, green, white, until settling into the most startling of all blues Elizabeth had ever seen. A few clouds that looked like raw cotton floated overhead, their gray bottoms turned a fiery red. It was, as Elizabeth later thought, a perfect time to gain one's first glimpse of Raven's Keep.

They had spent the day crossing the Marches, passing through towns with Celtic names and a land that still felt mystical, with its sweeping valleys and gently sloping green hills. Edward I had built a host of castles in Wales, and as they approached Raven's Keep from a tall vista that overlooked a windswept beach, Elizabeth realized that the duke's home was one of them. An island castle, she realized, for it sat upon a small patch of land that had long since disconnected from the mainland.

"The castle was built in the late thirteenth century," the duke explained. "'Twas considered an ambitious project at the time. Nearly twenty men died raising the outer wall alone."

Elizabeth simply stared. It *looked* like it'd been built in the thirteenth century. In fact, it looked like it'd been built before Christ. The fortress rose up from a small, grassy island. A wall surrounded it, and inside that wall was the castle, with what looked to be a courtyard in the very front. A bridge with three sweeping arches rolled out like a tongue to connect the castle with the mainland. Only the building didn't rise. It sort of . . . crumbled.

"It looks . . ." She searched for the appropriate word, not wanting to insult the duke, goodness knew why.

"Dilapidated," he supplied drolly.

She swallowed. "I was going to say old."

He snorted. It took Elizabeth a moment to realize it'd been a choked-back laugh. "That is putting it kindly."

And it was, she admitted, for though she'd seen many an old castle, this one looked to be more like a pile of rubble than anything else. The top of the turrets were eaten away, like giant bites had been taken out of them and then spit upon ground. The ocean had eaten at the outer wall, too, the blocks that made it up having long since fallen into the sea.

"You look a bit frightened, my dear," he said, and she could hear the laughter in his voice.

"I'm not frightened, just—" She searched for a word again.

"Concerned?" he offered. "Afraid you might be sleeping with no roof over your head?"

For some inexplicable reason she suddenly felt like laughing again. "Yes," she found herself admitting. "The thought had crossed my mind."

He smiled, the setting sun accentuating his bronze skin. And he did look bronzed, she realized, though she'd hardly paid notice to it before. The color turned his skin cinnamon and spice and bleached sienna streaks upon the tips of his hair. She stared, noticing the fine lines around his eyes, the way his mouth twitched when he fought laughter.

"Look," he said, pointing with his chin out the window again.

Elizabeth found herself hard-pressed to pull her gaze away. And yet, pull it away she did, gasping at what she saw.

"Oh, my," she breathed.

"We're going to repair the turrets next."

They had dropped lower, the carriage nearing the bridge that led to the castle. And yet, what a difference just a few hundred yards made. She shook her head, for one side of the castle had been repaired, the other side, the side they'd approached from, looked like a bizarre and twisted mirror image of the right.

"Amazing," she exclaimed.

"It has taken us years."

Elizabeth could understand why, for the castle was massive. Rectangular in shape, it had four round turrets across the front. The same number of turrets lined the back of the castle. Those turrets, oddly enough, appeared to be in good shape. She could even see glass in them. As the horses took their first steps onto the bridge, the sun hit the stones just right, turning them the color of parchment, the reflection of the castle walls shimmering off a calm sea.

"It will be beautiful," she said in awe. And it would be.

Like the castle of a fairy-tale princess. All it would need
was a lady with very long hair and a prince to rescue her.

Instead it had Ravenwood. Poor castle.

And her. The granddaughter of a cobbler. Poor, poor
castle.

"Why is it taking so long?" she asked, knowing the
duke had inherited a sizable fortune. Money that could
have bought and paid for repairs such as these ten times
over. And ten times as quickly, for all that they were
lengthy.

But like a sandcastle swept away by a wave, the pride
on his face vanished. His expression turned closed, grew
guarded.

"I am taking my time."

Elizabeth studied him, sensing there was more to it
than that. He held something back from her, though what
it might be, she couldn't imagine.

She turned back to the castle. They drew closer now,
the water as smooth as glass on either side of the bridge.

"Is it always this calm?" she asked, a part of her feeling the need to see his expression change.

Change to what? asked that annoying little voice Elizabeth wanted to choke.

Back to laughter, she answered herself. She liked the
smiling duke much better than the sarcastic one.

His eyes were still guarded when they looked back at
her. "Oftentimes 'tis smooth near the castle," he answered. "And quite choppy farther away. We're in a natural bay, however, one that holds back the worst of the
waves. Even during a storm."

"But I thought . . ." she let her words trail off.

"You thought 'twas the elements that had destroyed the castle?"

She nodded, relieved to see some of the light come back in his jade green eyes.

"No, 'twas the Scots."

"The Scots?"

"Aye. As you are no doubt aware, all of the castles in Wales were built to fortify the English borders. Unfortunately, Raven's Keep happens to be the castle closest to that border. As such, we sustained the worst damage, the Scots taking it personally that we would dare to build a castle so close to their homeland. Edward I was not a very popular man."

"Do you mean to say the castle has looked like this for almost six centuries?"

He nodded.

Elizabeth felt her brows lift.

"The ocean has helped to weather it, too," he said. "But for the most part 'twas my Scottish cousins who were responsible for the worst of it. They were quite adept with catapults."

"And none of your relatives thought to repair it?"

Once again, the light seemed to fade from his eyes. He looked away, his lashes squinting as he stared out the carriage window. "They wanted to repair it, but it wasn't until recently that my family's fortunes were made. A silver mine discovered upon an old plot of land that had been in the family for generations." His eyes grew distant. "When we realized we'd have the money for repairs, my brother offered to pay for them, even though by rights the castle belonged to me."

Elizabeth felt her heart pause. The oddest urge to reach out and touch his hand filled her then.

She must be going daft.

"Not once did he balk at the cost." He looked back at her, his gaze turning challenging. "When he died, I took over the project."

And received all his money, Elizabeth thought, only to look away, the thought somehow seeming a betrayal, though why that should be when it was the truth, she had no idea. "You've done a wonderful job."

She was rewarded with a startled, then pleased, expression before he turned to look out the window again. His brother had died nearly three years ago, she mused, and yet with all the ducal money at his disposal, all the time he'd had, he still hadn't finished the repairs.

How odd.

By then the carriage had nearly crossed the bridge, the water so close, it looked as if they rode upon it. As they drew closer to the main entrance, the larger the building looked. Rectangular arrow slits were cut into the outer wall. The curved opening they rode through seemed to swallow them up—so large it looked as if a dragon could pass through it. The carriage suddenly grew dark, the light blocked by the tall exterior walls. The sound of the hooves striking the ground *clip-clopped* off the stone. She felt the carriage turn, looked curiously toward the front of the castle, and blinked.

Not only had the right side of the castle been redone, so had the courtyard.

Large, ornate archways opened toward them like welcoming arms . . . the courtyard she'd seen from above. From between those arches one could glimpse the small bit of park that surrounded the castle, and on each post, lanterns glowed welcoming light. Above it all rose the castle, light shining from nearly every window. But it wasn't the Romanesque effect of the structure that made one blink, it was the sixty or so servants lined up before the large, double-door opening of what must be the castle's main entrance. Red-and-purple livery hung on the frames of men of every size and shape. Even the outdoor servants appeared well dressed, their dark brown half boots and tan breeches pristine with cleanliness.

"Are they expecting the queen of England perhaps?" Elizabeth queried.

She decided she quite liked the way her impertinent comments made him look.

"No," he said, an odd half smile lighting upon his face. "'Tis the way I am always greeted." His smile turned rakish and somewhat arrogant. "My servants adore me."

"Oh, I've no doubt," she drawled.

"Especially the ladies," he added with a leer.

She stiffened, her eyes narrowing. Her uncle would get along famously with him. And just as the sun sank below the horizon, so did her mood. How could she have forgotten what sort of man she'd married?

He seemed to realize that might not have been a wise thing to say, for he quickly added, "But only because I give them time off when they have their menses."

"You *what*?"

He nodded, his expression endearingly serious, so much so that she wondered if he might not be telling her the truth.

Do not be fooled, Elizabeth, he is merely trying to recover lost ground.

"Indeed. 'Tis an estate policy, from the lowest scullery maid to the ones who garden. They've taken to saying, 'If you bleed, you don't weed.' "

She stared at him in absolute shock, a part of her thinking he must surely jest.

"I see," she said, knowing that even in the faded light, he could see her blush. Dratted man.

She had decided he was quite having her on about his female servants and their menses as a crass way of making her forget her ire (to which he hadn't succeeded, she might add), but when the carriage finally came to a rocking halt, Ravenwood handing her down as gallantly as her aforementioned prince, one look at the expression on the servants' faces and she had cause to change her startled and stunned mind.

They cheered.

She just about came off the ground, the duke smiling as widely as a courtly knight.

The cheering grew louder, his staff greeting him like he'd tilted Cervantes's windmills . . . and won.

"John," Ravenwood called out over the sound. He stepped forward and offered his hand to the only formally clad servant on staff. The man had curly blond hair and wide, boyish blue eyes, although his tall frame and handsome features proclaimed him all man. He wore a black jacket and black boots that bespoke of a tailor, as did the fine cut of his dark gray breeches. "How goes repairing the west side?"

The man took her husband's hand, his smile nearly as wide as the duke's. "It goes well, though it would go better with you lending a hand."

Elizabeth started. *Lending a hand?*

And suddenly the reason for his callused touch presented itself. And on the heels of that notion came the reason why he was so tan, too. And just as quickly as that came the realization that *this* was the project he'd spoken of earlier. He hadn't been fabricating a reason to come north. He'd been utterly serious.

The duke of Ravenwood labored alongside his staff like a commoner.

And they loved him for it.

CHAPTER NINE

❧───────────────────────────────────

Lucien turned away from his old friend to see Elizabeth standing next to him with an odd expression on her face. She appeared to be almost in shock. No doubt because of his staff's effusive greeting. He nearly smiled. What could he say? He *was* adored.

Turning back to them, he lifted his hands. "Ladies and gentlemen," he called, the signet ring that shouldn't belong to him, flashing, "if I might have your attention."

One by one, the crowd stilled, then quieted. Lucien turned to Elizabeth, giving her a smug smile before facing his staff again. "I would like to present my wife, the Lady Elizabeth St. Aubyn, duchess of Ravenwood."

There was a momentary silence, and then smiles broke out, followed abruptly by cheers. Elizabeth was suddenly and completely surrounded by a barrage of servants, each of them greeting her with happy and courteous bows.

Lucien expected her to stand by woodenly, had anticipated some of his staff's disappointment when she did so. Instead, she utterly shocked him by smiling widely in return, even going so far as to offer her hand to some.

What was this?

He stood there, feeling a juvenile urge to gawk as his prim and proper duchess did the unexpected.

Again.

He straightened, watching her, the waning light turning her dark blue dress to purple. The shade was perfection upon her, for it made her eyes appear almost lavender, her skin translucent. There could be no more beautiful a woman in all of London, and yet as she stood there greeting his staff she acted as if she didn't know it. And perhaps she didn't, he surmised. It was well-known that she had a harridan of a mother, one who constantly criticized. Perhaps that mother had sapped the confidence out of her.

"She's not what I was expectin'," said his steward and longtime friend, John Thorsen in his Scottish brogue.

"Were you expecting a toothless old hag?" Lucien asked.

John shook his head, an answering smile lighting up his face. "Knowing your taste, no."

"Then what?"

"I was expectin' a lady with a stick so far buried up 'er arse, we'd be hard-pressed not to jerk it out and smack her over th' head with it."

Lucien laughed. "To tell you the truth, John, her ladyship is not what I expected, either." His laughter faded, saying almost to himself, "She is a mass of contradictions, constantly surprising me with her impertinent comments and equally impertinent behavior. I am hard-pressed to understand what, exactly, I've married."

A lifted brow greeted his comment. "How did you meet?"

"She called me a murdering whoremonger."

"She's astute."

"Why thank you."

"Now tell me the truth. How did you meet?" John asked.

"I *was* telling the truth."

John lifted a brow.

"But that was the first time. The second time I sank the ship she was on."

John's eyes narrowed. "Your brief stint as a pirate."

"Aye, though I never touched her. Barely spent five minutes in her company. The next time we met was recently. At a party."

"Ah, at last we come to it."

"I compromised her."

John laughed. "You never do anything the normal way, do you?"

"Apparently not."

"Did you get 'er with child? Is that why you married her?"

Lucien felt his blood grow cold at the thought. Some of his good mood vanished. "No. She is not carrying my child."

"Then why? Compromising a lady has never prompted you to marriage before."

He shrugged. "This time it did."

His friend held his gaze for a long moment. Oddly enough, it made Lucien want to turn away. He looked at Elizabeth, watching as she bent to greet a child. His new wife sank to the little girl's level, taking the flowers she shyly held out. He heard a husky, "Thank you," before she ruffled the girl's black curls.

And suddenly, Lucien felt anxious. John's dire expression, no doubt. And it also became impossible to tear his eyes away from the two, Elizabeth looking up at the child's mother and saying something he couldn't catch.

She was good with children, he noted. Another surprise. And the child appeared to adore her instantly, giving Elizabeth a worshipping smile.

"You look like a fairy princess," he heard her say.

He watched as his new wife laughed, her face filling with comely color.

"If I do," he heard her say, "'tis only because of my clothes."

"May I touch them?" the little girl asked.

"'Ere now," the child's mother said. "'Tis enough o' that. 'Er grace is terribly kind for standin' out 'ere and greetin' us, but I suspect she's tired after her long journey."

The child's face fell.

"Not at all," Elizabeth said. And then she did something that completely shocked him. She reached out and scooped the child up, the little girl giving out a whoop of glee at being so unceremoniously lifted and then settled into the princess's arms. "I am delighted to make everyone's acquaintance." She looked at the child, then smiled widely at his staff.

They smiled back.

Lucien stood transfixed. A tightening in his throat became an obstruction that made it damn near impossible to breathe. He turned to John, disconcerted to realize his steward watched him like a hawk.

"You're in love with her," he said flatly.

"In love with her?" Lucien shot, peeking to his right

to ensure Elizabeth hadn't heard the ridiculous comment. "Do not be absurd."

"That is why you married her."

"As you well know, the only person I strive to love is myself."

"So you're fond of sayin'."

"Yur Grace," the child's mother said. Lucien turned, forgetting for a moment that he wasn't the only "Your Grace" anymore. "Mrs. Fitzherbert is goin' ta show 'er ladyship inside."

Lucien looked at Elizabeth just as she gave the child a squeeze before gently setting her down.

You love her.

Hah, Lucien reassured himself, he did not. He had married her because he'd felt obligated to do so. Certainly, he enjoyed bantering with her. That itself was a surprise. But love her? Unlikely.

"A splendid idea," he agreed, shoving aside all thoughts of love, his past, and John's obvious dementia. "I shall go in with you. After all, I have much to discuss with her."

Naughty catcalls followed his words. Lucien straightened, giving his staff a censorious stare. They ignored him.

They were entirely too familiar, Lucien privately admitted. But as he eyed the unruly lot, he realized he rather liked his staff that way. His castle was his oasis. A haven away from the *ton*. He permitted no one to visit him here, the 'wild parties' often rumored to have happened here simply that—rumors. But as he reflected upon showing Elizabeth his home, a sudden, undeniably boyish enthusiasm filled him.

"Come," he said, giving her his arm. "I shall show you the way."

She didn't look like she wanted to take his arm. They stood there, surrounded by his staff, and Lucien wondered if she would publicly humiliate him. Like a fool he'd forgotten how much she despised him. But then she seemed to gather herself and slowly reached for him.

Something akin to disappointment filled him as he watched how hard it was for her to do so. He laughed silently. What did he expect? Certainly what she felt toward him was no worse than what he felt for himself.

Forcing laughter into his voice, he leaned toward her and said, "Try not to look so revolted by the prospect of touching me. I promise no cankerous sores will sprout upon your flesh if you do."

She glanced up at him, her marvelous blue eyes widening a bit. Then she looked away, finally, softly placing her fingers upon his arm.

Lucien stilled for a moment, curious and a bit taken aback by the way her light touch made him feel inside.

Ah, yes, he thought, suddenly feeling as buoyant as a cannonball. *The next few weeks should prove interesting. Love her, indeed,* he scoffed.

And yet as he led her inside, he couldn't help but feel a sense of pride. And who wouldn't with such a woman on his arm? Even at dusk her skin still seemed to glow. The jaunty cap she wore accentuated the classic shape of her face. Her eyes looked luminous as they swept the interior of the courtyard, and he found himself wondering if she was impressed.

He'd modeled it after one of Robert Adam's designs. The famous architect had been partial to archways.

Ravens and lions frolicked atop the arches. The effect looked rather Roman, the courtyard almost seeming to resemble a coliseum.

"Do you see the ravens?" he asked.

She nodded.

"I had a devil of a time finding someone to sculpt them. Seems they're not at all the thing."

"Whoever did them did a marvelous job."

"Do you think?"

And Elizabeth did. It was all so beautiful. There were at least four or five arches on each side of her, the only break in them near the castle's front door. It was to those massive double doors that Lucien led her.

"The doors are original."

They looked it, the ancient oak reinforced with steel and smooth-topped bolts. And then the duke showed her inside, and she forgot all about archways and ravens.

If the outside was stunning, the inside was breathtaking. There, too, they had used the Roman influence. Door moldings and casings were scrolled and rounded. Black-and-white marble crisscrossed the floor. The space was massive in size, although the left side of it appeared to be cornered off by hanging wall coverings. She would wager if the colorful tapestries were pulled down, the room would be half the size of a small cricket field.

"We've only done the right side," the duke said, explaining the presence of the tapestries. "I thought it looked better to hide the unfinished side of the castle with those. When we are done, they will go back up on the walls."

Elizabeth nodded. What amazed her was the amount of candlelight. The duke had given the interior all the modern conveniences of the time. Wall sconces. A large candle-filled chandelier. The largest fireplace Elizabeth had ever seen took up what looked to be half of the right wall. Gracious, one could place a bed inside of it. An ornately carved, wood mantel had been built around it, a gold-gilt mirror fixed above that. But the most amazing change had been to the corner tower to her right. The duke had cut an archway into it, an archway that mimicked the exterior ones. Through them, twelve-foot-tall windows looked out over an ocean and a blazing red sky.

Breathtaking.

That was the only word she could find to describe it. She looked straight ahead. Walls had been built in the back half of the castle, no doubt private rooms. She wondered if the back corner tower had been cut out, too. And as she looked around her, one thought penetrated. Goodness, she felt out of her depth. Certainly she'd seen many beautiful homes before, but as she looked around she realized the exact class difference between a duke and a poverty-stricken earl's daughter.

"We built support beams into the archway," he said. "Had a devil of a time concealing them beneath the stone, but 'twas the only way we could open up the corner tower like that without the walls above collapsing."

Too captivated by the view outside the round tower window, she didn't say anything. Ocean stretched toward a distant shore, the opposite side of the bay, she realized. The sky, which had been shielded outside by courtyard walls, scorched a rolling ocean, the water as fiery, terra-cotta red as the sky above.

"'Tis beautiful," she breathed.

"Aye," he answered.

"So this is your project?" she asked, turning back to him, the feather in her hat tickling her cheek as she did so.

"It is," he answered, his body only inches away.

"Why didn't you tell me?"

"Tell you what? That my home was crumbling about my ears?"

"No. That you were helping to rebuild it."

"Well of course I am supervising."

Elizabeth lifted a brow, feeling the urge to poke at him. "You do not supervise, duke. I suspect you work right alongside your staff."

She had the pleasure of seeing his face fill with guilt, just before he assumed a look of innocence. "Whatever gives you that idea?"

Steeling herself, she reached for his hands, grabbing them. "This," she said, turning his hand palm up, her fingers tingling where they touched. She swallowed and tried to ignore the sensation. 'Twas a big hand, she realized, the tips of her own fingers barely reaching to his second knuckle. "You have calluses," she said.

"They're from riding."

She looked up, still holding his hand. "Do not try to bamboozle me," she said softly. "These are not from riding. You labor on this project yourself."

He stared down at her, Elizabeth seeing a slow smile lift the edges of his lips. She blinked, told herself to step back.

"I see I am found out," he said softly, his breath drifting over her. Lemons again. He must have a basement full of the stuff, or a dungeon as the case may be.

"You are," she agreed.

He squeezed her hand. Elizabeth's mouth went dry. He leaned toward her, saying with a wicked leer, "You should see all the labor I've put into the bedroom."

And just like that, she found the ability to step back. His hand dropped. "Indeed," she said, straightening. "Why am I not surprised that you would concentrate your efforts there?"

"Because you know what a crime it would be to have my lair less than prepared for any female guests I might have."

"Oh, it would be a crime," she drawled. "I wager it would dampen a woman's mood to be tumbled in a room whose walls crumbled."

"Tumbled?" he asked on a laugh. "My dear, your first lesson in the art of seduction will be how to speak the proper language. One does not tumble. One has an assignation. One gives pleasure." He actually leaned toward her, his green eyes glittering. "One makes love," and was it her imagination, or did he actually growl that last word?

And in that instant Elizabeth knew. She knew she'd gotten in far above her head. Goodness, whatever had made her think she could match wits with the infamous Rake of Ravenwood? A man fabled for his skills as a lover?

She swallowed. He was trying to use those skills on her just then, she realized, his green eyes glowing with a sort of teasing promise that she understood all too well.

"I see," she managed to say. "I, er"—she swallowed again—"you are quite correct. I need to become familiar with speaking freely. To use words like, ah"—she searched for the naughtiest word she'd heard, saying—

"lobcock"—she swallowed, certain her face must look like a sunburned sailor's—"and, and meat whistle," she added, wondering where she'd heard that one before. "And sausage stick."

Though she wished she could sink through the floor, the look on the duke's face when she was finished made it all worthwhile.

"Where," he asked, curiosity lighting his green eyes, "did you learn words such as those?"

She stood up as straight as her mortified spine would allow her. "From a friend."

"Lucy," he supplied, monotone.

She nodded.

"I should have known."

"Are you terribly shocked?" she asked, unable to keep the hope from her voice.

"Oh, indeed," he drawled. "I am."

She smiled.

He smiled, too, a mouse-in-the-grain-room kind of smile. "Although I am partial to calling my shaft a one-eyed monster. Very apropos, wouldn't you agree, given its size?"

A one-eyed *what*?

His lids lowered slowly, his smile sliding up his face in a complacent way.

She told herself not to react. Dratted man. He'd out-done her again. "Er, ah, yes," she agreed, forcing a blasé expression upon her face. "I imagine most men think theirs is the largest one-eyed monster in existence. At least, that is what Lucy told me."

"Indeed," he drawled, his lips twitching now as he

apparently tried not to laugh. "Lucy appears to be quite a fount of knowledge."

"She is," Elizabeth agreed, quite certain that all the inhabitants of Wales must feel the heat radiating from her cheeks. "I suspect she could teach most courtesans a thing or two, especially now that she is wed."

He finally let the laugh escape, his chuckles a husky, masculine sound of pure amusement. "I do think you might be correct." He leaned toward her, his eyes sinfully teasing. "And I am ever so grateful to her for imparting that knowledge to you."

She was sure he heard her swallow. Sure he could see her pulse beat at the base of her neck. It felt as if someone was banging a stick there. "Best you remember it is not you who will benefit from that knowledge."

"Oh, but I do," he said silkily. His grin grew even more wicked. "For I can think of no other woman who would know such words as 'lobcock' and, ah, what did you call it?" He drew back. She felt instantly better. His expression turned thoughtful. "Ah, yes," he said. "Sausage stick. A most amusing term. I find myself quite anxious to hear what other unusual euphemisms you might know."

And to that she could think of absolutely nothing to say.

He must have known he had her at a loss for words because he straightened and asked, "Would you like to see the rest of the castle?" abruptly changing the subject as if he knew he'd won the battle. And he had. Handily.

She would rather saw off both her arms and go swimming in the Thames than spend any more time with him, but she forced herself to say, "Of course," in a polite sort of way.

"Good, then follow me."

He offered her his arm again. Elizabeth almost ignored it but she knew she would need to get used to touching him thus. Placing her hand on his arm, she tried not to jump when he covered it with his fingers.

"You know, my dear," he said softly, patting her hand. "I really do think we shall get along famously. You have quite managed to surprise me with your unusual tongue."

A tongue that felt suddenly tied, Elizabeth realized.

"I believe that prim and proper exterior of yours might hide a very naughty lady, indeed."

Elizabeth straightened. "I would not wager upon it, duke."

"No?" he queried, looking down at her at the same time as he patted her hand. Elizabeth tried not to pull away. "Hmm. We shall see, shan't we?"

Indeed he would, for she was a lady through and through.

Lobcock.

She started, telling herself that she'd said the word merely to shock him.

Oh? a voice asked, *then why have you been dying to use that word in a sentence since the moment you heard it?*

Nonsense, she told that voice. *I wished for no such thing.*

Sausage stick.

Her face flamed. Naughty, naughty words. Goodness

knew where she'd learned them, for she truly didn't think Lucy knew them.

She was about to think upon it further, but a sudden realization that he had stopped before the derriere of a deer brought her up short. Well, 'twasn't really just the hind end of one deer, it was several of the beasts. A tapestry hung before her, a tapestry featuring a herd of unfortunate animals running from men with muskets. Big muskets.

"Have you lost your way?" she asked, as Lucien stared at the rug.

"No," he said, letting go of her hand briefly to push the woven tapestry aside. "We are going in this direction."

She looked beyond, the difference amazing, for even in half-light, she could still see the mess the castle had been in. Dusty, gray stones as plain as cave walls made up the interior. Wooden walls tipped and sagged. At one time she supposed those rooms must have been parlors, but they had long since ceased to serve that function. Gracious, it was hard to believe the right side had started out looking like the left.

"We are going someplace special," he explained. He headed toward the back of the room, stopping before—of all things—a wall.

She lifted a brow. "Yes, indeed this is a special wall, Your Grace. I can see that at a glance."

He lifted a brow before turning to a stone that seemed to stick out more than the rest. He touched it. Something groaned. She stiffened. The wall seemed to move, the stones vibrating briefly before—gracious—it was moving.

She felt her mouth drop.

"A secret passage," he said. "It works on a complicated system of pulleys and levers. My ancestors were quite clever."

She snapped her mouth closed, staring at the black hole with a combination of dread and curiosity. There were stairs. They went down. A long way down, by the looks of it. "Pity they did not pass that intelligence on to you."

"Oh, they did. You just don't realize it yet."

Unfortunately, she knew only too well that the duke was hardly an idiot. All the more reason not to trust him.

"There is a torch just inside," he said. "Please be so kind as to hand it to me."

"You must be mad." She stared down at the dark hole the wall had drawn back to expose. Over the top of the tapestry, the candle chandelier cast a mellow glow upon steps that dropped down into cold, musty, dark space. "You cannot expect me to go down there."

"Why not?"

"It looks unsafe."

"Do you not trust me?"

She looked up at him, disturbed to realize she did. Gracious, the man was a rake and a suspected murderer. She shouldn't trust him.

"No." Something like static leapt through her, her skin twitching as if she'd stepped through a spider's web.

He smiled, though she realized that smile did not quite reach his eyes. "Very wise of you, my dear." He looked away, stepping away from her to grab the torch in question. Elizabeth looked around, hoping to catch the eye of a servant, though what she would have done if one had been nearby, she would never know. But she could see no one beyond the wall hangings, and so she swallowed instead, watching as the duke picked up a lucifer and lit the peat-tipped end with a *whoosh* of flame.

"Come," he said, the light glowing around him like a devil's halo. He waved her before him with a hand.

Why, oh, why did he suddenly seem like a fish . . . and she the worm?

CHAPTER TEN

Despite the torch that hissed and spit, only a few steps at a time were illuminated. Reluctantly, Elizabeth stepped onto a large stone landing, smooth walls rising on either side of her. A breeze stirred the feather in her hat, the vanes tickling her cheek. It smelled like fresh-tilled earth. And yet . . . salty, as if the ocean were nearby, which, of course, it was. Curiosity rose within her, which only served to confirm her worst fear: She'd lost her mind.

"Careful," he said, turning to close the door—if one could call it that—behind them. It sealed shut with a thud that set Elizabeth's heart beating. "The steps can get damp this time of year."

"Where are we going?"

"You'll see," he said.

She wanted to press the matter, but tilted her chin instead, turning to the first step. And indeed, it was wet, and the lower they traveled, the wetter they became. She could feel the dank coolness seep through her slippers. She paused on a glistening landing and wiggled her toes.

And nearly fell.

"Careful," he warned again, grabbing her by the arm.

She never, ever thought she'd see the day when she was glad for his touch.

"Gracious, that was close," she hissed, noting there were still several more steps for them to descend. Bother that. She still couldn't see the bottom.

"I would advise you to keep going until we reach the end."

"Is there an end?"

"There is," he reassured. "Though not as nice an end as yours."

"I beg your pardon?"

"Nothing. Nothing," he drawled.

She compressed her lips, grabbing her skirt as she gingerly took another step, mumbling, "Why could you not be like a normal person and own a home without secret passageways?"

"It is not a secret. All the staff know of its existence."

"The existence of what? What is this?"

"Worried, Elizabeth?"

"How did you guess?" she asked, "For all I know you could be taking me to the dungeon."

"The dungeons are in another part of the castle."

"How lovely."

"We can go there if you want."

"So you could have your wicked way with me? I think not."

She almost crashed into his back as he stopped abruptly. The flames from the torch cast his face in flickering shadows, and yet she could still see the flirtatious smile that slowly lifted the edges of his mouth as he turned back to her. Handsome. She found him handsome. What a nodcock.

"What a novel idea," he breathed, his teeth exposed as he smiled. "I confess, the thought never entered my mind."

"No?" she queried.

"Hmm," he said, stroking his chin with his free hand. "I wonder if I shouldn't, how did you say it? Have my 'wicked way with you.' "

"I wouldn't," she snapped.

"Are you quite sure?" He lifted a brow. "Could I not interest you in a chaining to the wall? I hear that is a most interesting way to tumble a lady."

She crossed her arms in front of her, staring up at him from beneath the brim of her hat. "If you do not behave, duke, you will find yourself tumbling down the stairs."

"That would hurt."

"Indeed, though I doubt you could crack that hard skull of yours."

"My skull is not the only thing that is hard," he said, wiggling his brows.

She drew away from him, surprised she hadn't done so before. He was terribly close.

He looked down at her, his expression one of poised anticipation as he waited for her next response.

"I'm sure I don't know what you mean."

"I'm sure you do," he contradicted with a devilish smile. "You forget, I have met your friend Lucy."

She compressed her lips, trying to tell him without words that she refused to converse with him about such matters "Lucy is not as base as you think," she said with a look that didn't work.

He snorted. Actually snorted. Elizabeth could scarce believe the ignoble sound came from him. Never mind that such a sound emerged from her upon occasion.

"I beg to differ, my dear," he said on a laugh. "I'm quite sure your friend Lucy has educated you on the exact size, shape, and various lengths of the male penis."

She gasped. Ooo, the utter crassness of the man. But she would not let him embarrass her. She would not.

She arched a brow. "How astute of you, Your Grace, for Lucy did, indeed, educate me upon such matters." She smiled up at him sweetly. "And you can be sure, I find yours sadly lacking."

She turned away, lifted her skirts, and took a step.

She was just in time to hear his laughter boom out. It startled her. She spun back to face him.

His laughter turned into a squeak. Ignominious sound. And she would tell him so, too.

"Get down," he suddenly ordered, covering her body with his own.

Get *what*?

He lay atop her on the stairs. She pushed against his immovable chest. "What are you—"

The squeaking grew louder. Only it didn't come from the duke, it came from—

"Bats," she shrieked, trying to squirm out from under him so she could run.

"Stay put," he ordered.

Bats, oh my goodness, bats. She squeezed her eyes shut. Fluttering wings flew around her. She could just picture their furry little vampire bodies, felt the air stir as hundreds, nay, thousands of the creatures flew around them.

"Elizabeth," Lucien warned.

They were all over her. Eating her.

"Elizabeth," he yelled.

It was only then that Elizabeth realized she was screaming. *Loudly.* She stopped.

A moment of silence, the sound of the fluttering bat wings fading. "Well," he drawled. "Now the castle bats are not only blind, they are deaf, too."

She clutched his shirtfront. "Bats. Oh my goodness, Lucien, those were bats."

He covered her hands with his own. "Quiet, they are gone now."

Were they? Elizabeth opened her eyes only to realize she couldn't see a thing.

The torch had blown out.

"Lucien, please tell me you have another lucifer upon you?"

"I'm afraid I do not."

Elizabeth became aware of him then. Aware that he leaned his weight into her, pressing her back into the edge of a step.

"Get off me," she urged.

"I'm not so sure that I shall. After all, this might be the last time I'm allowed to lie with you thus."

"The step is cutting into my back."

He lifted his weight off of her instantly. "I beg your pardon, my dear. Here. Let me help you up."

And to her surprise, his touch was gentle as he asked, "Are you alright?"

And gracious, was that his hand that lifted and some-how found her chin in the darkness . . . his touch soft, his fingers probing for injury. She stepped back and turned away.

"Where are you going?" he asked.

"Back up the stairs." She couldn't, wouldn't begin to think of him as a caring, gentle human being. That way was madness. Witness her aunt.

"I wouldn't if I were you."

She lifted her skirts, taking a step as she said over her shoulder. "And why is that?"

"Because all those bats are no doubt clinging to the ceiling above."

She froze.

"Thank goodness I closed the door behind us. Of course, you might be the type who likes the ghastly little creatures. I, for one, do not wish to have my eyes nibbled out."

"They eat eyes?"

"Some do."

She wished she could see him. Oh, how she wished she could see him. "Then what do we do?"

"We go down," he said.

"Down. But how? We have no torch."

"I know the way."

"Why does that not reassure me?"

"Because you don't trust me."

He was most correct.

"Which is a pity because it means you will be staying here for a very long time. Ta ta." He squeezed past her, the heat of his body startling.

"No wait," she cried, hating him at that moment. Ooo, how she wished she could just push him down the stairs. "I shall go down with you."

"Excellent idea," he approved. "Here, take my hand."

No. She didn't want to. Gracious, she truly didn't, but it was a necessary evil, she told herself. Lifting her hand, she felt for his own. Warm fingers suddenly enveloped her. She shivered.

"If you feel yourself falling, cry out. I will catch you."

And his voice had softened again, making her ask, "How far is it to the bottom?" because she didn't want him to be kind to her. It was far easier to think of him as the wicked duke.

"Not far."

They had already climbed down half a dozen steps. "Is this a scenic tour of the dungeon then?"

He stopped suddenly. She crashed into his back. He turned in time to steady her with his hands, his fingers lightly clasping her waist. Gracious, but she hated the way his touching her made her feel.

"If you must know, I was going to take you down to the beach to watch the sunset."

She didn't know why his words made her heart suddenly still, but they did.

"Unfortunately, this is the only way to get to it. Under the walls."

"Oh," was all she could think of saying. He'd been taking her to see the sunset. How . . . nice.

"I am only sorry that once we find the torch, get down to the bottom, then relight it, the sunset will be gone."

And he truly was disappointed. She couldn't see his face, but she could hear it in his voice.

For the first time since their marriage, nay, for the first time since meeting him, Elizabeth felt her heart soften.

Careful, Elizabeth, a voice warned. *You might find yourself actually liking him.*

But then he ruined everything by saying, "Of course, the last woman I brought here said the journey below the castle took away the enjoyment she might have received out of the view. Not surprising since this is hardly a romantic stroll. 'Twas originally built as an escape passage for my ancestors. Given the fact that I have done nothing to beautify it, I suppose you would have felt the same way."

She stiffened. "Do not compare me to one of your mistresses."

"Mistress?" he said, his tone sounding confused. She could see his face. Just barely, for he shook his head. "No, my dear. 'Twas not my mistress, but my nanny."

"Your nanny?"

"Yes. I was ten. She was twenty, and I was desperately in love with her. Unfortunately, she never saw my potential, though I did my best to convince her of it."

She could only gape.

"Speaking of mistresses," he said, and she could see him stroke his chin, "the thought occurs to me that since we shall undoubtedly miss the sunset, there might be another way to make use of this time."

Her heart suddenly stopped, then resumed beating at a furious pace.

"You want to learn how to entice men. What better way to teach you than instructing you on the sensory delights of touch?"

"Touch?" she croaked.

She could barely see him nod, felt her breath catch as she saw him lean toward her.

"Indeed," he said softly, his breath floating over her face. "When there is no light, one's senses are heightened."

"But I can see you," she choked out.

"As I can see you," he observed. "'Tis the light from the entrance to the cave we are near."

As if to give proof to his words, she felt a breeze stir against her cheeks, the salty smell of dank seaweed and sand filling her nose. She could hear a roar that faded in and out.

"But no matter, for instructional purposes, this should do well."

She stilled, felt every nerve in her body tense. And for all that the air had chilled, she suddenly felt very, *very* warm.

"Do well for what?"

"Why, this, my dear."

Her breath caught as she waited. For what? Asked a voice. She didn't know, but she knew she wouldn't like it.

And then she felt it. Just the softest of touches, though how he'd moved without her noticing she would never know. And then she realized he hadn't touched her. He'd blown on her neck. She could smell the lemons. She swallowed, the feel of his breath like the most intimate of touches. "What are you doing?" she asked. *Oh, gracious.*

"Patience," he said softly. "I'm teaching you something."

She tried to draw away.

"Don't move," he instructed, clasping her waist.

"Let me go," she ordered, her body stirring in places she knew it had no business stirring in. *Not with him.*

"Do you not want to learn about men, Elizabeth?" he asked, leaning toward her, his hands not releasing her.

No, she did not. Not this way.

"Do you not want to learn what it is that stirs their blood?" He blew on her again.

"No. I, I've changed my mind."

"Have you?" he whispered in her ear.

The hairs on her neck stirred as if brushed by an unseen hand. And in its wake, her skin warmed. Oh, heavens. She closed her eyes. Her knees suddenly felt as supportive as noodles.

"Let me go," she groaned.

"Are you sure?"

"Yes," she breathed.

He let her go. She almost fell.

He caught her, saying, "Careful."

She tried to catch her breath, was dismayed to realize she felt like she'd run a mile. He stared down at her as if he waited for her to change her mind. The air seemed to hum, she wondered if the bats returned, then admitted she didn't care.

And then he drew away from her. "Stay here," he ordered.

"Where are you going?" she gasped out, her heart pounding to the point that she felt out of breath. Gracious, what had he done to her? Just a mere breath had made her heart beat erratically.

"I am going to the bottom of the passage to collect the torch that rolled down there. Lucifers are kept at the bottom, so I should like to relight it so I can come back and fetch you."

She placed a hand upon her stomach and the strange flutterings. "I see."

And, indeed, she could see him turn, heard his steps fade away, only the sound of a water dripping nearby keeping her company. And suddenly, Elizabeth felt terribly afraid.

Ah, but was it from being alone? Or was it from his touch?

She closed her eyes, suddenly more confused than she liked to feel. And that bothered her. The man was a reprobate. A rogue. Someone a wise woman should keep a healthy distance from. But she was married to him.

Married to a rake just like her aunt had warned her against.

Sudden light made her eyes snap open. They must have, indeed, been near the bottom, for the duke was back in seconds, his smiling face staring down at her wickedly in the flickering torchlight.

"You lost your hat," he observed.

She clutched at her head. She hadn't even noticed.

"Would you like to go back for it?"

She tried to sound calm as she said, "If 'tis all the same to you, I'd like to go back to the main hall. I feel a headache coming on."

She didn't know why her words made his smile falter, what he meant when he said, "I see," in a tone of voice that indicated he might just be disappointed. "Very well. Follow me."

"What about the bats?"

"They won't stir because of the light. You will be quite safe."

And she was, the trip up the steps as uneventful as the

trip down was eventful. Yet when he opened the passage, she couldn't help but feel a strange sense of . . . what? Disappointment? Surely she wasn't upset that she'd missed his sunset? Or was it something else, something Elizabeth refused to identify?

"Have one of the servants fetch Mrs. Fitzherbert. She will show you to our room."

Our room. "Where are you going?" she asked when he turned back to the passage.

"To catch the tail end of my sunset," he said without looking back. Elizabeth watched him go, disconcerted to realize that she was, indeed, curiously disappointed.

It didn't take Lucien long to reach the mouth of the cave, nor the rock outcropping that overlooked the ocean. 'Twasn't really a beach, although there was a small strip of sand below the stone platform he stood upon. Rocks tumbled from beneath it, a boat able to be launched during high tide. But right now that ocean was far below him, the sea mirroring the color of the sky above it: Angry, vibrant red.

Elizabeth would have loved it.

He smiled wryly. How utterly silly to want to show her a sunset. Even sillier to think she'd want to spend time with him.

A salty breeze slapped his face. It bit hard at his cheeks, flung the lapels of his jacket open, the ends of the cravat he wore flying behind him. He splayed his legs and braced himself against the icy shock of it, crossing his arms in front of him to keep the cold air at bay.

And what kind of a bacon-brained idea was it to teach her how to seduce a man, he wondered? Although, truth be told, 'twas a most interesting sort of task. Even a wee bit devilish, for what man would be able to resist her once he was through with her.

And therein lay the crux of the problem. He desired her. Devil take it, he actually enjoyed *being* with her. 'Twas most disconcerting. And troubling, for one thing he did not want to do was bed his wife.

Turning his back on the sunset, he slid down the wall that had been erected around the cave's entrance to prevent erosion. The back of his jacket snagged on the grainy stones. Coldness crept through the material making it feel wet. He hardly noticed.

What to do?

Did he retract his offer to teach her the art of seduction? A humorless chuckle escaped. God, who would have thought she would affect him so? It had been a shock standing here on the stairs, a strange longing filling him as he touched her chin. Thank God she'd gone back to the castle. He'd been more than happy to let her.

Henry, my brother. What a fine kettle of fish I've landed in.

Henry undoubtedly laughed himself silly.

Wiping a cold hand over his face, his gaze turned unseeing as he pondered the problem of Elizabeth. Undoubtedly, she would leap at the chance to call his "lessons" off. She'd as much admitted that in the passage. Dare he let her? Dare he try to battle his desire for her? What a challenge that would be. Resisting one's wife.

Aye, but did he dare?

Lucien contemplated the problem for goodness knew how long, but in the end, he was no closer to a decision about what to do than when he'd first arrived.

"Where is she?" he asked after returning to the castle. His cheeks felt frozen, his limbs ached from the cold, and yet he felt curiously alive.

"Would you be talking about her grace?" the impertinent footman asked, a man who had shed his footman's attire on more than one occasion to help him labor upon the castle.

"No, Ian, I am talking about the potbellied pig I brought home."

"A pig is she?" Ian asked with lifted red brows. Technically, the man was supposed to be an underfootman, but the lines blurred when one was employed by the duke of Ravenwood.

"I was not referring to the duchess, and you know it," Lucien said impatiently. His servants truly had gotten shockingly familiar. "I was referring to *your* wife."

Far from being angry at the slur, Ian gave a bark of laughter. "Now, now, Yur Grace. I know ye fancy me wife, don't try to bamboozle me."

Lucien merely smiled. "You know I jest, just as you know I wish to know where my duchess is."

My duchess. Hmm, he liked that.

Ian stroked his chin, appearing to give the matter some thought. "Lemme think. I knows Mrs. Fitzherbert showed 'er to your room." He scrunched his brow. "Then I believe she took a bath."

Lucien's manhood, which had shrunk considerably in the cold, suddenly leapt to life again.

"Then I believes she was to take dinner in the dining room."

The dining room. Elizabeth eating food. Her tongue licking those wonderfully full lips.

You are a sorry, sorry man.

"Thank you," he all but croaked, turning toward the back of the castle.

"Will you be joinin' her?" Ian asked.

And suddenly Lucien realized that to play with his wife was to play with fire. The question was, how did one bow out of their "agreement" gracefully.

"I could arrange to have a romantic dessert sent up," Ian added.

And that was when an idea came to mind. An idea so excellent, so perfect, his heart leapt in glee. It might actually work. He didn't need to call it off, he would make sure *she* would. That way, he didn't lose face. Excellent.

"Yes," Lucien purred. "Have your wife prepare some fruit, that is, if she's visited the exotic fruit peddler recently?"

"She has," the little man said.

Lucien smiled. "Good." He thought a moment, his lips tilting wickedly. "Then have her send up some bananas."

Lucien could swear Ian knew his every thought. Lord love him, he probably did.

"Right away, Yur Grace."

Lucien turned again.

"Would you like some melons to go along with that?"

Lucien stopped, turned halfway, his sly smile growing. "No. I think her grace's melons are more than adequate."

Ian looked surprised, and then amused by the comment. "Aye, I think they are, too."

Lucien's smile abruptly faded. His servant's grin faded, too. "At least, that's what the men've been sayin'."

"Indeed," Lucien drawled, his eyes narrowing. "Well,

you can tell the men that her grace's melons are not for discussion."

Ian nodded, his expression at once horrified and contrite. Lucien realized he might have been a bit harsh with the man. After all, 'twas he that'd brought up the subject. But he wasn't about to apologize.

He turned away, not seeing Ian's happy smile. "Got it bad, 'e has," he mumbled. And as the servant turned to the kitchen, an astute observer would have noticed the little man skipping. "Got it bad, indeed," he chirped.

CHAPTER ELEVEN

Elizabeth all but jumped when she heard the door to the dining room open. It wasn't that she didn't expect company. Goodness knew a bevy of red-and-purple-garbed servants had been in and out. One still stood to the right of the door, his back ramrod straight. If the door opened too hard, he'd be smashed like a fly. But what jolted her was seeing her husband.

"My dear Elizabeth," Ravenwood said, his green eyes back to their mischievous norm. "I see you washed the bat dung out of your hair."

Elizabeth, whose damp hair hung long and clean down her back—narrowed her eyes. Bat dung, indeed. She had dried her hair in front of the fire. There was not a speck of bat dung around . . . other than the two-legged variety that stood before her.

She laid her fork down, gently, gracefully putting the silver fork next to the silver-and-beige plate that sat between the silver hors d'oeuvre, salad, and dessert forks. "Actually, duke, I left it in. It does wonderful things for one's hair. Do you like the smell?"

He missed a step, or at least she thought he did. The

roguish look in his eyes faded into one of genuine humor. "Indeed," he drawled. "I shall have to try that sometime."

The servant leapt forward to pull out a chair. Raven-wood sat down, not at the opposite end of the rather long table. No, he took the seat to her left, his leg all but brushing hers as he did so. She blushed, turning her legs in the opposite direction.

"Thank you, Colin," he said to the footman. "That will be all."

The servant bowed smartly, straightened, and turned with military precision.

"And, Colin," the duke called. The man turned on his heel with graceful precision again. "You can dispense with the royal equerry act," he said drolly. "You look ready to asphyxiate, that jacket is so tight."

The servant's whole demeanor changed. His shoulders slouched, his neck relaxed, his black hair fell forward over blue eyes. "Can I, Yur Grace? Lord love me, me shoulders was beginnin' ta hurt."

"I am not surprised," Lucien drawled. Elizabeth stared between the two in shock. "Where the devil did you get that livery?"

"Mrs. Fitzherbert made 'em. Said a proper duchess would expect it."

Lucien caught her gaze, his expression seeming to say, "Do you believe this nonsense?"

Oddly enough, Elizabeth felt the urge to smile back.

"Well, you can tell Mrs. Fitzherbert your normal mode of dress is acceptable." He turned back to her, his brow lifting. "Unless, of course, you prefer otherwise?"

Elizabeth looked between the duke and Colin. "Of course not."

That seemed to be the right thing to say, for Lucien smiled at her approvingly. Elizabeth blinked, telling herself she shouldn't care to have his approval. And yet, she did.

She looked away, her gaze fixing upon the silver candelabra whose arms stretched toward the ceiling. Candles dripped wax upon the flowers that surrounded it, the smell of the pungent blooms noticeable even over the smell of food.

"There, you see," Lucien said. "Straight from the duchess's mouth. You may tell that staff that unless the Prince of Wales is hiding in a closet somewhere, they will be free to wear and behave however they wish."

The servant's face filled with relief. "Thank you, Your Grace," he gushed. "Knew you wouldn't marry no priggish London lady. Told the old bat that, but Mrs. Fitzherbert wouldn't have none of it." The man smiled, bowing in her direction when he neared the door. "Welcome, Yur Grace," he said to her. "'Tis glad I am that you wed this wretch."

"I beg your pardon?" Lucien shot, swiveling in his seat. But the servant had already gone. Elizabeth found herself biting back another smile, something that surprised her given the fact that her knee still burned where Lucien's leg had pressed against the maroon fabric of her gown.

He faced her again, his eyes frowning, but his green gaze glinting as he stared across at her. "I should fire the lot of them."

"They are—" She searched for the word.

"Beyond the pale," Ravenwood supplied.

"Indeed they are," she said, finding a bit of a smile leaking through, despite her best intentions.

He leaned back in his seat, the front legs of his chair no doubt lifting. "That color becomes you."

"Thank you," she murmured, looking at her half-eaten plate of food.

Silence descended. Elizabeth wondered if she should get up and leave. She folded her hands in her lap.

"What do you think of this room?" he asked.

She looked up sharply. "'Tis beautiful." But, of course, he must know that. The dining room was in the back corner tower. Since it was dark, she couldn't see much from the glass windows that stretched to her right, but she imagined the view would be lovely come the morn. A fireplace to the right of the door sent a mellow glow over the table, and the cherrywood side table to her left was covered with ornate dishes that matched her plate. The serving dishes each had the Ravenwood crest on the side. Very impressive. It all made her feel very much a commoner.

She met the duke's gaze again, only to notice him staring. Her knuckles turned white beneath the table.

"It occurs to me, my dear," he said softly, "that you are at a crossroads."

Her gaze snapped to his. He'd sat forward again, his elbows on either side of his silver charger, his hand cupping his chin in a manner of extreme relaxation. The pose irritated Elizabeth given that her own pulse pecked at her chest like an angry chicken.

"What do you mean?" she asked.

He tilted his head, his expression turning pensive. He traced an invisible pattern upon the plate with his other hand. "Well, you can tell me you've changed your mind about my teaching you how to seduce a man." He smiled. "Or, we can continue."

Her hands clenched then unclenched in her lap. Leave it to him to state everything so plainly.

"Do you not agree?" he asked matter-of-factly.

She gained the courage to look at him. A half hour ago she'd steeled herself to tell him she'd given up the idea. A half hour ago she'd convinced herself that it was her only choice. A half hour ago she hadn't been sitting next to him, staring into green eyes that all but dared her.

"Which will it be, Elizabeth?" he asked, leaning back with a smile upon his face. That grin seeming to mock her determination to quit. "I confess, I am all agog to hear."

She swallowed, then slowly, deliberately, stood. She'd dressed in her finest this eve: satin evening gown, fancy lace-embellished slippers, her trunks having arrived from London. Only now did she realize she'd done so to give her courage. After all her failed seasons, she'd learned to dress to give herself more confidence. Mock her would he? Call her a coward, would he? Well, he hadn't exactly, but he may as well have. "Why, Your Grace," she said, her posture meant to remind him that she'd come face-to-face with far worse than a randy duke. She'd stared down all of society. "I'm surprised you would think me ready to give up the notion." She smiled tightly.

Was it her imagination, or did his green eyes widen? She couldn't be sure, for in the next moment he straightened, too. "Good, for the next phase of your training begins now."

Had a servant been listening at the door? At that exact moment, one entered with a large tray of . . . fruit?

"Here you go, Your Grace," the man said.

She saw the duke eye the tray. "Ah. Excellent. I see we had the bananas."

A devilish smile lifted the edges of the servant's mouth. "Cook found 'em at market last week, though they're a wee bit small." Lucien and the servant exchanged a look Elizabeth didn't understand—the servant setting the tray down and then turning.

"Fruit?" she asked, when the servant left.

Lucien turned to face her.

A twinkle had entered his eyes. "Aye. Fruit."

She hated to ask the question, she truly did. "What, may I ask, are you planning to do with fruit?"

He lifted a black brow. "Oh, but 'tis not what *I* am going to do with it. 'Tis what *you* are going to do with it."

"I beg your pardon?"

"Have no fear, Elizabeth, this shan't hurt."

"What are you planning?" she asked suspiciously.

"You shall see." Slowly, he stood. Elizabeth told herself to relax as he stared down at her. When he turned to the tray of fruit, he all but cracked his knuckles. When he faced her again, he had a banana in his hand, the look on his face one of gleeful anticipation.

"One of the things you need to learn, my dear, is that there is a multitude of ways to seduce a man."

She supposed the fact that he was a man and holding a banana should likely worry her. She stared at him.

"Bananas are a favorite of mine"—his eyes glinted—"for many reasons."

"Indeed," she drawled. "I confess, I've only ever had the fruit upon a few occasions."

"We get them regularly, thanks to our proximity to the

ocean." He slowly took a seat. Elizabeth felt some of her amusement fade at the look in his eyes.

He leaned back. "Since you claim to know more than the average lady would know about the male appendage, I'm sure you recognize its similar shape to this." He held the banana up.

No, Elizabeth had not ever noticed the resemblance. Heat made her cheeks sting.

"I can see by the expression on your face that you haven't ever made the connection." And was it her imagination, or did she see him bite back a grin. "Then, you see, 'tis good I am educating you, for a banana can bring a man to his knees."

She knew she wouldn't like where this went. She just knew it. But it was far too late to protest. And so she merely stared, trying not to squirm.

"Pay attention," he said, leaning forward.

Elizabeth told herself not to lean away, she truly did, but she couldn't help herself.

"As the banana markedly resembles a chap's manhood, one need only pick one up and hold it thus"—he encircled the fruit with his fingers—"to make a man think of *your* fingers wrapped around his shaft."

Elizabeth combusted . . . at least, that's what it felt like. Her whole body burst into flames, starting with her cheeks and ending with her toes.

"Now," the duke said, the twinkle in his eyes increasing, "if one peels the banana thus"—he broke the top off then began tugging at its skin—"then lifts it to one's mouth thus"—he slowly put the fruit to his lips—"one should take care to eat it gingerly. If you bite the end off, you are apt to ruin the mood."

Elizabeth watched as he gently, slowly, opened his mouth, his tongue flicking out to nibble at the fruit.

She couldn't look away. Her eyes stared, transfixed, as he worked upon the fruit. She grew light-headed, only to realize 'twas because she'd forgotten to breathe.

"Now," he said, his eyes suddenly warm, "you try it."

She couldn't. Elizabeth almost said the words aloud, but the look in his eyes, coupled with the challenge she saw there, made her slowly, reluctantly, reach for the fruit. Her hands shook. Their fingers brushed. She jerked both the fruit and her hand away.

"No, no. Do not hold it that way," he scolded, and she could see him bite back a smile. "Lord, Elizabeth, you will make your lover wince with pain."

For some reason, his words got her back up. He had fun with this, at her expense. Cad. Fiend. Miscreant.

"How is this?" she asked. She shifted the banana to her other hand, caressing the smooth flesh softly.

The tables had turned. She saw him swallow, the humor in his eyes instantly fading.

"And this?" she asked, bringing the fruit to her lips.

Did she hear him groan as she mimicked his earlier movements? Certainly, she saw his nostrils flare. Saw his lips compress. She licked the side.

He met her gaze. Elizabeth felt her body jolt at the heat in his eyes. "Don't lick it, stroke it," he ordered.

"The banana?"

"Yes."

"Like this?" she asked, rubbing her finger up its side.

"Encircle it," he ordered, "with your thumb and index finger, then stroke it up and down."

Warnings went off in Elizabeth's mind, but she did as

asked. "Now don't move." He reached for a plum off the tray, lifted it to his mouth, took a bite of it, the fruit hanging over his lips.

"Take it."

Take it?

She almost drew back. He stilled her with a hand. The contact jolted her, made the heat that had waned suddenly burst through her again. And with that heat came the realization of what he wanted. He wanted her to take the piece of fruit that hung over the edge of his lips. With her *mouth.*

No, a voice warned. *Don't do it.*

But something in his eyes, some power that seemed to hum between them, made her dip toward him, made her do something completely naughty and thoroughly against every ladylike behavior drilled into her head. She took it, their faces closer than ever before.

The tough skin didn't break. She tugged, her breath coming in sharp gasps. Lucien tugged back, their lips touching. And then they kissed.

Elizabeth groaned, stood, a half-formed notion of fleeing entering her mind. But Lucien followed her up, pulled her to him, and then he deepened the kiss. He licked her. Licked at the fruit. Or was it she? Gracious, she didn't know. Instead she . . . oh goodness, she licked him back. The taste of the fruit blended with their kiss. Gracious, oh, gracious. It was heaven. It was naughty. It was wicked.

His tongue entered her mouth. Her body pulsed at the apex of her thighs. He cupped the back of her neck, the fruit disappeared, though she had no recollection of swallowing, only of him. Of his tongue filling her. Of the need, nay, the craving for him to fill her in other ways.

"Elizabeth," he moaned.

She clutched at him, pressed against him. *Closer,* a voice urged. She wanted him closer. Wanted their bodies to touch in places they shouldn't. Her breasts ached to be pressed up against him. She shifted. His manhood pressed into her mound, and she almost cried out.

Yes, her mind screamed. *Yes.* This was what she wanted. And then his hand replaced his manhood and she did cry out, her body pressing into his fingers of its own volition. He stroked her. Something began to build. She strained against him.

And then he abruptly let her go.

Green eyes burned into hers. She stared back. It was no consolation that his breath seemed as labored as her own. No source of comfort that his voice was raspy as he said, "And that, my dear, concludes this lesson. As you can see, touching fruit can arouse even the most jaded of men."

He turned, his back ramrod straight as he left the room. But before he exited, he turned, his hand resting on the door handle. "I shall meet you upstairs for another lesson."

Elizabeth turned, too, her hands clutching the edge of the table. Her eyes stared blindly at him. What in heaven's name had just happened?

CHAPTER TWELVE

H e didn't think he could do it. Didn't think he could continue with her 'lessons'. And, by God, that surprised the hell out of him. Just as everything about Elizabeth Montclair had been a shock.

He threw out crass sallies. She threw them right back.

He tried to frighten her with bananas. She ended up frightening him.

Aye, he sighed. No sense in denying it. He'd begun to be charmed by his new wife and it simply wouldn't do. She beguiled him with her sweet smile. Made him laugh with her sassy tongue. Made him wonder what life might have been like if things had been different.

But things were not different. The title was not his to pass on. Elizabeth would have been the perfect wife for Henry. Not him. Never him.

And so the question remained, had he scared her enough to call it off? Lord knew he hoped he had. He'd almost lost control in there, didn't think he had the willpower to go through another lesson.

He grabbed the banister rail, slowly lifting himself, surprised how out of sorts he felt. But as he climbed the

steps, a part of Lucien knew he couldn't face her again.
But what shocked him, what had him pausing with one
foot on the step above him, was the realization that he
didn't seek to avoid her out of a need for self preserva-
tion. No. What had him turning around and sinking to the
step again to his consternation was the realization that he
sought to comfort her by not appearing in their bedroom.

Good lord, he wanted to make her happy.

Only he knew he never would.

It took Elizabeth forever to gain the courage to leave
the dining room, and even then she had to pause at the
base of the stairs to take a deep breath. How could she
face him? What would he think of her?

He would think you are an apt pupil, that's what.

She shushed the voice, for all that it had a point. This
talking to herself had become quite annoying.

The staircase was sweeping, the steps wide, the railing
ornate. She focused on these details as she climbed. On
the wall sconces that were recessed into the walls. On the
landscape painting that hung in the hall that led to her
room. Their bedroom, she corrected. It was over the dining room, and so she turned to her right, her steps slow-
ing as she neared the door.

Gracious, she didn't think she could do this. She
couldn't go inside. What if he was—she swallowed—
naked. What if he expected her to sleep that way?

Elizabeth, a voice scoffed. *He cannot force you to
sleep naked. Do not be a ninny and go inside.* She
touched the handle.

He stuffed his tongue inside my mouth.

Her hand fell back to her side. Gracious, *he licked my tongue. And I licked him back.*

She couldn't do it, she thought. She just couldn't embark upon another lesson. Or any lessons, she admitted. She needed to call their agreement off.

"Did you need help undressin', mum?"

Elizabeth whirled. The same maid who had helped her dress earlier stood there, the pixie-faced servant having said more words to her than her former lady's maid had said in an entire lifetime.

"His grace told me you weren't feelin' well. Likely because of your long journey. Told me to tell you he's changed his mind about playing a game with you. Said you can go to bed instead."

The relief was so great, she almost collapsed where she stood.

"He's not here?"

The little maid came forward, her red hair peeking out from beneath a white mobcap. She opened the bedroom door for her. "No. Left the castle using the back stairs." She stood aside to let Elizabeth enter. "A good man ye married, if you don't mind me sayin'. Not many would forgo a night of pleasure with 'is new bride to let 'er sleep."

A night of pleasure? Oh, gracious, if the maid only knew.

And on the heels of that thought came the notion that she wondered if Lucien had been affected by what had just happened?

Well, of course he'd been, you dolt. You could feel *that.*

She blushed again.

And from that thought came another. He didn't trust himself.

She didn't know what to make of that. Should she be frightened? Happy that he obviously thought it wise to stay away? Worried?

"Come along," the maid said. "You'll catch a chill standin' out 'ere in this drafty old hall."

Elizabeth blindly followed her into the room. Instant warmth enveloped her. A fireplace stood in the room's corner to her right, with a large bed with a red-and-gold coverlet against the opposite wall. She tried not to think about that bed, nor the images of her and the duke sleeping in it.

Lord willing, he'd given up the idea of sleeping with her, too.

No wall coverings decorated the room, just heavy, ornate red-and-off-white drapes that hung alongside the massive round tower window to the bed's left. A cherry side table stood on ornately carved legs to the window's left. A door to her immediate right led to a large dressing room. It was there that the maid headed.

"Did you an' the duke have a pleasant dinner?"

Had she eaten? Elizabeth couldn't remember.

"Cook likely outdid herself. Truth be told, the whole staff were excited to 'ear about the duke's marriage. Never thought we'd see the day."

She turned to her, her blue eyes filled with friendliness. "The staff thinks yur lovely."

Elizabeth felt her brows lift. "I—" She swallowed, not quite sure how to respond to a servant's praise. *Did* one respond? "Tell the staff thank you."

The maid smiled, turning her around with gentle hands

on Elizabeth's shoulders. "What do you think of the castle?" she asked, quick with the catches.

Elizabeth had to force away memories of the duke doing the same thing. "It's lovely," she heard herself answer.

"Aye. 'Twill be as grand as a palace when 'tis finished. 'Eard the duke tell John that he had the money for more repairs. Guess the crop that came in was a good one."

"The crop?"

"Aye," the maid said. "The townspeople are excited. Means more work for the menfolk. Times were tough afore the duke took to repairing the castle with money from these lands."

Elizabeth turned to face the maid, unable to contain her curiosity a second longer. "What do you mean, 'money from these lands'?"

The little maid looked pleased at finally hearing words emerge from her mistress's mouth. "Money from Ravenshire," she said.

"You mean from all his lands, do you not?" Elizabeth affirmed.

To her shock, the maid shook her head. "No. Just from his land, the estate he inherited as a lad. He doesn't touch none of the other."

He didn't what?

The little maid must have noticed her shocked expression, for she grabbed her arm, the familiarity of the gesture startling Elizabeth. "You didn't know?"

"I, I didn't," Elizabeth found herself saying.

The maid looked up at her with a thoughtful expression, some of her friendliness fading. "He's never touched the other money, from what I 'ear." She stared up at her, eyes narrowing. "And I 'ear tell, he's vowed he never will."

It dawned on Elizabeth then why it was she stared up at her so challengingly. "I didn't marry him for his money."

The maid didn't look like she believed her, not surprising since servants knew everything. Like as not this one knew of the duke's dastardly reputation, undoubtedly assuming the only reason a lady would marry a man of such character would be for his money. Or his title.

"Well, 'tis a good thing then," the maid said, her expression very near a scowl. "For he refuses to touch the ducal money. Says it's blood money."

Elizabeth shook her head. Drawing away from the maid, she sat down on a nearby settee, uncaring that the top of her dress sagged around her elbows. "Blood money," she whispered. She looked up, her surprise apparently obvious.

"You thought he mighta killed his brother, like they said, didn't you?"

No, she didn't. Or perhaps she did. Heavens, she didn't know what to think. A part of her had wanted to believe in the duke's innocence. And yet another part of her had followed the flow of society's thinking; that the duke could easily have arranged his brother's murder. Such a thing had been done before. Undoubtedly, it would happen again.

But if Ravenwood didn't do it, why did he not protest his innocence?

"I just assumed . . ." Elizabeth's words faded.

"Aye, as have others," the maid said, glowering at her. And then she did the unthinkable. She turned her back to her, her expression that of a cat whose tail had been stepped on.

Heavens, she was about to walk out on her. Her mother would dismiss her on the spot.

She was not her mother.

"Wait," Elizabeth called. "Please."

The woman slowly turned, a scowl marring her brow. "What is your name?"

"I told you earlier, mum," she all but snapped. "Polly." Had she?

One does not speak to servants.

Her mother's voice rang out in her head, only this time Elizabeth shushed it for good.

"Polly, I'm sorry if I offended you." She took a deep breath, meeting Polly's gaze head-on. "I did not marry the duke for his money, nor his title, you see. He compromised me. We *had* to get married."

The suspicion didn't fade. If anything, it grew. "*Had* to, ma'am?"

Did maids get compromised? Elizabeth wondered. She had no idea. She'd been schooled in how to hire servants. Schooled in how to treat them, but she was chagrined to realize she actually knew nothing *about* them.

"Yes, had to. If I hadn't married him, my family would have been ruined, my father a laughingstock. *I* would have been ruined. We were forced to wed and I fear neither of us is happy about it."

Polly's expression remained skeptical.

"So you see," Elizabeth added, "I am not the fortune hunter you think."

The maid drew herself up, eyes blazing. "Yur a fool."

Elizabeth drew back, shocked to be snapped at thus.

"The duke is one o' the nicest employers a person could ask for. He doesn't chase th' maids. He doesn't ask for special 'services.' 'Tis fair and decent, he is, and a lady like you should be grateful for his attentions."

The ferocious little maid took a step at her. "The poor man's heart fair broke clean in two when his brother died. He spent hours on 'is beach. We had to drag him away one night after he near froze himself ta death."

Elizabeth's eyes went wide.

"But what fair broke me heart, what had the whole lot of us cryin' in the kitchen, was the sight of the duke's tears. The cold had frosted them upon his cheeks in twin tracks." She clenched her hands. " 'E's a good and decent man, and he didn't kill his brother. And if you doubt me words, just be 'ere on the anniversary of his brother's death. 'Tain't none of the staff what goes near 'im round that time, despite the love we all have for him."

No one, least of all Elizabeth, could doubt her words.

Polly's hands unclenched as she straightened, her expression irate. "So forgive me if I take offense at yur *havin'* ta marry the man. Half the women on staff would love to be in your shoes."

And with those words she whirled again. Elizabeth could only stare blindly at the spot where she'd been.

He'd *cried*?

She didn't know why the words startled her so, but they did. Perhaps because the duke always seemed so cavalier about everything. So unfeeling. It was hard to believe he could care about anything enough to cry over it.

But who wouldn't cry over the loss of his brother?

A man who'd cold-bloodedly killed that brother, that was who.

It was then that Elizabeth admitted to herself that she might have been wrong about him. Oh, goodness.

She'd called him a murdering whoremonger. Her hand lifted as she covered her mouth, her fingers shaking. She'd said the words to his face in full view of society, ignoring the brief glint of something she'd seen in his eyes.

Pain.

Only now would she admit to herself that she'd seen pain.

Gracious, what had she done? What had they all done, for she wasn't the only one to think him guilty of the crime. Society did, too. And yet, the duke had never once denied their accusations. He made a joke of it, Elizabeth having heard tell that he'd once dressed as an executioner at a masquerade ball. It was a morbid thing to do given the circumstances, and all of society had been agog because of it. There were some who had said his costume had been his way of admitting his guilt. Why else would he do it?

Why else, indeed?

The maid had undone enough catches for Elizabeth to shrug out of her gown and to strip down to her chemise. She crossed to the round tower windows, rubbing suddenly chilled arms. It was a long time before she turned away, her eyes burning from the length of her stare. As she reviewed her time with him, Elizabeth had to admit Lucien had behaved far from dishonorably toward her. Certainly, he had compromised her, but that was more the result of his bad judgment than any true desire to do her ill, for no matter what he said, she truly doubted he'd meant to go through with any sort of seduction. It had been a game, one that had gone horribly awry. Yet, in the end, he'd done the right thing. He'd married her. She turned, staring at the bed . . . a bed she would share with him soon.

Sleep was long in coming to her that night. A part of her wondered if he might go back on his word after their passionate interlude below. But, as she finally drifted off to sleep in the early hours of morning, not even a mouse stirred in their rooms. That was her last thought before her eyes closed . . . Only to open moments later.

"Good morning, my dear," a masculine voice purred.

She came up in bed, nearly colliding heads with him, only to slam back on the feather mattress again. The wretch leaned over her, arms on either side of her body, a wicked smile upon his face, his pepper-colored eyes glittering with that daredevil's gleam.

"Did you miss me last eve?"

Their interlude in the dining room came rushing back to her with a speed that made her cheeks flush. It didn't help that he wore no jacket, his shirt in shocking disarray. A half-formed notion that he might not have changed last eve penetrated, only to fade away when she noticed that his shirt was half-undone, a light sprinkling of hair showing through the crack. The intimacy of his dress shocked her, as did the way he lowered his head toward her, his wicked green eyes mere inches away. "I am more than willing to pick up where we left off, if you've a mind."

God help her, but all she could think about was the feel of him against her, his body pressed against hers intimately. The urge to close her eyes overcame her. She fought it.

"Get off me."

"But, my dear. I am quite comfortable."

And she was distinctly *un*comfortable. His breath wafted over her cheeks, making her body tingle. It also made her realize that she was in a bed with him for first time. Bother that, with *any* man for the first time.

She fought a groan, fought the urge to look away. "Get off me."

"Are you sure?"

She'd begun to tremble, though not from fear.

"I thought you might like to continue your lessons." He leaned even closer, his lips mere inches away, and was it her imagination, or did his body tremble, too? "They promise to be"—he leaned even closer—"amusing."

"Please," she whispered, her head sinking back into her pillow. The scent of him filled her nostrils. He smelled different this morn. No lemon. More like fresh-cut grass.

He tilted his head—and dear God—did he come even closer? "If you insist." Instantly, he rolled off her.

It was as if she'd escaped from beneath an elephant. A six-thousand-pound elephant. Good heavens.

He stepped back from the bed. Elizabeth realized why he smelled like the out of doors. He'd been riding. Hard, by the looks of it. His hair hung loosely around his head, part of his shirt drooping from his rust-colored breeches that were tucked into brown-topped riding boots. Flecks of grass dotted the surface of those boots, the green nearly the same color as his conniving eyes.

"Since you don't want to pick up where we left off,"

he said, his eyes glinting roguishly, "how about another kind of lesson, eh?"

She couldn't think. All she wanted to do was sink beneath the covers and hide her head. She watched as his eyes swept over her. Of its own volition, her hand smoothed her hair. She usually braided it at bedtime, but last night she'd been so rattled, she hadn't touched it. As a result, it hung around her shoulders, bits of it clinging to her face. She swiped at it. His eagle eyes followed the motion.

"Well?" he asked.

Think, Elizabeth. Think. "What kind of lesson?"

He straightened, the morning light illuminating half his face. He hadn't shaved as yet, a fine dusting of dark hair clinging to his chin. "A lesson in dress," he said.

"A lesson in *what*?"

Lucien tilted his head. "I haven't decided yet."

"Haven't decided what?"

"My dear, has your hearing gone bad again?"

"My hearing is quite fine, as you well know. I simply cannot believe—" Her words trailed off, her mind having a hard time deciding on the best way to phrase her concerns.

"Cannot believe what?"

She forced her gaze to meet his own head-on. "That you mean to continue with our lessons."

"Why wouldn't I?" he asked with lifted brows.

Because you almost snogged me silly on the dining room table, her mind fair screamed. But she didn't say the words aloud, though her face flamed as brightly as if she had.

His eyes narrowed. "Are you, perhaps, referring to our time in the dining room?"

He knew she was. The cad. Wretch.

"For if you are," he continued, "I would not think too much of it. 'Twas nothing more than your virginal reaction to a master's touch."

"I beg your pardon?" she said between clenched teeth.

He waved a hand in the air, his posture that of a tutor instructing a pupil. "It would be like a stable master teaching a horse how to canter. The horse doesn't canter because it wants to, it does so because it's instructed. Last night I taught you how to kiss a man. 'Tis nothing to be ashamed of."

He sounded so cavalier about it, so absolutely unaffected, Elizabeth felt her hands clench the coverlet. She might be innocent, she might be naive, but she was no fool. He'd desired her. Only he tried to bamboozle her into thinking he hadn't.

"Indeed?" she drawled in disbelief.

"Indeed," he agreed, inclining his head.

"Well, that is a relief," she said, "and here I thought you had lost control."

"Lost control," he shot. "Good heavens, no."

She studied him through narrowed eyes.

"'Twas only my body's natural reaction to your touch. All men react that way to a woman's touch. 'Tis the way of things. We can't control ourselves, heaven help the man who tries."

Hmm, methinks he doth protest too much. "So what you're telling me then is that if we move forward with our lessons, I shall have to get used to our"—she searched for the right words, sitting up in bed a bit just to see what would happen—"reaction to each other."

She watched as his gaze dipped down for a second, then swept back up. Was it her imagination, or did his eyes heat? "Indeed," he said.

She stared up at him unblinkingly.

He smiled, but it looked a bit forced. "Of course, I will understand if such a thing frightens you. In fact, if you would like to call it all off, I will certainly understand."

Ah-ha. So that was the lay of the land? He was trying to goad her into calling it off, just as he'd tried to bribe her into calling off their marriage.

Seize the excuse, Elizabeth.

But something held her back, something that had to do with some silly ridiculous hope that maybe, just maybe . . .

"No," she said softly, "I do not think I shall call it off."

She had the pleasure of seeing his eyes widen, of seeing him look momentarily shaken. Just like he had been last night when she'd declined to back down. And as soon as she saw that look, she knew she'd made the right decision. Wherever it might lead.

"You don't?" he asked.

"No, Your Grace, for 'tis obvious by last eve's performance that I have a lot to learn."

And, yes, his voice was definitely a croak when he said, "You do?"

She bit back a smile. "I think we should continue."

"You do?"

"Indeed. I am completely at your disposal."

"You are?" He took a step back, almost as if she'd begun to spout poisonous bugs from her mouth. But then he seemed to get ahold of himself. His eyes caught on something. She followed his gaze. Her dressing gown. "You *are*," he repeated, and his green eyes narrowed, their color turning almost black. "Very well," he said. "We can get started straightaway then. Get out of bed."

And suddenly, the tables had turned.

"Go on, I promise not to thrust myself upon you in a fit of uncontrollable lust. Takes more than that to arouse a man of my experience."

He was trying to goad her. Again.

Her lips compressed into a line. She felt her hands clench. "Very well," she said. Taking a deep breath, she forced herself to crawl from beneath the covers. Forced herself to place her feet on the floor and reluctantly stand.

It was like standing before him naked, the thin chemise affording little cover. But some of her embarrassment faded at the look on his face. She watched it happen. Watched the way his breath caught. The way his whole body seemed to resonate.

Force her into backing down, would he? They would see about that. Proudly she stood before him, knowing that the morning light turned the fabric near transparent. She knew it for certain when she saw the way his eyes slowly lowered and then narrowed infinitesimally. She threw her shoulders back, watching as a glint of heat entered her eyes.

And that was when Elizabeth got her first taste of what it was like to control a man's desire. The duke didn't *want* to desire her. And yet he did.

It made her feel naughty. Made her feel saucy. And it was a feeling she'd begun to like.

CHAPTER THIRTEEN

Lucien felt like a young lad gazing at his first naked woman. But the sight of Elizabeth standing before him in nothing more than a chemise, her hair flowing around her shoulders like a river of mink, made him seriously consider a career in the clergy. Damnation.

"Are you quite—" He coughed, chagrined to realize his throat, and subsequently his voice, had gone raspy. "Are you quite certain," he began again, "that you want to put your hands on me, ah, put yourself in my hands?"

Did her eyes sparkle? Could she truly be looking at him in the same devilish way he usually looked at her?

She walked toward him, and she'd obviously picked up a thing or two in the ensuing hours since she'd last tried to walk like a strumpet. Her hips swayed enticingly. Her shoulders drew back to reveal pert breasts. Her lips smiled cockily.

And for the first time in his adult life, nay, the very first time *ever*, Lucien found himself fighting the urge to retreat from a woman. The master of seduction was in danger of becoming the master of . . . nothing.

"But, my dear husband," she drawled in the exact

same tone he himself liked to use, "I believe I need to get comfortable with a man's stare. Who better than to practice on than you? A man experienced at controlling his base needs. Or so you say."

It hit him then, what this was all about. She'd called his bluff . . . just as he'd called her bluff earlier.

And from nowhere came the urge to say, *brava*. She hadn't backed down. In fact, she'd turned the tables on him. Nicely.

A spurt of admiration filled him. By God, she was full of surprises. If he hadn't been married to her, he would have found himself liking her.

"Indeed," he said, as she stopped before him. And— good God—were those her nipples he could see? He almost groaned, for it was, the dusky hue teasing him. Not only that, but he could see the curve of her breast. The pale flash of her stomach. And—God help him—the small indentation of her navel.

For a second Lucien wondered if this was God's punishment for the part he'd played in his brother's death. Who would have thought he'd desire his new wife? But he did. What was more, she seemed to realize that. Elizabeth the shrew was gone; in her place was a woman that would do a courtesan proud. Devil take it, she leaned toward him. He found himself tilting away. His hands clenched, then unclenched, Lucien trying in vain to remind himself that he was the one supposedly in control. He had the upper hand.

Didn't he?

"Very well," he forced himself to say, hard-pressed to remember where the conversation had just left off. "If you wish to parade around dressed thus, feel free. I would, however, suggest you put on a wrap. Wouldn't do for you to catch a chill."

And make your nipples hard.

He bit back a groan.

If she grows chilled, you can warm her up.

"No, I cannot," he warned himself.

"Cannot what?"

Damnation, she had him addled.

"Cannot—" he struggled for a suitable reply. "Cannot fetch your wrap for you."

She lifted a brow, and he realized then and there that she knew that wasn't what he meant. Good Lord, how had this happened? She was supposed to have been so frightened by his presence that she would call the whole thing off. That had been the plan anyway. Only, somewhere, things had gone horribly wrong.

He turned from her, knew that if he didn't, he would surely scoop her up and toss her upon the bed.

"Come," he instructed.

Argh, he'd come alright.

His hands clenched again as he crossed to their dressing room. Not much adorned the room but wardrobe closets and a settee. It was to one of those closets that he crossed, the dark oak door opening soundlessly.

"Since you're already in a state of *déshabillé*, let us see what other items you can use to your advantage."

He stopped before their wardrobe closet, opening the doors with more force than necessary. Undergarments hung there. He reached in and pulled out a corset, turning to her just in time to see her eyes widen.

"Come, my dear. Let me show you the proper way to

lace this up so that your breasts are shown to their full advantage."

"I beg your pardon?"

He bit back a smile, noting the telltale teeth marks in her lips. "Come, come," he urged, wiggling the garment. "This is what you want, is it not?"

It didn't look like it was, but he'd just called her bluff, and she knew it.

Check.

"Very well," she said, her shoulders stiffening as she brazenly faced him. "Show me."

Check*mate*.

He held the corset out before him, studying it for a second before he gleaned how to put the thing on (he'd only ever taken them *off*). When he looked up, he saw her staring at him. "Turn around," he ordered.

She looked ready to balk.

"Go ahead. I shan't bite."

Oh, yes, he would if given the opportunity.

Slowly, reluctantly, she did as instructed. Lucien stifled another groan. If the front of her had been stunning, her back side was simple perfection. A narrow waist curved into a heart-shaped rear. Sunlight projected through her chemise, revealing long, slender legs.

He didn't think it was possible to grow any harder for her, but he did.

"Move your hair."

Slowly, and in a way that seemed almost sensual, she lifted her waist-length hair, pulling it over one shoulder. Damnation, but he loved the way craving her made him feel. Out of control. Excited. On edge. He wanted to do things to her. Wanted to plunge inside of her. Wanted to hear her rhythmic groans of pleasure. Wanted to feel her body contract and contract and contract around him.

Only, he couldn't.

But the pleasure, oh the pleasure of coming up behind her, right behind her. He stayed there for a second, inhaling the sweet scent of her. Roses. She didn't move, although he could tell by the way her chest heaved that she was far from unaffected by his presence.

And then—God help him—he couldn't resist moving closer.

She gasped, turned. Wide, violet eyes peered up at him in shock. She only jumped an arm's length away, and yet the essence of her stayed with him. Aye, and the desire.

The air stilled, grew heavy. He told himself to go to her, to kiss her, touch her.

But he knew if he did, he would have her, and that he must never do.

Ever.

"Touch me, Elizabeth," he said instead.

She didn't look like she understood his words. Truth be told, if she felt anything like he did, she would be hard-pressed to think at all. "What did you ask?" she said, her voice breathless.

"Touch me," he said, discarding the corset, stepping forward and grabbing her hand.

Her eyes flickered, lips parted.

"Here," he said, placing her hand against him.

"Lucien," she gasped, drew away. "You go too far."

"Do I?" he asked, frustration making his words terse. "Is this not what you want, Elizabeth? Do you not want to learn how to entice a man?"

"No. I mean yes." She looked away from him, her eyes

darting from left to right. "You were going to teach me how to dress."

"I've changed my mind."

She peered up at him, her eyes wide.

Run, little girl, he silently told her. *Run away and never come back, for if you do not, you will start something neither of us will be able to finish.*

But she didn't run. She stayed right where she was, her hands at her sides, her hair concealing her left breast. He almost turned, but something wouldn't let him. Maybe pride. Maybe determination. Whatever.

"Touch me," he ordered again.

Why, oh why, didn't she run? Why didn't she do what any other virgin in her place would do?

He studied her. Watched the way her chest rose and fell, her plump breasts pearly globes. Watched the way her pulse beat at her neck, the skin throbbing rhythmically. The way she trembled.

"Do it," he ordered.

"I can't."

"Do it or my lessons are over, for there is no point in instructing you in the art of seduction if you cannot touch a man without blushing."

She lifted her chin. He thought he might have done it then. Thought he might have convinced her to turn tail. Instead, she lifted a hand and, God, she touched him.

A gasp escaped from his lips. He almost closed his eyes. Almost picked her up and carried her to the bed there and then, but that odd pleasure/pain had begun to build again. That excitement that made him want release and not want release. The feeling of hovering on the brink.

And all she'd done was touch him. It defied belief. But he was closer to a release than he'd been with his last three lovers.

She drew her hand away.

"No," he ordered, pressing her hand against him again. "Stroke me."

"I can't," she gasped. "'Tis not right."

"We are man and wife, Elizabeth. What could be more right?"

She didn't answer, her mouth parted, eyes gone topaz blue.

He pressed her hand against him again. "Stroke me, Elizabeth. Stroke me and learn the power that a woman can have over a man."

She closed her eyes. He pressed harder, showed her how to move her fingers over him. And, God, the pleasure it gave him. "Yes," he hissed. "Like that."

And she did it. Bloody hell, she did it, her eyes staring at him in wonder and curiosity. He tilted his head back, feeling a release build.

"Harder," he instructed.

The pressure increased. Sweet Jesus, she touched him exactly right. And then, against his will, he was coming almost as quickly as he had the first time he'd had a woman.

"Lucien," she gasped.

But Lucien didn't hear her. He was too busy containing his cry. Too busy trying not to fall to his knees. Too busy enjoying a woman's touch for the first time since his brother's death.

CHAPTER FOURTEEN

"Thank you, Elizabeth," she heard him moan what seemed an eternity later but was mere seconds.

Elizabeth stared up at him, her body trembling, her mind whirling, mortified by what she'd done, empowered by how she felt.

She'd made him lose control.

It was exactly as he'd said. It made her feel splendid. Potent. *Desired.*

And aroused. Her body trembled, her woman's mound tingled. She herself hovered on the brink of something, something she felt sure he'd just experienced.

"And now it is your turn."

Her body pulsed at his words. At the look in his eyes. She moistened in a place that burned and throbbed in a way that made her legs tremble.

"No," she said, even as her mind whispered, *yes.*

He ignored the word, his right hand reaching for her. And then he touched her right breast. Just a light touch, but it felt like fire. Her nipple stung, as his thumb worked the tip of it.

No, screamed a voice. 'Twas not supposed to be this way. *She* was the one in control.

And yet she wanted to be out of control. Wanted what he had had moments before, whatever "it" was.

"Lucien," she moaned.

"Stand still," he ordered. "Do not move, for if you do, I shall stop."

It sounded like a threat. Her mind balked at the words, but she didn't move, feeling rooted to the floor. She didn't flinch as he reached out with his other hand and lightly stroked her left breast. Her eyes closed. A low moan filled her throat.

"Don't move," he warned again.

Had she moved? Heavens, how could one tell when one's whole world spiraled toward . . . something? She felt as light as air, and as wild and untamed as the Welsh coastline.

One of his hands dropped lower, skimming the flesh of her belly, caressing the circle of her navel, stroking her softly in a spot no man had touched before.

Another moan escaped.

"Yes, Elizabeth," he said softly. "That's it. Let it go. Let it happen." His hand dropped lower, cupping her.

"Lucien," she moaned again.

"I'm here, Elizabeth. Right here. Hold on to me."

And she did. She'd lost her willpower. Lost her sense of right and wrong. All that mattered was this, this *thing* that built inside her. This need for, for *something.*

"Let it go, Elizabeth," he ordered again, his voice right by her ear, his hand rubbing her rhythmically. "Open for me."

God help her, she did. She spread her legs. Allowed

him full access. His fingers fondled her. Teeth nipped at her neck.

And then light flashed before her eyes. She moaned. Then moaned again and again.

"Yes," she heard him say. "Yes, Elizabeth. That's what I wanted."

She clutched at him, would have fallen if he hadn't caught her. 'Twas like she flowered from the inside out, as if she gave him all of herself. Throb after throb after throb pulsed between her legs. She wanted to call out, wanted it to go on forever. Alas, it ended far too quickly.

And with it, reality returned.

She stood in their dressing room, her chemise caught between her legs, his hand still cupping her, moisture dampening the place where his hand pressed.

He stared down at her, his chest heaving, eyes blazing. And then he turned and calmly strode to the door, leaving the room as soundlessly as he'd come.

An hour later Elizabeth was no closer to making sense of the tumultuous event than she had been before. If anything, she was even more confused and upset by all that had transpired both this morn and last evening.

She paced the castle's dark and drafty halls, wondering where he'd gone and, more importantly, what he was thinking. She paused before a portrait she'd discovered in the library, a man riding a black horse with a docked tail stared arrogantly down at her, a pack of hounds frolicking at the horse's hooves.

"He was my father."

Elizabeth just about came off the ground. She turned sharply, disconcerted to see the object of her thoughts glide into the room as calmly as a ship to harbor, no trace of what had happened showing on his face. It was as if he'd forgotten it. As if it had meant nothing to him.

Would that she could act the same.

He'd touched her between the legs.

She blushed at the memory.

"His portrait used to hang at the Ravenwood family seat. I brought it here to remind me of all the reasons why I do not eat chicken."

"I beg your pardon?" she asked, having to force herself to follow his words and *not* remember the incredible pleasure he'd given her. And *she him.*

"He died choking on a chicken bone."

She watched him come toward her. Volumes of books lined the walls from floor to ceiling. Tall, oblong windows shot sunlight directly on him. The white shirt he wore was unbuttoned, his bronze skin glowing from exertion. And still no trace of what had happened flickered in his charming eyes, at least, not that she could tell.

She, however, felt ready to ignite.

"How unfortunate."

"Yes, it was."

They lapsed into silence, a silence that made Elizabeth uncomfortable. That must be why she blurted, "Where have you been this morning?" like a jealous wife.

He lifted a brow. "Why? Did you want another lesson?"

She stiffened. "Of course not. I was merely trying to be polite, as you apparently are."

He stared down at her, clasped his hands behind his back as he looked up at the portrait again. He seemed to be grappling with himself, for he appeared almost nervous. It was another few seconds before he turned to her. "Elizabeth, we should likely discuss this unfortunate attraction we have for each other."

Unfortunate?

"I think in light of it, you should call off our lessons."

She stared up at him, her whole body humming at his presence, her heart beginning to thump in fits and starts only to burst into a frantic rhythm. He turned up the heat of his smile, and she wanted to melt. Instead, she stiffened.

"*Me* call it off?"

"Yes, you," he said, "for it was you who lost control."

"Me?"

"Yes, you. But do not take it personally, my dear. You are inexperienced. I forget about that when I am around you. But surely you can see that continuing with our lessons might cause you to lose control again. I would hate for that to happen, for I am, after all, only a man, and if you throw yourself at me, I might not be able to resist."

Throw myself at him!

Lucien watched as her face filled with outraged color, his heart pounding as he waited, nay, *prayed* for her to call it off. "I can assure you, you are in no danger of that," she said.

"Oh, and how would you know that?"

"Because I am not as innocent as you think. Because I know you were just as out of control as I."

"I was not," he lied, utterly determined to keep the truth from her; wouldn't do for her to realize she made him feel as edgy as a trapped bee.

"The evidence points to the contrary."

"Beginner's luck."

"Do you think so?" she asked.

"I do," he said.

"Well, I think you are wrong."

She did? "Do you now?"

"I do. I would wager my skills have taken you quite by surprise."

"Indeed?" And he cursed her ability to read him so easily. Demme, now what?

"Indeed."

"Prove it," he said.

She stiffened. "Prove what?"

"That it was not beginner's luck," he smiled, an idea suddenly coming to mind, an idea so simple, so cunning, he knew it would work. He hoped. "That you could arouse another man, one perhaps, less willing than I."

"I beg your pardon?" she found herself gulping.

"John," he said matter-of-factly, liking the idea more and more. "If you think yourself such a prime article, try your skills on John Thorsen, my steward."

She looked appropriately shocked. "You want me to seduce John?"

"Why not? We'll make a wager of it."

"You're mad."

"Why not?" He waited for her to say the words to back down and, god willing, give the whole lesson thing up.

"Because it's, it's . . ." She appeared to have to search for the appropriate word. "Unseemly."

Yes, it was, and lord willing it would give her a revulsion of him so great, she wouldn't want a thing to do with him ever again. "But my dear, aren't you the one that wants to take a lover? Are you telling me now that you think the idea unconscionable?"

"That is not what I'm saying at all. I am saying that to seduce *John* would be unseemly."

"Not at all," a part of him disbelieving that she would entertain the notion this long. "In fact, it would be John's very reluctance that would make this all the more a challenge." He smirked down at her. "Of course, if you are too afraid to do so, I will understand."

"I am not afraid."

She wasn't? "Then what is stopping you? Surely you can't be ashamed of trying out your newfound skills?"

Lucien felt his chest still as he held his breath. Any minute now she would snap. Any moment she would tell him he went too far. All he had to do was retain his smirk and she would run screaming from the room and never want another thing to do with him.

"Very well," she said. "I will try to seduce John."

What?

"However," she added, her eyes filled with pique. "Since you want to make this a wager, you will need to do something for me should I win."

He couldn't believe she'd said yes. Now what the devil did he do?

"And what would that be?"

He watched her eyes dart around, catching on a portrait of a long dead aunt behind him. "If I win, you shall wear a dress for a day."

"I beg your pardon?"

"You will dress as a woman," she repeated. "I insist upon it, for, quite frankly, you and I both know this is not about my skills as a lover but about our pride, yours and mine. If you lose, I want you to suffer." And she looked like she did. Truly. "In a very public way. This should do nicely."

"That is not very kind of you, Elizabeth."

"Afraid you might lose?" she threw back his words.

"Of course not. But what do I get if I win?" he asked, furiously searching for another way to make her back down. And then he had it. The ultimate way of scaring her off.

And once again, she must have read his face. "Oh, no," she said.

He wiggled his brows.

"Oh, ho, ho, no," she said, lifting her hands in protest.

"Just one night," he said. "One night of lessons such as you've never imagined."

"You're mad."

"Afraid I might win?" he taunted back.

Her eyes narrowed. He'd backed her into a corner. "Very well," she said. "Invite the man to dinner."

It was then Lucien realized he fought a losing battle. But if it was a battle she wanted, a battle she would have. "When?"

"Tonight."

"So soon?"

"Why not?" she asked, Elizabeth hating that he seemed a bit taken back by the speediness of the wager.

"As you wish." Then he came forward. "Of course, I shall require some proof that you were successful in your seduction."

"You want to share a bed with us then?"

He drew back, looking, *well*, shocked. "Heavens, no. I merely wish for you to prove that you've seduced him."

"I see."

"Do you, my dear?" His eyes glittered.

"I do, duke. And I shall delight in proving to you that I am more than up to the challenge."

"Let us pray for your sake that 'tis John who is 'up' to the task."

He was being crude, and in a way she finally understood. She didn't know whether to be repulsed or angry by the realization.

"Until tonight then, my dear." He picked up her hand, dropped a feather-light kiss upon the back of it. Her body stilled. Shimmering energy danced down the back of her neck. It irked her no end that all he had to do was touch her to elicit a reaction. "We dine at six."

She couldn't stop staring at their hands, hands that had stroked each other so intimately.

Stop it, she told herself. Do not think of it.

And she didn't. At least not for the next ten seconds.

Slowly straightening, he stepped back, his hand dropping away. Her fingers rubbed together as if her flesh stung. His eyes remained fixed upon her. "I look forward to our wager, my dear."

"Until tonight," she answered, her voice hoarse.

His smile grew in volume. Elizabeth watched him turn, watched him walk away. Wondered if she'd just agreed to do something terribly foolish.

CHAPTER FIFTEEN

Nine hours later Lucien surveyed himself in his dressing room mirror.

"Perfect," he said, straightening to his full height so that he could get the full effect.

"If I might say, Your Grace, you do, indeed, look smashing."

"I do," Lucien agreed, smoothing his black jacket. "Although I do wish this cravat looked more full. If that poor sod Brummell were still around, he would be aghast at the state of it. It's as floppy as a fisher wife's breasts."

"Indeed, sir," Phibbs agreed, his lips unmoving. The man was of the old guard, much to Lucien's dismay. Try as he might, Lucien couldn't get the chap to unwind.

Stepping back from the mirror, his eyes swept down, observing the pristine crispness of his black cloth trousers. Next he eyed the way his black jacket hung right to his waist, open in the front, tails in the back. At the glorious shine upon his black dress shoes.

He looked, quite honestly, as good as a man could look.

He turned to Phibbs. "Have you seen my wife?"

The servant gave him a half bow. "She is with her lady's maid, Your Grace. In the guest bedroom. I believe they are concocting a surprise for you tonight."

No doubt they were, Lucien thought, smiling in anticipation, though not a surprise for *him*. How shocked Phibbs would be if he knew, Lucien thought. He even contemplated telling the man, just to see his reaction, then changed his mind. Word would reach his staff about this evening's events without his help.

"Tell me, Phibbs," he said, tweaking with his cravat again. "Why do they call a manservant a manservant and a lady's maid a lady's maid?" He turned to him again. "Should she not be a lady's *servant*, instead?"

Phibbs's gray brows lifted, rheumy old blue eyes lowered humbly. "Why, I'm sure I do not know."

"No?" Lucien asked with an answering lifted brow. "Pity, I've always wondered."

With one last adjustment to his cuffs (tailored to the perfect length just below his wrist), he turned for the door.

"Do not wait up for me, Phibbs. It might be a late night." For he knew Elizabeth would not give up on her seduction easily.

He almost pitied John. Almost.

Instead, Lucien smiled. Quite honestly, it surprised him how much he looked forward to this evening's events. It wasn't so much that he anticipated Elizabeth's failure—and he was sure she would fail—no, it was more that he couldn't wait to see the look on her face when she realized she would be spending the night with him.

Of course, he wasn't actually going to spend the night with her. Heavens, no. He would scare her a good bit, though. Enough so that she would leave him alone. Forever. That way he could save face, make sure she never bothered him again, and lay the blame all at her door.

Perfect.

He smiled, pleased with his plan and taking the steps two at a time, the heels of his shoes clicking on the marble floor in the main hall.

The door to the dining room lay open, Lucien spying John inside. What Elizabeth didn't know was that he and John had been friends since university. In fact, he was the only friend of his who hadn't died, a fact that made Lucien distinctly nervous, for he truly liked John. He'd also been one of the few people to stand by him after Henry had died.

So it was that he entered the dining room in a jovial mood. John turned from his spot by the tall windows, the flames in the hearth to the right reflecting back in the glass. Outside another orange sky blazed.

"See you're all dressed up for your pretty new wife," his friend said in a Scottish brogue.

The words gave Lucien pause. Had he gotten dressed up for her? Truth be told, he hadn't given it a thought. But John was quite correct. Usually he adopted a more casual dress for dinner at home.

"Yes," he admitted. "I suppose I did."

"I don't blame you, for a prettier lass I've yet to see."

Just wait until she turns her charms upon you, old friend, Lucien thought, wanting to chuckle slyly.

"Yes, she is rather pleasing to look at."

John's brows lifted. "She is a great deal more than mere pleasin'."

Lucien shrugged, joining his friend by the window, his

hands folded behind his back in a casual manner. "Truth be told, I hadn't noticed. This is, after all, a marriage of convenience."

"So you tell me."

Lucien smiled. While he wouldn't tell John outright to have a go at his wife, he didn't want him to get the wrong idea about their relationship. Love her, indeed. He still couldn't believe his friend had said that.

"My wife and I are . . ." He searched for the right word. "Friends, but not lovers. Not ever. I know you might find that hard to fathom given my reputation, but 'tis the truth. In fact, we have each agreed to go our separate ways once a respectable amount of time has passed."

Surprise and shock filled his friend's blue eyes. "Then you're a fool, Lucien, for I do not believe you could find a woman more your match."

"And how have you gleaned that?"

"One need only observe her briefly."

"That may be true," Lucien agreed. "But you know how I feel about matters of the heart."

"Yes, though I've always thought you shouldn't judge other women by a previous lover's cover."

"If by that you mean I should not think all women devious just because of the actions of one, you are quite correct. Silly thing to do. No, that is not why I have vowed not to love again, and more on the subject I am not prepared to say. Simply accept that is the way it is."

John's eyes narrowed. "As you wish."

They lapsed into silence, but not for long. "In any event," John said, " 'twas kind of her to invite me to dinner."

"Yes," Lucien said, biting back a smile. "My wife is the epitome of goodness."

John looked a bit surprised. Lucien wondered why, only to realize it wasn't his comment that had taken him aback. It was something behind him, and he had a feeling he knew what . . . or *who*.

Slowly, he turned.

And there she stood, and even his jaded eyes near bulged at the sight of her.

She wore a gown that suited her coloring perfectly. It wasn't sinful scarlet, as he'd assumed she'd wear. It wasn't mauve, nor any other shade of red. No, she wore black. Simple, elegant, *plain* black. And yet on his wife it looked far from plain. It matched her upswept hair perfectly. Made her blue eyes appear huge with the way it accentuated her black lashes. Her skin looked as creamy as first snow. Long, elbow-high gloves, the skin above the black fabric a startling contrast, completed the outfit. And while her gown wasn't sleeveless, it might as well have been, for the short sleeves were made of black lace, allowing for a delicious peek at her shapely arms. She looked like Harriet Wilson, only with more class, and the result was quite splendid.

"My dear," he said, coming forward to greet her, hands outstretched before he thought better of touching her. His arms dropped to his sides. "Well done. You look smashing." He darted a sly glance at John. "Good enough to eat, I daresay, eh, John?"

John looked incapable of speech. That gave Lucien pause, for he knew from their days at Eton that John was as much a connoisseur of women as Lucien felt himself to be. Certainly a pretty face and an elegant smile shouldn't give him pause.

But my wife's are.

It was that moment that Lucien got his first inkling of trouble. Looking back on it, he should have likely said goodnight then and there.

"Lady Elizabeth," John said gallantly. "Thank you for inviting me."

His wife swept into the room. And that was the other surprise. He'd expected her to use that three-legged gait of hers, the one that made her look silly. Instead she appeared to have given that up. She walked like a lady . . . And yet, not. Her chest was plumped up a bit too much for that. Almost as if she held her shoulders back. And perhaps she did, he thought, eyes narrowing. Or perhaps it was the dress. The damn thing was so tight around her bosom, John would be hard-pressed not to gauge the exact size, shape, and weight of the things. Odd's teeth, he realized, she'd wetted her petticoats, too, for they clung to her luscious legs like paper to wet glass.

"I'm glad you could join us," she said, coming to stand before John with an inviting smile.

Inviting him to do *what*?

Careful, Lucien old boy, 'tis the object of the game. Besides, you'd best get used to her looking at men thus.

Yet to his complete and utter shock, he found himself *not* liking it. Not liking it one bit. He watched, arms crossed, fingers drumming on his sleeve as John pulled out a chair for his wife. But Elizabeth didn't take the seat next to Lucien as was proper. No, instead she smiled charmingly, and said, "But I would like to sit next to you, John. I can talk to Lucien anytime."

John appeared flattered by her words. Lucien stewed. He sat down at the chair a servant held out for him, John to his right, Elizabeth on John's right. She smiled in a coquettish way as she took her seat, removing her gloves before a servant placed a beige napkin in her lap. Dinner trays were then placed before them. The servants had dispensed with the livery this eve, Lucien noted, but they still held themselves as if they waited upon the queen of England.

But what piqued Lucien the most, what bothered him more than anything, was that his wife and his friend didn't seem to notice the parade. They were too busy making small talk.

"Most pleasant weather," John commented.

Please, Lucien almost said aloud. *Can he not think of anything more original to charm my wife?*

But Elizabeth didn't seem to mind. "Indeed," she answered. "The view from our room was most spectacular this evening. Nary a cloud in sight." And, demme, if she didn't all but bat her eyelashes. "Is the weather always this fair?"

John smiled. "Alas, no. I believe the sun shines down upon the castle solely in your honor."

Lucien snorted. He couldn't help himself. What a bloody foppish thing to say. And Elizabeth. She was worse. She tilted her body in such a way as to draw John's attention to her breasts, picking up a crystal glass just filled with red wine. Firelight turned the liquid amber. She licked the rim of the glass. Lucien jerked. *Where the devil did she learn to do that?* His pique increased when he realized neither his wife nor John happened to have noticed his ignoble sound. They were too busy making eyes at each other.

The doomed feeling within Lucien worsened. "Wine," he called to a hovering servant, watching as his own smooth-faced crystal goblet was filled.

He eyed his dinner guests, half-tempted to make a face at them. He cleared his throat instead. "The castle repairs are going well, are they not, John?"

Elizabeth and John, who had moved on to other subjects mundane, both stopped midconversation to peer over at him as if surprised at his audacity to interrupt them.

"Yes," John agreed. "They are."

Silence descended. Lucien felt like a schoolboy who'd been caught muttering obscenities at the dinner table. Devil take it, was that a blush he felt darken his cheeks? He reached for his glass, saying, "Bloody hot in here this eve. Anyone else care for some wine to cool the palate?" He tugged at his cravat.

His observant little wife's eyes narrowed.

Witch.

"John," she said to his friend, "do you like fruit?"

Lucien, who'd been in the process of swallowing, promptly spit it out, spattering fluid all over.

"Lucien," his wife chastised. She scooped up her napkin from her lap, dabbing at John's face. "Are you alright, John?"

Of course he was alright. He was looking down his wife's dress.

"Lucien, you should apologize to our guest."

"My apologies, John," he gritted out. "Swallowed wrong."

"Here," Elizabeth said, "lean forward. There is a spot near your mouth."

Lucien watched as his steward and soon to be ex-friend did as asked. Nay, he even looked pleased to receive the new duchess's attention. And could he blame him? Lucien wondered. When she leaned forward Lucien wagered John could see down to her petticoats. He found his breath catching in his throat as he waited for one of her breasts to pop out like a peach from a produce cart. When it didn't, he looked up in time to see his wife wipe John's brow.

And Lucien, who prided himself on not caring a whit for anything but himself, suddenly minded very much the way John and Elizabeth stared into each other's eyes.

"Thank you, Your Grace," John said huskily, his eyes never leaving hers.

"You're welcome," she murmured back, with a smile.

Lucien almost waved a hand between them. Bugger that, he wanted to smack John's brain box. Didn't the man know that 'twas his *wife* he flirted with? Didn't he care?

Apparently not.

But Lucien did. Terribly. Never mind that during their college days he and John had often tried to woo the same lady. The truth of the matter was, he truly hadn't expected John to respond to Elizabeth's flirtation, no matter what their past was. In fact, he'd been hedging his bets that John wouldn't respond simply because Elizabeth was his bride. His *new* bride. Yes, yes, yes. He'd spouted all that rot earlier about a marriage of convenience. Only now he suddenly wondered if he'd really meant it.

Instead, the two smiled at each other in a silly fashion as Elizabeth dabbed at his face. Still.

"There," she said, removing the napkin, much to Lucien's relief, only to—good God—suck on the end of that napkin before dabbing at John's chin and saying, "'Tis a stubborn spot here."

Was it he who'd groaned, or John? Lucien couldn't be sure.

Damnation. Where had she learned such a thing? What had happened to the virginal Beth?

And when had she become *Beth*?

"Roasted beef, sir?" a servant asked near his ear, placing a serving tray to his right, the smell of it wafting up.

Lucien nodded mutely.

Elizabeth looked up, apparently finished with her task, for she and John leaned away from each other. Smiled. And he could have sworn his little wife fanned her lashes at him again.

"Ian," she said, seeming to pry her gaze away from John's to look at the servant. "It is, Ian, isn't it?" she asked.

The servant must have nodded for she smiled. "Ian, would you be sure to bring me some bananas and plums for dessert?"

"Elizabeth," Lucien shot, standing up abruptly and nearly knocking Ian off his feet. "I must speak to you immediately."

Elizabeth stared up at him, her lips damp from wetting the bloody napkin, her eyes wide and innocent. Argh. As innocent as a black widow.

"But, Lucien, dinner is just being served."

"'Twill take but a moment," he insisted.

Elizabeth looked at John, the two exchanging glances. Lucien's temper flared even more. And he *was* angry, he admitted. Bugger it. He felt furious. And the devil of it was, he didn't know why. His wife merely did her part. But, demme, she did it too well. She wasn't supposed to. But she did, he thought grimly as she reluctantly got to her feet. He held his hand out toward the door, indicating she should proceed him. With a sultry, apologetic smile at John, she turned. The servants, who'd been in the midst of placing trays upon the table seemed to freeze in their various places.

He slammed the door in their faces.

"What the devil are you doing?" he snapped.

Elizabeth turned, looked up at him and he could have sworn he saw amusement flicker in her eyes. She-cat.

"Why, Lucien, I should think it obvious. I am seducing your friend."

Bloody hell, he hated it when she behaved like he did.

His hands clenched. "Yes, I know. But dabbing at his face like that. Elizabeth. What will the servants think?"

She tilted her head. "Perhaps you should have thought of that before you suggested the wager."

He *had* thought of that. That's what made the whole thing worse, for at the time, he hadn't thought she could win. Now, much to his amazement, it appeared she would.

"Of course I thought of our servants' reaction," he snapped. "However, I was not expecting you to be so, so *blatant*."

Her brows lifted again. "Why, Lucien. Haven't you heard the expression all is fair in love and war?"

He felt his temper flare. "Do not give me that, Elizabeth. There is a line, and you have crossed it."

She drew back, her expression falsely confused. "Why, Lucien, I am only doing what you taught me to do."

Odd's blood, she tried his patience. Never mind that he knew he hadn't a leg to stand upon. Not even half a leg. Nor an eighth.

"I am not asking you not to do it, Elizabeth," he clipped. "Just not"—in front of me—"in front of my staff."

"Very well. I shall only seduce John when the servants are out of the room."

She turned, conversation apparently at end.

"Wait," he called, suddenly realizing that her agreement appeased him not in the least.

She turned back to him, her manner one of impatience. His gaze dropped down. He couldn't help himself, he just looked at her breasts, stifling a groan as he recalled how'd they felt in his hands.

Would John find them soft, too?

Stop it, Lucien. You should not act the jealous lover.

"I'm waiting, Lucien," she said, crossing her arms in front of her and—God's teeth—lifting her breasts up even farther.

"I—" he struggled for something to say, his mind boggled by the realization that his tongue was tied. "I want to know where you got that dress," he improvised.

Her brows dropped. " 'Tis one of my gowns. Altered, of course."

"Did Polly do it for you?"

She nodded.

He would fire the maid. "I see."

"She did a remarkable job, did she not?" She turned around for his inspection, arms held out, the gown clinging to every luscious curve as she slowly spun before him.

Jezebel. Strumpet.

"Yes," he croaked, having to force his gaze away.

"I'm quite pleased my mother insisted the maid we shared stay behind, for Polly is an admirable replacement."

"Indeed."

"Yes," she said smugly, turning toward the door again.

He seethed, trying to come up with another reason to stall. But he could think of nothing, and so he reluctantly opened the door, granted, with more force than necessary, wondering what the devil had happened to him. One moment he'd married a diminutive shrew. The next she'd turned into Cleopatra.

She swept into the room, her skirts—damp as they were—clinging to her delectable legs. He held her chair out for her, shooting John a look of warning over her shoulder. John merely smiled in a thoroughly irritating way.

Lucien's hands clenched around the back of the seat.

He returned to his own chair, the servants having placed all the dishes upon the table. The smell of duck ragwood mixed with beef and apple loaf.

Lucien had lost his appetite. He watched as if from a distance as Elizabeth nibbled at her dinner, John solicitously serving her.

She laughed. She flirted. John appeared to be captivated.

Lucien spoke nary a word. The two completely ignored him.

An interminable half hour later, the table was cleared. The cloth changed. Lucien tensed as he waited for dessert to be brought in. Sure enough, Ian entered the room with a heaping tray of bananas and plums. He set them down in front of Elizabeth with a flourish.

Lucien vowed to fire Ian right after Polly.

There could be little doubt what Elizabeth intended, for her eyes grew as smoky as the fireplace pit, her eyes glittering just as vividly as she slowly, inexorably peeled the skin back.

"Would you like some?" she asked. Lucien looked up from the banana, thinking it was him she offered it to. Alas, she had eyes only for John. John whose gaze had ignited.

"They're quite good," she said, but she didn't nibble the fruit as he'd taught her. No. She sucked on the damn thing. Sucked! pushing the fruit in and out of her mouth. Odd's teeth, where had she learned *that*?

"I," John croaked. "No. I believe I shall watch you suck, er, eat it."

She smiled as she nipped at the fruit, her eyes wicked.

If Elizabeth had asked both men to take off their clothes and jump into a volcanic pit, they likely would have done so at that moment. Both of them stared at her in mute fascination as she lifted the banana to her mouth again, her tongue whipping out to lick the side of it suggestively.

"Elizabeth, that is enough," Lucien shot, standing abruptly. "You win," he found himself admitting, fighting the urge to adjust himself. He turned to his steward. "John, you may have her with my blessings."

"I beg your pardon?" John asked, his expression falsely aghast.

Lucien turned to his wife. She smiled. Not a ha-ha-isn't-this-funny smile. No, she smiled in a smugly superior way that set Lucien's teeth on edge.

"Why, Lucien," she drawled. "Are you saying I've won the wager?"

"That is exactly what I'm saying," he snapped, throwing his napkin down on the table. He turned to John. "We had a wager that she could not seduce you. Obviously, I was wrong. I should have known that not even the bond of friendship would stop you from succumbing to my wife—"

"Lucien," John began to protest.

"No. Do not tell me you were unaffected. For I could see with my own eyes that you were all too willing to succumb to her charms. But I do not care. Take her, my friend. With my blessings." He turned on his heel, uncaring that it was rude to give his dinner guests his back. If he didn't leave, he would do something dire.

"Where are you going?" Elizabeth asked.

"Out," he snapped, not looking at her. "I will see you in the morning."

"I'll send Polly to you at nine," she called after him. "We've picked out a lovely gown for you to wear."

Lucien stopped, spun on his heel, about to say she could take her bloody gown and her bloody wager and go to the devil. But he refused to let her see how much her winning the damn wager irked him. So instead he smiled, having to work harder at that smile than he'd ever had to work at anything in his life.

"Indeed, my dear. I look forward to it." He kept the smile on his face, though he still couldn't meet her eyes. Bowing, he left the room, taking great pleasure in the fact that he didn't slam the door as he did so.

Had he turned back at that moment he would have seen the pleased smiles John and Elizabeth exchanged. Gone was the flirtatious manner.

"That went smashingly well," Elizabeth said gleefully.

"Aye," John agreed, giving her a smile back. "But what I want to know is where the devil you learned to eat a banana that way?"

"Why, from Lucien, of course."

Small chuckles escaped from John. He shook his head. "I almost pity the day my friend gained you as an adversary."

"Ah, but you enjoy watching him squirm."

"That I do," John said. "That I do." And if Elizabeth had looked at John closely, she would have seen the way his eyes lingered on her, the way, for just a moment, his gaze filled with envy.

CHAPTER SIXTEEN

And, indeed, the next day Elizabeth woke up in a bright mood. Of course, a part of her wondered where her husband had spent the night. But no matter. Her plan to knock Lucien off his high horse had gone splendidly well. So much so, that she told herself she didn't care if he'd spent the night with another woman.

That was what she told herself.

So as she dressed for the day in a high-waisted red dress with a ruffled neckline, she and Polly exchanged conspirator's glances. She and the maid had called a truce when she'd explained things to her, and a good thing, too, for it was Polly who'd helped put the finishing touches on her seductive skills.

Almost as if she read her mind, Polly entered. "Sleep well, ma'am?"

"Indeed, Polly," Elizabeth said with a smile. "Most well."

Polly smiled, too. "Thought you should know, the duke spent the evenin' with the stable hands. Word is he got jug bitten, then fagged out in a stall."

The words made Elizabeth's shoulders relax, her relief undeniable. "Is he up yet?"

"Aye. Demanded 'is breakfast a bit ago."

"Did he now? Well, we shall just have to see about him eating that breakfast dressed as he is."

"You mean to go through with it then?" the maid asked, wide-eyed.

"Aye, Polly. If the gown is ready."

"Spent 'alf the evenin' sewin' it," she said.

Throaty chuckles escaped. She came forward and clutched the maid's hands. "You're a dear for doing it."

"No thanks be necessary, m'lady.'Twas the thought of seeing his grace in that gown that kept me going. Like as not I'd have stayed up all night if I'd needed to."

"And did Mrs. Fitzherbert mind the donation?"

This time the maid chuckled. "Once she heard what we were up to, no. She said you could have the dress with her blessing."

Elizabeth all but danced upon her toes. "Good. Then what say you go fetch my husband? He has an outfit to don, *non*?"

They both laughed.

Lucien was in a cankerous mood. No doubt about it. He stabbed at his eggs and bacon, thrusting his fork into each piece as if it were John's head. It didn't help matters that his stomach rolled with every bite and that his head hurt every time he moved. He would eat his bloody food if it killed him. Lord willing, it just might.

"Beggin' your pardon, sir," a feminine voice trilled. "But the duchess is requesting you meet her in your dressing room."

Lucien looked up. Polly, the little traitor. A maid he'd promoted from under maid to lady's maid, a grand step up in pay and respect. And look how she'd done him wrong.

"She does, does she?" he asked, caring little that he sounded surly. He *was* surly, damm it.

"Aye, sir. Right away, sir."

Well, they would just see about that. She could bloody well wait.

"Sir?" the maid said when he didn't move.

Lucien looked up, giving her a look reminiscent of his dark days. It should have sent the maid scurrying.

"Are you coming sir?" she asked, odd's teeth, and she actually sounded impatient with him.

Lucien set his fork down, his fingers fisting over his plate of food. "Polly, how long has your family served the St. Aubyns?" He drummed his fingers.

"Three generations, sir."

Another drum. "Well, my dear, if you do not want such a grand history of servitude to end with you, I suggest you run upstairs and tell my little wife that I will be up when I finish my repast." He unlaced his fingers, calmly lifted his fork again.

The maid went still. "Yes, sir. Right away, sir."

That's more like it, Lucien thought, feeling a bit better when the door closed, although he supposed he ought not take out his black mood on his staff. Then again, it was because of the little traitor that his wife had been so successful last eve, for Lucien had no doubt that Polly, who was known as something of a flirt amongst the male staff, had helped her.

So it was that he took his time, enjoying the vision of

his wife cooling her heels upstairs. But like a child dreading his first day of school, the moment came when, inevitably, Lucien had to go to her. Not for a moment did he think about reneging upon the wager. His pride wouldn't allow it. No. Instead he slowly straightened, slowly stepped away from the table.

Ian walked into the room just as he rose. "Don't let 'er grace pull your corset too tight."

Lucien froze. One of his staff members out in the hall—Lord knows who—erupted into laughter.

"You're fired," he said to Ian. "The whole lot of you. Pack your bags and leave my home."

"Oh, no, Your Grace. Not gonna miss this for the world. Fire me if you want, but I'll stay long enough to see you in a dress."

Lucien stared at the man, trying to decide just when, exactly, he'd lost control of his staff. "Does the whole staff know?"

"The whole lot o' them."

Marvelous. Superb. Absolutely lovely.

"From what I hear, her grace is gonna parade you before all o' us."

Over his dead body.

"If I may be so bold, sir. Whatever made you wager such a thing?"

"Overconfidence, old boy. Pure and simple overconfidence."

"Well, that'll teach you."

Lucien didn't respond. What could he say? He had, indeed, learned his lesson, although he felt better than he cared to admit upon being told his wife had spent the night in their bed. Alone.

He found her reclining in their dressing room, calmly reading a book, a flowered white-and-blue dress with a solid blue pelisse reminding him all too quickly of what he'd come up to do. He would not wear a pelisse, he privately vowed. One must draw the line somewhere.

"Ah, Elizabeth," he drawled. "Your maid tells me you requested my presence." He loomed over her, enjoying the way she seemed to sink back into the settee. "Couldn't wait to see me again, eh?"

She slammed the book closed, those lovely cheeks of hers filling with rosy and—he didn't mind saying—flattering color. "On the contrary, duke, you know very well what I summoned you here for."

He leaned over her, her eyes widening as he placed a hand on either side of her body. Damnation, but he liked the way she smelled. All night he'd thought of her, alternating between anger and being impressed at the way she'd won the wager, and dismay that she'd won. She'd turned the tables on him. Handily. Now it was time to turn them back.

"Why, yes, I do," he said silkily. "Another lesson in the art of seduction? Shall I teach you more of my tricks?"

Somehow, Lucien hadn't the foggiest notion how, she slipped out from beneath him, standing before he had time to react.

"Thank you, no. As I illustrated last night, those types of lessons are hardly necessary."

Oddly enough, disappointment filled him. Ridiculous. "Are you sure?" he said, just to cover the reaction.

She nodded.

"Hmm. Pity." He straightened. "Very well. It must be

that other thing then." He hated to say it. "The wager." He sighed.

"Indeed," she agreed, pointing to a second door in the room, the one that led to the hallway beyond their rooms. And by the doorframe, nay, taking up most of the doorway, was the most hideous brown dress Lucien had ever seen.

"Surely you jest?" he found himself saying.

She shook her head. "No. I do not."

"But, my dear, I must protest. I have a reputation to uphold where matters of dress are concerned."

"And surely *you* must understand that given your size, we were limited in our selection of gowns?"

"Yes, but still—" he protested. "You cannot expect me to wear *that*."

"Why not?"

" 'Tis hideous."

"Mrs. Fitzherbert obviously does not think so."

"Is that who you pilfered this from?"

"Yes."

He glanced at the dress critically. "Mrs. Fitzherbert must have been a great deal smaller when she was younger."

She gave him a look of reprimand. "She is a very dear woman who was most kind to give me this dress."

"What if it doesn't fit?"

"It will fit," Elizabeth reassured, taking the dress off the peg on the door. "I had Polly alter it to your size."

Yes. He most definitely needed to dismiss Polly.

"Here," she said, handing him the gown.

He took it, the cloth actually scratchy to the touch. She

smiled like a cat with a mouse in its mouth. "Enjoy your-self," she said, turning to leave the room.

"But are you not going to help me put it on?"

She paused, turned, lifted a brow. "Phibbs is going to help you."

"Phibbs? What does he know of lady's dresses?"

She smiled. "I suppose you two will find out."

She turned again, heading for the hallway door. He couldn't believe she would really make him go through with it. He truly couldn't. Perhaps he'd been in denial up until then, but as he watched her head for the door, he realized she did, indeed, intend to see this through.

"You shall regret this, my dear."

She didn't turn, just placed her hand upon the door handle.

"I shall look hideous."

She swung the door wide.

"I shall frighten the staff into quitting."

She paused, turned back to him. "You have half an hour." Then she gave him a smile, a smug, self-satisfied smile just before she turned and exited the room.

Lucien narrowed his eyes. She would come back any second, he thought to himself. Come back and tell him it was all a hum.

He didn't move.

One minute faded into two.

Any second now.

Two minutes faded into three.

Come on, now. Open the door.

But five minutes later she hadn't returned.

"Bloody hell," he cursed as he crossed to the bellpull to ring for Phibbs.

* * *

If Lucien thought his daily toilette as a man tedious, 'twas nothing compared to a woman's. New respect and admiration for the opposite sex filled him as he donned an itchy chemise, tight petticoats, and—worst of all—a whalebone corset surely used in medieval times to torture unsuspecting women. It didn't help matters that his charming, ever-so-thoughtful Phibbs seemed determined to turn him out as spectacularly as a woman as he would a man, flitting and fussing here and there.

"Phibbs," he grunted, as he pulled upon the corset. "That is quite enough."

"Just trying to make your waist smaller," the man grunted.

"Well, enough is enough. Get to the dress, man."

His pique must have reached Phibbs because the pressure on his corset lessened. Enough so he could breathe at least.

Phibbs came around the front of him, eyeing him up and down. "Would you like me to dampen your petticoats before you don the dress?"

"Yes, please," Lucien drawled sarcastically before he erupted with, "Of course not, you silly man. Just put the bloody dress on."

"As you wish, sir."

The dress was fetched, the servant opening the neck hole. "Duck your head."

Lucien eyed the dress one last time. "I cannot believe I am doing this," he muttered, ducking his head only immediately to straighten with an exclamation of, "Ouch. Damnation. The bloody corset stabbed me."

"If you use your knees, it will not pinch you then," Phibbs said matter-of-factly.

"Phibbs, your familiarity with women's clothing is quite disturbing."

"I was married for thirty years, sir. Alas, I did not make enough coin to hire a lady's maid for my wife. I often helped her to dress."

Lucien wasn't sure if that was meant to be a jest, wasn't sure because the world became a brown sea of fabric as the gown was lifted over his head, and he couldn't see the man's face.

God's teeth, he couldn't believe he was going through with this.

Phibbs went around to his back side, pulling the dress tight as he did the catches.

"I see you have no pelisse," Phibbs observed dryly.

"Demme, if there was a pelisse, I would set it afire."

Phibbs didn't say anything in return, merely finished his task, then bent down to pick up two pairs of slippers.

"Black shoes or brown."

"Brown," Lucien gritted out. *Unbelievable.* Slippers, too.

Phibbs bent, slipping the things on. They were a perfect fit, which made Lucien wonder which female on his staff had elephant feet.

"Very good, sir. I believe we're done." The servant stepped back and eyed him critically.

"Well?" Lucien snapped.

"You would need a bonnet to be truly fashionable."

"Devil take it, Phibbs. Do not be ridiculous. I'm not trying to be fashionable." He turned to the mirror, and gasped. "Good Lord, I look like—"

"Beau Brummel in a dress," Phibbs finished.

"A strumpet," Lucien corrected, outraged. "You've given me cleavage, Phibbs. *Cleavage.*"

"Indeed, sir. Corsets can do wonders for a flat chest. I believe that is the point."

Lucien couldn't pull his gaze away from the dressing room mirror, staring in mute horror at the picture he made in Mrs. Fitzherbert's brown dress. The thing had a wide, dark brown sash just below his—his eyes narrowed— masculine breasts. Off-white lace garnished the neckline and wrists. It had long sleeves and a straight-cut skirt that brushed the floor at the perfect length.

Polly.

"She will pay for this," he muttered.

"You look charming, sir."

And so would his wife. "I look like a fool," he corrected.

"That is the point, I believe, sir."

"Do not remind me."

"Shall I fetch her grace?"

"Yes. Let her come up here and get a good look. The sooner she does, the sooner this bloody nonsense will be over."

The servant bowed. "As you wish." He turned to the door.

"Phibbs, if you tell anyone how I looked in this gown, you will be dismissed on the spot."

"Of course, sir," the unflappable servant said with a nod. Lucien glared at him in warning, but the moment the door closed, he went back to eyeing himself in the mirror, spread his skirts wide, swished them a bit just out of curiosity. Even tried a curtsy. *How in God's name do they move in all this rot?*

But five minutes later Phibbs returned, and was it Lucien's imagination, or did the man's countenance all but sparkle with—could it be amusement?

"Beggin' your pardon, sir, but her grace wishes for you to come downstairs."

A horrible suspicion filled Lucien then. Ian's words came back to haunt him.

"Phibbs, how much do you enjoy working at Raven's Keep?" He dropped his skirts hastily when he noticed he still held them and that Phibbs stared at him oddly because of it.

"Very much, sir."

"Then you understand I need you to be completely honest with your response to the next question." He tried to intimidate the man with a moment of silence, despite the dress. "Is the household staff assembled at the foot of the stairs?"

Phibbs bowed. "They are, sir."

Lucien hopped up and down, all but tripping on his hem as he stomped around. "Rot and bother." He clenched his hands in his skirts. "Blast that woman. She truly means to humiliate me."

"She does, sir," Phibbs agreed, not meeting his eyes.

Well, they would just see about that.

"Is the duchess with the staff?" he clipped, calling upon the intellect that had gotten him in this whole mess in the first place, which wasn't terribly reassuring.

"No, sir. She is in the drawing room."

"Ah. Good." There was only one drawing room, and

two ways to enter it; a staff's entrance and the public entrance. He took a step forward.

And fell flat on his face, his hands slapping the floor with enough force to make his eyes water.

"Damnation," he cursed, shaking his stinging palms.

"I believe you need to pick up your hem, sir."

Lucien contemplated firing the man on the spot. *Bloody hell, I should fire all of them. What happened to their loyalty? What happened to their love for me? Since my wife's appearance, they've turned.*

"Thank you, Phibbs. I believe I'd gleaned that for myself."

Phibbs didn't reply, just offered him a hand. Lucien wanted to slap it away, except he'd suddenly realized that the corset wouldn't allow him to move, not to mention that his skirts appeared to be twisted around his petticoated legs.

"She will pay," he muttered again, his eyes widening in horror as he realized he was about to fall out of his own bloody gown. He had to adjust himself when he stood.

Five minutes later—and a near tumble down the servant's stairs later—Lucien had worked up a truly good head of steam. So much so, that he very nearly didn't spy the man who stood a the base of the narrow corridor.

"Going somewhere?" that person asked.

Lucien froze, his skirts clenched in his hands, little brown slippers peeking out from beneath his gown (although he still wondered where Elizabeth had gotten them from. The things were *huge*).

John eyed him up and down, a low whistle escaping from between smiling lips.

"Ach, Lucien, you make a passably fine-looking woman."

Lucien dropped his skirts, hands clenching, charging the man before he knew what was good for him. Unfortunately, his legs got caught up in his skirts again. He almost fell to the floor, but his tormenter saved him.

Hearty chuckles greeted him as he helped him to straighten. "Lord love you, Lucien. Your wife had a notion you might try this. She positioned me here in the event you did come this way. I've half a mind to take pity on you and tell your wife I didn't see you pass, or forcing you out in the main hallway so you can face the consequences of your wager."

"You wouldn't dare," Lucien growled, noticing John's black jacket and buff breeches with envy.

"Wouldn't dare what?"

"Make me face my staff like this?"

John eyed him up and down. "Ach. I'm half-tempted to do so. Truth be told, I never thought ta see the day when my flirting with a woman o' yours would produce such dramatic results."

"You were not flirting. You were all but drooling."

"Aye, but only because she asked me to."

Lucien stiffened, his corset tightening around him uncomfortably. "I beg your pardon?"

John nodded. "I ought not to be tellin' you this, to be sure, but the sight o' you in that dress raises tears of pity in me eyes. Either that, or the devil in me makes me want ta stir the kettle a bit."

"Drop that Scottish brogue of yours, John, and tell me what you mean," Lucien clipped.

John smiled. "Your wife came to me yesterday afternoon," he said in perfect, unaccented English, a trick he did remarkably well, thanks to Eton. "Said she wanted to knock you off your pedestal a bit. Asked me to help her by acting smitten with her at dinner." The smile grew. "I confess. Her grace made it easy." He shook his head. "Whatever made you teach her that trick with the banana?"

Lucien merely stared at his friend. No. Ex-friend. "It was all a hum?" he asked.

"A big hum," John admitted.

A trickle of disbelief turned into a flood of it as he eyed John. His back stiffened in outrage. How could she do something so low, so underhanded, so utterly crafty? Why, it made him incapable of speech. But following his pique came a spurt of admiration for her cunning. What a stroke of genius to ask John for his help.

"Where are you going?" John asked.

Lucien hadn't even realized he'd picked up his skirts and turned. "To change, then find my wife."

"Oh. Aye," John said, chuckles escaping as he watched him head back upstairs. "Won't mind me peeking in the keyhole when you confront her, will you?"

"Do as you like," Lucien called. "But we shall not be in the drawing room for long. I'm taking her to the bedroom."

And to that, John said nothing.

Phibbs helped him change at a rate of speed he wouldn't have thought possible given the intricacies of female dress. Less than fifteen minutes later he pushed open the servant's door.

Elizabeth spun on an armchair's dark green seat, her breasts nearly spilling out of the dress she wore. A large, black brooch was pinned on the red bodice of the gown, right beneath the V of her cleavage, the dress's white skirt accentuating her narrow waist. Clever puss thought to distract him with her breasts, did she? "Where's your dress?" she asked, her expression clearly disappointed.

Lucien moved toward her slowly. "I had an interesting conversation with John just now," he said smoothly. "One that made me change out of the dress I spent an hour lacing myself into."

She lifted a black brow, the morning light allowing ribbons of sunlight to streak her black hair. It played with her eyes, too, turning them more purple than blue.

"Oh?" she asked.

"Indeed," he said. "Would you like to know what he told me?"

"No," she answered, and he could tell she'd discerned something was very, very wrong. Her eyes even darted to the door as if seeking an escape route.

"He told me about an interesting conversation he had with you yesterday afternoon," he said, ignoring her.

She tensed, though one would hardly notice it if one hadn't been looking closely. But he could see in the way her fingers flexed. The way her eyes widened just a bit.

"What conversation?"

He contained a triumphant smile. The mouse was about to be caught by a very large, very fierce cat. And though it surprised him to admit it, he rather admired the handy way she'd orchestrated everything. If John hadn't shared what had happened to him, he'd be parading in front of her in a dress instead of a brown coat and buff breeches.

"My dear, there is no sense in denying it, for I heard directly from John about the deal you made."

Not by word or deed did she give her misconduct away.

"What is more, I believe him. John—while boyish-looking on the outside—is something of a reprobate. 'Tis why we get along so well."

She licked her lips, something he knew from experience meant she felt nervous.

"But there is no sense worrying about it, for I shan't punish you. After all, the penalty for cheating on a bet is simply that you forfeit the bet. Thus I win."

"What are you talking about?"

"I'm talking about the fact that you owe me a night of pleasure."

She shot up from the chair. "I do not."

"Ah, but you do." He smiled. "You cheated, Elizabeth." He lifted a brow. "Or do you deny your perfidy?"

He had to give her credit. In his experience, a woman lied as easily as she changed gowns. And yet Elizabeth didn't. He could see the battle being waged within her, see the moment when she realized truth would likely be better than fiction.

"Very well," she said softly, her shoulders thrusting proudly. "I cheated. But only because you deserved to lose, Lucien. How dare you suggest I seduce your friend?"

"You agreed to the wager."

She lifted her chin. "Yes, I did. You deserved to lose. Whatever the cost."

Honesty. How refreshing. He smiled, a very naughty

smile, for it was time to make his move. He held out his hand.

Her eyes widened. "No, Lucien."

He invaded her space, leaning toward her a bit. "My dear, Elizabeth. You see before you a man who honored a wager no matter what the cost. Call Phibbs if you do not believe me. Five minutes ago I was wearing a dress. And I wore it proudly as penalty for losing my bet. Will you do less in honoring the loss of your wager to me?"

"Yes," she shot.

He almost smiled. "Then I suppose I must take matters into my own hands."

Pupils dilated as he suddenly lifted her in his arms. "Lucien," she cried.

He smiled down at her, the sweet smell of her filling his nostrils. "We are going upstairs," he said.

"No, Lucien. This, this wager is void. Defaulted," she gasped. "Rendered moot. You can't do this," she huffed, as he opened the servant's door. Nobody stirred beyond, likely because the whole traitorous lot of them were at the foot of the main stairs all agog as they waited for the duke of Ravenwood to come down the bloody steps.

"Elizabeth, will you be still? You shall break both our necks if you cause us to fall."

"I should be so fortunate," she huffed.

He looked down into her panicked eyes. Panicked, not frightened. "Relax, my dear. 'Tis only for a night." He allowed his smile to spread farther up his face. "Or a day, as the case may be."

She began to struggle in earnest.

"Elizabeth, settle down. You act as if I am about to rape you."

"Aren't you?" she gasped.

He stopped in his tracks. "No, Elizabeth, I shall not." She looked up at him with wide, disbelieving eyes. "I will end it right now, if you but ask. I'll set you here where we stand. But I will be sorely disappointed in you if you do. I thought you woman enough to accept your fate. As I was man enough to accept mine."

She didn't blink. Didn't move as she processed his words. He could feel her body tremble. Could see the way her pulse beat at her temple.

"What are you going to do to me?" she asked.

He held her gaze. "Nothing that you don't want me to do." He wiggled his brows lecherously.

"Are you going to bed me, Lucien?"

"Oh, yes," he said fiendishly, his manhood stiffening at the vow. Odd's blood, but that was unexpected. And unwanted, for he only meant to teach her a lesson, not actually go through with the deed.

"Then I beg you to go slowly."

He almost dropped her. "I beg your pardon?"

"Be gentle," she said.

He didn't know what he'd expected her to say, but certainly not that. He stared down at her, wondering if she'd lost her mind. Surely she must have.

"You are quite serious?" he asked.

"Aye," she said, her blue eyes huge and luminous.

Demme. Now what?

CHAPTER SEVENTEEN

Elizabeth stared up at the duke's face, knowing what she'd just agreed to must shock him. And yet she knew, too, that consummating their relationship was the only chance their marriage had. She had no idea when that had become important to her. Likely when she realized she'd so badly misjudged him. But in the past twenty-four hours she'd come to admit that he wasn't the rake and the reprobate everyone thought him. And if that was true, then there was a chance this marriage might work. Just a chance.

And wasn't it a chance worth taking?

The option was living the life of a strumpet, of flirting with one man after another. Her flirtation with John had shown her that she didn't have the stomach to behave thus. Deep down inside she'd always known that.

"Very well," he said, staring down at her with the oddest expression on his face. "If that is truly the way you feel, then I shan't ask you again."

She stared up at him, too, his eyes a jade green today, eyes that had grown so good at concealing emotions from the world. What did he feel now? She would give anything to know.

Instead, she waited for him to proceed to the bedroom, her heart beginning to pound even more so than it had before.

"If you're absolutely sure?" he said again.

"Yes, I'm sure," she reiterated.

"There's no going back once this is done."

"Lucien," she said impatiently, beginning to think that he stalled, "at this rate the Prince of Wales will ascend the throne before we consummate our marriage."

She heard him swallow. Actually heard him swallow.

'Twas then that she realized he didn't want to go through with it. She could see it in the way a tiny bead of sweat had sprung upon his brow. The way he suddenly wouldn't look her in the eye.

He'd been bluffing.

And on the heels of that thought came the realization that he was good at bluffing. He'd bluffed his way into making society think he hadn't cared about his brother's death. Had hoodwinked society into thinking he was a rake, for Polly had confirmed that no licentious behavior had ever happened at the castle, nor anywhere else that she knew of.

He had duped society about a lot of things. The wild parties. The fiendish behavior. Well, perhaps that was true at times.

"Why, Lucien?"

"Why what?" he asked.

"Why do you pretend not to be affected? Why do you pretend that you are all set to consummate our marriage when in fact you want anything but?"

He started. "I beg your pardon?"

"Set me down."

He stared down at her for a moment longer before slowly letting her slip from his grasp. She met his gaze directly, trying to piece together the puzzles she knew of him.

"Do not try to bluff, Lucien, for I have gleaned the truth. You don't want me. The question is, why? I know you desire me." She lifted her chin proudly. "Even I am not *that* innocent. Why then, I ask myself, do you not want to bed me? Are you afraid?"

He gave a bark of laughter. "Don't be ridiculous. What man doesn't want to bed his wife?"

"Then why are you stalling?"

"I'm not stalling," he said. "I am merely thinking on the best way to initiate you, my sweet."

And there he went with the lecherous rake routine. Another defense mechanism, she realized.

"I see," she said, forcing herself to place a hand against his cheek, wondering what his reaction would be.

He acted like she'd slapped him. "What are you doing?"

"Touching you. Trying to let you know that you don't need to pretend with me. If there is a reason why you do not wish to go through with this, you can tell me why."

He had stiffened at her touch and leaned away from her. Elizabeth waited, breath held, heart pounding, for him to make the next move.

"Come," he said, grabbing her hand and dragging her toward the bedroom.

Her heart, which had steadied, burst into a nervous rattle against her chest. When they entered the room, he let go of her near the door.

"Where are you going?" she asked, when he turned away from her, a half-formed notion that he'd lost his nerve after all crossing her mind.

He paused, halfway between the massive bed and the dressing room door, sunlight shining into his enigmatic green eyes. "I am going to remove my clothes," he said drolly. "You may remain dressed, for I shall remove your clothes for you."

He was back to trying to frighten her. Odd how she could read him so easily now.

"Do not go away, Elizabeth my dear. I shall be right back." His smoky gaze lingered on her breasts.

Tilting her chin to a courageous angle, she said, "As you wish," serenely clasping her hands in front of her.

He stared at her for a long moment, almost as if he expected her courage to desert her at any moment, and when that didn't work, he let a slow, lecherous smile slide up his face.

And yet Elizabeth wasn't afraid. Not in the least. 'Twas odd, but she felt filled with a fierce resolve to see this through. To *reach* him. She watched as his smile faded a bit just before he exited the room. Elizabeth's shoulders slumped.

"Gracious." She took a deep breath, crossing the massive room to halt before the window. A dark blue ocean stretched to a distant horizon, small, white-tipped waves coasting one after another toward the shore. The view from the window was spectacular, another sunny day having dawned. Funny, but she'd always envisioned her first time with a man to be in the evening, perhaps a few candles burning, white sheets turned back. Instead, the sun shone brightly in the room, the red bedspread pulled up to cover the pillows she'd slept upon for the past two nights. No fire burned in the grate to her left. No candle lit the room. But they wouldn't need any light. There would be no concealing her body with soft beams of sunlight illuminating the room. The thought didn't frighten her. Rather, it excited her, her heart beating an irreversible countdown until his return.

She had no idea how long she stood there, only knew she seemed locked in a paralysis of anxiety and resolve.

"Did you miss me, my sweet?" he asked.

Elizabeth whirled to face him, her hands shaking as she swiped away a few strands of loose hair. "No," she answered bravely.

"Hmm. I shall have to work to change that." He wore a dark purple satin dressing gown with foppish wads of lace sewn around the arms and neckline. Gaudy turquoise-and-red embroidery decorated the fabric. The thing looked like something worn in a boudoir.

Another prop, she realized.

"I have a surprise for you," he said, smiling in a self-satisfied way.

He looked more in control of himself. That worried her.

He reached into his pocket.

Elizabeth tensed.

He pulled out . . . silk?

"Wh—" She forced herself to breathe. "What are those for?"

Lucien smiled. "They're for you." He came to her,

holding out his hand so she could get a better look. "To tie your hands."

She jerked back, her eyes darting to his. "Tie my *what*?"

"There goes your hearing again," he said happily. "My goodness, Elizabeth, I believe we should have a physician come and look at you. Perhaps you have wax balls."

"Stop it, Lucien. What do you mean tie my hands?"

He lifted his brows, giving her a lecherous smile. "Why, Elizabeth, 'tis done all the time. It's to heighten your pleasure." The smile, if possible, grew bigger. "I also brought you this."

He reached into his pocket.

Elizabeth tensed again.

He pulled out . . . A *feather duster*?

She didn't want to know what that was for, she truly didn't. The thing was small. In fact, 'twas oddly small. She tried to formulate a response. "Do you intend to dust my body?" she asked, trying to act as cool as he did.

"Why as a matter of fact, I do. With this." He shifted the ties to the hand with the feathers, reaching into his other pocket for a small pouch.

She hated to ask. She truly did. "And what is that?"

"Sugar," he said, his smile still firmly in place. "Powdered sugar." He shook the bag a bit, puffs of the stuff escaping. "I intend to lick this off your body."

She jerked. He wanted to frighten her into backing out of this, she realized. But she refused to do so. "I see," she said, steeling herself as she crossed to the bed. "Shall we begin then?"

To her utter delight, he looked momentarily flummoxed.

Hah, she told him with her eyes. *Your ploy did not work.*

Ah, he silently answered back. *But I am not finished yet.*

The battle lines had been drawn. The gloves were off. Who would be the first to back down? They each vowed it would be the other.

"Just let me set this over here," he said, turning from her to place the objects on the side table near the window.

She felt her breath quicken. Knew the moment of truth was coming. Odd how she still wasn't afraid. Anxious, certainly. But who wouldn't be with his medieval scare tactics? Still, she knew he wouldn't hurt her. That consoled her a great deal as she waited for him to come to her. And he did come to her, although his walk was more of a slink, a diabolically roguish smile upon his face. When he stopped before her, he held her gaze for a moment, then slowly lifted a hand. She tensed.

He stroked his chin. "I'm trying to think how I want to do this. Tie you up now, or take off your clothes first?" He looked her up and down. "Do you have a preference?"

She had to swallow before she answered, her throat— for all her resolve—suddenly dry. "Not at all," she answered smoothly.

He lifted a brow. "Hmm. Pity. I suppose *before* then. Goodness knows with you tied, those catches in the back might be a problem."

She tensed. He seemed to tense, too. Elizabeth knew he did though he tried to conceal it by placing one of those sublimely complacent looks upon his face. He lifted a hand. Elizabeth's breath caught. He motioned with his index finger. "Turn around," he said.

She felt oxygen desert her brain, only to inhale deeply as she slowly did as he asked.

"Closer," he ordered, putting a hand around the front of her and pulling her up against him, his hand brushing her neck as if to swipe away a lock of hair.

"Ah. Buttons. Very good. Never did like the eye hooks. They're damnably hard to see."

Elizabeth barely heard the words, her blood rushing through her ears in a residual effect of being pulled up against him. She felt her dress move, felt him step back, the brooch she'd pinned beneath her breasts weighing it down. Her aunt's favorite pendant, she remembered, the realization giving her courage.

"You know," he said, "I can't decide if I should tie just your hands or your legs, too. I suppose you have no preference for that, either?"

"No," she said, surprised at how level her voice came out.

He sighed, undoing another button. "My dear Elizabeth, your unwillingness to comment on this matter is most distressing."

"Is it, duke? I beg your pardon, then, for I mean no offense."

"Lucien," he said, leaning next to her ear, his breath brushing the side of her cheek. Lemons again. "With what we are about to do, you should certainly call me Lucien. Duke sounds so terribly . . ." He searched for the right word. "Impersonal." He undid another button. "And I assure you, my dear, what I'm about to do will be very, very personal."

He'd done it to her before, she reminded herself. And she to him. Still . . . She told herself not to move, even though every nerve begged her to grab him by the lapels of his foppish dressing gown and shake him. Instead, she felt the last few buttons give, felt the red dress slip off her shoulders, then drop to the floor.

"Ah," he said. "More buttons."

She tensed even more, reminding herself that as he had already touched her as intimately as he ever would, surely she shouldn't be nervous?

He meant to tie her up.

But did he really? He'd bluffed before. Perhaps this was yet another.

She waited, her breath coming faster as she felt him undo the buttons of her dress. All too quickly she felt it fall to the floor.

"Hmm," he observed. "I must say, your corset looks a great deal better on *you* than mine did on *me*."

She felt his hands on her shoulders, all but jumping at the feel of them through the thin gauze of her chemise.

He leaned close to her again. She could feel the heat of him next to her nearly naked body. "You know, I've decided to watch you take off your petticoats. There's nothing more exciting to a man than watching a woman strip."

She closed her eyes, clenching her hands, as close as she'd ever been to fleeing. Then she caught sight of the brooch again and a great calm came over her. She released a breath she hadn't known she'd been holding, then forced herself to take another one, to make her shoulders relax, to make her body feel loose beneath him.

"Is that so?" she asked, stepping away from the discarded gown and toward a new future. "If that is true, then I wonder why you didn't have me strip for you from the very beginning?"

"But my dear," he said silkily, "you couldn't have undone the catches in the back. But now that we are finished with those, I wish for you to entertain me as I will entertain you in the coming hours."

She opened her eyes, tilting to the right so that she could peer up at him. She saw him draw back before he checked the action. Ha. Try to frighten her, would he? They would see about that.

"Then let us be done with this, shall we?" She turned suddenly, only inches away. She tugged at her chemise, and despite her resolve, she felt her breath catch as she slid first one shoulder free, then the next. The lightweight fabric slid down. She saw his nostrils flare. Saw his eyes narrow as she stood before him in nothing but her petticoats. She turned a bit, giving him her profile so she could stare up at him as she placed a leg upon the bed, then released the strings one by one, starting at the bottom and working her way up. But he wasn't staring into her eyes. No, he watched her every move, his eyes almost a caress as they moved over her. He watched as she slowly, inexorably, pulled on the strings. When she was finished, she did the other leg, slowly tugged the last, tiny string until her petticoats, too, fell away. She stood up.

He stared.

Elizabeth felt the warming then, that heat that had suffused her yesterday when he'd kissed her so intimately. Except this was more intense.

She reached up, slowly taking the pins out of her hair. She felt the weight of her tresses shift, tugged at the last pin. Her hair tumbled around her shoulders.

"God, Elizabeth," she heard him say.

She, didn't move, knowing he fought himself. He tried to maintain his composure, but his words and stance belied his expression. His chest rose and fell. His hands clenched. His body hardened.

"Very nice," he said. "Very, *very* nice."

Lucien the rake had returned.

She didn't know how he'd done it, but she knew he had.

"Lie down on the bed," he instructed.

She had her answer then, an answer she hadn't even known she'd been searching for. He meant to go through with it. Meant to tie her up.

He will not hurt you, Elizabeth.

Ah, but he did not know she knew that. She held the realization close to her heart, knowing he still tried to intimidate her. She wouldn't let him.

She went to the bed, taking her time as she climbed up on the massive mattress. When she looked back at him, he'd moved, having crossed to the side table. He turned back to her, the silk ties in his hands.

"Lift your arms."

She almost closed her eyes, then felt the stain of embarrassment cover her body. But there was that other heat, too. Persistent. Building. Pulsing. She did as instructed.

His nostrils flared again. She could see him battle for control again. She bit back a triumphant smile.

"And your legs," he added.

She almost told him no. Almost resisted. But that was his point. He wanted her to resist.

She spread her legs.

He turned away from her then. Elizabeth knew it was because he fought for control, not because, as he pretended, he needed to fiddle with the silk ties. It was a moment before he turned back to her again.

"You surprise me, Elizabeth, for I truly thought you might balk at this."

She swallowed. "I am full of surprises."

"So I've noticed." He came toward her.

She stiffened, despite her resolve. He seemed to have to gather himself as he reached out to pick up her arm. But he didn't clasp it normally. It was like he touched something he didn't want to touch, his contact light as he drew her arm toward the massive headboard. With his other hand, he wrapped the fabric around her wrist, then placed her arm back on the bed as he used both of his hands to tie the silk around one of the bedposts.

And it was done. She studied his face as he drew back, observed the way his skin appeared chiseled from stone. The way his eyes burned into hers for a moment before he looked away, turned, and did the same thing to her ankle.

Elizabeth's heart began to flutter in her chest. Her chest rose and fell rapidly, no matter that she urged calm upon herself. How could one be calm when one felt the oddest mix of anticipation crossed with fear?

He came around the foot of the bed, his eyes stabbing into her own once more as he lifted her other ankle.

"Almost done," he said, though he didn't give her that rakish smile. His face looked like it would crack if it did. He tied her ankle, shifted, moved to the head of the bed, reaching for her free wrist. Did she see him hesitate just before he touched her? Yes, she was sure she did, for he almost seemed to flinch as their flesh made contact. He made short work of the last wrist, stepping back to observe his handiwork when he was finished.

"I never thought I'd see the day when an earl's daughter lay prostrate before me."

Was he trying to anger her? She didn't know, didn't care. A multitude of emotions filled her as he stared down at her. Shame. Embarrassment. *Desire*. 'Twas the last that coursed through her the most. The emotion shocked her, heightened her awareness of him standing over her.

"Do I please you, Lucien?" She didn't know where the words came from, had probably read them in Lucy's wicked book, but they had the right effect. He lost his composure then. She saw the mask slip, saw a layer of fierce desire become revealed.

"Oh, yes, Elizabeth," he murmured in a way that seemed pried out of him. "You please me."

She lay there, her nipples feeling odd. Her body dotting with goose pimples. More vulnerable and more fiercely excited than she could ever remember being in her life.

He eyed her up and down, his breathing no longer regulated. And then, almost as if he couldn't stand the sight of her anymore, he wrenched around, crossing to the side table and placing his hands upon the edge of it for a moment before he picked up the feathers and the bag of sugar.

His hands trembled.

She could see it from where he lay. Her eyes closed in a moment of victory. When she opened them again, he stood over her. She expected him to sit on the edge of the bed, expected him to cover her body with his own, to do any number of things she'd read about. What was more, she wanted that. *Mon dieu,* how she wanted that.

But instead he moved to the foot of the bed, his eyes never leaving hers. And instead of being horrified that he could blatantly see the most intimate part of her, she felt even more aroused, the heat increasing to the point that it caused moisture to build, caused her woman's mound to fill, to swell. She trembled, too, closed her eyes because of it, wanting him to touch her with a longing that made her feel embarrassed.

Was she so base?

Apparently so.

And then he *was* touching her—on the leg—his fingers suddenly tipped with velvet. Her body convulsed, her eyes sprang open. But he hadn't really touched her, the feathers had. She watched as he dipped them in the bag, then lowered the feathers to her calf again.

"Lucien," she moaned, helpless to act unaffected. She didn't care what his intentions had been in tying her up like he had, she only wanted what his touch promised.

"What, Elizabeth?" she heard him ask, his voice unnaturally low and husky.

She didn't answer, couldn't for he was dusting her again. And then . . . Oh, Lord, he bent down, his tongue lapping at the sugar. She jerked in her bonds.

"Sweet," he murmured, his hot breath all but scalding her. "So sweet."

Her body spasmed. She felt that familiar pressure build, that wonderful pressure he'd raised within her.

She saw his eyes flicker, saw the mask slip again. Almost as if he had to prove to himself that he was the one in charge, he licked her calf. She threw back her head. His left hand moved to the inside of her thigh.

"Yes," she murmured, as he moved ever closer to the place that burned for his caress. Uncaring that she begged for the pleasure she knew he could give her. "Yes," she said again, writhing in her bonds.

He used the feathers on her inner thigh, followed the trail with his tongue, higher this time, then higher still. She trembled so fiercely now she felt ready to explode, every nerve straining, begging for his touch. She waited, body held poised. "Please, Lucien. Please."

"Please what?" she heard him moan.

She opened her eyes then, met his gaze. He was poised over her, his body in between her thighs. "Touch me. Touch me like you've touched me before."

She saw his eyes close, saw him tilt his head back. His whole body seemed to sag. "I can't fight it," she heard him groan. "God help me, I cannot fight it."

"Don't, Lucien," she ordered. "Please don't."

She felt him shift, and then—oh, gracious heaven—his mouth covered her woman's mound. She screamed, her whole body tensing, then expanding into ripples of pleasure. "Lucien," she cried and then moaned, and moaned.

He sucked at her, nibbled at her, and she died a sweet death as her body flooded his mouth. And when he was done, he drew back. She could see the heat in his eyes as he knelt between her legs. Could see the evidence of his arousal jutting out before him.

He must have known what she looked at, for she saw his eyes fill with heat. "Did you enjoy that, my dear?"

He'd gotten control of himself again. She knew he had. And yet, she also knew that losing control lay a heartbeat away. And she wanted, oh how she wanted him to lose it.

"Did you enjoy the taste of me?" she asked right back.

She saw his eyes narrow, saw his body twitch.

"Let me taste *you*," she said.

His eyes flamed. She waited, breath held, to see what he would do.

"Is this what you want?" he asked, throwing back his purple robe to reveal his erection . . . and more. For the first time she spied the utter masculinity of his chest. Ridges of muscles rippled down his bronze chest. Perfectly carved, those muscles flexed as he rose above her. He was no soft gentleman. Lucien St. Abyn was all hard, sinewy man.

"Yes," she said, refusing to let him intimidate her.

"Where?" he asked.

She lifted her hips. "Here," she said, spreading her legs.

He threw back his head then, groaned as if in pain, the muscles along his shoulders tightening.

"No," he said, though the word seemed to be uttered for himself. "No," he repeated.

"Take me, Lucien," she said, sensing her victory. "Take me," she repeated, spreading herself as far as she could.

His eyes opened. And she knew she'd won.

"Curse you, Elizabeth. Curse you for what you've done." He pressed into her, his body covering her own. She could feel the hairs of his chest brush her nipples. They hardened almost painfully, but it was an erotic pain, one that made her press into him. And then he began to kiss her, his body slowly pushing into her even as his tongue entered her mouth. She gave back to him, sucking at him frantically, tasting what could only be herself on his lips. He pushed farther. There was pain, brief pain, and then the pressure of his body inside of her own, a tight fullness that made her begin to spasm all over again.

"Elizabeth," he murmured against her mouth. "Damn you, Elizabeth."

She lifted her head to capture his lips, jerked her hips as she sought to recapture the friction. He pulled out. She moaned in protest. He pushed into her again, harder this time. Her nipples grew more and more taut. And despite her body's innocence, she met him thrust for thrust, cursing her bonds, exulting in his domination of her.

Yes, her mind screamed. *Yes.*

And then they both cried out, Elizabeth's moans matching his thrusts. Once, twice, he pumped into her. And then, almost as if he were jerked off of her, he pushed away. Her eyes sprang open. He climbed off the bed, stood over her, the evidence of his pleasure glistening on his maleness. His chest heaved. His hand lifted to wipe at his mouth. "What have you done?"

Elizabeth strained at her bonds, her body still undulating.

"Damn you, Elizabeth, what have you done?" He turned away from her.

"Lucien," she called. She thought he would leave her here like this, panicked for a moment at the thought, even as her body still hummed from the pleasure he'd given her. Over and over again. But he stopped, suddenly turned back to her. She looked into his eyes, waited for him to do the same, but he didn't. Instead he crossed to her, undoing her right wrist. She waited for him to untie her legs, too, but he didn't. Instead he turned, heading back to the dressing room.

"Lucien?" she called.

He didn't answer.

"Lucien," she called again. But he was gone.

CHAPTER EIGHTEEN

It took Elizabeth almost five minutes to untie herself, but by the time she raced to the dressing room, it was already empty. She clung to the doorframe, stared into the empty room, her body burning in secret places.

Where had he gone?

But she knew. Knew it with a certainty that belied the shortness of their time together. Rushing back to the bedroom, she ignored the evidence of what had transpired— the silk ties still hanging from the bedposts, the mussed sheets—and hurriedly cleaned herself up before pulling on her chemise, then her gown, uncaring that she wore no corset, nor even her petticoats beneath.

A quick stop at her dressing room to pull on a cloak and she was off, hoping against hope that she could manage to find the stone that would open the door that led to his secret beach.

But as she gained the bottom of the stairwell, John was there.

"He's left the castle," he said, holding out a hand to stop her.

Elizabeth didn't want to believe him. After all, the

man had betrayed her to Lucien. But she couldn't deny the truth in his eyes. She collapsed on the last step, her eyes watering suddenly as the aftereffects of what had just happened hit her with a suddenness that robbed her of breath.

"Where?" she asked.

He shrugged. "Likely to town, but I've no way of knowing for sure."

She couldn't meet his eyes, merely nodded in mute misery.

"Elizabeth," he said, looking uncomfortable for a moment, "he does not want an heir."

She jerked her head up.

"Thinks the dukedom is not his to pass on since he was never meant to hold the title."

Didn't want children? Her hand moved to her chest. But in a blinding flash she admitted it all made sense. The empty threats. The way he fought his desire for her. His anger when he'd lost control.

"I had no idea," she said, realizing there were many things she hadn't known about her husband.

"So you can understand why he's so upset. You might be with child."

Her gaze jerked to meet his. "What makes you say that?"

He smiled tightly. "Half the castle heard the two of you upstairs."

She let out a small gasp of embarrassment, her body warming. "Oh?"

"Oh," he said back.

She looked away, her chagrin fading in the face of her problems. "What do I do?"

"Have patience. I always thought his vow was a damn foolish one. Now that the beans have been spilled, so to speak, he's going to have to rethink everything. Give him a day or two to acclimate himself to the notion."

She nodded, realizing there was little else she could do. And yet as she waited for Lucien to return, she mulled over what she'd learned. The duke's vow only reaffirmed her suspicion that he had loved his brother deeply. So much so that the guilt at playing a part in Henry's death had nearly destroyed him. No pictures of that brother hung in the castle, Elizabeth realized as she found herself strolling the rooms yet again. Just the one portrait of his father, the look on the old duke's face one of rebuke. Elizabeth wondered if it'd been placed in the castle to do exactly that: remind Lucien of what he'd done.

And what had he done? Elizabeth wondered. Her knowledge of the day's events was sketchy at best. Just snippets of conversation she'd overheard. There'd been a duel. Lucien's brother had been a second. That meant he'd been standing nearby, though certainly not within the duke's pistol sights. So why was it assumed Lucien had been responsible for Henry's death?

"Because it seemed very coincidental that Henry should be shot during Lucien's duel with another person," John explained. He was working on the castle walls outside, Elizabeth supposing she should be abashed by his shirtless body. Other workers hovered nearby, a pile of freshly carved stones to her left.

"But it was obviously an accident," she observed. "Pistols are terribly inaccurate. He could well have been struck by a ball that went astray."

John wiped at his brow. "Aye."

"But no one believed that."

John dropped the shirt he'd used as a rag, his body nearly as tan as Lucien's. "When an old title and a large fortune are at stake, people think the worst. No one wanted to believe that Lucien was capable of such a thing, and yet in the end they did. It didn't help matters that Lucien never defended himself."

"Why, I wonder?"

"Because," John said, his face grim, "at first grief made him too numb to care. Months passed, and by the time he returned to society, it was too late. The rumors had circulated for too long." He met her gaze. "The damage had been done."

Elizabeth looked at the ground, her mind mulling over what she'd just learned.

"Do you think he did it?" John asked.

"No," Elizabeth said, instantly meeting his gaze. "I will admit, before I got to know him, I had my doubts. But not now."

John held her gaze, an expression in his eyes she couldn't quite catch. But then he looked past her, his shoulders stiffening. "Your husband returns."

Elizabeth whirled. And, indeed, Lucien came at them. Not walked, not strolled. He stormed, his green eyes as cold as the Atlantic, his face tight.

"I need to speak to you," he said, ignoring his friend as he reached for her arm without even so much as a by-your-leave.

Elizabeth looked at John, but the man just smiled tightly. "Offer him some fruit," he said to her. "That might settle him down."

Elizabeth almost choked on a burst of hysterical

laughter, but her husband didn't seem amused. He turned her away, his hand clasping her elbow as he all but dragged her back toward one of the archways that shielded the crumbling part of the castle from visitor's eyes.

"Where are we going?" she asked, telling herself to be calm. Whatever he had to say, he would say. There was not much to do but wait. But he kept quiet until they'd nearly reached the courtyard, pausing just inside an archway. She shivered at the feel of his touch, helpless not to remember how his hands had felt against her flesh earlier.

"Your parents are here," he clipped.

"Here?" she gasped.

He nodded.

She looked through the arch at the courtyard, trying to find evidence that what he said was true. A man led a black horse toward them.

"They rode?"

He followed her gaze, his eyes narrowing when he saw the horse. "Damnation," he muttered under his breath. "Not now."

"Here you are, Your Grace," the groom called as he arrived near them, turning the horse for their inspection. "Got the gelding just a few moments ago. Thought her grace would want to ride straight away."

Her grace.

Elizabeth stiffened.

It was hers.

"The duchess doesn't feel like riding at this moment," Lucien clipped.

She stiffened in protest. "No. I want to ride."

"And keep your parents waiting?"

She'd forgotten. Her shoulders slumped. "I . . . No. You're correct." She searched his eyes as she struggled for something more to say. "Thank you. He is quite beautiful."

For a moment she saw his anger fade, but just a brief moment. "You're welcome."

She bit her lip, turned toward the house again. "Where are they?"

"In the drawing room."

"I see." He'd bought her a horse. A horse. Of her very own. She didn't know why, but the realization made a lump rise in her throat.

"Before we go in," Lucien asked, his voice suddenly harsh again, "answer me this."

She tensed.

He waited until the groom was far enough away before asking, "When were your last menses?"

She felt her jaw slacken.

He appeared to struggle with himself for a moment, the battle lines drawn again. "I spoke with a midwife today. She told me that a woman is more apt to get with child approximately ten days after her last menses. So when did you last bleed?"

She shook her head, her mind spinning. "Three weeks ago." She lifted her chin. "So I doubt you have to worry."

His relief was palpable, his shoulders losing their strain.

"Afraid you've gotten me with child?" she asked with a proud tilt to her chin.

His eyes swiveled back to hers. "Obviously."

"I know why."

His eyes moved past her to where the workers labored. "John."

"Aye," she agreed.

" 'Twas not his knowledge to share."

"Yes, it was, Lucien," she said, losing her bravado and switching to reason. "You should be proud of your heritage, despite how you obtained it. The title has belonged to your family for generations. Can you not see past your guilt and realize that it needs to be carried on?"

"Guilt," he spit, his voice raised until he lowered it to a hiss. "Guilt? What do you know of guilt?"

"I know you would never have killed your brother."

"Do you? And how do you know that?"

"Because you're not capable of it."

He smiled mirthlessly. The grin sent chills down the nape of her neck. "But I did kill him, Elizabeth."

He bluffed. She was sure he did. And yet . . .

She could see none of the usual signs. There was no teasing glint in his eyes. No devil-take-it glare. His eyes looked utterly serious for the first time since she'd met him, and she felt alarmed.

"You didn't."

"Oh, yes, Elizabeth. I did. Pointed the pistol at him and fired. What do you think of that?"

"No," she said, shaking her head.

"No," he mimicked. "Such a tedious word. 'Twas what I should have told myself when I first laid eyes upon you."

He tried to wound her with his words, his anger causing him to lash out. She knew that, but the words still stung. She realized now that they'd come too far for her not to feel hurt by what he might say, for while they'd been married less than a week, this morning had changed everything.

She looked away.

"Go freshen yourself. I refuse to have your parents meet you when you still reek of sex."

She snapped her eyes upon him. "Then you'd best clean yourself, too."

She thought he might say something crass, for his eyes narrowed in that particular way he had, but he didn't. Instead, he turned on his heel and left. Elizabeth followed his departure, debating with herself whether to do as asked . . . no *demanded*. But a streak of defiance made her lift her head. Made her decide that no matter how nasty he sounded, she would not let him intimidate her.

He had killed his brother.

Well, there had never been any question about that. One way or another, Lucien had been responsible. The question was—and still was—had he *meant* to kill him? Lucien almost made it sound like he had. And yet she knew. She just *knew* he couldn't have done it intentionally. 'Twas simply not possible.

So she stood there, mulling over all she'd learned and coming to the realization that what he'd just done was actually quite masterful. He'd made himself sound like a devil, and she'd been filled with the appropriate horror. Only, he wasn't a killer. He only wanted her to *think* he was. And he did it because he obviously wanted her to leave him alone.

Intimidation again.

Well, she would not have it. She would not meekly go away. She would force the dratted man to confront his guilt. To tell her *his* side of the story. He *owed* her that.

She drew herself up, squared her shoulders. and tilted her chin. Her hands clenched in determination as she stared at the castle door he'd just walked through.

His grace would soon learn that she was not like him. *She* did not walk away from her problems.

Lucien's hands shook as he poured himself a drink, uncaring that it was early afternoon, nor that his wife's parents were in the room as he tipped the glass back and downed the whole thing in one gulp. Nor even that he re-filled the glass again. God willing the alcohol would help him to forget the morning. There'd been a time after Henry's death when spirits had worked remarkably well. He'd woken up six months later to find that society be-lieved him a murderer. He smiled grimly. Well, he was.

Someone cleared a throat, the earl by the sound of it. Lucien slowly, reluctantly turned toward them.

Two haughty faces stared back, the both of them standing with their rears to a window, four dark blue arm-chairs and a low cherrywood table between them.

"I beg your pardon," Lucien drawled. "I was quite parched."

The earl's nostrils flared. Quite remarkable really, for the man resembled a horse to the point that Lucien was surprised no one had offered to halter the fellow. He took another swallow. The liquid burned down the back of his throat, heat spreading through him. He welcomed that heat and the looseness that warmed his muscles.

"Please have a seat," he invited, motioning with his glass, some of the liquid sloshing out.

"No thank you, duke," the earl answered, his long chin tilting up.

Lucien lifted a brow at his arrogant attitude. Quite cheeky of the man, really, especially given that his family still inhaled the scent of feet for a living. Had he forgotten that Lucien descended from royal blood? That his cousin—distant, of course—was the Prince Regent? That he could lay claim to half a dozen royal relatives?

Apparently so.

Lucien rolled the glass between his thumb and forefinger, smiling tightly.

"Did you have a pleasant ride up from London?" Lucien asked, his throat tingling from the liquor.

They didn't answer. "Where is my daughter?" the countess asked instead, her face like that of a bull terrier—perpetually in a scowl—her tone just slightly short of accusation.

"Chained up in our dungeon, of course," he answered with a polite smile. "Where else?"

She drew herself up, her jowls all but quivering.

"I'm right here, Mama."

Lucien almost dropped the glass. He turned to the door. God, but his hands shook just at the sight of her.

"Finally," her mother all but accused. "Elizabeth, where have you been?"

"What a surprise to see you," Elizabeth said, ignoring her mother's harsh tone as she crossed the plush blue-and-white carpet toward her mother. She bent, placing an air kiss next to her cheek. "Has Lucien offered you some refreshments?"

Lucien watched her, his hand tightening around the glass. She looked composed. Defiant, even, as she shot him a glance. His nails dug into the glass. "Alas, no," he said as evenly as he could. "I did offer them a seat, however. They declined."

"I'll just ring for some tea then."

"Elizabeth, we do not want refreshment," her mother said with a nervous glance at Lucien. "We need to talk to you." She straightened. "Alone."

Elizabeth darted a glance up at him, brows raised. "Indeed?" she asked, facing them again.

"Yes. Alone," her father agreed.

Icy tendrils of foreboding coursed through Lucien. 'Twas more than Elizabeth's treatment of him. It was the looks her parents kept sending him. Even when he'd offered for Elizabeth's hand they'd never openly shown hostility. Now they did. Why?

"What you have to say to me can be said in front of Lucien," Elizabeth said. She shot him another look, tilting her head stubbornly as she said, "He is, after all, my husband." And her tone seemed to be a reminder of that fact.

Silence greeted her words. Lucien debated with himself if he should leave.

But then her father said, "Very well. If that is how you feel." He straightened, shooting a look between them. "Elizabeth," he said sharply, "we've come to tell you that Lucien is to be brought up on charges of murder."

CHAPTER NINETEEN

The words rocked through Lucien, the words he'd lived in fear of since his brother's death.

"No," his wife said.

"Yes," her father said, his face filled with loathing as he shot him a glance. "I heard it from the Lord Chancellor himself. They had to clear it through him as your husband is a peer, not that he acts like one."

He expected her to whirl on him, to look up at him with horror and accusation. Instead she kept her gaze on her parents.

"Impossible," she said.

"I wish it was," her father snapped, "but I tell you 'tis true." His glance fell upon Lucien again. "I am sorry, Ravenwood, to break the news in such a fashion, but there you have it."

Bloody bastard wasn't sorry in the least.

The earl held his gaze, his expression turning almost challenging. "In light of this, Your Grace, I'm sure you will do the right thing and grant Elizabeth a separation. She will, of course, keep the title of duchess."

"Separate," Elizabeth shot. "Father. No."

"Elizabeth," her mother said, "listen to your father. You need to get away from this man. 'Tis your only course of action. Why, already we have suffered the repercussions of *our* association with him. Yesterday Lady Haversham told us that she would no longer receive us as we were now affiliated with a murderer."

He watched as Elizabeth's face hardened. "I am sorry for that, Mother, but my husband can hardly be blamed for people's misapprehensions of him. You should have told the lady good riddance and cut her in return."

Her mother gasped. "Elizabeth, do not be ridiculous. Lady Haversham is a pillar of society, almost as influential as Lady Jersey. I cannot cut her."

"So you would have me leave my husband instead?"

They didn't answer. Lucien waited to see what Elizabeth's reaction would be. He had it an instant later.

"Well, I thank you for coming all this way. But I'm sure you understand that leaving him is quite out of the question."

And Lucien simply stared.

"Don't be a fool," her father snapped. "I insist upon it. No one will think ill of you for doing such, Elizabeth. He is a murderer, 'tis only a matter of time before it is proven."

"No, he is not," Elizabeth answered. "And how dare you. How *dare* you come here and say such a thing? And to Lucien's face, no less?"

Lucien felt his heart swell in an odd way as she stepped toward her parents, tiny hands clenched. She looked as ferocious as a cornered barn cat. "He is my husband and, God willing, the father of my unborn child if the seed that he has planted takes root."

"Elizabeth," her mother gasped. "You are too common."

"Have I embarrassed you, Mother?" she raged, turning on the countess. "Well, you have embarrassed me, too," she added, swiveling on her heel to cross to the door, jerking upon the polished brass handle with enough force that her hand slid off it. The wood door hit the wall. "You will both leave."

The earl and countess looked incapable of speech. Lucien knew how they felt. He stared at his wife, emotions he couldn't name filling him, as she glared, nay, all but growled, at her parents.

"Don't do this, Elizabeth," her mother urged. "You will need us in the coming months. Why, it could take years for Lucien's case to be heard. What will you do in the meantime? You will be an outcast. No one will associate with you."

"That is a chance I will have to take."

"Elizabeth—" Lucien warned, about to agree with them, but her father interrupted him.

"You're a fool," her father repeated with a growl. "I will not stand by and watch you do this. If you refuse to leave with us, then we will have no choice but to cut our connection with you."

He saw her stand tall, saw her tilt her chin in that stubborn way of hers, watched steely resolve turn her spine into iron. And then she said the words that must have cost her more than he could imagine. "Then I bid you goodbye, Father." She looked at her mother. "And you, too, Mama. Do have a pleasant journey back to London."

No one said a word, least of all Lucien. Lucien, who found himself fighting to keep from pulling his wife into his arms. Lucien, who, for the first time in years, felt not quite so alone.

"If that is how you feel," her mother said. "Come, George." She lifted her nose in the air, gliding by her daughter without even a farewell. It was the coldest, most heartless good-bye Lucien had ever witnessed. Her father did the same.

"Elizabeth—" Lucien tried again.

"Lucien," she said, "quiet."

Quiet? She followed her parents out, turning to him and ordering, "Stay."

She returned a few moments later, her parents, apparently, gone. "Answer me this," she said, throwing his earlier words back in his face. "Did you intend to kill Henry the day of the duel?"

And just like that his heart began to race. He debated how to answer, but in light of her championing him, he felt he owed her a straight answer. "If you had asked me that an hour before the duel, I would have said yes."

Her eyes went wide.

And perhaps this was the way to make her leave, for her parents were right. If he was to be brought up on the charge, it would be best if she left. Now. Before she was tainted by the stain of his guilt.

"There is more to the story than you know, Elizabeth. But, no, I did not mean to kill Henry if that is your question."

She seemed to sag a bit before she recovered, saying, "Then what happened?"

And yet oddly enough, he found himself not wanting to tell her the truth. But he must, it was the only chance he had of making her see the wisdom of leaving. "The ball from my pistol didn't go astray," he said. "It *was* aimed in Henry's direction, however."

She didn't say anything, just stared at him as if repeating his words in her mind. "But . . . how?"

"I fired at him. Directly at him, or near enough that there was a good chance it would hit him."

"No," she said, shaking her head. "That is not possible. Even John confirmed your brother was hit as he stood by."

"A lie."

And God help him, he saw some of her compassion flee. It shocked him how much that disappointed him. Devil take it, he hoped he hadn't started to care for her. That he must never do. "No lie."

"But everyone knows you were fighting Lord Chalmers—"

"I was fighting my brother."

She stepped back as if he'd threatened to hit her. "Your *brother*?"

He faced her squarely. "We were fighting over Melanie, countess of Selborn."

"Selborn," she gasped, for all of society knew of the woman's banishment to the Continent. She'd been branded a murderess, much as he would be branded a murderer.

"I fancied myself in love with her back then. But Henry didn't approve. Said she was a trollop. Said he could prove it."

Elizabeth shook her head, her expression that of someone clearly unwilling or, perhaps, frightened to believe the words they heard.

"I called him out."

"No."

"But I did, Elizabeth," he said, the steel he'd erected around his heart fracturing as he fought to contain emotions he'd managed to keep hidden for so long.

"We fought at Putney Heath. But by the time we were back-to-back, Chalmers and Greshe, the seconds, had made me see the ridiculousness of our dispute. I intended to delope, as did Henry, I thought." He paused for a moment as it all came back. "And then I heard a shot. I couldn't believe it. Henry had turned and fired early. At me. I resolved to fire, too. But at the last second I pulled up. I couldn't do it. I couldn't shoot my own brother in cold blood. But something happened. My pistol went off. My brother fell." Bile rose in his throat as he recalled the sight of his brother falling, a shocked expression on his face. 'Twas a memory he'd worked so hard to forget, and yet one he would never be able to banish.

"He died within minutes. Bled to death. Clutched my hand the whole time. He tried to speak, but the ball had pierced his lungs, for he was only able to pronounce one word, and only then to describe how he felt." He swallowed, forcing himself to go on. " 'Empty.' I shall never forget the word as long as I live."

He waited for her to say something, and when she didn't, he looked away. Having known this would be her reaction, it surprised him how much he hated seeing the look of shock and revulsion on her face.

"Afterward, the countess came up with the idea of concealing the duel. It was she who suggested we give out the story that I was fighting with Chalmers, the man who had been acting as my second. 'Twas he that swore my brother's pistol must have misfired, for Henry hadn't been facing me," he repeated, his hands clenching. "His pistol must have misfired while we were counting paces, and when it had, he must have known what I would do, spun around to stop me. Perhaps cry out a warning." He shook his head. "I don't know. I'll never know."

"Oh, Lucien."

He took a deep breath, fighting to keep his voice even. "As it turned out, my brother had been right. Melanie was a scheming bitch for by then she'd decided to blackmail me."

"She needed your help to cover up the murder she'd committed," Elizabeth guessed.

"Very good, my dear. Yes. She'd never loved me. The duel had all been part of her plan. By killing my brother, I played right into her hands. She had me over a barrel, and she knew it." Anger came over him again, anger at the way she'd so expertly outmaneuvered him. He'd defended the slut's honor, and she'd turned around and made him pay for it, with Henry's life.

"So I pretended to help her," he said. "And in doing so I became the person society thought me. Cold. Heartless. Capable of anything."

He looked down at Elizabeth. "I didn't care what I'd become. I would have done anything to make her pay. Anything. And I did."

To his utter amazement, she placed her hand upon his arm. "You did what you needed to do."

He couldn't believe she would defend him. "No, Elizabeth. I did what I *wanted* to do. I enjoyed being the blackguard. Several times in the past year I've wished to go back to that life, but to do so would make me as bad as the countess, and now that she has paid, I have tried this past year to behave as I ought. Until I met you.

"It will all come out in the trial, Elizabeth. My affiliation with Melanie. The duel. All of it. I will be convicted of murder. And you will be tainted by my crimes . . . unless you leave."

"I'll not leave. You need me."

"I need no one."

His words hurt, as she supposed they were meant to do. "You will need me to be on the outside if they decide to imprison you."

"Decide?" he snapped, his patience obviously at an end. "Of course they will imprison me. I am to go to trial, according to your father. I shall be imprisoned in Newgate, tried before my peers. If I'm lucky, my conviction will be stayed, and I shall be transported to Botany Bay. If they decide to make an example of me, I shall be hanged."

"You won't be hanged. We'll fight it."

"*We* will do no such thing."

And again, his words hurt. "Then what am I to do? Stand by and watch them hang you?"

"If you are wise, yes."

"Oh, that is a marvelous idea," she went on a touch hysterically. "Perhaps I should sell sweetmeats at your trial. Mayhap offer the *Morning Chronicle* an insider's look at what it's like to be the wife of the duke of Ravenwood. They could title it 'Life with a Diabolical Duke.' "

He didn't say anything, just stared down at her with steely resolve.

She lost her patience then. "You do realize you are sunk if you go through this alone? You need someone to speak for you, someone unbiased—"

"A wife unbiased?" he cut her off with a cynical laugh. "Oh that is rich."

She stiffened.

"You're a fool, Elizabeth. Just as your father said."

If he'd slapped her, he couldn't have stung her more.

"You would be no help at all for, believe me, I have given the matter serious thought over the years. If there was a way out of this, I would have thought of it by now. No. I will face the charges, be convicted, and then—" He splayed his hands. "Who knows."

"Who knows?" she cried. "You said it yourself, they will hang you."

"Perhaps."

"And I am not supposed to be bothered by that?"

"Why should you care?"

She drew back, her eyes stinging for some unfathomable reason. Goodness, she wasn't going to cry, was she? "After what happened this morning, you could ask me that?"

"What happened was sex, Elizabeth. Nothing but sex. You're too naive to realize that, but I assure you, that was all it was. I seduced you. And in doing so, I certainly hope you're not going to bore me with protestations of love."

"Love?" she hurled back, hurt by his callousness. "I think not."

"The first *wise* thing you've said all morning."

"I do not love you," she said, but God help her, something felt wrong inside as she said it. "And what happened earlier might have been sex, as you say, but it does not change the fact that I am your wife. As such, I intend to stand by your side."

He came at her then, his eyes blazing in a way she'd

never seen before. It wasn't like upstairs after they'd
made love. This was different.

"No, you will not," he gritted out. "You are leaving,
my dear. The game is over. You've gotten your reputation
back. You are now a duchess. Do as most women in your
position would do and use the title to your advantage."

She could only stare up at him, shaking her head.
"What kind of person do you think I am?"

He didn't answer, merely stared down at her.

"Have you so little faith in me then?" she asked. "So
little faith in humankind?"

He didn't answer.

"Lucien, you might be cleared of all charges. They
could judge you innocent."

To that, he merely lifted a black brow. It dawned on
her then, what he was doing. It hit her in a flash that made
her unable to breathe for a second. "You *want* to be found
guilty, don't you?"

He drew back. "Do not be absurd."

"You do," she accused. "What is more, you're afraid
to let me help you."

His eyes flashed fire as he glared down at her. "Poppycock."

"No," she breathed, feeling an odd sort of desperation
fill her. "It's true. You *want* to hang."

"Enough," he shot in a voice loud enough that the
crystal brandy glasses hummed. "You will leave my
house. And in doing so, you will save yourself."

"Save myself because your cause is lost? That is what
you mean, isn't it?"

"That does it," he gritted out, swiveling on his heel.

"Where are you going?" she called, a sudden spurt of

anger stemming from helplessness making her follow him.

He spun to face her again, his eyes enraged. "I am going to order your things packed. Then you are going away."

She lifted herself to her full height. "No, I am not."

"We will see about that," he clipped, turning again.

She watched him go, watched the door close behind him. Only when she heard his feet hit the stairs did she turn, and then to cross to the window and stare out, a habit of hers, she realized. Something she always did in times of trouble. And this was most definitely trouble.

She wiped away a tear of frustration. Perhaps she should just leave. Certainly staying wasn't much of an option. But if she did that, then he'd have no one. And damn it all to hell. The man could have left her at the altar. He could have deserted her. Caused her ruination. But he hadn't. He'd married her. That spoke volumes to his character, she admitted. And while she didn't agree with the way he'd handled his brother's death, for the first time she could understand why he'd done what he did. The man had been wracked by guilt. Now, in some odd way, he'd decided it was time to pay.

She couldn't let that happen.

Turning on her heel, she followed the path he'd taken out the door, pausing for a second in the main hall. Should she confront him again? But, no. It was too soon. Besides, she needed to get her thoughts in order. Needed to present him with an indisputable reason as to why she should be allowed to help him.

And so she went to the front door instead, deciding she

would ride her new horse. She'd be damned if she stayed here and let him force her from their home.

When Elizabeth returned, he was gone. It happened so fast, so suddenly, she could barely comprehend it as she stood in the drawing room she and Lucien had occupied less than an hour ago.

"Came for him with a cart," John was explaining, his face grave. "Just showed up at the door with a Writ of Indictment and took him away."

Elizabeth felt her legs give way. Fortunately, there was a chair nearby. She clutched at its back. "What do I do?"

"What he wants you to do. Stay out of it."

"But I can't." She looked up at John. "He needs me. Surely you understand that?"

"I understand that he cares enough for you that he doesn't want you to become involved."

"But I am involved."

"No, you are not. You're married to him. That is all."

"Devil take it," she swore aloud for the first time in her life. And it felt good. "You sound just like him."

John gave her a small smile, but only a small one, and she had to remind herself that he'd known Lucien a long time.

"What will you do?" she asked.

"Testify on his behalf."

"Has he asked you?"

He shrugged. "No, but he will."

"How do you know that?" She got up from her chair, clutched his arm. "John, I don't think he wants to fight the charges. I think he wants to be convicted of the crime."

John drew back from her, almost as if he didn't like her touch. "Don't be ridiculous, Elizabeth. Of course he doesn't wish to hang."

She shook her head. "You don't understand. I could see it in his eyes. He's convicted himself of the crime; now I think he's decided to pay for it."

"You're wrong."

"I wish I were."

"You don't know Lucien. He may be a saphead at times, but he is no dunderhead. He knows what happened was an accident."

She came forward, clutching his arm again. "Has he told you what really happened?"

He drew away from her again. "What do you mean?"

She stared up at him. "He was dueling Henry, not Lord Chalmers."

John drew back, his blue eyes wide. "Impossible."

"I assure you, it is not."

"How do you know?"

"He told me."

"When?"

"Before they came for him."

John looked momentarily incapable of speech, his eyes growing unfocused as he stared off. "I never knew."

She drew herself up, wanting to touch him again. To get through to him. "Do you see what I mean? Do you understand now why he would be so guilt-ridden?"

He didn't answer, just stared blindly at the floor. "He never told me."

"He would not," she said. "Frankly, I think he buried the event deep inside."

But John wasn't paying attention. "It all makes sense now."

Elizabeth tilted her head at him. "What do you mean?"

Turning to face her, John said, "Lucien's cousin came here to visit once. I overheard part of a conversation they had. Greshe was saying to Lucien that he had much to lose by not agreeing to his terms. I thought they were talking about business, but then Lucien said he cared not a whit if he agreed for it was never in his plans to wed. He said that Greshe could have the title, for all he cared." He looked her in the eye. "I never understood what Greshe had been talking about, and when Lucien married you, I assumed it was nothing. But now I realize Greshe was talking about the duel."

"Blackmail," Elizabeth whispered. "Twice."

"What do you mean?"

She told him about the countess, shaking her head as she did so. "No wonder Lucien doesn't trust people easily. Everywhere he's turned, people have let him down."

"But not us."

Elizabeth looked up sharply, hope setting her heart pounding. "Will you help me?"

"What say you I escort you to London?"

She flew at him, throwing her arms around him. "Oh, John, thank you."

But he pushed her away abruptly, his voice gruff and filled with something harsh as he said, "Best you save your hugs for Lucien. He will need them."

All sins cast long shadows

—IRISH PROVERB

CHAPTER TWENTY

The trip to London was one of the most uncomfortable and excruciating in Lucien's life. There were no stops. No rests, just a ceaseless charge broken up only by Lucien's need to pee, something he was sure his captor would rather have not remembered judging by his near unwillingness to let him use the facilities. Compounding it all was the fact that his wrists were bound with iron chains, the magistrate charged with bringing him in having forged them onto his wrists at first opportunity. Standing in the blacksmith's yard, people gawking as he was put in chains, was not an experience Lucien cared to repeat. It didn't help matters that his captor had the personality of a stepped-on snake, the man having an obvious chip on his shoulder where "swells" were concerned.

And through it all, God help him, he thought of Elizabeth. Thank God she'd been out of the castle when they'd come for him, for he had no doubt she'd have thrown herself upon the carriage, pushed the magistrate out the door then found a way to set him free.

She was that kind of woman.

But now John would take charge of her. And he had

no doubt his friend would do as instructed and keep her away from London. Oddly enough, the thought depressed him.

Silly of him, he knew, but it was all for the best. 'Twas why he'd been so harsh on her. Why he'd said such callous things. She needed to realize that she was better off without him, for the way he saw it, his conviction was a foregone conclusion.

They crossed the Thames over Blackfriar's Bridge, then turned right toward Newgate. All too soon they came to a stop before the prison's main entrance, the stone-and-mortar building stretching four stories high. The reality of what he was to face hit him then, even though he would have sworn it'd hit him several times before. But as he stepped into Newgate's tall shadow—the smell of it all but bringing him to his knees—he realized life as he'd known it was over.

He tilted his head back. *Henry, old man, do you see how I go to my fate?*

He closed his eyes, thinking that this might be his last glimpse of freedom for a while. The magistrate grabbed his chains. Lucien opened his eyes, feeling rather doglike as he was led toward the main gate.

"Name?" asked Newgate's keeper as they paused before his heavy oak desk. 'Twasn't a desk, really, but rather an oak board with four legs. Years of use was scratched into its surface, the corners broken away as if it'd been tipped by one too many unruly prisoners.

"Lord Lucien St. Aubyn, duke of Ravenwood."

The keeper looked up from his equally beaten chair, his elderly face pinched into an expression of disdain. Little light penetrated through the rat's maze of corridors

that was Newgate, but what light managed to filter in illuminated a face and eyes devoid of any humanity.

"A lord, eh?" the man drawled, his ancient gray wig a
throwback to past times. Lucien had no doubt that here
was a man who enjoyed his position of power. "What's
he charged with?"

"Murder," the magistrate answered.

Gray brows that matched the wig lifted. "Bored with
being a pampered duke, were you, so you went and
killed a man?"

For the first time since he'd been taken from his
home, Lucien felt his anger return. "Actually, I shot my
brother, which is an urge I've no doubt your own siblings feel on a regular basis."

Whether the man didn't realize he'd just been
insulted—rather smartly, too, if Lucien didn't miss his
mark—or if he were inured to such remarks, Lucien
didn't know. But whatever his reaction was, he hid it
well, merely picking up his massive black quill to write
down the prisoner's name, the tines on the feather dipping and swaying with the motion.

"Admission fee," he snapped.

Lucien lifted his brows. "I'm afraid I don't have any
coin on me, my good man. Care to advance me a loan?"

The man looked up, eyes narrowed. "No, sir, I do
not."

"Then I'm afraid I'll have to miss this evening's fes-
tivities."

The man blinked up at him, the right side of his face
twitching. "Put 'im in with the rest o' them," he snapped.
"We'll collect 'is money later."

A man stepped out of the shadows, as big and burly as

the magistrate was tall and thin. He took the chains, Lucien smiling at the magistrate. "Quite a pleasure making your acquaintance."

The man didn't so much as crack a smile. Not that Lucien blamed him. He didn't feel particularly like smiling, either.

"If ya balk, I'll clobber you over the 'ead," said the turnkey.

Looking away from his former captor, Lucien lifted a brow. "That sounds rather appealing, my good man, given the fact that I would then be unable to smell."

The man just grunted in response, tugging on the chains as he led Lucien away. Unfortunately, the stench as they moved deeper into the prison was reminiscent of being downwind from a pen of bovines. Only worse. A horrible clanging rattled down the narrow passages, prisoners calling out obscene words as they banged upon the bars with metal spoons. All of the prisoners were men, though they varied in age. The young interned with the old. Hardened criminals put in with first-time offenders. Each room holding between five and fifteen prisoners, some of them mere children.

It was toward one of those rooms that they stopped, the only light that from the torches that flickered and sputtered a sooty mess onto the filthy floor. There were eight men in the yard the turnkey opened up. Each and every one looked him up and down as he entered, the turnkey sliding the chain out of the rings forged to his manacles.

"'Ere now," drawled a pale-skinned man. "What 'ave we 'ere?"

"A regular swell," a younger man said.

"Aye," said yet another. "Wager that jacket alone would cost more than all me belongings combined."

The door clanged shut behind him.

Lucien had never felt so alone.

He drew himself up, wishing he'd taken up boxing in previous years. But he'd refused to risk damaging his face. Only now did he realize that perhaps the object of boxing was to learn how to *protect* one's face.

"How do you do, gentlemen?" He bowed. "My name is Lucien St. Aubyn, and I am the duke of Ravenwood. Ten shillings to each man who keeps away from me, money that will be paid when my money arrives."

His words had the desired effect. They looked less like an advancing pack of wolves than curious hens as they stared him up and down.

"Speaks like a swell," one observed.

"Smells like a swell," said another.

"By George, I must *be* a swell," Lucien finished.

They didn't look amused, but they stayed away. That was a relief. But his legs felt like wilted lettuce, and his pulse thumped in his chest as he turned to stare at the turnkey's retreating back. Another yard of prisoners stared back at him. He looked away, trying to ignore their calls and clattering.

God, how did he get here?

He'd killed his brother.

It felt unreal. Like a bad dream, all the clichés he'd ever heard. Only this wasn't a cliché. It was real. He was in Newgate, indicted on charges of murder, the result of an inquest the London magistrate had told him about, one run by the Attorney General, a man who Lucien knew didn't like him. Nobody liked him, the result of leading a hedonic life that had outraged more people than he cared to admit. Now they would get even.

Well, bully for them, he told himself. He'd suffered their ill behavior before. This time it wouldn't be so painful.

Or so he told himself.

The trip to London was interminable, but Elizabeth relished the freedom being a married lady evoked. And a duchess, no less. She used that to her advantage, spending the coin John had brought with them to ensure their quick passage.

Only, it was all for naught.

"What do you mean he refuses to see me?"

They had decided John should approach Lucien first, speak on her behalf, then come get her at the inn they'd stopped at. Only it hadn't worked. "He was furious with me for bringing you here."

Elizabeth stared up at John. They were close to Newgate, Elizabeth in too much of a hurry to drop her trunks off at Lucien's town house. Thankfully, they'd secured a private parlor, the hum of conversation and the stale smell of old food wafting around them.

"He should not be furious. He should know I would bring myself to London with or without you."

"He trusted me to stop you from doing that."

"I am not a puppet to dance at men's strings."

But John shook his head. "There is more."

And the dire look in his face made her face pale. "What?"

"The Bank of England has frozen his assets."

They were not the words she'd been expecting, so it took her a moment to process them.

"They will not let me draw money. After our trip here, I only had enough coin to pay for Lucien's admission at Newgate and then his bedding."

She looked up at him, her face feeling frozen. "But how can that be?"

John shrugged. "I spoke with the Attorney General. Elizabeth, the man is out for blood. He claims Lucien orchestrated everything. That he acquired the dukedom and his fortune by improper means. Therefore, he has the legal right to freeze those assets on behalf of the legal heir, whoever that might be, once Lucien is executed."

"Executed?"

John nodded. "Aye. They are pushing for him to hang."

It was worse than she'd thought. She sank down onto a window seat. The glass overlooked a narrow alley from the second floor. A black and white cat made figure eights around wooden crates, its nose lifted as it smelled the remnants of what had been inside. The sloshy sound of carriage wheels pulled through mud echoed down the alley.

"What do we do?" she asked.

"There is more."

She turned to face him. "What more could there possibly be?"

John's expression grew dire. "When I attempted to go to Lucien's town house, that, too, was closed off to me."

The words robbed Elizabeth of breath.

"The Attorney General had closed it off as well. I went to the man, tried to explain to them that Lucien had never touched his brother's money, but he didn't care. Their investigation is complete, they told me. Lucien is to be formally charged before the House of Lords tomorrow, tried before Parliament next week."

"Next week! But that is impossible. 'Tis too fast."

"They are expediting matters in the hopes of stemming the frenzy that will no doubt surround Lucien's trial and because there is a session scheduled for the week after next."

Elizabeth's breath escaped in a rush. It was inconceivable.

And yet obviously true.

Lucien had already been tried and convicted in the eyes of the Attorney General. Now all the man had to do was convince his peers. And Lucien. John told her next that Lucien had decided to represent himself during the proceedings, further proof in Elizabeth's eyes that he didn't want to fight the charges. But they had to. They needed to hire a barrister. The finest one they could find. Then convince Lucien to allow the man to speak for him.

Yet where to get the coin?

"Sell the carriage horses," she said suddenly. "Get as much money for them as you can," though the thought of losing Lucien's beautiful animals made her ill. It couldn't be helped. "Use the money to find a barrister for Lucien, and to pay for better lodgings for him in Newgate."

John nodded, and did she detect a note of approval in his eyes?

"If that does not raise enough money, then sell the carriage, too."

"I have a cousin you could stay with," John said. "It would save the expense of your lodgings."

She nodded. "That would be appreciated."

"'Tis the least I can do."

She came forward, clasping his hands. "You are a good friend."

He didn't pull away, just stared at their entwined fingers. Elizabeth grew uncomfortable for some reason, so she pulled away. "In the interim, I shall apply to my parents for a loan."

"Do you think they will help?" he asked, having been told of their disapproval.

"I should hope so. And if they say no, then I shall sell my ring. Or go back to Raven's Keep. That is Lucien's by birthright, surely they have not seized that as well. And there is money there. Objects we can sell—"

"There isn't time, Elizabeth," John interrupted. "Four days there and back, plus the time it will take to sell the items. Lucien will be put to the bench by the time you return."

She stared up at him mutely, her eyes filling with tears of frustration. "They have us over a barrel."

"That, I'm sure, was their intent."

"But why?"

"Because Lucien is to be an example," he theorized. "One does not kill a duke without repercussions, and now that the truth has been revealed, nothing will do but that he is made to pay."

"Who told them what happened?"

John's face grew hard. "Greshe."

"So it's true? We have Lucien's cousin as an enemy?"

"He wants the title."

"Betrayed again," she mused.

"Aye," John agreed.

"Then there's nothing left to do but pray," Elizabeth said softly.

"Aye," John agreed. "For a miracle."

And Elizabeth did pray, though it did little good. During the next few days she did all she could to help Lucien—even though he still refused to see her—including the humbling task of applying to friends and family for loans.

No one would give her money.

Instead, they each encouraged her to separate herself from the duke, and when she refused, they each of them politely and oh so civilly showed her to the door.

Elizabeth stung from it all.

She knew now what Lucien must have felt when society had shunned him before. Knew how it felt to be condemned without benefit of a trial. It was the worst sort of betrayal, for it was a betrayal of friendship. She learned too late that even those that professed themselves as family could be far from that.

Now, as she stood in her room, a room lent to her by one of John's relatives, she felt unable and unwilling to believe that this could truly have happened.

And yet, it had.

There could be no denying it for it was all over *The Times*. Lucien St. Aubyn, duke of Ravenwood, would be tried for murder Tuesday next. Thank goodness Lucien had no access to the paper, Elizabeth thought, and that he was unable to read about the atrocities he had purportedly committed. But what truly made her ill was the way they portrayed her as the poor, duped wife. They claimed he'd married her as a way of gaining respectability. That he'd known he was to be brought up on charges and that he'd hoped their marriage might gain him sympathy with his peers. And most ludicrous of all the paper stated that perhaps he'd hoped his marriage might gain him more clout, for her father, while new to the peerage, was well connected to the crown.

Connected? Hah?

Her father was a cobbler's son, a business they still owned. His only connection to the crown was a mad king who likely wouldn't recognize him. But they made it sound like truth. And everyone believed it. The *ton* treated her with a combination of pity and condemnation— the poor cobbler's daughter who had married above herself. She could barely stomach it all, but she stuck by her vow to see this through, stuck by it because she refused to let Lucien down. Enough people had done that, she reasoned. She would not do the same. So she worked behind the scenes, preparing herself for the coming trial with more grace and courage than she'd thought herself capable of, and all the while Lucien refused to see her. He stay interned with the common criminals, reasoning that he was a criminal himself.

Elizabeth wanted to scream in frustration.

The day of the trial dawned cold and overcast, drizzle casting a sheen on the leather tack of the swaybacked horse pulling the hired hack she rode in. The backs of the horses were wet. As were the windows to her left and right. She snuggled a scratchy wool carriage blanket closer, chilled to the bone, and not just because of the weather. John, next to her, glanced her way for a second. She mustered a brave smile that, sadly, wobbled and ruined the effect.

She'd dressed well for the occasion, her attire meant to remind those who would watch her testimony that she was a nobleman's daughter, for all that she was of common stock. She'd worn rose, the color bright, cheerful. The pelisse over the gown was maroon, the neckline moderate. She had piled her hair atop her head as best she could, although she feared she'd done such a poor job of it, the whole thing might come tumbling down as she stood at the bar.

"Did he appear nervous last eve?" she found herself asking without even realizing she would.

"He seemed well in control," John answered, Elizabeth wishing for his thick brown trousers and black wool jacket to keep her warm.

"How are *you* doing?" he asked.

She lifted her chin, trying hard not to let loose the silly tears his words evoked. "I am fine."

She was terrified. The fact of the matter was, she'd been called as a witness, but not by Lucien. No. Rather, she'd been called by the prosecution and that terrified her. Granted, she was under no obligation to testify for the law prevented a spouse from doing so. She, however, had agreed to do so of her own free will.

"You are not a very good liar, Your Grace."

"I am nervous about testifying," she admitted, "but who would not be?"

She could feel his gaze as he stared at her, but he said nothing in return. Elizabeth felt grateful for that. The horses sloshed through a puddle, water kicked up onto the carriage's floorboard with a splash.

"I admire your courage," he said, his kind blue eyes meeting her own. "You have held up admirably well given the circumstances."

She held his gaze. "Thank you." But she had to look out the window lest the tears that threatened fell. Frankly, she felt ready to shatter. With the exception of John, she had no one in all of London on whom to lean. And even then, she didn't know John well enough to use him for the support she desperately needed.

"I will feel better once I give testimony."

"Will you?"

She told herself she would. What she said at the trial might be the only positive thing someone would say about Lucien—if the Attorney General let her—with the exception of John, who also was to testify. As a result, her nerves stretched taut; her stomach rolled like a pot of boiling water. She didn't know what she would be asked, but she knew that whatever it was, she needed to turn it somehow into a defense of Lucien.

They both lapsed into silence. The ride was short, but as they neared Westminster, they slowed to a near crawl.

"Spectators," John observed from his side of the carriage.

She nodded wordlessly as she looked outside. The Abbey rose to her right, people dotting the streets as they hurried toward the proceedings. They pulled up before the Hall. Less ostentatious than the Abbey with its plain stone facade and low roofline, the structure still set her heart to beating like a panicked horse. She wiped her hands on the carriage blanket, knowing that the next few hours would be difficult, at best.

The crowd outside nearly mobbed them once they recognized her. One of the benefits of having one's face plastered upon newspaper covers as well as being immortalized in satirical drawings featuring her in a wedding dress and Lucien as the devil incarnate. The drawings had appeared in nearly every London print shop to the point that Elizabeth was afraid to venture out. She had no such luxury now.

Cries of, "There she is," followed her into the building as well as, "The Duchess of Death."

A Charlie stopped her near the entrance, but once he recognized her, he let her pass. She barely noticed the interruption so intent was she on escaping the crowd.

"This way," John said, his voice swept up by the noise around them. The general public would not be allowed inside although there would be a few spectators. A vague impression of gray halls and muted light penetrated her vision as he led her toward the gold-gilt and oak-beamed room that was the *House of Lords,* or more correctly, to the narrow pit in the center of it. She stared straight ahead as those lords already in their seats noticed her arrival, the crowd of crimson-robed peers quieting. The chairs they sat in rose up at a steep angle, circling the pit, a walkway intersecting them midway like a longitude line around the circumference of a globe.

Someone called for attention an interminable amount of time later. And with those words, it all began. Ceremonial proceedings first, the Lords' Speaker entering followed by the Purse-bearer and other officials. Elizabeth sat in her seat, every nerve strained, her heart pounding hard enough to be heard outside her chest. The commission appointing the earl of Glashow as Lord High Steward was read, the Garter and Black Rod made their reverences and proceeded to their places on the right of the Lord High Steward. The indictment was read, the Lord High Steward then directed the sergeant at arms to make his proclamation for the yeoman usher to bring Lucien to the bar.

Elizabeth sat forward in her red velvet seat. A door opened. She held her breath. Lucien entered. She fell back into her seat. He looked—well, not like she'd expected. His black jacket fit tight against his broad shoulders. Beneath the coat he wore a white shirt with a pointed collar and a lavish cravat. Light gray trousers with black half boots completed the ensemble. 'Twas the uniform of a man trying to look in control, of one who wanted to appear unfazed by what he now faced, but Elizabeth knew better.

Her hands clutched as he was led forward.

"He looks calm," John observed, sitting next to her.

"'Tis an illusion," she murmured in an aside, knowing Lucien must surely want to wilt beneath the scathing looks directed his way. She watched as his lips tilted in his isn't-this-amusing smile. But tension resonated from his shoulders, barely discernible, but there if one looked hard enough.

Or knew Lucien well enough.

And amazingly, she did. She tried to will him to look at her, but he merely stared straight ahead as he took a seat on a stool within the bar. The Lord High Steward moved to a table near him, preceded by the Garter, the Black Rod, and the Purse-bearer. It was all very tedious, this moving about, the positions they took undoubtedly meant to intimidate the accused. The Lord High Steward sat at the middle of the table, the Black Rod sitting on a high stool behind him and to his right, the official staff now held in his hands. The Garter took a seat upon a similar stool to the Black Rod's right, the sergeant at the lower end of the table. They resembled a king and his court, which, Elizabeth conjectured, was exactly how they were supposed to appear.

And then Lucien looked her way.

Elizabeth felt instant tears slide onto her lower lashes as their eyes met, even though a part of her wondered why she cried for a man she told herself she didn't love. She supposed 'twas because she could see the brief flash of anxiety that shone in his eyes. And so she smiled, trying to tell him without words that she was here for him.

He didn't smile back; if anything, his gaze hardened. Elizabeth almost choked.

"You love him, don't you?" John asked, keeping his words low so no one could hear.

Did she? Could she love a man who didn't care enough to see her? Who didn't want her help? Who seemed to want to hang and leave her a widow? "I don't know," she admitted aloud, even as she suspected she knew well and good the answer to the question.

"Well, if you do, I don't know whether to congratulate you or pity you."

She glanced over at John. He looked as noble as any of the men in the seats below, but, she reminded herself, he *was* a nobleman's son. Like Lucien, he'd been born too late to benefit from his father's station. Unlike Lucien, he hadn't dueled his brother and gained the title.

"My lords, ladies, and gentlemen," the Attorney General began. "Let me explain today's proceedings . . ."

And so it began, each member of the court coming forward to state their case. The indictment was reread, evidence was presented. Lucien stood up to speak. He nodded to the Lord High Steward, then the members of the House. And despite their obvious antipathy, they all nodded back, ever so civilly. Elizabeth felt hysteria rise in her throat.

And then Lucien recounted the events of the duel, spoke publicly for the first time as to why he was innocent, but he didn't sound like he believed himself, and that hurt his case, Elizabeth could tell, her hands clenching in her lap as she noticed the hardening of the faces around her. When he was finished, the Attorney General came forward to question him. Lucien responded in a clear, calm voice, his answers direct and to the point, even when the Attorney General implied Lucien might be responsible for more than one death, Elizabeth hearing for the first time the number of loved ones Lucien had lost. She waited for Lucien to turn and look at her, but he never did. Not even once. And for the first time Elizabeth understood where the word "heartache" came from. Her heart quite literally ached with a pain and made her eyes well with tears.

The first witness for the prosecution was called forth. Elizabeth's nerves stretched to the point that her stomach churned with anxiety and made her ill. Man after man was called forward to state in no uncertain terms that Lucien had often remarked upon his brother's good fortune to be born first. The Attorney General had gathered five to every one of Lucien's witnesses. John disappeared as he was called.

And then it was her turn. She placed her hands upon the bar, the wood it was made of reflecting back the gold-gilt trim of the room. She told herself to relax, and had the insane urge to stick her tongue out at them all.

"Elizabeth St. Aubyn," the Lord High Steward said. "You have been called as a witness for the prosecution. Will you testify of your own free will?"

"I will, my lord," she answered, surprised at how utterly confident and relaxed she sounded when inside she quaked like a shaken bottle.

The Attorney General came forward, a studious-looking man if ever there was one. His gray barrister's wig looked too small for his head, his robes unable to disguise his large girth. He had a ruddy face and even ruddier blue eyes, the man looking as if had spent most of his life in a state of drunkenness. Elizabeth disliked him on sight.

"Elizabeth St. Aubyn, how long have you known the duke of Ravenwood?"

She licked her lips staring at the assembled peers. One by one, she tried to meet their gazes. "I have known *of* him for many years. In fact, he first came to my attention when rumors surfaced that he'd seduced your daughter, Lord Glashow." She picked out his lordship from the sea of crimson robes and smiled. "Over the years I heard of a great many more women he supposedly seduced, so many, in fact, that I wonder how his grace would have had time to plot a murder, much less execute it."

There were a few chuckles at her comment, as was her intent.

The Attorney General did not look amused. "Can you

describe to me the circumstance under which you met at
Lady Derby's ball?"

She had been expecting the question and so met it
head-on. "He compromised me." She gave him a wry
smile.

"Ruined you?" the man clarified.

"Indeed, sir. Most thoroughly."

More chuckles. The Attorney General never cracked a
smile. "And would you describe your husband's behavior
that night as honorable?"

"That night, no. His marriage to me, yes."

"That wasn't the question."

"No? I suppose what you want me to say is that my
husband behaved anything but honorably that eve, and
that is true, but in my eyes and the eyes of society, he redeemed himself."

"Redeemed himself, you say? Why, my lady, I'm surprised. I myself know of the difficult position you hold
amongst society. The daughter of a nobleman, and yet not
really noble."

Her cheeks reddened. Vile man.

"I know that you've worked hard to give yourself the
best of reputations. You've been out now for what? Two
seasons? And yet in one night this man"—he pointed at
Lucien—"the man you claimed redeemed himself in your
eyes, undid all your hard work. Is that the behavior of an
honorable man, would you say?"

She lifted her head, thanking the heavens above for the
training she'd received that allowed her to smile civilly.
"No, it was not honorable, sir. However, given my ques-
tionable position amongst society—a position you yourself just alluded to—how easy it would have been for my

husband to turn his back on me. He is a duke. And I, as you say, all but a commoner. He did not have to marry me. And yet he did."

The Attorney General stared. It was as if by not commenting he tried to make a point of some sort, though what it could be, Elizabeth was too anxious to note. "And has the duke treated you well since your marriage?"

"Like a queen."

He lifted a brow, and something in the way his eyes glittered alerted her to the coming question. "Your grace," the man said calmly. "Have you ever heard of a ship called the *Revenger*?"

Elizabeth felt her cheeks grow numb. "I have."

"And what kind of ship is it?"

"A big one," she stalled.

The Attorney General's eyes narrowed. "Let me rephrase that. Was the *Revenger* a pirate ship?"

She sat up as tall as she could. "It was."

"And can you tell me who captained this ship?"

"A man called Jolly."

"Was Jolly a pirate?"

"He was."

"And was your husband on good terms with this man?"

Elizabeth didn't want to answer. Lord, she would have given anything not to, but she knew the Attorney General had her in a corner. He knew it, too. "He was."

"And did your husband participate in the sinking of a ship called the *Swan* while friends with this man?" He curled his lip. "This *pirate* called Jolly?"

Who had told him?

"Lady Ravenwood?" he prompted.

She swallowed, knowing to lie would be futile. Like as not, the prosecution had learned of the incident, how was anyone's guess. "He did," she admitted.

"He did?" The Attorney General affected surprise. Keats would have been proud of his playacting. "But you claim his lordship is honorable."

"He is," she said.

"A man who sinks a merchant ship honorable?"

"He was different back then."

"Different enough to kill his brother in a duel?"

"No." She shook her head. "I mean, yes."

"Which is it, Your Grace?"

"No, he was not capable of killing his brother."

"You knew him well enough to judge that?"

"I did."

"And that would be why you called him a . . ." He walked slowly to his desk, moved a piece of parchment around so that he could read it. "What was it . . . ah, here it is, a 'murdering whoremonger' when he asked you to dance at a ball."

Those words. Those awful words.

The Attorney General looked up at her. "Did you call him that?"

She looked away.

"Did you?"

She shook her head.

"You didn't?" the man asked.

She looked up, met his gaze scathingly. "It would seem, sir, that you know I did. But I never meant it literally."

His eyebrows lifted again. "Ah," he drawled mockingly. "I see. You call all men who ask you to dance a murdering whoremonger, do you?"

She didn't answer.

"Do you?" he asked.

Damn the man. Damn them all. They would twist her words and Lucien's until they had the slant they wanted.

"Well, Your Grace?"

"No, I do not."

"So it would be fair to say that before you married your husband, you believed him guilty of murder?"

Her mind spun with a possible response that would change the slant of his words, but none was forthcoming.

"Your Grace?" he sang, clearly at a loss for patience at her reticence.

"I did."

"What was that?" he asked, cupping his ear. "I didn't hear you."

She lifted her chin. "I did," she repeated.

The man turned away from her, facing the Lord High Steward. "No more questions."

But she wasn't finished. She wanted to tell them about Lucien protecting her. About why he'd taken up with pirates as revenge against the evil countess of Selborne. But, she realized she wouldn't be given the chance.

"Lord Ravenwood, do you have any questions?" the Steward asked.

But Elizabeth knew he didn't. Frustration made her stand abruptly "Don't do this to him, my lords—"

"Lady Ravenwood—" the High Steward cried, turning to her, aghast.

Elizabeth ignored him. "Don't convict a man for murder because of an accident."

"*Lady Ravenwood,*" the Steward tried again.

"I might be of common stock, but at least I treat a fellow human being with respect until there is just cause for me not to do so."

"That is enough," the Steward said.

"Let her speak."

All eyes turned to Lucien, whose face had gone tight as he eyed the assemblage, his body half out of his chair. He kept his gaze firmly averted from hers. "Let her speak her piece. Trust me, gentleman, the lady will speak her mind with or without your permission."

She waited for Lucien to look at her, but he didn't, merely nodded as he sat down. Some of her triumph faded, but she forced herself to stay erect, forced herself to act as if Lucien had just asked her to speak on his behalf.

"My husband did not kill his brother for the title," she began, looking around her. "He told me the truth of what happened that day and, I might add, he had no reason to do so. In fact, he had much to lose, for who was to say I would not go to the authorities with all that I learned?" She felt tears rise, cursed herself for being such a watering pot when she had need to appear in control. "Before you is a man who has lived with the horror of his brother's death for years. Alone. For whom could he talk to about the events?"

She clenched her hands upon the bar, straightening to her full height as she willed her words to be believed. Damn Lucien's reticence. "That day, when he told me what had happened, my husband's countenance was that of a man who had been witness to a horrible accident, one that had claimed a family member's life." She searched the room, her eyes picking out one man in particular. "He acted the way you must have acted, Lord Stanton, when the carriage you drove overturned and took your tiger's life. Do you remember the horror and anguish you felt upon realizing that you'd inadvertently killed a man? For those were the emotions on my husband's face when he relayed the story of his brother's death."

She leaned forward, her hands clutching the edge of the bar. "Henry St. Aubyn's death was not an act of murder. I would stake my life upon it."

Silence followed her words, a silence that was so complete, one could hear the shifting of bodies in their seat.

"But you have it easy, my lords," she said. "Because for some reason my husband has decided to put up half a fight."

"Elizabeth," Lucien growled.

"I believe he is tired of the guilt. And I believe he wants to pay for that guilt with his life."

"Elizabeth," Lucien half stood again.

"It's true," she said, meeting his gaze.

Tell them, her eyes implored.

I will not, he answered back.

She gave up then, wilted back upon the bar. What was the point in saying anything further when he refused to fight? Tears rose again in her eyes. She closed them to keep them at bay.

"Are you through?" the Steward asked.

And Elizabeth knew she'd lost. She hadn't gotten through to him. Or the peers. She opened her eyes, wiped at a tear that flowed before anyone noticed. "Aye," she murmured.

"Redirect?" the Lord Steward asked the Attorney General.

But apparently the Attorney General deemed he had enough. "No further questions."

"You may leave the bar, Lady Ravenwood," the Steward said.

Her legs felt like pudding as she stood, turned away, too disappointed to risk another glance at Lucien. Likely he wouldn't be looking at her anyway.

Lord Chalmers was called next, but all he did was explain the happenings on the day of the duel. Greshe, Lucien's cousin, followed and 'twas he that gave the most damning piece of evidence, for he told the assemblage about a wager Lucien had placed, a wager wherein Lucien bet that his brother would be dead by the age of thirty.

It was over. Elizabeth knew it the moment she heard those words. A look at the peers' faces only confirmed her supposition.

It took only an hour for the verdict to come in, an hour during which Elizabeth waited alone in an antechamber, Lucien having been dragged away by the sheriff to be given back to the keeper of Newgate. There was no fanfare, just the Lord High Steward asking, "How do you find, my lords?"

"Guilty," the Speaker announced.

CHAPTER TWENTY-ONE

They sentenced him to hang. Elizabeth felt like collapsing when she heard the news, for all that it was expected. Now as she looked out a second-floor window, she wondered how her life could change so irrevocably in so short a time. Ruined. Married. Widowed.

The cousin of John's she was staying with lived on the east side of London. As such the view was less than spectacular: muddy streets with cart tracks crisscrossing the road like snail trails on a dirty road. Clods of muck hung upon all nearby surfaces, including the brownstone facades of the homes and businesses that huddled next to each other like bedridden siblings. A steady stream of work carts, hired hacks, and the occasional gentleman's coach passed beneath her window. She followed one of those carriages with her eyes now, noting the crest, wondering distantly if it was one of the lords who'd sentenced Lucien to hang. But of course it was.

She turned away, a box atop a worn chest of drawers catching her attention. They were the dueling pistols, the Attorney General having given them to her after the trial. Unnecessary evidence, he'd said, referring to the fact they hadn't needed them to convict Lucien. Elizabeth's face stung with anger at the memory.

Steeling herself, she crossed to them, lifting the oak lid and eying the pistols inside. They had a gold-gilt design around the end of the barrel, the rest of the pistol brushed with an ornate pattern. The stock was made of carved ivory, the handle etched with a crisscross design for better gripping. They'd never been used prior to the duel, or so Lucien had told her, but one could see that they'd been fired. The stain of powder dimmed the area around the flintlock. She brushed her finger against one, wondering which had killed Henry. Then the morbidity of her thoughts made her slam the lid closed.

"Are you ready?"

Elizabeth turned, meeting John's concerned gaze. "Aye," she said softly. She had cried the whole way home, John doing his best to console her. Lord, could she have muddled her testimony any more? Worse, she knew that testimony had been instrumental in sealing Lucien's fate. Heaven help her, the Attorney General had gotten her to admit that she'd thought her husband a murderer.

"Elizabeth, I cannot guarantee he will see you."

She lifted her chin. "I know."

John looked ready to argue with her about why she shouldn't go, but in the end, he must have realized she meant to try with or without his support.

And so once again they found themselves in a hired hack. Elizabeth pulled the heavy wool cloak she wore tight around her; the black fabric warm against London's chill. Lately, she could never get warm, as if a permanent cold had entered her bones and her heart. She felt tears rise again, but firmly batted them away. She would not cry. She had words to say to her husband, words she would say without evidence of tears.

All too soon they pulled up before Newgate's colorless facade.

"I'll be back in a moment," John said.

Would Lucien see her? Elizabeth wondered. He had no reason not to now that the trial was over. She could no longer shame him into defending himself. No longer hire a barrister and force him to use the man. The only reason he would not see her now was if he'd decided to wash his hands of her.

One look at John's face when he returned convinced her that he had. She jumped out of the carriage.

"Elizabeth," John called as she stormed past.

"No, John," she said, turning back to him. "I will not take no for an answer."

"He will not see you."

"Yes, he will," she gritted out.

She thought John might try and stop her. To her surprise, he didn't. She crossed the muddy road to get to Newgate's main entrance, dodging freight and hay carts as she did so. The stench was unimaginable. Not even the smell of the manure piles that lay in the street penetrated it. Inside was even more frightening, for at least from the outside the place had looked clean. Inside was a gritty, dank mess whose stench was the one she smelled outside, only more pronounced.

"I'm here to see Lucien St. Aubyn," she said to the Keeper, a man whose desk stood just inside the main door.

"And you are?" the man asked, his elderly face colder than the stones beneath her feet.

"His wife."

Brows lowered over impatient eyes. "He won't see you."

In desperation Elizabeth threw down a bag of coins. It was the money she'd raised from selling the carriage and the horses, money she had held on to in the hope that Lucien might have a last-minute change of heart. She should have known better.

"This bag is yours if you secure a private cell for my husband and myself."

The man stared at her for a while, but greed must have won out for he said, "Give me some time."

Elizabeth resolved to wait a lifetime if she had to.

Lucien knew when he saw the turnkey outside that something strange was about to happen. He knew it by the way the man's eyes scanned the interior of the cell, coming to rest on him before he lifted his keys to the door. For half a moment he wondered if they'd come to take him away. Perhaps they'd moved his execution to today instead of the day after next. Oddly enough, the thought frightened him not at all. Instead he felt . . . numb. A numbness that had settled over him as he'd watched Elizabeth ride away from the castle all those days ago.

"'Ave ya come for me then?" asked one of his cellmates, a man with more hair above his eyes than he had on his head. "'As me miserable wife finally decided to fetch me outta 'ere?"

The turnkey ignored him, pulling open the door and pointing to Lucien. "Yur ta come with me," the man said.

Lucien pushed away from the stone wall he'd been leaning against, his cellmates saying not a word. There was a strange pecking order amongst the men, and it seemed as if a murdering brother ranked quite high. They'd left him alone since his crime had become known.

"I'll leave your chains off, but if you make a move, I'll clout you over the head," the turnkey said.

He must say those words at least a hundred times a day, Lucien thought. He'd heard them himself a dozen times as he'd been taken to and fro. And so he meekly followed the gentleman, and by now he hardly noticed his surroundings: the other prisoners, the dark corridors, the smell. But the turnkey didn't lead him to the prisoner's door, as much as Lucien had suspected he might. Nor even to the chapel, a place they usually took condemned men in a final effort to save their souls. No. He led him up, to a tower room, opening a door to a reasonably clean and moderately bright cell. It didn't have bars on the front; rather, it was a corner cell with stone walls and a single wood door with a small, barred portal in the top half of it.

And suddenly, Lucien felt alarmed.

"What is this?" he asked.

The man ignored him, just opened the door. "Get inside."

For a moment he almost balked, but reason won out. What did he have to be afraid of? Perhaps the Regent was about to visit? Perhaps he was going to stay his execution after all?

But it wasn't the Prince that came into the cell a few moments later, it was his wife.

Lucien stiffened.

"Hello, Lucien."

He blinked, thinking surely her presence was an illusion. He'd given strict instructions that he didn't want to see her. But, he supposed, anything could be had at Newgate. For a price.

"Elizabeth," he said, steeling himself as she came into the cell, the sweet smell of her nearly sending him to his knees.

"Surprised to see me?" she asked with a tight smile.

"No. Your resourcefulness never ceases to amaze me." He looked her up and down, trying not to notice the sad tilt of her lips. The pained look in her gaze. The redness around her eyes that bespoke of tears. But he'd be blind not to notice those things, or the way the black cloak she wore turned her eyes almost silver. The way her hair smelled, the floral scent startling against Newgate's stench.

She stared at him, her upswept hair seeming to glisten. Moisture, he realized, noticing for the first time that the light shining down from the small window high above was muted. Mist. 'Twas foggy outside.

"Why have you refused to see me?" she asked softly.

"I'm sorry." He feigned polite sorrow. "Didn't my butler tell you? I was not receiving."

She tilted her chin. "I have been trying to see you for days."

He smiled. "I have been a bit indisposed."

She walked toward him, a pity, for as she drew nearer the heavenly smell of her enveloped him again. It shocked him how much he'd missed that scent . . . how much he wanted to inhale it now. To simply drink his fill of her. Instead, he held himself erect.

"Stop it, Lucien. Stop treating this as if it's all a joke.

You always do that. When you're uncomfortable, you cover it up with humor."

His smile turned sardonic. "I assure you, my dear, Newgate is hardly a humorous place to be."

"That is not what I meant, and you know it."

"No?"

She lost her patience then. He could see it in the way she stiffened suddenly. The way her little hands clenched. The way her mouth trembled as if she fought back tears. "How dare you?" she said. "How dare you do this to me?"

"My dear, I don't know what you're talking about."

She went from anger to rage then, coming at him with her hands lifted as if she'd strike him again. But she didn't, just came to a halt before him, then dropped her arms to her sides as if embarrassed by her outburst.

"You know very well what I'm talking about. You gave up. Judged yourself guilty. Made a jest of the whole proceedings by refusing to allow me to hire someone to defend you."

He didn't say anything. Truth be told, he was afraid if he did, she might give in to the urge to hit him. Lord knew it looked like she would.

"At least when you compromised me I didn't run away from my problem. I faced the consequences of what happened with my head held high, even though I knew every member of the *ton* was nodding his head saying, 'See, I knew this would happen to her. She's *common.*'"

Her eyes had begun to glisten. "But you! You bowed your head and accepted your fate without a fight. You will make me a widow. And all because you were too wrapped up in your own self-pity to realize there were

people who cared for you, who—God help them—*love*
you. People like John. Like your staff. Like your tenants,
who have worked alongside you for years. People who
couldn't afford the price of a post, but who wrote to me
nonetheless, somehow managing the fee so that they
could tell me what a good man you are and how they
were praying for you." She swallowed back more tears.
"And after reading their missives, I had to go to Westminster and watch you give up."

"I did not give up."

She came at him then, grabbing the lapels of his dark-
gray jacket. "Yes, you did," she all but screamed, a tear
breaking free. "Damn you, Lucien, you did."

She let go of him then, turned away, her shoulders
shaking in a way that gave evidence to tears.

He stood there, numb, and yet, *not*. His heart beat
against his chest hard enough to vibrate the fabric.

"You did give up," she said through her tears, slowly
turning to face him again, the smell of her drifting on a
breeze to reach him once more. But it was the sight of the
tears running down her face, that nearly broke him. "You
gave up on us all."

She took a deep breath, her hands swiping at her face.
"But the worst of it is that I can forgive you for giving up
on me. I knew you, after all, a short time. But I can't forgive you for letting everyone else down." She shook her
head. "You let down John, your best friend, a man who
cried for you as I did when he heard the verdict. Pity
yourself, Lucien, but pity those who love you more, for it
is they who will weep the hardest when they hang you."

She stood there, facing him, more tears running down
her cheeks. For the longest time, their gazes held, her

eyes unwavering. Lucien stood there, feeling emotions he refused to name or identify. And then her shoulders slumped, only to be pulled erect an instant later.

"That is what I came here to tell you," she said softly. "And also, I think, to say good-bye." She took a deep breath, her hands unclenching then clenching again. She closed the distance between them, lifting herself on tiptoe and pecking his cheek. Her lips were wet. Yet warm.

"Good-bye, Lucien," she said as she drew back, her sweet breath wafting toward him. Her hand lifted as she patted smooth the jacket she'd clutched. "I wish you Godspeed on your journey." She swallowed, another tear fell. "I hope you find peace wherever that journey might end."

She turned then, the bottom of her cloak flaring so that it lightly touched his legs. The turnkey must have been waiting right outside the cell, for the door opened. She was halfway through it before he heard himself call out, "Elizabeth?"

He thought she might ignore him, saw her take another step as if she would. But then she stopped, slowly turning to face him.

"Will you weep for me, too?"

He didn't know why he asked the question. Silly thing to ask.

He watched her grapple with her answer before saying hoarsely, "Yes," and the word was hardly more than a croak. "God help me. I will. I will cry at the unfairness of it all. I shall cry for the people who love you, but most of all, I shall cry for *you* and the life we might have shared together . . . if you'd but had the courage to fight."

She turned again. He heard the door clang close, her words hitting him in a way he'd never thought possible.

If you'd but had the courage to fight.

Only when it'd grown quiet again—well, as quiet as Newgate could get—did he move, and then only to collapse against the side of the wall.

She would cry for him.

Lucien didn't know why, but the words hit him hard. Why would she cry? It wasn't as if she loved him.

Did she?

Something burned within him. Something that he refused to let escape.

You gave up, she'd said.

No, he hadn't, he reassured himself. He'd done his best.

He stood up abruptly, refusing to dwell on the matter. What was done was done. She was gone. It was over.

I'll cry for you.

His fist balled. Something coiled within him.

"Stupid bastard."

He thought he'd imagined the words. Thought it was his subconscious speaking.

But it wasn't. It was John.

His old friend stood on the other side of the door, and Lucien could see his eyes glow with unholy rage.

"Do ya ken what you've done to her?"

Lucien didn't answer.

"Do ya ken what you've put her through?" John's voice was a physical lash, his rage stinging Lucien, the Scottish brogue more pronounced as it always was when emotionally charged. "She begged people she hardly knew fer money fer you. I watched her go out day after day, only to cume back beaten. And fer what?" John asked. "For you to turn your nose up at her."

"Hello, John," Lucien said woodenly. "Nice to see you, too."

"Dontcha give me that, ya bastard. If I trusted meself not to beat you to a pulp, I'd come in there and knock some sense inta you. She's crying 'er eyes out down there. Crying in a hired hack because she sold everything she had ta help you. Or did you not notice her wedding ring gone?"

No, he hadn't noticed.

"But never you fear. I'll be only too happy to put another ring on her finger once you're gone. She'll deserve some happiness after this. Lord knows, you've only given 'er heartbreak."

"Don't you dare." The growl that emerged from Lucien's lips surprised even him.

"Don't I dare do what, Lucien? Marry meself a wife you've all but given away? Too late. I'm already 'alf in love with her, or hadn't you noticed that, too?"

"You? In love? I hardly think so."

"Don't ya be judging me by your own idiotic behavior."

"Speak English, man."

"Go ta hell, Lucien. But then, that's where you be wantin' ta go anyway, ach?"

"You act as if I could have fought the charges."

"You could'a," John snapped. "And you know it. At the very least, you could'a tried to get the charges reduced ta manslaughter. That, at least, does no carry the penalty o' death. But, no, you let yourself hang outta some twisted sense of obligation. Well, think you again,

Lucien. Henry be dead. An' nothing you do will bring him back. Not even sacrificing yur own life."

"I didn't—"

"You did," John snarled, but then his eyes narrowed. "But I will no complain because it means I shall have 'er." He leaned toward the door. "So 'ave fun at yur hanging, Lucien. Elizabeth and I will no be attending. I'm going ta take her away from the mobs that've been houndin' her, take her away from memories of you because, despite what she may have told you, she's in luv wi' you, though God knows why."

In love with him?

Not bloody likely.

"Good-bye, old friend. 'Ave fun at your bloody hangin'."

"John," Lucien called, but his friend ignored him.

Lucien went to the bars. "John," he called again. But there was no one there.

CHAPTER TWENTY-TWO

Rain spilled chilly tears down the room's single window, not that Elizabeth cared. There was no fire in the room John's cousin had been kind enough to let her use, but who needed to be warm when one knew one would never be warm again? Elizabeth clutched an off-white shawl around her, knuckles blanching as she fought to maintain control.

"Elizabeth, if there's anythin' I can do—"

She stayed his words with her hand, her body beginning to shake uncontrollably. She clenched her hands to stop the shaking. "No, John, I will be fine."

She took a deep breath, knowing if he didn't leave the room soon, he would be witness to a horrible display of tears. Again. But at least she hadn't broken down completely in front of Lucien. Lord knew she'd wanted to crumple in a heap on the cell's floor.

"Please," she said softly, her voice near a groan. "I would like to be alone now."

She felt a hand on her shoulder, nearly shattered at the touch of it, but somehow she held on.

"I'll be belowstairs if you need me."

She didn't trust herself to say anything, merely nodded. He kept his hand on her shoulder for a second longer. She felt her control slip even more, never having felt more alone, more terrified in all her life.

And then he pulled his hand away. She took a deep breath, one that caught in her throat. The door clicked open, then just as quietly, closed.

And yet she didn't break down. It was odd, for she could feel the sobs inside, but they didn't come. She walked forward, placed her hand against the glass, the tips of her fingers turning white as she remembered a time when she'd looked out her own bedroom window and seen Lucien's carriage. How long ago had that been? It seemed a lifetime ago.

I want to cry, she told herself as only a single tear dribbled out. *Cry at the injustice of it all.*

She felt her stomach lurch. Willed the tears to follow the sick feeling that coursed through her.

Her eyes caught on a woman who walked down the street, a woman who suddenly reminded Elizabeth of her aunt.

Promise me you won't marry one of them.

But she had married one of them. She'd done exactly as her aunt had warned her not to do, and look where it had landed her.

And suddenly the dam burst, the tears she'd craved to shed erupting into a flood of sobs that robbed her of breath, that made her drop to the floor. She cried for her aunt, who had died a bitter and broken woman. She cried for herself, but most of all, she cried for him.

Damn him, she sobbed. *Damn him for doing this to me.*

She stood, her legs all but collapsing beneath her weight, but with an inhaled breath she wobbled on her feet. The dueling pistols caught her attention. Rage such as she'd never felt rose within her then. Her legs carried her to the chest of drawers. All of her anger centered on that box, her hand a near blur as she flung them to the floor. But when it struck with a clatter, she felt no better. And that drained the anger from her as quickly as it'd come. She dropped to her knees again, sobbing.

How long she lay there, Elizabeth had no idea. She heard John knock once, had just enough strength to call out to him that she would be fine even as she knew nothing would ever be "fine" again.

Her eyes burning from spent tears, she picked herself up off the floor. The pistols still lay on the floor, the two of them at odd angles. She needed to put them away before John saw them, or worse, the staff. Wouldn't do for rumors to surface that the duchess of Ravenwood had tried to do away with herself. That would be the next headline.

She reached for one just as the sun broke free.

Odd how such a simple thing could change the course of someone's life.

For as the sun hit the barrel, it flashed. Elizabeth saw it glint. She picked the pistol up, examining it, wondering what it was about the firearm that caught her notice. She moved to pick up the other one.

But something . . . something made her drop the second pistol, then hold up the first pistol again. She studied if for a second, a frown wrinkling her brow, turning it this way and that. A part of her thought she must be mad, for what could she find that the Attorney General hadn't found? Still, she tilted the barrel. Sunlight arced around the inside of it. She leaned closer, her eyes straining.

And that was when it hit her.

No powder stains.

She drew back, her heart racing.

There were no powder stains and no remains of lead shot streaking the inside of the barrel.

Be calm, Elizabeth, perhaps the other pistol was the one Lucien fired? But, no, they had both been fired, or so the witnesses had reported. But just to be certain, she checked the other pistol. Clean too.

By now her hands had begun to shake with a different kind of emotion. Very well, she conjectured, perhaps Chalmers had cleaned the barrels. But why would he not clean the firing pins, too, for they were still dirty? And even if they had been cleaned, would not the passage of a lead ball make some mark upon the barrel?

She all but threw both pistols back in the box, slamming the lid closed before shoving herself to her feet and racing downstairs.

"Elizabeth," John called just as she reached the front door.

She spun in the narrow, dark hall. John had emerged from one of the home's small antechambers.

"Where are you going?" he asked.

She shifted on her feet, wanting only to be off. "To see Lord Chalmers."

"I didn't clean them before putting them away."

Elizabeth reached out and clutched Chalmers's hand. "Are you certain Lucien did not?"

They were in Chalmers's elegant and ornately furnished parlor, its pretty yellow-and-white wall coverings and fresh-cut roses bespeaking a woman's touch.

"No." Chalmers instantly shook his head, firelight catching on the rim of his spectacles. "He didn't want a thing to do with them. Told me to dispose of them for all he cared. I didn't. Instead, as you know, I put them away. Where they remained at the family estate, until fetched for the trial."

"Thank you," she said squeezing his hand once again.

He shook his head. "All this time. All these years, I believed they'd been fired."

"As did everyone, Lord Chalmers," Elizabeth reassured him. "And why wouldn't they? There are powder stains around the firing pin."

"But then who took the lead shot out of them before the duel?"

"One of the duelists," she answered.

"Henry?" Chalmers shot, his brows lifted.

"Aye," she said. "For something has bothered me. Lucien told me how Henry had struggled to tell him something before he died. He'd said the word 'empty.'"

"Aye," Chalmers said. "I remember."

"Lucien took it to mean that was how Henry felt. But I think he was trying to tell him something else. I believe he was trying to tell Lucien that the chamber was empty."

Chalmers instantly looked thunderstruck.

She leaned forward. "Now I need you to think, Lord Chalmers. Was there a time, no matter how brief, when Henry could have had access to the pistols?"

Chalmers' eyes grew unfocused as he leaned back. "There was," he said, his body suddenly tensing. "When Greshe and I were trying to talk Lucien out of the duel.

The pistols were in the carriage, Henry standing by it. He could have easily pulled the balls from the chambers."

"But he didn't empty the powder," Beth surmised.

"Do you know how hard it is to remove packed powder?" Chalmers asked. "It would have taken more than the time he had."

She leaned back, relief making her limbs weak. But just as quickly, she rose.

Chalmers looked up as she did so, his eyes wide. "He is innocent."

"Yes," she answered. "As I have always known."

"Someone else must have shot Henry."

"Yes, and I believe Lucien confused that shot with Henry firing upon *him*."

"But then would not Henry's pistol be *unfired*?"

"Yes, but if, as I suspect, I know who the murderer is, it would have been easy for her to have fired the pistol at a later date, to cover her actions, little realizing that the pistol wasn't loaded. I doubt, after all, that she checked the chamber."

"*She?*"

"Yes, the countess of Selborn."

Chalmers's eyes went wide.

"Now, one last question. Did anyone check the pistols to ensure they'd been fired after Henry was wounded?"

Chalmers drew himself up. "Of course not, we were concerned with helping Henry."

"*Thank you*, Lord Chalmers."

"Where are you going?" Chalmers asked as she stood up.

"To a gunsmith."

But she had to hurry, and she went alone, despite

Chalmers's protestations. John had protested, too, but this she needed to do by herself. If she was wrong . . . well, she didn't want any witnesses to her disappointment.

The ride to Milburn's was short, the shop located near the heart of London. She had gotten the name from John, but only as the hack pulled to a stop before its glass facade did she think the shop might be closed. Her palms began to sweat as she disembarked, the pistol case clutched to her chest. She sank a good three inches into mud as she stepped down, puddles and refuse clogging the gutters, if one could call them that. But Elizabeth would have stepped through the gates of hell to gain her objective and so she hardly noticed as she slogged her way to the front door, pulling open the oak door as she carried the box under her arm. The acrid smell of gunpowder and iron filled her nose. A cat meowed at her feet. The feline's owner, a man with as little hair as he had size, looked at her through wire-rim glasses. He stood behind a wooden counter, pistols hanging on the wall behind him. Hundreds of them, each a different shape and size. Some were ornate, others merely serviceable.

"May I help you?"

She hadn't thought to change, knew that her appearance was far from that of a duchess. Her upswept hair was wet, her gown spattered with mud, but that hardly mattered as she faced a man who could well save Lucien's life.

"I need to speak to Mr. Milburn."

"I am he."

She felt her shoulders sag. Her feet left muddy tracks as she crossed to the counter where he stood. The door slammed shut on a sudden breeze.

"Look at these," she said.

He drew back, and she could tell he was offended by her demanding tone.

Careful, Elizabeth. Best not to get off on the wrong foot.

She drew a deep breath, tried to compose herself. For the second time in her life she had cause to be grateful for her mother's training. She straightened to her full height, not very impressive, to be sure, but it was looks that counted, or so her mother said.

"I am the duchess of Ravenwood," she said.

She saw the man's eyes widen, saw the way he scanned her face, doubtful at first, but he must have been privy to those awful drawings for realization dawned.

"These pistols were used by my husband in a duel, one which I'm sure you have heard of."

"Aye, Your Grace. Who has not?"

Who indeed? "I need you to tell me if they've been fired," she said.

He looked thunderstruck again. "Fired?"

"Yes. Fired."

"But I thought—"

"That they had?" she finished for him. "So, apparently, does everyone else, but I would wager no one thought to check that they actually had."

"But surely someone examined them for powder stains?"

"I'm sure they did. But it is my guess that they saw the stains around the firing pin, which would be enough to prove to the examiner that they'd been fired. I doubt they looked to see if there were powder stains in the barrel."

The man's brow furrowed. "But the barrel would not be stained by powder."

Elizabeth felt as if the floor beneath her had been yanked away. "No? But what about marks inside the barrel? 'Tis plain there are none."

The man shook his head. "The barrel of a pistol does not scar easily, Your Grace. It would be hard to prove the pistols had not been fired using that theory."

She closed her eyes in a disappointment so stinging, it actually prickled her eyes in pain.

"But let me have a look at them just the same," the man said, obviously reading her face.

She'd told herself not to get her hopes up. Lord, how she'd warned herself. Blindly, she hefted the box.

He opened the lid almost reverently, peering inside with eyes that went suddenly wide before they met hers. "But the stock is made of ivory."

She nodded, her gaze turning blurry as she fought back tears.

"And this has never been noted before?"

She shook her head, something in his gaze setting her heart racing. "Not that I know of," she said, her body quickening at the look on his face. "Why? Is it important?"

"Of course it is, my dear lady," he said, his expression that of a man who'd opened a paper box only to spy gold inside. "Ivory stocks are notoriously weak, thus they are used for pistols that are meant for decoration only. Firing them would have broken the stock, the force of the blast causing cracks to appear around the barrel. These, as you can see, are still intact."

Elizabeth could only stare, the words he had spoken

slowly sinking in. "Then I was right? They have not been fired?"

He shook his head. "Powder might have been ignited from the flintlock, but only a small bit of it . . . enough to make them look as if they'd been fired. But, no. If a ball had passed through the barrel, the recoil would have caused the stock to break. I would stake my reputation on it."

Elizabeth almost collapsed.

"And in looking at these, there is likely one other way to prove it. A way that could not be disputed."

She tensed, waiting for him to explain.

"The barrels of these pistols are very narrow, the ball that would have come from it easily matched, I would think."

"Matched?"

He looked up at her, his eyes blinking behind his spectacles. "Aye. By exhuming the murder victim's body."

CHAPTER TWENTY-THREE

Hangings, Lucien decided, were not for the faint of heart. Especially when one was the person about to be hanged.

The scaffold creaked, the floor beneath a fellow prisoner's feet gave way. A thick rope twanged under the weight of a body.

Another man had met his end.

Lucien almost lost the contents of his stomach. His bound hands clenched behind his back, the shirt he wore beneath his black jacket drenched with sweat. The sun beat down upon him with the relentlessness of a purser's whip. It made him dizzy. Or perhaps it was the smell. Or the roar of the crowd as hundreds, nay, thousands of people shouted at him, spit at him, threw things at him.

Lucien swallowed back bile.

"Would you like me to say a prayer for your soul?"

Lucien turned. A clergyman stood to his right, his robes as black as the executioner's, a poor choice of color, Lucien thought a touch hysterically. He wore the high-pointed collar that all men who served the cloth wore, the wig upon his head looking a great deal cleaner than the clergyman's at Newgate who had given the condemned's sermon.

"If you like," the little man added, his own forehead beaded with sweat. "I will pray *with* you."

"What I would like," Lucien said, "is for you to get me out of here." And he did, for it was one thing to resign yourself to your fate, quite another actually to face it.

The clergyman's brows had risen. "I'm sorry, but I cannot help you with that, my son."

"But I thought all things were possible with prayer."

"They are," he said, placing a hand on Lucien's arm. "Given time."

"I don't need your time, old man," he said, wrenching away. "I need to get out of here."

The expression on the man's face turned pained. "You cannot leave, but you can repent. Your end is near. Confess your sins so that peace will rule your heart as you prepare to meet your Maker."

"My dear man," Lucien snapped, "the only peace the good Lord is likely to get from me is a piece of my mind. And I assure you, if I was, indeed, guilty of the cold-blooded murder for which I was accused, it would be far too late for me to make amends with the good Lord above."

"It is never too late."

"I assure you, it is, but since I don't intend to meet my Maker just yet, your prayer would be wasted."

But he *was* going to meet his Maker, he thought, turning away, only to be yanked back by a nearby guard. Oh, well. At least he'd tried.

"I will pray for you, my son."

"Yes, do that," Lucien said. "And while you're at it, ask God to show me the easiest way to escape."

He ignored the man's look of pity and his guard's tightening grip.

He didn't want to die.

The thought hit him hard.

Henry, old man, you shall soon have your vengeance on me. And face-to-face, no less.

The crowd let out another roar as the limp body was cut down. Lucien kept his gaze averted. Odd's teeth, what a fool he'd been. Why had he been so deaf to Elizabeth's words? She'd been right. He'd not fought the charges as hard as he could. He'd given up. Caved in, and as a result Elizabeth would suffer the stigma of his death for the rest of her life.

"Bring on th' duke," a spectator yelled.

"Duke," another person echoed.

Duke, duke, duke, the crowd began to chant.

Bloody idiots. Bloody infidels.

"Your turn, Your Grace," the clergyman said.

Lucien glanced at the scaffold. It stretched high above him, the beams L-shaped. The previous victim had finally been removed, a new rope hung.

"Any last words?"

Lucien eyed the executioner, the oddest urge to poke his fingers through the slits of his hood overcame him. Too bad his wrists were tied behind his back.

"Yes, my good man. I do have a few last words." He faced the crowd. They were in a near frenzy now, their eyes all but glowing, their drab, gray clothing seeming to blend together so that it looked like the sea near Raven's Keep on a stormy day.

Raven's Keep. His home. One he'd never see again.

"Quiet," the executioner called. "He's got somethin' to say."

They quieted marginally, Lucien feeling his heart beat to the point that it hurt.

Come on, old boy. Buck up. There are worse ways to go.

Yes, he mentally answered. *Like dying of plague or being torched alive.*

"Quiet," the executioner repeated.

Slowly, the crowd obeyed.

Lucien took a deep breath. "My dear friends," he called out.

"Speak up," someone yelled.

A hysterical urge to laugh overcame him. "I beg your pardon," he bellowed, then waited to see if that was loud enough. When no one protested, he assumed it was, hysteria clogging his throat yet again before he tamed it.

"First of all, I would like to thank each and every one of you for coming to my hanging today. You've no idea what it means to me."

When you're uncomfortable, you cover it up with humor.

He shoved Elizabeth's words to the back of his mind. He refused to think of her. Not now. "I realize it must have been quite a crush to get here, so your attendance means that much more."

"Get on w' it," someone yelled.

"I beg your pardon, old man," Lucien said in the general direction of the person who'd spoken. "But this is my hanging, and I shall speak as long as I wish."

No one said anything. That was good. Very good.

Delay. That was what he needed to do, though why when the outcome was a foregone conclusion, he had no idea.

"Before I go," he said, "I would like to say good-bye to my tailor, without whom I could not have obtained such a sterling reputation as a *pink of the ton*."

He forced a smile.

One lone guffaw greeted his words.

A start. "And to my valet at Raven's Keep, who is surely the stodgiest man alive, but who never clothed me wrong."

"Ahh, get on wi' it," another person yelled, a woman this time.

He ignored her. "And to my staff at Raven's Keep, who I understand are praying for me." And his voice broke on the last, his satirical humor fading as the reality of what he faced grabbed hold of him with both hands. "Thank you. I appreciate your prayers more than you know."

He had to swallow a few times before he could continue, the crowd strangely quiet now. "To my tenants, who worked their fingers to a nub for me. Thank you. It was a privilege to get to know you."

His hands clenched as he forced himself to say the next. "And John." Odd how his anger at his old friend had faded suddenly. "Good luck, John. Take care of her for me."

Her. Elizabeth.

He had to take a deep breath. What the hell to say to her?

I was a fool. An ass. I should be shot.

You're going to be hanged.

Fear dragged icy fingers over his skin, leaving a cold

sheen of sweat in its wake. He lifted his head, knowing he had to say something. He owed her that much.

"Elizabeth," he said, his voice having lowered. Was she even here? God, he wished he knew. "My wife. You know how hard it is for me to admit this, but I find suddenly that you were right." He shook his head, overcome by such a sudden burst of emotion he could barely think, and so he said the first thing that came to mind. "I was wracked with guilt, just as you said. I didn't want to fight the charges. I don't know why, but I didn't."

Bloody idiot, you know why. And you should admit it, too.

"I was afraid," he said softly, and the people near the front of the platform leaned toward him in a group wave. "I was afraid that if I confessed to my fears, I would have had to admit something else, something that terrified me equally as much."

He straightened, his bonds tugging at his wrists. "I would have had to admit how much I'd come to care for you." There. He'd said it aloud. Only it was far too late. The world grew blurry, but he didn't care.

"You are a remarkable woman, Elizabeth. You faced marriage to a disreputable bore like me without fear. You stood up to me. Matched wits with me. And you are witty, my dear. Sometimes I would marvel at your charm. You are wonderfully brave; something I noticed about you prior to our marriage. I can only imagine 'tis because of the way you were forced to stand up to society's derision of you." He felt tears come to his eyes as he admitted the last. "Would that I had faced my brother's death with as much courage.

"You are remarkable," he repeated, having to fight to

keep his voice even. "I want you to know that. And that I was an utter fool for not seeing it before. It's too late for us now, but I would give it all, my dear. Everything. Raven's Keep, the land, the castle, *everything* for another chance."

"Are ya finished?" the executioner interrupted, clearly fed up with such a maudlin speech.

"Well," Lucien said, near hysteria again, "I suppose I should thank my boot maker, too, but I never did like the man."

"Good, then let's get on wi' it."

And just like that, it was time. No fanfare. No cries from the crowd. Life would soon be over.

"Bow your head," the executioner said.

Lucien closed his eyes. He toyed with the idea of struggling, but what was the point? He was a condemned man. Nothing would change that now.

He did as asked. The crowd erupted.

A hood dropped over his head. Remarkably clean-smelling, he noted, another part tensing as he waited for the rope to be lowered, too.

Elizabeth, are you watching?

He felt a tug on the hood.

Did you understand what I was trying to tell you?

A rope tightened around his neck. Not even the crowd could drown out the sound of his heart.

I was trying to tell you that I fell in love with you.

The executioner stepped back.

I fell in love with you as you stood on the stand, so righteous, so outraged that anyone could think me guilty. I fell in love with you as you tried to seduce John, just so you could win a wager. I fell in love with you when I saw your reaction to that bloody horse. You looked as if I'd given you diamonds, as if no one had ever given you something so precious, something so silly. But perhaps no one has given you things before. And I'm sorry for that, too, little one. So sorry.

And then an odd sort of peace overcame him. 'Twas strange. He focused on the memory of Elizabeth's face, wished for a second that he'd taken the clergyman up on the offer of a prayer.

He would have prayed for happiness. For her *happiness.*

The executioner gave the call. He tensed. She'd looked so beautiful the day of their wedding. He could picture her perfectly, the damn musicians playing the wedding march so loud. He could still hear the cacophony in his head as they'd tried to keep up with her outraged pace.

He straightened.

Cacophony?

"Make way!" a man yelled. "Make way by order of the Prince of Wales!"

Horns blared. A sweet, melodic sound that blended with the crowd's cries as they were made to move out of the way.

"Make way."

Every nerve in Lucien's body froze. Was that a carriage he heard? It was hard to tell and it took what seemed like hours to reach him.

"Do not hang that man."

And Lucien almost dropped to his knees.

The voice sounded out again, nearer now. "He has

been cleared of all charges by order of His Majesty, the Prince of Wales."

"Remove his bloody hood." Was that John's voice? He waited, nearly blinded by the sun as the fabric was abruptly pulled from his head, his bonds cut in nearly the same motion.

He blinked, focused. A carriage stood near the base of the platform, and not just any carriage, but the Prince of Wales's own personal carriage, judging by the crest on the open door. Two outriders rode behind it, the black horses they rode twisting and spinning about at the crowd. But what caught Lucien's eye was the sight of John coming toward him, his long legs making short work of the steps up the scaffolding.

"Well?" John asked. "Have you nothing to say?"

"Yes," Lucien instantly responded, then he socked his friend.

"Lucien," Elizabeth yelled, jumping down from the carriage as John dropped to the floor.

The crowd went wild.

And yet oddly enough, the first thing he thought as he saw her was that she hadn't heard his speech.

Well, that was a relief. Or was it? It was hard to tell while he was bombarded by a myriad of emotions as he stared down at the woman he had thought never to see again.

And then he realized he didn't care if she'd heard his speech or not. He'd meant every word of it. He straightened, giving her a blinding smile, holding out his hand as he did so.

She collapsed.

"Elizabeth?" Lucien cried.

People crowded around her. "Elizabeth," he teased. "This is hardly time for theatrics." But she was below him, and so she couldn't hear.

He jumped down off the platform. The crowd parted, the same crowd that had thrown tomatoes at him moments before. Lucien found that wildly ironic.

"Elizabeth," he called when he spied her in the arms of a stranger. "Devil of a time to swoon." He went to her, gently—no, lovingly—touching her cheek.

Shock made him jerk back.

Her flesh burned. "Get a physician," he moaned in horror, his hand still warm from her skin. "Get a physician *now*," he roared, looking up at the gawking crowd.

"Gaol fever," the physician pronounced, looking at Lucien gravely. "Likely caught it whilst visiting you. I've bled her twice in the past hour, but it hasn't helped. Like as not it's not up to me whether she makes it."

Lucien could only stare. He felt John's hand on his shoulder.

"Is there anything I can do?" Lucien asked, ignoring his friend.

The doctor shook his head, his spectacles glinting from the reflection of firelight. "I'm sorry."

Lucien's knees almost gave out. "Sorry," he croaked. "Sorry for what? That the woman I love is sick from a fever that she got visiting me? That one of the few people to believe in me might die as a consequence of her faithfulness? That despite my absolution of guilt, I am still to be punished if God takes her away?"

The physician merely blinked up at him. John's grip tightened. "Go," Lucien ordered, uncaring that the man could see the tears in his eyes. God help him but half of London knew his feelings for his wife. He would not hide them now. "Go and leave me in peace."

"Lucien," John said.

"Go," Lucien snapped, turning on him. "Or have you forgotten that I know of your true feelings for her?"

John looked pained, and in his eyes Lucien could read that he truly had fallen in love with Elizabeth. Bloody bastard.

"Out!" he screamed.

John looked ready to balk, but the physician motioned with his head that he should not. They both left the room.

Lucien turned back to the bed. They were in his town house, a place he had shared with nobody but himself in previous years. The massive oak bed near a corner window now encompassed the small form of his wife. Muted light shone from behind drawn, gauzy curtains to cast a pale glow upon her face. White sheets were drawn up to her shoulders, her black hair loose on the pillow behind her, firelight catching the strands and burnishing them auburn.

John had told him everything. Of how she'd pawned all of her gowns but the one she stood in in order to pay for the gravedigger, and the physician, and the hack she had hired to take her to his family seat and back. She had moved heaven and earth, literally, to prove him innocent, and now she was paying for it.

God help him.

Sitting down next to her, he clasped her hand. So hot. And yet her body was wracked with chills. He could see her shiver beneath the dark blue coverlet. Her veins glowed a matching shade of blue beneath her pale skin, her pulse beating at her neck in a rhythm that was far too rapid. He closed his eyes, feeling out of control.

What had the clergyman said? Prayers would be answered in time? *Well,* he thought, *here's my prayer, God. Will you answer it? Will you keep her safe for me?*

He dropped her hand, templing his fingers in prayer, hoping the gesture would prove his sincerity to the powers above.

Please, God, don't take her.

She murmured something, her head beginning to thrash. Without thought, he climbed into bed next to her, pulling her into his arms. She burned, but he didn't care as he held her.

"Must hurry," she murmured. "Hanging him," she cried out. Her arms began to flail.

"Shh, Elizabeth," he soothed. "'Tis all right. You made it in time."

But the feverish nightmare had her firmly in its grip. "Dig. Dig," she cried.

His own tears felt nearly as scalding as her own, her blue eyes opening to reveal a panic-stricken gaze. He relived every moment of her quest to clear his name. She had demanded admittance into Carlton House, John had said, her feverish words confirming the action. She had ordered the Prince up from his bed. Only his attendants refused to rouse him. Only Elizabeth's steely determination, along with the clutching of one of his dueling pistols—those damn dueling pistols—had convinced them to do otherwise.

And look where it had gotten her.

Had it been worth her life?

He shook his head, uncaring that a sob escaped. Not

even the thought of death had filled him with as much fear as the thought of losing Elizabeth.

How long he held her thus, he had no idea, but eventually the bedroom door opened. He looked up. John stood there, his black jacket and buff breeches spotted with rain, the low heels of his boots covered in mud.

"Get out of here," Lucien growled.

"Not on your life," John said.

"Go away," he ordered again.

"I am your best friend, Lucien. And I care fer your wife, too. I'm no leaving."

"You would have married her."

"No," he said, his eyes filling with something . . . sadness. "For she only ever loved you."

Lucien felt as if the breath were knocked out of him. His arms tightened around Elizabeth.

"Aye, she does. Though I doubt the lass realizes it."

Loved him.

Did she?

Stinging hot tears fell down his face as he clutched Elizabeth to him. He closed them, ashamed to let John see them.

But his longtime friend knew him too well. He came over to the bed, placed a hand on his shoulder, and this time Lucien didn't fling it away. "You need to be strong, Lucien. You will do her no good if you get no rest this eve. Go," John ordered. "I will watch her for you. Lord knows if I let anything happen to her, I'll never forgive myself, either."

He didn't want to move.

"Come."

And Lucien gently, so as not to wake her, laid Elizabeth down. He placed her under the covers, hands shaking as he tucked the covers around her, then patted them gently. He stood.

"I will call you if anything changes."

Lucien nodded. A peace was struck then, one that was forged out of necessity, but one that strengthened as hour after hour passed while Elizabeth fought. The fever came and went, racing across her body with the speed of a grass fire, leaving behind a coldness that seemed to grow more and more pronounced with each feverish outbreak. Lucien willed her to fight, but there came a time when she had little strength to do so.

"Shall I fetch th' physician?" John asked.

They were unshaven, both fighting a fear they refused to name.

"Aye," Lucien said, his voice a mere croak. "I think—" He couldn't go on, his tears long since spent, his body unable to produce another drop. "I think she might be dying."

John nodded, and there were tears in his eyes, too. "I'll be back."

Lucien didn't look up, as he had eyes only for his wife. Her hair had gotten mussed with the last feverish outbreak. He picked up a brush from the side table and began to brush it out.

"You need to keep fighting," he told her matter-of-factly, even as he knew such urgings were all for naught. "You need to get well, my love." A tear blazed a path down his cheek. "Lucy sends her love, by the way. She can't be here for fear of getting the baby ill." He couldn't go on for a moment. "It's a girl, Elizabeth, and she named her after you."

She didn't move, and a sudden frustration made him throw the brush across the room. "Damn you, Elizabeth. You can't leave me," he croaked. "Everyone I have ever loved has left me. My father. My brother. I can't." His breath hitched. "I can't lose you, too." He shook his head. "God, please don't take her away from me, too."

Her breath grew more shallow. *Where was the damn physician?* He grabbed her hand, held it to his cheek. She took a deep breath.

And then stilled.

Lucien stared at her, willing her to breathe.

But she didn't.

"Elizabeth," he called, panic making him rise.

She didn't move.

"Elizabeth?" He grabbed her shoulders.

She still didn't move.

"Elizabeth," he cried. "Elizabeth."

"Lucien," he heard John call. "Let her go."

"No," he growled, suddenly clutching her to him. "No. I'll not let her go. I'll not."

"Lucien," John ordered.

Lucien fought him, his eyes blurred as he stared at Elizabeth's lifeless face.

"Lucien," John ordered. "Calm yourself."

"She's gone," he howled in pain.

"Lucien," John snapped.

Lucien whirled on him. John socked him in the jaw.

"She's not dead," John explained, his look one of apology. He shook his hand. "*Look* at her, at her face. The fever has broken. She is in a deep sleep."

Lucien stared. "What?"

"She is in a deep sleep," John explained. "Go, look for yourself."

And if he doubted John's words, he had only to turn to the bed, to see the doctor's smiling face.

"This is good," the bespectacled man said. "This is very, *very* good. 'Tis not like the other times between fevers. This time her body is cool." His smile increased. "She is going to make it."

Lucien looked down at the bed, at the still form of his beautiful wife.

And collapsed to his knees in thanks.

EPILOGUE

The carriage rolled to a halt, the lamplight flickering as the coach swayed in its place before Lord and Lady Jessup's residence. Inside, Elizabeth and Lucien held hands as they waited for the door to be opened.

"Are you ready?" she asked, staring into Lucien's lime-colored eyes.

"Do I look like I'm ready?" he asked wryly.

Elizabeth peered up at him, pretending to consider his words. He'd been consuming lemon drops again. She could smell the sweet scent of them, the realization making her conceal a grin. "Hmm. I see, no sweat on your brow, nor upon your upper lip. So I suppose you appear ready to go."

"Looks can be deceiving." He patted her hand. "But with you by my side, I am ready for anything."

They stared at each other, Elizabeth awed yet again by the turn her life had taken. He loved her. It still amazed her. Sometimes she pulled out the copy of *The Times* she kept in her drawer, the one that recounted, word for word, what he'd said the day of the hanging. Even now, she still had a hard time believing it. But what astonished her more, what made her smile in secret bemusement, was the mutual love she felt. She didn't know when it had started, although she sometimes wondered if it hadn't been that silly dress he'd donned. Or maybe before that, perhaps when he'd tried to take her to see his sunset. Or when he'd bought her the horse. Whenever, it'd come to full bloom as he'd nursed her back to health. No woman could be proof against the kind of devotion Lucien showed her. Still showed her.

So she'd named the horse Thunder, a name Lucien claimed was entirely girlish. Elizabeth had replied that he was just jealous of certain male parts of her horse's anatomy, to which Lucien had said . . . nothing.

She adored making him speechless.

Such was the nature of their love, full of smiles and laughter. And not a day went by that Elizabeth didn't thank God for it.

"Are you ready, duckies?" the coachman said, Elizabeth's thoughts scattering like a late summer breeze.

"One moment, Cedric, I need to put on my boxing gloves," Lucien replied drolly.

Moments later they stepped down, the cool night air filled with the scent of evening fires, long-eaten dinners and pampered bodies. A quadrille played, the sound of violins mixing with voices as gaily dressed people walked in and out of the open double doors. Inside the massive main hall, Elizabeth could feel the stares of the other guests, could see the way their hostess started a bit when she spied who stood before her.

"Lord and Lady St. Aubyn," she said, her smile seeming to be sincere. "I'm so glad you could come tonight. I confess, when I received your acceptance, I about fell over in shock."

"Thank you for inviting us." Elizabeth gave her a smile.

Their hostess smiled back, the corners of her blue eyes crinkling in a way that could only be genuine. "My pleasure." But then her eyes narrowed a bit and she leaned forward. Elizabeth thought at first that she stared at her aunt's brooch she'd pinned on her dress. "What an unusual necklace, Lady Ravenwood. I don't believe I've ever seen gold . . ." she leaned even closer. "Balls like that."

Not the brooch, her necklace. "Do you like them?" Elizabeth asked, touching them with her gloved hands. "They used to hang between my husband's legs. I wear them to remind him of all that he owes me."

Her ladyship drew back. Her mouth dropped open.

"Elizabeth," Lucien chastised, but she could hear the strangled laughter in his voice. "I do wish you'd quit telling people that."

"I'm sorry, dear, but you know it is the truth."

It was Lucien's turn to smile at the poor woman. "Alas, it is."

What could their hostess say to that? Nothing, apparently, for she merely blinked.

Lucien crooked his arm through hers, smiling again as he led her away, but they both heard their hostess's titter of laughter. "That went well," he said.

"I couldn't help myself."

But their smiles faded a bit as they neared the ballroom.

"Their graces, the duke and duchess of Ravenwood," the majordomo boomed.

Conversations stopped. People turned. Heavens, 'twas as if someone had called out, "Fire!"

Elizabeth straightened to her full height. She could feel Lucien do the same.

A man came forward, the earl of Glashow, Lord High Steward from the trial. He looked momentarily hesitant as he approached, but when he stopped before them, he bowed. And was it her imagination, or was that bow a bit deeper than it should have been. "Your gravedigger, er, Graces," he said. "Good to see you looking so well."

He looked up. And, yes, there was definitely a twinkle in his eyes, and a look of apology.

"Indeed?" Lucien said, recovering first. "I wonder if you might know where my wife can put her shovel?"

And that was that. Conversation resumed. Good gracious, people smiled. The music started again. Glashow laughed, as did several people around them. And then the well-wishers came forward. People asked how she felt. How Lucien was faring since the trial. Her husband answered the questions with a good-natured smile.

Apparently, society had put Lucien's past behind him. Thank God Lucien had, too.

"Move out of my way, I say," someone grumbled, a someone whose voice sounded very familiar.

Beth turned, hardly daring to hope . . .

"Lucy," she gushed, "Oh my goodness, Lucy."

Elizabeth felt tears come to her eyes as she and her friend embraced, right there, in the middle of the ballroom, something Elizabeth would never have deigned to do a few months before. Now, however, she'd discovered she didn't care what other people thought, she only cared that she and the people she loved were happy. She drew back to stare into her friend's sparkling green eyes. She was most definitely happy.

"Beth, oh my goodness, Beth. It *is* you. When I heard your name announced, I couldn't believe it. Why didn't you tell me you'd arrived in town?"

"I didn't know *you* were in town. I thought you were still nursing the babe."

"I am, and you wouldn't believe what happened to me earlier. My breasts started leaking right through my ball gown—"

"Lucy," Beth interrupted, laughing. "Please, there are some things I do not wish to know." She turned to Lucien. "You remember my husband."

Lucy drew herself up, and Elizabeth had to admit, her friend looked . . . different. More mature. Content. *Loved.*

"Ravenwood," Lucy said, giving him a curtsy. "I trust you received my letter?"

Letter? Elizabeth thought, drawing herself up. What letter?

"I did, my lady," Lucien said, and she could tell he was fighting back a smile. "And I duly promise to cherish Elizabeth for the rest of her life."

Lucy stared at him a moment longer, then nodded in apparent satisfaction, a lock of her red hair falling loose. "As long as we understand each other."

"We do."

And Elizabeth tried not to laugh.

"What do you understand?"

All three turned at this new arrival. "Garrick," Lucy

said to her husband, a blond-headed giant who towered over men. Right then his blue eyes stared at his wife suspiciously just before he turned to Elizabeth. An instant smile sprang to his lips.

"How are you, Lady Beth?" he asked.

"Very well," Elizabeth answered, turning to Lucien. "You remember my husband?"

The two stared at each other, neither man making a move. "Aye," Garrick said, and it was apparent he had yet to forgive Lucien for sinking his ship. Children.

"I was just reiterating to the duke," Lucy said, "that if he doesn't behave, I shall hang him from the rafters by his balls."

"Lucy," Elizabeth gasped again.

"That might be hard to do since she wears them around her neck," Lucien offered.

Lucy and Garrick both lifted their brows. Elizabeth pointed to her neck. And then all four of them laughed.

"Elizabeth," a different voice called.

Elizabeth stiffened. She turned. Her mother stood next to her, her father nodding at them. "Lady Cardiff," her mother gritted out, nodding at Lucy. "Lord Cardiff," she added. Then she turned to her. "Why have you not called upon me, my dear? I wonder if you have forgotten my existence?"

Elizabeth felt her mouth drop open, almost saying something derogatory, but the bond of family—no matter how tedious—was simply too strong to break. To give her credit, her mother had tried to visit her while she'd been ill, but Lucien had shooed her away, and then later they'd wanted time alone . . .

"I will be by tomorrow, Mother. This is the first week back in town." And she'd been procrastinating. A lot.

Was that emotion she saw on her mother's face? Emotion from a woman who prided herself on showing none? "I was concerned for you, Elizabeth. Deeply concerned. I hope your husband conveyed that to you. You are feeling better, are you not?"

Elizabeth's heart instantly softened. "I am."

"Good. Then I shall see you on Thursday." She looked uncertain for a moment. Then, she leaned forward and gave her a peck on the cheek, quickly, as if afraid someone might see. "You may bring Lucien, too, of course, despite the fact that he would not let me visit your sickbed."

Elizabeth almost laughed. "He was worried you might catch my illness."

"Yes, so he told me."

"If it makes you feel any better, I was refused admittance, too," Lucy said.

Her mother turned to Elizabeth's friend. "Yes, well, that I understand."

The look on Lucy's face indicated she wasn't sure if she'd been insulted or not. Garrick choked back a laugh as Lucy covertly jabbed him with her elbow.

The countess straightened. "Well," she said, "I am glad you're better."

"As am I," her father added, his first words. He peered up at Lucien. "And that the charges were dropped."

Lucien nodded politely. It was as close to an apology he would get from the earl.

"Come, George," her mother said to her father. "Let us be off. I see Lady Haversham over there. The woman is all agog to hear how you are doing, Elizabeth."

"And I would like to dance with my wife," Garrick said. "Now that she has said hello to you, Elizabeth, mayhap she will join me."

Lucy looked up at her husband, his face softening as she said, "Hmm, perhaps I shall."

They watched them walk away, Lucy so small, Garrick so tall. And yet they were perfect for each other.

"Would you like to dance, too, my dear?" Lucien whispered in her ear.

She turned, smiled. Lucien found himself smiling back. God, but she was glorious, the blue of her eyes nearly matched the topaz coronet that nestled amongst her upswept hair.

"I'm not so sure," she murmured teasingly. "After all, you are a known rake."

He didn't respond, merely pulled her to the dance floor. A waltz played. Ah, yes, perfect timing. He looked around, clearing a spot on the floor with a mere look. It paid to be a former dastardly duke.

"I am *your* rake," he said earnestly.

She shrugged, sighed, her right hand lifting her skirts as he pulled her to him. Their bodies connected with a familiar jolt, his hand clasping her left hand. The wedding ring she'd pawned—the one he'd moved heaven and earth to find whilst she recovered—glinted in the candlelight. Odd how he'd been so picky when he'd chosen it. A part of him must have known even then that she was special.

"My aunt told me never to marry a rake," she teased.

He spun her gently, enjoying the feel of her in his arms. "Your aunt never met *me*," he replied.

She laughed again. He watched her, the other dancers

receding away. She was like a painting he'd once seen. That of a pearl. Perfect. Brilliant. More lovely than any grain of sand had a right to be. And she was *his* pearl, a jewel he hardly understood how he'd obtained. But not a moment went by that he wasn't grateful that they'd been brought together.

"You're staring at me," she said.

"Am I?"

"You are."

He smiled down at her, loving the way she smiled back. "I was wondering if you're as happy as I am?"

She pursed her lips. "I might be."

"*Might?*"

"Indeed, for my happiness depends a great deal on your ability to furnish me with bananas."

He stared at her in shock for a second before throwing back his head and laughing. People turned to look at them, but Lucien didn't care. He had Elizabeth in his arms. And that was all he'd ever need.

"Indeed," he drawled. "And what will you do with these bananas?"

She stood on her toes, whispering the most shocking and titillating thing in his ear. He almost fell to the dance floor.

"Scandalous," he said, as she drew away.

"But intriguing," she added.

He chuckled. "And when you're done doing that, ahem, *thing* to me, then what?"

But it was later that night before she showed him, and it wasn't a *thing*. She rested her palm against his cheek, her eyes filling with love as she said, "What I'm going to do," she whispered softly, her mouth still moist from his kiss, "is love you forever."

He kissed her palm, drawing back to place his hand on her enlarged belly. The dress she'd worn tonight had concealed her pregnancy well. Granted, she was only two months along, but it still filled him with wonder as he stared at the small bulge. His child grew there. His eyes misted, his gaze moving back to hers. "Love me?" he questioned softly. "Is that a promise, my dear?"

She nodded, her own eyes misty.

"Then I suppose there's nothing for it but that I must love you back." And he tilted his head down, sweeping his lips over hers. "But first," he said, kissing the crook of her neck, "I shall seduce you."

She laughed softly, the sound vibrating beneath his lips. "Oh, I beg to differ, my lord, for 'tis *you* who has been seduced."

And, indeed, he had been. Most thoroughly. Seduced. And *loved.*

AUTHOR'S NOTE

Researching Regency London criminal trials when one lives in California is like trying to build sand castles in Antarctica. Oh, the pain. The pain (to quote Dr. Smith). I did my best, but please forgive me if I blundered in any way. My thanks to the University of Texas for posting the Newgate Calendar on line. Without it, I would have been horribly lost.

I'd also like to thank my husband, Michael, for taking care of our little family so that I could write and do research. You're appreciated more than you know, hon. You make me understand the words to Martina McBride's "Blessed" in a way I never would have thought possible. I wuv you.

Also, thanks go to the employees and owners of two restaurants where I wrote this book: The Faultline and Elegant Touch, both in Hollister, California. Thanks for all the cookies, guys.:)

I hope you enjoyed your time with Lucien and Elizabeth. As always, my goal is to bring you wacky, zany stories that make you laugh out loud and (hopefully) sigh at the end.

Happy reading,

Pamela

ABOUT THE AUTHOR

Bestselling author Pamela Britton blames her zanny sense of humor wacky story ideas on the amount of Fruity Pebbles she consumes. Not wanting to actually have to work for a living, Pamela has enjoyed a variety of odd careers such as modeling, working for race teams—including NASCAR's Winston Cup—and drawing horses for a living.

Over the years, Pamela's novels have garnered numerous awards, including a nomination for Best First Historical Romance by *Romantic Times* Magazine and Best Paranormal Romance by *Affaire de Couer* Magazine. Pamela's second book, ENCHANTED BY YOUR KISSES, was an Amazon.com bestseller resulting in Pamela having to choose between writing full-time or selling insurance. Difficult decision.

When not imbibing Fruity Pebble milk, Pamela enjoys showing her horse, Peasy, and cheering on her professional rodeo cowboy husband, Michael. The two live on their West Coast ranch (aka: Noah's Ark) along with their daughter, Codi, and a very loud, very obnoxious African Grey Parrot prone to telling her to "Shut up!"

Please visit me at my website at: www.pamelabritton.com.

More
Pamela Britton!

Please turn this page

for a preview of

TEMPTED

available

in early 2004.

CHAPTER ONE

N o red cape.

No pitchfork.

No horns.

All in all Mary Elizabeth Callahan would say that the Devil Marquis of Warrick didn't look a thing like she expected.

Oddly, she felt disappointed. Of course, she couldn't see his lordship all that well what with him sitting upon a bleedin' throne of a chair behind his bleedin' monstrosity of a desk.

"Please have a seat," he said without looking up, his eyes firmly upon a document before him, a clock on a mantel behind him *tick-tick-ticking* in an annoyingly sterile way. Muted sunlight from the right reflected off the flawless, polished perfection of that desk. The ink blotter lay exactly square, almost as if someone had used a measuring tape to place it. Papers were stacked at perfect right angles. A fragrant, rather obnoxious-smelling tussy of red roses and rosemary squatted in a fat vase. And yet there were also black stains on the front of that desk, as if someone had thrown a jar of ink at his lordship here. And not quite erased from the desk's surface she could just make out . . . a smiling face that looked to have been finger painted when the ink spilled.

She bit back a smile as she took a seat, nearly yelping when the plush blue velvet did its best to swallow her whole. She had to jerk forward, looking up as she did so to see if his lordship had noticed. No. The swell was still engrossed in his work. Hmph.

She waited for him. Then waited some more. Finally, she began to tap her foot impatiently, her toe ticking on the hardwood floor in time with the clock.

The scratching of his quill stopped abruptly. His head slowly lifted, his eyes widening a bit as he caught his first glimpse of her.

Two things hit Mary at once. One, Alexander Drummond, Marquis of Warrick, had the prettiest eyes she'd ever seen. Blue they were, the color of a seashell when you turned it over.

Two, he was not the ugly ogre she'd been expecting, which just went to show a body shouldn't believe all the things they hear.

He blinked at her, frowned, then said, "I'll be with you in just a moment," slowly and succinctly—as if she had wool in her ears—before going back to work.

She narrowed her eyes, studying him, seein' as how there were nothing else to do. His high-and-mightiness had an angular jaw with a cleft smack-dab in the middle of it, she noted. Wasn't anything slug-faced about him, which was how most peers looked, to her mind at least. *This* peer had midnight black hair with twin streaks of gray that started at both temples ending somewhere in the back, his dark hair pulled back in a queue.

"Did your daughter give you that?" she found herself asking.

Once again he looked up. Once again, his quill stopped its annoying scratch, the black jacket he wore tightening as he straightened again. Thick, very masculine brows lowered. "I beg your pardon?"

"The gray hair," she said, pointing with a gloved hand at his hair, and then motioning to her own red hair in case he needed further clarification.

And now those black brows lifted. "As a matter of fact, no. 'Tis a genetic trait inherited from my father. All heirs of Warrick have it."

She pursed her lips. "Just the heirs? What do you do if a nonheir is born with it? Shoot him?"

His lips parted. His jaw dropped, but he was only struck all-a-mort for a moment. "No, Mrs. . . ." He looked down, his white cravat all but poking him in the chin as he pulled sheets of papers toward him. She recognized them as being the ones John Lasker had forged. John had the best penmanship in Hollowbrook. Actually, John had about the only penmanship in Hollowbrook. "Mrs. Callahan. We do not shoot our children."

Got his lordship's ballocks in a press, hadn't she?

"And," he continued, "since it would appear as if you're determined to interrupt me, I suppose we should just begin the interview for the position. That way, you can be on your way, and I can get back to work."

Mary perked up. At last. Two, maybe three minutes and she'd be out of here and on her way back to Hollowbrook. For one thing Mary Callahan didn't want was to nurse his lordship's daughter. She'd only come today to appease her baboon-brained father, a man who'd gone a wee bit crackers in recent months with his plot of revenge against the marquis here for shutting down the town's smuggling operations. Although now that she'd met the man, she could well understand her father's aversion to the cull. Fact is, she didn't particularly want the job. It entailed lying, and she loathed doing that. But it was her duty to do as her father asked, and so she'd come even though she knew she'd never get the job. She didn't qualify, but that suited her just fine, even though she knew the people of Hollowbrook would be disappointed when she came back unemployed. They were just as determined to gain revenge as her father was.

"I see you're from Wellburn, Mrs. Callahan?" he asked.

She leaned forward, placing an arm nonchalantly on his desk as she pretended to look at the papers. He smelled nice. She took a big whiff of him. His brows lifted again. He looked at her arm, up at her, then at the arm again. Pointedly.

"Is that wha' it says?" she asked, not removing her elbow, and not trying to smooth her Cockney accent, something she could do, if she had a mind to. She tilted her head, and Lord knows why, but when their gazes met, she smiled. Mary Callahan had a bonny smile. Truth be told, she had a lot of bonny traits—or so she'd been told. Fine green eyes. Dimples. And an endearing way of looking at a man from beneath her thick lashes, not that there was any reason to look up at his lordship that way.

The marquis, however, didn't appear fazed. "You're not from Wellburn?" he asked, his face blank.

He had the composure of a corpse.

"If that's what it says, then I suppose I am." She leaned back, noticing that his eyes darted down a second, as if he'd glanced at her breasts. But she must be mistaken, for even if they were a fine, ripe bushel, his lordship here wouldn't be noticing. That kind of thing was beneath his hoity-toity nose.

"You suppose?"

She shrugged, one of the seams in the blue dress

Fanny Goodwin had sewn popping a bit at the shoulder. Mary should have insisted she let it out a bit more, but the woman had been all agog to show Mary to advantage. Who was Mary to protest? She planned to keep the dress once she got back to Hollowbrook. "Been travelin' a lot. Hard to keep track."

"I see," he said through gritted teeth. He went back to studying the papers. "Do you enjoy being a nurse, Mrs. Callahan?"

"No."

His head snapped up again. He was going to get a bleedin' neck ache if he kept that up.

"No?"

She shook her head. "Can't stand children."

She had the rum-eyed pleasure of seeing his mouth drop open. "But it says here you love them."

"Who said that?" she asked, and she really was curious.

"Mrs. Thistlewillow."

Mrs. Thistlewillow was one of her neighbors in Hollowbrook. A perpetually cheerful sort of person. "Mrs. Thistlewillow would claim Beelzebub loved children."

His lordship had fine teeth, she noticed. She had occasion to study them because his mouth hung open again. Not a rotted one in the lot.

"Mrs. Callahan. I get the feeling that you have not read your references."

She snorted. Couldn't help it. 'Course she hadn't read them. She couldn't read. "I make a point not to read what others say about me." And she was bloody proud of that fact. She might be a poor smuggler's daughter. She might be a wee speck on his lordship's bootheel, but Mary Callahan stood on her own two feet. Damn the rest of the world.

He shook his head as he picked up her references. "Mrs. Callahan. Thank you for coming, but it appears as if I've made a mis—"

"Papa!"

Mary's arse fair puckered to the chair. Blimey, what a screech. The door swung open with a resounding boom. She swiveled toward the door. At least, she tried to. The bloody chair held her backside like a bog.

"Papa, Simms says you're interviewing another nurse."

A little girl of about eight ran by, her hair streaming behind her. Black it was, and in sore need of a good brushing. She landed in a heap in her father's arms. "I don't want a nurse. I *told* you that."

Ah. The little termagant herself, and no doubt the finger paint artist, too.

Mary held her breath as she waited for his lordship to look up, to dismiss her, which she was sure he'd been about to do before the hellion had come in.

"Gabby," the marquis said. "Be polite and say how do you do to Mrs. Callahan."

Polite? Bugger it. Mary wanted to *leave*.

"No," the little girl snapped.

"Do it, Gabby. Now."

The little girl drew back, her face only inches away from her father's. They were practically nose-to-nose, the marquis's face stern and disapproving. Lord, the man could scare kids on All Hallows' Eve with a look like that.

The bantling wiggled on his lap. She shimmied down, landing with a thud. The gray dress looked stained with juice, Mary noted, her slippers muddied. But she was a cute little moppet, with her father's startling blue eyes and dark, curly hair.

"How do you do," she said, dropping into a curtsy that somehow seemed, well, *mocking*. And then she rose, looked sideways out of her eyes, and that cute little moppet with the pretty blue eyes stuck out her tongue.

Mary stiffened.

The hellion gave her a smug smile.

Mary's eyes narrowed. Never one to be gotten the best of, especially by some pug-nosed whelp, she stuck her tongue out, too.

"Papa." The little girl breathed without missing a beat. "Did you see that? She stuck her tongue out at me."

Mary looked up at the marquis. What? Wait a bleedin'—

"Gabby," he said. "I know well and good that you stuck your tongue out first. Apologize to Mrs. Callahan immediately."

"No," the little girl snapped, her tiny hands fisting by her sides.

"Do it," he ordered.

"No," she yelled.

Mary covered her ears. "Land's alive, m'lord. Don't argue with her. I'll lose me hearing. 'Tis plain as carriage wheels that she's not going to apologize."

For the third time that day—the first being when he'd caught his first glimpse of the stunning Mrs. Callahan—Alexander Drummond, Marquis of Warrick, felt speechless. It defied belief, the things that kept coming out of her mouth.

"I beg your pardon?"

The nurse arched red brows, and was it his imagination, or did her pretty green eyes twinkle?

"She's not going to apologize. What's more, I don't want her bloomin' apology. Fact is, I don't want to be her nurse, either."

Alex thought he'd misheard her again, but then Gabby said, "Good. Leave."

"I will," she answered right back, rising from her chair.

"Sit down," Alex ordered.

"Please," he added when—good Lord—the woman looked ready to defy him.

She slowly sat, but she didn't look too pleased about it.

"Gabby, you may leave. I will speak with you upstairs."

His daughter's lips pressed together, something he knew from experience meant a tantrum. "I'm a bastard," she yelled in a last-ditch attempt to put the nurse off.

Alex winced. He knew the child was inordinately sensitive to the fact that her mother had left her on his doorstep. He could sympathize, still incensed himself that a woman could do such a thing.

He looked at Mrs. Callahan to gauge her reaction, but she merely lifted a brow. "Are you now?"

"I am."

"Is that the excuse you use for having such poor manners?"

Gabby sucked in a breath. "Did you hear that, Father? She said I have poor manners."

"Well, you do," Mrs. Callahan said.

"Do not."

The nurse snorted, the inelegant sound somehow seeming to fit the redoubtable nurse perfectly. "You don't even know how to curtsy properly."

"Do too."

"Not by the looks of the one you just gave me."

To Alex's absolute and utter shock, his obstinate daughter took a step back, straightened, and then gave the nurse a curtsy that would have done her mother proud . . . if she'd had one.

"There," she said upon straightening.

Mrs. Callahan wrinkled her tilted nose. "Hmm. I suppose that was a *wee* bit better, but no proper little girl disobeys her elders."

Gabby glared. So did the nurse.

Alex decided he'd had enough.

"Gabby, go to your room."

His daughter opened her mouth to give her standard protest. But an odd thing happened. He saw her stiffen again. Saw her clench her fists. Saw her straighten. "As you wish, Papa."

Alex just about fell off his chair.

She turned, gave him a quick, *perfect* curtsy, nodded to Mrs. Callahan—who, of all things, stuck her tongue out again—then left.

Silence dawned. Alex could only stare.

"If that's the way she behaves, 'tis a wonder someone hasn't given your daughter a basting." Her full lips pressed together. "Fair wanted to do it meself."

He blinked, found himself clearing his throat. "Mrs. Callahan, how long, exactly, have you been a nurse?"

"Long enough, m'lord," she answered with a tilt to her pert little chin and a sparkle in her eyes.

"How long?" he asked again.

"Long enough to know you must be desperate indeed for someone to fill this post if I'm still sitting here."

He drew back, once again startled by her frankness.

But the way she'd challenged Gabby into behaving . . .

It was a remarkable technique. "Where did you learn to handle children that way?"

"Handle 'em like what?"

"So expertly."

She snorted, her pretty eyes lighting up once again. And, yes, there was no sense in denying it. She was very pretty. Far better-looking than the old crones he and his steward had been interviewing the past week.

"It's the way I raised me younger brothers. Four of them I have. I assume what works for the poorer classes works for the nobility, too."

Rather a pert answer, but there might be some truth to her words. He stared at her for a second longer, a bit disbelieving that he was actually contemplating the idea of hiring her. She disliked children. Well, he knew a blacksmith that didn't like horses, but he was still a fine farrier.

"Let me explain Gabby's unusual circumstances."

And was it his imagination, or did she actually look impatient? No. That couldn't be. "She is my daughter, that I do not deny, left on my doorstep for me to raise when she was only days old. I've done my best, but my duties as a revenue commander ofttimes take me away, smuggling being rampant this time of year. When I am gone my two cousins look after Gabby. I'm afraid my cousins haven't been a very good influence on her making me lament my lack of female family. One of them taught her to shoot a pistol during her last visit." He frowned. "As such she has grown up rather independent and strong-willed. No nurse has stayed beyond a week. No governess, either. Since my last mission, my house steward has hired a total of twelve good ladies, all of whom have left in a huff." He eyed her critically. "Knowing what I've just told you, are you still interested in the job?"

"No," she said.

"It pays a pound a week."

Her eyes widened.

He nodded. "If you take the job, and I am in no way convinced you are right for it yet, you will receive one pound a week for your troubles, and believe me, Mrs. Callahan, my daughter is trouble."

"A pound a week," she whispered, her whole expression undergoing a change. "And all I need do is nurse the bantling?"

"Indeed. However, your response to my earlier question puzzles me. If you do not like children, why do you nurse them?"

She stared at him hard and he had the oddest feeling she was mulling over something. "I was lying," she said at last.

"I beg your pardon?"

She nodded, her eyes having lost some of their earlier impatience. "I'd decided on my way here that I didn't want the job. I ain't never worked for no nobleman before, and I didn't want to start."

He felt his brow wrinkle in surprise. "Then why did you apply for the job?"

She stared at him for a moment. "My father made me do it."

His brows lifted. Well, he could certainly understand one's father's influence on one's life. "I see. So you decided to botch the interview."

"Yes, sir. I mean, me lord."

He studied her for a few seconds before asking, "Have you ever struck a child before?"

"No." She stiffened. "No, wait. Tommy Blackford. He'd plucked all the feathers off a chicken. Made the thing look like a poodle with mange, he did. Have you ever seen a poodle with mange, me lord?"

"No, I have not."

"Ugly, it is. And to my way of thinking, Tommy's lucky I did no more than clout him on the backside. I'd half a mind to pluck all his own hair out just to see how he liked being bald."

An unexpected urge to laugh tickled Alex's lips. "I see," he said, batting the urge back. How common. "And have you worked with difficult children before?"

"Only me father."

That did shock a bark of laughter. Gracious, what the devil was wrong with him? "That is not the kind of child I had in mind."

"No? Well then, the answer is no."

"How about difficult people?" He held up his hand quickly. "Aside from your father."

She pursed her lips in thought. "Old man Mathison were a real handful. Used to hit me in the backside with a slingshot whenever he'd catch me crossing his field. Hurt like the dickens, it did. A regular scaly old cove. So one day I built myself some armor. Used ash bin covers. Strung them together with twine. Worked like a charm. Old man Mathison didn't know what to do when his rocks bounced off my body. Eventually, he gave up, though I never did understand why he didn't just ask me to stop trespassing. I would have if he'd asked."

He stared across at her unblinkingly, a part of him wanting to laugh again, another part of him rather intrigued by her tales.

Still . . .

He looked back down at her résumé, reviewing her qualifications. There could be no doubt that she had the experience necessary for the job. And the way she'd handled Gabby . . .

He looked back up at her. The redoubtable Mrs. Callahan was once again tapping her foot as she shot covert glances at his furnishings.

"I shall give you a trial," he said at last. "Two weeks, at the end of which we shall evaluate your performance. Of course, that is assuming you are still interested in the position?"

The foot stopped tapping. "A pound a week?" she reiterated, eyes narrowed.

"Over fifty pounds per annum."

"And all I have to do is keep an eye on the hellion? Feed her? Dress her?"

"That is, I believe, rather the point of being a nurse," he said dryly.

She scrunched her face. Perversely enough, it did nothing to detract from her beauty. When she straightened, Alex felt a surprising stab of hope.

"I'll take it," she finally said.

"Very good. When can you start?"

"When do you want me to start?"

"Today."

"*Today*?"

"If your affairs are so in order."

"But I—"

"If not, next week will be just as well."

She blinked, stared at him for a long moment, then said, "I'll start today."

"Good," he said, rising. "I'll have Miss Grimes show you to the nursery."

THE EDITOR'S DIARY

Dear Reader,

Discover romance at its sexiest and history at its grandest with our two Warner Forever titles this month. Find a cozy spot, put your feet up, and escape—to Regency England and seventeenth-century Scotland.

When Amanda Quick says that **SEDUCED** by **Pamela Britton** is "everything a historical romance reader could ever want," it's time to pay attention. When she adds that **Pamela Britton** "writes the kind of wonderfully romantic, sexy, witty historical romance that readers dream of discovering," it's time to read the book already! Here's what you'll find in this Regency-set tale: Lucien St. Aubyn and Elizabeth Monclair loathe each other. Elizabeth sees Lucien for the scoundrel that he is. Lucien finds Elizabeth too straitlaced, if only because she's the one woman who has ever resisted his charms. When he devises a plan to seduce her and the two are caught alone, their worst fears come true—they must marry each other!

If a spectacular drama set in seventeenth-century Scotland is your fantasy, then get ready to be swept away by **Kathleen Givens'** **THE DESTINY**. This story involving an ancient prophecy about twin brothers began with THE LEGEND and continues with the tale of Neil MacCurrie, Highland chieftain and enemy of the Crown. When Neil is captured in the home of a foe, the owner's royal-blooded daughter, Eileen Rowley, has her passion awakened by the handsome stranger and helps him escape. Fate brings them together again in London's gilded court, where their star-crossed destiny is tested by Neil's duties to his clan, the lure of the crown and the desires of Eileen's heart.

To find out more about Warner Forever, these April titles, and the authors, visit us at www.warnerforever.com.

With warmest wishes,

Karen Kosztolnyik, Senior Editor

P.S. Mother's Day is coming up, so be on the lookout for these perfect gifts: **Leanne Banks** offers some not-so-traditional mother's advice in the hilarious romantic comedy **SOME GIRLS DO**; and in **LAST BREATH** romantic suspense writer **Rachel Lee** offers a chilly reminder of things our mothers warned us about.